GOODBYE, PICCADILLY

GOODBYE, PICCADILLY

War at Home, 1914

Cynthia Harrod-Eagles

Little, Brown

LITTLE, BROWN

First published in Great Britain in 2014 by Little, Brown

Copyright © Cynthia Harrod-Eagles 2014

The moral right of the author has been asserted.

*All characters and events in this publication, other
than those clearly in the public domain, are fictitious
and any resemblance to real persons,
living or dead, is purely coincidental.*

A CIP catalogue record for this book
is available from the British Library.

ISBN 978-0-7515-5626-1

Typeset in Plantin by
Palimpsest Book Production Limited, Falkirk, Stirlingshire
Printed and bound in Great Britain by Clays Ltd, St Ives plc

Papers used by Little, Brown are from well-managed forests
and other responsible sources.

MIX
Paper from
responsible sources
FSC
www.fsc.org   FSC® C104740

Little, Brown
An imprint of
Little, Brown Book Group
100 Victoria Embankment
London EC4Y 0DY

An Hachette UK Company
www.hachette.co.uk

www.littlebrown.co.uk

To Tony – for so much tea and sympathy

THE HUNTER FAMILY
of The Elms, Northcote

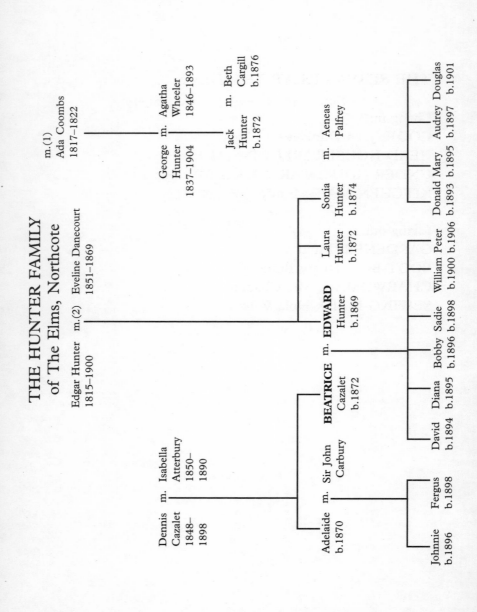

THE SERVANTS AT THE ELMS

Living in:
COOK: Joan Dunkley
HEAD HOUSE/PARLOUR-MAID: Ada Cole
UNDER HOUSE/PARLOUR-MAID: Ethel Lusby
KITCHEN-MAID: Emily Conaghan

Living out:
GARDENER: Munt
BOOT-BOY: Henry Binns
CHARWOMAN: Mrs Chaplin
SEWING-MAID: Nula Wilkes

CHAPTER ONE

July 1914

It was another beautiful summer day, clear and hot. The distant wooded hills were brushed with shadows of mauve and indigo, the dusty road shimmered, and behind the hawthorn hedges to either side, the hayfields, long cut, were beginning to flush again with flowers. Swallows were skimming back and forth above them; their shrilling and the faint rustle of the hedgerow were the only sounds in Sadie's world, aside from Arthur's steady hoofbeats. One motor-car had passed them since they had left the forge; and they had passed a cart loaded with straw coming the other way, scattering golden chaff in its wake.

Sadie loved riding, but keeping horses was not within her father's means, so she had to take rides where she could get them. Arthur was one of Simpson's Dairy's horses, and she had offered to ride him down to the forge to have a loose shoe seen to. He was large and white and bony, with a pendulous lip and a docked tail, and he had only one plodding pace. But he gazed round and pricked his ears now and then, and she believed he was enjoying the break from routine – until a stone shot out of the hedge and hit him on the stifle.

He jumped, and snorted in protest. Sadie soothed his neck, and looked round. 'Come out, you boys!' she said sharply; and then, 'I see you, Victor Sowden! Come out this minute!'

A group of boys pushed through the gap in the hedge: boys unkempt of hair and grubby of face, in hand-me-down suits and sagging stockings. They were all around eleven, except for the ringleader, Victor Sowden. He was big for his age, which was thirteen: a knuckly, raw-faced boy, the only one in long trousers. Wherever there was trouble, it was a fair bet that Victor Sowden would be at the bottom of it.

He lived in a tumbledown cottage on Back Lane with a large family of siblings. His father was – intermittently – a farm labourer, a frequenter of the Red Lion and not unknown to the police, and his mother was a hopeless slattern, worn down by childbearing and her husband's fists.

Victor cared for nobody but, unusually, he loved animals. Sadie had a reluctant half-liking for him, ever since he had fought a bigger boy who was stoning a cat. And perhaps it was because of Arthur that, instead of running away, he remained there, glaring at her sulkily.

'How dare you throw a stone at my horse?' she said. 'You should know better.'

'Never frew it at you,' he said. 'Frew it at *them*.' He jerked his head towards the other boys, ready to run but lingering on the edge of the scene, gripped by the eternal boyhood longing to see someone else 'catch it'.

'Why?' Sadie was moved to ask.

He shrugged his bony shoulders. 'Chuckin' a grenade. Never meant it to 'it yer 'orse,' he added.

The largest of the other lads, Olly Parry, from Parry's Farm, spoke up. 'We're sojers. Germans an' English.'

The smallest boy, whom she recognised under a fine mask of dirt as Victor's brother Horry, complained shrilly, 'He always makes us be the Germans.'

Sadie addressed Victor: 'Shouldn't you be at work?' He shrugged again, and she surmised that he had been 'let go' from his latest employment. He ought to be put into a job with horses, she thought, but with his reputation, few

2

people were willing to employ him. She felt oddly sorry for him, so she just said, 'Don't throw stones. It's dangerous,' and rode on.

Germans and English! she thought. Ten years ago, at school in Kensington, she had sat next to a German girl, Bertha, who used to jab her in the ribs with her ruler and whisper, 'Our king's going to come over and fight your king, and our king's going to win.'

Sadie, of course, had had to return the jab and whisper, 'No, our king's going to win.'

So the exchange would go on until Miss Madison glared them to stillness. All those years later, and it was still Germans and English!

Arthur turned off the road on to the track that led to Simpson's stables without her help. The stableman, Gallon, came out, took the rein, and asked, 'How did he go, then?' rather in the manner of a head groom enquiring after a prize hunter's performance to hounds.

'Very well,' Sadie said obligingly. 'And he stood like an angel in the forge.'

Gallon stroked the white neck with quiet pride. 'Ar, 'e's a good old 'orse, is Arthur. Shows these young 'orses a thing or two.'

She agreed, indulged him in a brief chat in payment for her ride, then set off on foot for home – The Elms, in Highwood Road.

Diana was on the sofa in the morning room, flicking through the magazines. Aunt Sonia Palfrey in Kensington sent them to her when she had finished with them. The *Illustrated London News* and *Ladies' Home Journal* came regularly, some-times *Vogue* and *Tatler* too, given to Aunt Sonia by a wealthy American neighbour.

The fashion in Paris this season, apparently, was for unre-lieved black. She wondered how that would go down. Black

3

suited her, fair as she was, but wouldn't people think you were in mourning? Not that it mattered here, in Northcote: though it was only twenty miles from London, it was hardly a hub of fashion. People who moved here seemed to forget the capital existed, let alone any world further off.

But this evening, at least, the wider world was coming to them. Cousin Jack and his wife Beth were to visit, and Jack was giving a magic-lantern lecture in the village hall on their recent walking tour in Switzerland.

He was only a year or two younger than Father, the son of Father's much older half-brother, George. Uncle George had died years ago. Diana remembered visits to his large, dark house in Hampstead. A tall and portly figure with a gold watch-chain straining across the widest part of his middle, he used to let her light his cigars for him: she loved the first smell when the tobacco caught. And there was a drink he had given them one Christmas, dark red and tasting hotly of cinnamon. It had seemed at the time the essence of Yuletide. Diana had taken the fancy that Uncle George, with his full beard and moustache, was really, secretly, Father Christmas.

There had been no Aunt Agatha on the scene – she had died before Diana was born; and Cousin Jack had already been out in the world. He had always seemed exciting to the children, a meteor that streaked across their everyday firmament. He had been a soldier, and served in exotic places; and when he left the army, having inherited Uncle George's fortune, he had indulged his great passion for travel. Luckily he had married a woman who shared his tastes. They had always brought fascinating souvenirs from China or Mongolia, Mexico or Afghanistan. Sadie still had her doll from Japan.

Switzerland seemed a mite less exotic than their usual destinations – she imagined it full of mountains and cuckoo-clocks – but it was still a far cry from Northcote. And

4

everyone loved a magic-lantern show: the village hall would be packed. Best of all, he and Beth would be staying overnight, and there was to be a supper at home after the lecture, to which all the important people of Northcote were invited.

The question was, would the Wroughtons come?

The Wroughtons of Dene Park were the most important family in the area by a long margin, barons from the seventeenth century and elevated to the earldom in 1910 by Lloyd George. Dene Park, their country seat, was a Palladian mansion in extensive parkland, whose gates were only half a mile from The Elms. It was another mile from the gates to the house itself, a fact recorded with pride in the local guidebook. Still, by any measure they were neighbours.

And in addition, Father was acquainted with the earl: Edward Hunter was a senior manager of Hutcheon's Bank, and the Wroughtons had always banked with Hutcheon's. The Wroughtons did not spend a great deal of time at Dene Park, and so far the contact had all been between the earl and Father – and not very much of that. There had been one or two notes passed between them, the odd present of game or hothouse fruit, and invitations for the occasional day's shooting.

But there was no reason why that should not change. Even Mother, moving serenely, it seemed to Diana, in another world, had seen the possibility offered by Jack's visit. The Wroughtons had been invited to the lecture and the supper afterwards. But would they come?

Or rather – since Diana's interest in the Earl and Countess Wroughton was limited – would *he* come? Their son, Charles, the Viscount Dene, to give him his title: the eldest son – the heir. He had been just a vague figure on the distant horizon until she'd had the good fortune to meet him, twice, in London, when she had been staying with the Palfreys in Kensington. Oh, thank God for the cousins! Always willing to have her to stay, which gave her access to proper shops, theatres, dances, and always an excuse, when Northcote grew too cramped, to catch the train up to London for a breath of less-than-fresh air.

She had first met Charles Wroughton last December, in Belgravia, at a party of some connection of the cousins, where the crush was dreadful and you could hardly hear yourself speak. He had been introduced to her and she had managed to mention that they were neighbours in the country, but she wasn't sure he'd taken it in through the din. He'd given her no more than a polite nod and an apologetic look when he was dragged away by the hostess.

Mary, the Palfrey cousin closest to her in age, had told her he was famously stiff and stand-offish, and she had not expected the encounter to lead anywhere. But he had been present at a hospital ball at Grosvenor House in May, and when she caught his eye across the room, she had seen a look of puzzled recognition, to which she had replied with the sort of smile that said, 'Yes, we are acquainted, it's quite safe to come over.'

And he had come. Explanations were given, acknowledgements exchanged; he had asked her to dance! It was a moment of triumph. She had seen looks following her as he led her on to the floor: Viscount Dene, so aloof and difficult to get to know, and Diana Hunter, merely a banker's daughter. She had known she was at her best that evening, she had been out for two years and an acknowledged beauty for two before that, but still she was nervous. She had to find some way to make an impression on him. Asking her to dance had been a big first step for him, but he did not seem to be much of a talker, and it was hard to be charming with so little to work on. Yet she felt he had noticed her. He didn't smile, but there was something in the way he looked at her . . .

He had danced with her twice, but he was there with a party and had been obliged to rejoin them, and since then she had not happened to meet him. Two dances two months ago was so little to hold her in his memory. He must dance with so many girls. She could almost *feel* herself fading from his mind, like a ghost at cockcrow. She *had* to see him again soon, to have any chance.

'Why should you care?' Sadie had said, when Diana wondered if he would remember her.

'Oh, you don't understand,' Diana had replied.

Ordinary-looking girls always envied Diana. They said, 'Oh, you are lucky,' and 'It's all right for you,' and imagined her life to be easier than theirs. But with great beauty came great responsibility: she *had* to marry well. It was expected of her. Sadie could wait, and marry anyone she liked, as long as he was respectable. But for Diana, waiting was an unaffordable luxury. Beauty, like a rose, had its season. Year by year it diminished, and day by day it was threatened. Sometimes she woke in the night in a panic. And when she stared in the looking-glass, it was not vanity but anxiety.

Since she had come out, plenty of local boys had chased after her. But even those she liked, she did not encourage. She had to marry well, and Charles Wroughton was her best chance. If only he came tonight . . . She knew he was at Dene Park, because their charwoman, Mrs Chaplin, was aunt to the blacksmith, Jack Chaplin, who had done a small repair on Lord Dene's motor-car, which he liked to drive himself. He had taken it to the forge in person and, standing chatting to Chaplin while the repair was done, had mentioned that he was down at Dene Park for the whole summer.

The Wroughtons had not replied to the invitation, but that meant nothing. They might still come. If only he accepted the invitation . . . Especially the supper . . . She could manoeuvre him to a quiet corner of the room where they could talk. If *only* he came . . .

Sadie's route home led her past All Hallows Church and the rectory. The rector's wife, Mrs Fitzgerald, was in the garden

7

cutting roses. She beckoned to Sadie as she went past, coming over to the gate to meet her. Sadie obeyed with sinking heart. Mrs Fitzgerald, whom one was obliged to admire for her energetic philanthropy – she was an example to them all, not least according to herself – always meant trouble.

'How is your dear mother?' she enquired. 'Busy getting ready for this evening, I imagine?'

Sadie gave a noncommittal sort of 'Mmm.'

'You will please tell her,' Mrs Fitzgerald went on, 'that if she needs any help, I will send my Aggie over to led a hand.'

'I'll tell her,' Sadie said, knowing full well that the famously sharp-tempered rectory maid would cause more trouble than she was worth, and that her mother's servants would resent the notion they couldn't manage. 'Thank you. But I'm sure she's all right.'

She had a fair idea that the offer was made less in the spirit of generosity than from a desire to meddle. Mrs Fitzgerald couldn't bear anything in Northcote to happen without her, and used her position as rector's wife to ensure it didn't. Sadie had the middle child's quickness at summing people up, and she absorbed things when people thought she wasn't listening. She knew that Mrs Fitzgerald felt that the magic-lantern lecture should have taken place in the church hall rather than the village hall. That would have put her in charge of all the arrangements, and allowed her and the rector to hold the supper party afterwards. It was more fitting, since they could fairly be held to represent the village: Mrs Hunter was taking advantage of the completely irrelevant fact that the lecturer was Mr Hunter's nephew.

It would be interesting to hear all this from Mrs Fitzgerald herself, but Sadie knew, without actually thinking it out, that egging someone on to expose themselves was not a sport for someone low down in the social order, like her. Wounded top dogs were likely to bite. Instead, to deflect the rector's wife, she asked, 'How is Dr Fitzgerald's throat?'

'Much better, thank you. Dr Harding said there wasn't any infection. It was just a strain. He advised Rector only to talk in a whisper for a few days, and says he will be back to normal by Sunday.' Mrs Fitzgerald, not wholly deflected, was examining Sadie even as she spoke. 'I expect you're going home now to help your mother, aren't you? It must be nice for her to have you at home on an occasion like this. But, my dear, what are you going to do with yourself? Idling about the countryside like this . . .'

'It's the summer holidays,' Sadie said.

'You know I don't mean that, child. You're how old? Sixteen, isn't it? So school is finished for you now. It won't do to get into idle habits. I assure you, men want active, useful wives. Does your father mean to send you to a finishing school?'

'I don't know,' Sadie said, trying to edge away. There had been talk of a finishing school in Vienna, the same one Diana had gone to, but nothing had been said recently.

'Well, dear, you must do something. There's your sister at home already,' the rector's wife pursued. 'Not that Diana will have any difficulty finding a husband, so truly beautiful as she is. But you – well,' she concluded, having given Sadie another up-and-downer, as her brother William called such looks, 'you will have to work that bit harder, as I'm sure your mother knows. It must worry her to have you thumping about the countryside like a hoyden. You should take up some lady-like pastime – the piano, or flower-arranging, for instance.'

Sadie had fidgeted herself as far away as she could without actually leaving, so she broke in now in desperation and said, 'I'm so sorry, Mrs Fitzgerald, but I have to go. Mother's waiting for me.'

'Oh, quite, quite. Well, give her my regards, and don't forget to tell her I'll send Aggie over if she needs her.'

'I won't,' Sadie said, pleased with the ambiguity of the answer, and made her escape. She hurried until she was round the corner and out of sight, then slowed, and mouthed a silent 'Phew!' at the sky. She supposed she was going to get a lot of that sort of thing from now on. A finishing school – which might or might not be fun – would only be postponing the inevitable. What, after all, could a girl of her class do except get married? You couldn't have a career, like a boy. If a girl didn't marry, the prospect was grim. She 'stayed home and helped Mother', and eventually looked after her parents in their old age.

Well, nothing would happen until September, anyway. She had the last bit of July, and all of August . . . It was a shame the older boys weren't at home to make fun for them. They had gone, David straight from university and Bobby straight from school, to stay with friends for the summer. That left only Diana, who was too old to be of any use to her, and Peter, seven, who was too young. William, who was fourteen, had lately developed an obsession with engines, especially aeroplanes, and went off with other boys of similar bent to 'spot' them in whatever places these things could be spotted.

There was the annual trip to Bournemouth in August to look forward to, but she had an idea that Diana might get out of it this year, which would leave her with just William and Peter and the faint suspicion that she was getting too old for seaside holidays, rock pools, sandcastles and donkey rides. Was it possible, she wondered, rustling her hand through the long grass of the verge as she ambled along, that sixteen was the worst age of all to be? Too old to play and too young to be grown-up . . .

At the corner of Highwood Road she met their dog, Nailer, turning in from the other direction. They halted and looked at each other. Nailer was a white, terrier-type mongrel, a square-ish, bustling kind of dog, with a coarse coat, cocked ears, bushy eyebrows and stiff white moustaches that hinted at a drop of Scottie in the general mix. He somehow managed to combine

10

contempt for his humans with ingratiation, so that he always ended up being forgiven for the shortcomings in his character, which were many. He loved digging, fighting, stealing food, chasing cats and killing rats. Pursuit of his pleasures led him widely over the countryside, and his carnal reputation was high – or low, depending on your point of view. There were few farms or hamlets within a range of, say, five miles where an apologetic bitch had not at some point given birth to a litter of squirmers sporting those distinctive whiskers, the badge of her shame.

Nailer looked at Sadie cautiously from under his frosty overhang, keeping a judicious distance, stiff tail wagging, until he determined his welcome. A dog with a clear conscience might have come forward with open friendliness, especially to Sadie, but Nailer knew that, for some mysterious reason, almost everything he did was frowned on by the two-leggers.

Sadie smiled. 'Good dog,' she said. 'Where have you been, then?'

Relieved, he came up to greet her, discovered traces of Arthur and gave her a full and frank going-over.

'You and I are the only ones who like the smell of horse,' she said. 'Diana will turn up her nose at me until I change.' She sighed. 'I hope I don't get as silly as her when I'm her age. Come on, let's go home. I'm starving.'

Nailer bared his teeth in what passed with him for a smile, and fell in beside her.

There was a fine big copper beech in the garden of the Oliphants' country house. David Hunter was lying on the grass in its dappled shade; his friend Oliphant was sitting with his back against the trunk, smoking a gasper and watching the fumes drifting gently up into the leaves. They had been taking turns in reading Ovid aloud, and talking, as men at university throughout the ages always had, about

Life, and love, and women. Their experience of all three was necessarily limited to the intellectual rather than the practical, and some time ago they had lapsed into silence.

At last David said, 'Don't you think this life of ours is sterile? Reading books, theorising, the whole academic world . . . Look at our dons: shut away in cloisters. None of them knows what's really going on outside. We ought to be *living* life, not endlessly discussing it.'

Oliphant considered. 'But isn't some kind of preparation for life necessary? An apprenticeship of thought?'

'Good phrase,' David said.

Oliphant tried not to smirk. He didn't often get compliments. 'After all,' he went on, 'ignorance means you don't know how ignorant you are. Until we *know*, we can't tell what we need to know.'

'Oh, more words! I'm tired of living through words. I want to *do* something.'

'What sort of thing?' Oliphant asked reasonably.

'I don't know!' David cried in frustration. He sat up. 'I want the chance to do something glorious and noble. There must be honour somewhere in the world. We've become decadent in this country. We need to shake off the shackles of ease.'

'Good phrase,' Oliphant offered him back.

'Civilisation is smothering us! You see it everywhere – the base, ignoble concerns of earthbound creatures.'

'But doesn't one have to earn a living somehow?' Oliphant said doubtfully.

'I suppose so,' David said restlessly, 'but must it be the whole of existence? We need to get back to a simpler, cleaner state of being. Like the noble savage . . .'

'I say,' Oliphant protested.

David took a breath, and let it out. 'Was I getting carried away?'

'No, it's good. You make me think. Much more than old Ovid does, anyway.'

'So much for Life,' David said lightly. His saving grace was that taking himself seriously was an intermittent fault. 'Now, about Love.'

'I'm not sure I shall ever fall in love,' Oliphant said. 'Women are too mysterious. Dark and dangerous.' Down by the house he saw his mother and his sister Sophy arriving back from their afternoon of visiting. 'Except one's family, of course, but they don't count. And even they can be very peculiar.'

David looked and saw them, too. The sight of Sophy's slender form, seeming to float in white summer muslin, illuminated briefly by the sun as she passed in through the french windows, caused a tremor somewhere inside him. It was only on this visit, the most recent of many to the Oliphants' home, that Sophy had seemed to step out from the background into sharp relief.

'I sometimes wonder if they are so very different from us,' he said, more in hope than conviction. 'If you could get a girl away from everything and talk, *really* talk to her—'

'But you can't, that's the whole thing,' said Oliphant.

'Don't you believe in love?'

'I don't think it's a matter of believing,' Oliphant said gloomily. 'I think it's just something that happens to you, like tumbling down a mineshaft.' David shook his head disapprovingly. 'You're too romantic,' Oliphant went on. 'It's not the Crusades. It's dances. Tea parties. Mixed doubles.'

David drew up his knees and wrapped his arms round them. 'I don't care,' he said. 'I firmly believe my life is on the cusp of something tremendous. I don't know what it will be, but I'm ready for it.'

'You've another year at Oxford, don't forget,' said Oliphant. 'I wouldn't recommend falling in love before you've settled into a career. You may despise money-grubbing, but women come expensive.'

'Dark, dangerous and expensive. Your women sound most uninviting.'

'If you'd met my cousin Hetty . . .' said Oliphant. 'I wish you were coming with us to Scotland. I'm sure she has designs on me. You might act as a buffer state.'

'Thanks, but I've no wish to throw myself into the path of a rampaging cousin.'

'Well, you wanted adventure. And there are other females as well.'

Sophy, for one, David thought.

'Come for the shooting, anyway,' Oliphant pressed.

'I'd like to, but I'll have to ask my parents. Will yours mind?'

'Of course not,' said Oliphant. 'The more the merrier, Ma always says. I think she feels about Aunt Cratty the way I feel about Cousin Hetty – buffer states always welcome.'

'You paint a most inviting picture,' David said. 'Toss me a ciggie, won't you?'

CHAPTER TWO

'Servants' hall' was a generous term for their sitting-cum-dining-room off the kitchen, but it was good sized and comfortable, with a long table covered in a brown chenille cloth, several armchairs clustered round the fire, and various ornaments and knick-knacks giving it a home-like feel. Some belonged to individual servants, but others, like the mantelpiece clock, the Japanese fire screen and the framed prints on the walls, had been donated by the family, objects they had no more use for.

The servants at The Elms had their elevenses at half past ten, but in accordance with local practice they called it 'lunch' (their main meal at midday being 'dinner'). All except the gardener, Munt, that was, who called it 'beaver'. His first job had been as under-gardener to a retired don. One day during his first week the boy Munt had been toiling in the borders in the hot sun when his extravagantly bearded employer came upon him and said, in the rich and fruity tones that the little Munt had thought would suit God Himself: 'Good heavens, boy, don't you know the others have gone for their beaver? Scurry along now. The labourer is worthy of his hire, you know.'

Thus had been born a lifelong hero-worship, though as the professor had even then been in his eighties, little Munt had had only two years to incubate it before the old fellow died and he'd had to move on to another place. But still he

15

was wont to say, 'Ar, he was a *real* gentleman, was Professor Scrimgeour. He wouldn't have had no truck with this 'ere,' whenever some slackness of modern manners provoked him, which was often. The rest of the staff had heard as much about Professor Scrimgeour as they ever wanted to, and generally told Munt to 'shut up about the old geezer', thus neatly proving Munt's point.

Just before half past ten Emily, the kitchen-maid, had spread the cloth and was vaguely smoothing out the creases when Ethel, the under-housemaid, came in and gave her a sour look. Emily was a skinny little Irish thing and widely agreed to be half witted – though a kitchen-maid's life was such hell that generally only a half-witted girl would stick it out.

Emily knew what they thought of her, and both did and didn't care. She thought it was mean, but life had never taught her to expect any better treatment. And she wasn't half witted, though she couldn't read or write: her apparent vagueness came from her habit of retreating from the harshness of real life into a world of richly stocked imagination, where characters from the stories of her rural Irish childhood frolicked. Here, where the real Emily lived, were fairies and demons, talking animals, hidden gold, tricky elves and wicked witches, magic transformations, and sometimes – best of all – happy endings.

Ethel saw only 'that girl' bending across the table and smoothing the same place over and over like a faulty automaton. 'Haven't you laid the table yet?' she demanded. 'There's no time for your nonsense today, with all there is to do, big party tonight an' all. I'm not getting left with your work as well as my own because you've gone potty again.'

Emily turned to face her. 'I've not gone potty,' she protested, in her soft Donegal lilt. ''Twas tonight I was thinking about. Magic-lantern show! Oh, Ethel, won't it be lovely? I've never seen one before. I can hardly wait.'

16

'It's not real magic, you know,' Ethel said impatiently. 'I s'pose you think electric light is magic, too. And motor-cars.'

'I'm not daft,' Emily said reproachfully. 'Even if it's not magic, it's something new. Can't a girl be excited?'

'You can't be excited about nothing till you've laid that table. Come on, bustle about! The others'll be here in a minute.' She gave Emily a shove in the direction of the cutlery drawer and, by way of priming the pump, grabbed a stack of plates from the dresser and began putting them out.

Emily got only halfway to the drawer. 'At the show tonight, Ethel – can I sit next to you? Ah, go on! I don't want to sit next to Cook. She'll keep telling me off and I won't hear what the man says. *Please*, Ethel!'

Ethel stopped laying plates and gave her a tight, smug look, like a cat. 'You can sit where you like. I shan't be there.'

Emily was shocked. 'But the missus has given us the time off for it, and it's awful kind of her. You have to go.'

'I can do what I like with my own time off,' Ethel said, and pushed at the hair under her cap in a preening sort of movement. 'I'll be back in time to help at supper, but I've got better things to do than look at pictures of some ol' mountains.'

'Where you going?' Emily pleaded. Her eyes widened. 'You're goin' sparkin'! Is it that Billy Snow?'

'Never you mind who it is,' said Ethel.

'Oh, Ethel,' Emily breathed, her eyes bright with visions. What would it be like to be Ethel, and pretty, and to go sparking with a man? Billy Snow, shop assistant at the grocer's, Williamson's, transmogrified easily in her mind into a prince, and his bicycle into a white horse. Oh, the glory of it! But the danger . . . 'You be careful. If they find out, you'll catch it!'

Ethel could pounce like a cat, too, when she wanted. She caught Emily's wrist in one strong hand, and hissed, 'No-one's goin' to find out. And you're not goin' to tell.'

17

'I won't tell. I wouldn't,' Emily cried.

'You'd better not,' Ethel said. She gripped the thin wrist tighter and felt the bones grind together.

Emily didn't cry out. She'd learned that much over a lifetime of being bullied. 'I won't,' she said. 'I promise.'

'Swear on yer mother's grave,' Ethel insisted.

Emily looked alarmed. 'Ah, I don't want to do that,' she whimpered. 'It's unchancy.' The bones were ground harder. Emily's eyes filled with tears. 'Don't make me. I promise, really I do.'

'Mother's grave,' Ethel said menacingly, adding a little twisting motion to the grip. 'Say it.'

Emily knew she was beaten. 'I swear on me mother's grave I won't tell.' Ethel released her, and she rubbed her sore wrist dismally.

'Right,' said Ethel. 'Now if you tell, she'll die, so remember!'

Cook came in in time to hear Emily's little cry of alarm. She took in the scene. 'Stop tormenting that girl and fetch the milk in,' she commanded Ethel. 'And, Emily, go and fill the teapot. I don't know! Have I got to do everything myself? You'd think with all I've got to do today I'd get a bit of consideration, but no. Nothing but laziness and selfishness . . .'

Her audience had already gone.

By the time Munt arrived, and stood in the open doorway regarding them sardonically, the rest of the servants were assembled round the table: Cook – her real name was Joan Dunkley but no-one ever called her by it – the housemaids, Ada and Ethel, in their morning uniforms of lavender and plain caps, and the kitchen-maid, Emily, who was so skinny Munt felt sure she had worms and liked to expatiate on the subject especially at meal-times. As it was a Friday, the charwoman, Mrs Chaplin, was also there (she came on Monday, Wednesday and Friday mornings), sitting below the salt and eating bread and butter with the slow but unstoppable determination of – Munt thought – a slug eating its way through his delphiniums. And finally there was the boot-boy, Henry, who was twelve and had just left school after seven years of education, of which at least five were wasted, in Munt's view. He was a gormless-looking boy, whose no-coloured hair seemed to grow in several wrong directions and whose mouth hung permanently open – 'catchin' flies', Munt said disparagingly.

Cook, plying the enormous teapot, turned her head to him. 'Oh, there you are. Thought you weren't coming.'

'Where's that boy bin?' Munt growled. 'Ent seen hide n' hair of him this morning.'

'He's been cleaning the silver,' Ada answered sharply. Of them all, she was the one who disliked Munt the most. 'And then the missus sent him on an errand to the village.'

'Errand? Shirkin', more like,' Munt said. 'S'posed to be helping me. Peas to pick.'

'Pick 'em yourself,' Ada suggested.

'Not my job,' Munt retorted. 'That's boy's work. Or woman's,' he added significantly to Cook. 'Them as wants peas should fetch 'em theirselves.'

Cook bristled. 'Don't look at me. When d'you think I'd have time, with all I've got to do – even if I wanted to, which I don't? And may I remind you that Henry's the boot-boy who helps out in the garden. Not the gardener's boy.'

Munt's eyes gleamed with malice. 'Help'd be a fine thing. Neither use nor ornament, that boy.' Henry hunched down in his seat, waiting for the storm to pass. Munt poured the scorn directly on his bent head. ''Enry!' he scoffed. ''Enery the Eighth, that's who 'e is. Won't last five minutes. We'll be having a ninth any day, the way he goos on – and a tenth, and a 'leventh. Boys! All as bad as each other. They don't know the meaning o' work, these days. When I started with Professor Scrimgeour, we didn't have none o' this—'

19

'Oh, give over with your Professor Scrimbleshanks,' Cook interrupted. 'We know all about him. Are you having your lunch or not?'

'What is it? Bread and butter?' Munt surveyed the table suspiciously. 'What, no cake?'

'There's biscuits. I didn't have time to make cake, with all I've got to do for tonight.'

'You bin making biscuits, though.'

'They're quicker.'

'Don't like home-made 'uns. I like them bought biscuits,' Munt said, more for the love of dispute than from conviction. 'Them Digestives. And them Mah-ree.'

Cook breathed out hard through her nose. '*Once!*' she addressed the table. '*Once* we had bought biscuits, when the range broke down and they had to shut off the gas stove at the same time. But he never stops going on about 'em.'

'No time to make cake!' he scoffed. 'Idle, that's what you are. Soft an' idle, like all you wimmin. You wait till your precious socialists take over. They'll sort you out all right, make you jump to it.' He liked to twit her, because once, back in 1910 at election time, she had said if she had the vote she would vote for the Labour Party. It had been one of his favourite themes ever since. ''Ave you running round like 'ens, the lot of you.'

Cook reddened. 'Don't you talk such rubbish!'

'And you wanted to vote for 'em!' he scoffed. 'Show you what real work feels like, they would. Send you down the mines for a bit, like they used to in the old days.'

'There's not going to be no going down mines!'

'No, and there's not goin' to be no votes for wimmin, neither,' he asserted, his eyes gleaming. 'Fine mess we'd be in if we was run by cackling wimmin!'

'Couldn't do worse than men,' Cook snapped.

'Revolution. That's what we'd 'ave,' he said. 'Like the Frenchies. Gutters running blood.'

'Don't talk so disgusting. Now, do you want your lunch or not? It's no skin off my nose either way.'

'Put some bread and butter on a plate,' Munt said. 'And some o' them biscuits, if that's what you call 'em. And give us me tea.' He pulled an enamel mug out of his pocket.

'Aren't you having it here with us?' Mrs Chaplin asked. She liked male company, even Munt's. He might be a grumpy old devil, but he talked about different things. She knew everyone else's conversation by heart.

But he retorted, 'I'll 'ave it in me shed. Can't be doing with wimmin's nattering.' He took the mug, balanced the plate of bread and butter on top, and headed for the door.

'And bring the plate back!' Cook shouted after him.

Munt started singing 'I'm 'Enery the Eighth, I Am' as he went out, well satisfied. Women needed gingering up from time to time, else they forgot their place. Boys, too. He stepped out of the garden door, and came face to face with Nailer, who had left Sadie at the front door and come round to the kitchen to see if there was anything he could steal. They both stopped and stared at each other warily.

Munt had come to The Elms when it was first built and the grounds had been nothing but marked-off fields. Over the past nineteen years, he had created the gardens with the sweat of his brow and the bending of his back, and precious little help had he got from the succession of boys who had passed through. The garden was his, more than it could ever be the Hunters', and he defended it like his own. Munt hated most living creatures, who were all in league to destroy his precious plants, but most of all he hated boys, cats and dogs, who were the most intractable pests.

Nailer, however, he sometimes granted amnesty to, because Nailer chased all three out of the garden if he spotted them. Munt almost approved of Nailer who, he felt, shared his functional and misanthropic view of the world. Sometimes he kicked out at the dog for form's sake, and sometimes he ignored him, but occasionally he welcomed him into his shed and even gave him a bit of whatever he had to eat.

Nailer's small, round, dark eyes, like two blackcurrants under snow-covered bushes, watched the hands and feet for clues as to what his reception would be today, while his nose twitched to catch the scent of what was on the plate. A devilish thought came to Munt. He smiled. 'Like biscuits, do yer? Home made 'uns?'

Nailer's tail said he liked the tone of the question, at any rate.

'Just about fit for dogs,' Munt said, and winked. 'Don't tell 'er inside where they're going. Come on, then,' he concluded, and stumped off down the garden. Nailer balanced the greater resources of the kitchen against the likelihood of being hit with a frying-pan like last time (a regrettable incident with a string of sausages), then trotted after him.

Northcote had hardly existed before the railway came, though it was mentioned as a hamlet in the Domesday Book. Three hundred years later it became a village with the addition of All Hallows Church. But by the mid-nineteenth century it was still just a cluster of cottages, and a handful of farms scattered along either side of the old turnpike road that ran from Harrow to Rustington and on to High Wycombe. It had a population of a few hundred, two public houses, three shops and the old forge, set up next to where the toll gate had been.

There were two 'great houses' within the parish. Dene Park was one. The other was Manor Grange, once owned by the monks of a long-defunct abbey, which had since passed through a succession of secular hands. Aside from them, until 1887 Northcote had been nothing more than an anonymous village twenty miles from London, set in rolling, handsome countryside, well wooded, with fine pastures, and extensive hayfields that provided fodder for the capital's ever-hungry population of horses. History had streamed gently past without disturbing it. It was like any settlement in England, part of the ancient fabric of a largely peaceful land, whose shapes, habits, rhythms and assumptions would have been instantly recognisable to a time-traveller from any age.

And then the Metropolitan Railway had extended its lines north-westward from Harrow-on-the-Hill and, in 1887, opened a station at Northcote. The village stirred in its thousand-year sleep, opened one eye, then sat up in astonishment as the speculative builders who followed the permanent way bought land from both the landowners and started to construct. The railway meant it was now possible to work in London and live in the country, and people of all conditions made the move. Up went neat brick terraces for the working classes; smart semi-detached villas for the middling sort; and large detached houses in their own grounds for the better-off. Two schools and a hospital swapped the grime and choke of London for the fresh air and sweet water of the chalk hills, and more settlement followed. And the villagers of Northcote took a look at the invasion and decided it was good: there would be jobs for their sons and daughters; new careers for the bright ones; and commercial opportunities for the enterprising.

By the time Edward Hunter took the decision to move his wife and family of five from the tall, soot-streaked house in Kensington, the old village of Northcote had extended itself, first to join up with the station, and then engulf it, so that the station now stood pretty much in the middle of the built area instead of a short walk away. There were more shops, with all the delivery services – milk, meat, groceries, etc. – that could be desired; a large hotel with assembly rooms that could be hired for entertainments and dances; and the better houses had electricity as well as town gas laid

23

on. It made it easy for him to persuade his wife, Beatrice, that they would not be sacrificing the comfort and convenience of London.

The Elms, in Highwood Road, had been built in 1895, and had been lived in by the builder himself, so all the initial faults had been ironed out by the time he, having become extremely rich from his speculation, elevated himself and his wife to an Elizabethan manor near St Albans and sold The Elms to the Hunters.

It had four good rooms on the ground floor – drawing-room, dining-room, morning-room and what had been the builder's business-room, which Edward took as his study and smoking-room. There were extensive and comfortable domestic offices: kitchen, servants' hall, scullery, drying-room, boot-room, pantries, gun-room (the builder had been a keen sportsman), rear lobby and servants' cloakroom. Upstairs there were ten bedrooms, a bathroom and a WC. The grounds covered nearly an acre, with a large pleasure garden, a kitchen garden, a tennis lawn and, at the far end, a rather wild and dense shrubbery, perfect for growing boys to play in.

The move was made with no more than the usual degree of hellishness, exhausting labour, broken treasures, tears, anguish, hair-tearing, mislaid indispensables and lost tempers. Edward, at the bank all day and indulged ('Don't trouble your father!') by evening, missed the crises, and was able to say, at the end of the first weekend at The Elms, 'Well, that wasn't too bad, was it?' without the least intention of irony.

Beatrice was able to persuade her cook, the senior house-maid Ada and the children's nanny to come with her; otherwise she didn't think she could have coped at all. Fionnula O'Fearghail, which translated into English as Nula O'Farrell, had been much more to her than just her children's nurse. Nula had been with her ever since her come-out in Dublin – Beattie's father had been an army officer and was serving at Dublin Castle at the time – and had come with her on her marriage to Edward, first as personal maid and then, as the children started arriving, as nanny. When the youngest finally went to school, Nula married a local Northcote man and became Mrs Wilkes, but still kept her connection with the family by coming in, when required, to do sewing.

For Edward, there was never any question that the move to Northcote had been worth it. He slept like a baby in the country silence every night, woke to breathe clean air. His walk to the station was through pleasant, tree-lined streets, and his journey by train was an opportunity to read the newspaper without being interrupted. His bank's headquarters in Old Broad Street were a short walk from Broad Street station, and even after he was given the privilege of opening a new branch in Piccadilly, the whole journey to work took very little longer than when he had lived in Kensington. And he went home every night to the loveliest scenery in the country, to peace and quiet, to a garden in which he could potter, or sit and do nothing but listen to the birdsong, as the fancy took him.

The adjustment was not so easy for Beattie. She liked London: she liked to look out of her windows and see people going by, and traffic. She liked the noise and bustle, the sense of neighbours being close, a shop on every corner, and theatres and galleries only a cab ride away. She liked street lamps and fog, the sound of horses, and the trains that hooted in the night as they went back to the depot; the rattle of trams in the early morning and the sound of milk bottles on doorsteps as the world wound up again.

But a wife goes where her husband goes, so she just had to get on with it. With Cook and Ada to get the routines set up, and Nula to confide in, she could hold her own; and Edward's manifest happiness at coming home to his rural idyll at the end of each day was her compensation. Before the first anniversary of the move arrived, their five children had become six, testimony to Edward's content and the rejuvenating effect of country living.

The Wroughtons hadn't come. Beattie hadn't really expected them to, and there was no need for Mrs Fitzgerald to lay a hand on her wrist and say, in that poisonously sweet way of hers, 'Don't be too disappointed, my dear. You couldn't expect the earl and countess to come to a *standing* supper.' The implication was that if *she* had organised the thing, it would have been done in a way that met the local nobility's exacting standards. Beattie only smiled vaguely – her air of serenity was a great defence against those like the rector's wife who couldn't be snubbed.

In any case, she was too busy checking that everything was as it should be to pay much attention. The folding doors between the dining-room and the drawing-room had been thrown back, making an adequate space, and the evening was so warm the french windows from the dining-room into the garden were open, so that the gentlemen could step outside to smoke. The buffet supper looked beautiful – Cook was an artist, and it was all elegantly laid out with floral decorations. The hired waiter and waitress knew their business, and the maids were circulating quietly.

There had been a slight ruffle of the surface waters at the beginning when Ethel did not seem to be present, then appeared in her afternoon black and frilled apron but wearing her morning cap. Beattie had raised her eyebrows at her across the room as high as they would go, and fortunately Ada had looked round, spotted the error and hustled her out to come back properly attired a few minutes later. She could trust Ada to get to the bottom of it. Ethel hadn't been with them long, and Beattie suspected she might be trouble. She *seemed* perfectly all right, but long experience of servants taught you to spot little warning signs, and there was something about the set of Ethel's mouth and the tilt of her head . . .

26

But everything was going splendidly now. Mrs Oliver came up to congratulate her. The Olivers of Manor Grange were affable and unaffected, though John Oliver was an Honourable and Mrs Oliver was the daughter of a baronet. They enjoyed entertaining and being entertained, and were a much more tangible asset to the neighbourhood than the haughty Wroughtons. They were in their fifties, an energetic couple often to be seen out on invigorating walks, always surrounded by a selection of their many dogs. Though childless themselves, they both came from large families, and often had parties of nephews, nieces and cousins to stay.

'What a splendid party!' Mrs Oliver said now. 'I did so enjoy the lecture. And what a good turn-out! I think the whole village was there. We ought to have more of that sort of thing, don't you agree? We should get up a series of lectures on intelligent subjects.'

Mrs Oliver loved getting things up, with the overflowing energy of the childless woman. Often these schemes came to nothing, so it was only necessary at this stage for Beattie to smile and say, 'What a good idea.'

'Do you think so?' Mrs Oliver said. 'I do believe we ought to encourage the lower orders to widen their horizons. A lecture series might get them talking about something besides the weather and the harvest and Mrs Brown's baby. We could invite speakers from different disciplines to come down. Oh, and at the end of each series we might publish all the lectures in book form!' Her imagination was soaring now. 'We might start a national movement of improvement: village lectures. The Northcote Programme, we could call it!'

'Well,' Beattie said cautiously, the gentlest tug on the reins. Fortunately Mrs Oliver had a light mouth. She laughed. 'Yes, of course – first things first. We must start small and see where it goes. But there's no harm in aiming high, is there? What an interesting man Mr Jack Hunter is!' She looked round and lowered her voice. 'My dear, do you think he needs rescuing from Dr Fitzgerald? I rather think the good rector has managed to turn the topic from Swiss mountains to African jungles.'

'Oh, good heavens, yes,' Beattie said. The rector could talk about Africa until his victims' eyes glazed, and he had a devilish skill in making any conversational opening lead straight to the heart of the Dark Continent. As well as boring, he could be embarrassingly graphic sometimes when his enthusiasm for tribal customs overcame him, particularly on subjects like nudity and nuptial rites.

Mrs Oliver patted her hand. 'Fear not! I'll go and interrupt them.'

Beattie watched her perform a neat cutting-out operation, taking Jack by the arm and turning him with a 'Now I *must* ask you,' and a gay smile of apology at the rector. It was beautifully done. Seeing the bereaved rector's eyes wander in her direction, Beattie declined to become his next victim and slipped away to talk to the Gordons.

Diana had swallowed her disappointment. The Wroughtons had been a long shot anyway, and at least she had Alec Gordon to fall back on. He was the son of neighbours who lived at Highwood House, just a little further up the road, and one of her long-standing admirers. He had just gone to fetch her something to drink when she heard the sounds of a late arrival, saw a little ripple near the door, and heard a man's deep voice in the hall. Her heart jumped. Could it be . . . ? Her mother was nowhere in sight, and her father was at the back of the room talking to Cousin Jack and Mrs Oliver. She slipped through the crowds and stepped out into the hall in time to see a flustered Ada taking the silk hat and gloves of Charles Wroughton.

Ada turned to her with relief. 'Oh, Miss Diana!' She gathered herself to remember his correct title. 'The Viscount Dene, miss.'

Diana dismissed Ada with a nod and stepped forward. 'How nice to see you again. I'd rather given you up for lost,' she said.

His voice was deep and curiously without inflection. 'I'm afraid the invitation went astray somehow. I only found out at the last moment. My parents had a prior engagement, otherwise I'm sure . . .'

Diana had a pretty clear picture of what had happened. The earl and countess had tossed aside the invitation without any intention of accepting, never thinking of mentioning it to Charles. He had somehow found it, or found out about the evening's entertainment some other way. But he had come, that was the thing – had stepped down off his pedestal. It was a big first step. She extended her hand and smiled graciously. 'It doesn't matter in the least,' she said. 'I'm very glad you were able to come. Let me take you to say good evening to my mother. And then we must get you something to eat.'

He followed her, his face giving away nothing. 'I'm sorry to have missed the lecture,' he said.

'It was very interesting,' she said. 'But I shall tell you all about it.' She led him towards her mother, whose head she could just see through the crowds, and passed, without seeing him, Alec Gordon, who was holding the glass of lemonade he had fetched her.

CHAPTER THREE

When Mrs Oliver left them, Edward said to Jack, 'Would you like to step outside for a cigarette?'

Jack was a handsome man, not tall but with an upright, soldierly look about him. His skin was rather brown from his travels, and he had thick dark hair that wanted to be unruly and was barely tamed with oil. There was not much resemblance between him and Edward, apart from the dark colouring, and not very much in character, either. They had both been to Eton, but Jack was several years below Edward, and their careers there had been very different. Edward, shy and sensitive, had been a scholar; Jack had been popular and sporting. Their memories in later years had come from opposite directions.

'Badgered to death by gerunds!' Jack would cry. 'What's the use of Latin and Greek?'

'Hacked about in the mud! What's the use of soccer and rugger?' Edward would reply.

In fact, Edward was not entirely unsporting. He liked cricket, was quite a pretty bowler and a useful catcher at slip. He rowed cleanly, though without great power, and was an adequate partner at tennis. What he didn't have was the unflinching courage to excel in the muddier sports, or the ambition to succeed in athletics. And Jack, while he liked the quick and sure results sport bestowed, was no dunce: where he saw the purpose of a lesson he could apply himself well enough.

But while Edward had gone to Oxford, Jack was too restless for university. He wanted adventure, and the army seemed his natural home. India and Afghanistan gave him a taste for mountains, and when he inherited his fortune he was able to dedicate his life to his pleasures, travel and mountaineering. He had written several well-received books about his travels, illustrated with his own sketches, and did the occasional lecture-tour. He was welcomed everywhere, and never seemed to age. He and Edward had always remained friends, and kept in touch by letter. They met in Town, at the club, about twice a year, or whenever Jack happened to be in England, and he and Beth occasionally visited Northcote.

He felt now for his cigarettes, but Edward was quicker, got out his case and held it open. 'No, have one of mine.'

Jack took one and said, 'Thanks, Uncle.'

'Don't you think it's about time you dropped the "uncle" nonsense?' said Edward. 'You used to roast me with it at Eton, but now we're both mature men . . .'

Jack grinned. 'I only do it to embarrass you,' he said, lighting them both.

Edward drew on his cigarette and said, 'Before the rector interrupted us, I thought you were about to develop some hints I detected in your lecture.'

'About the situation in Germany? You're quite right. You never hear it talked about over here. You'd think we were all asleep!'

At that moment Beth came out into the garden. 'All asleep? Darling, they were on the edge of their seats.' She was small and neat, with a quick, athletic form from all the walking and climbing; fairish, prettyish, with no striking beauty but rather large dark eyes. 'Mmm!' she said, taking the cigarette from Jack's fingers and drawing on it. 'I was gasping too!'

'Beth!' Edward exclaimed, scandalised.

31

'Oh, don't look so pained,' she said. 'Lots of women smoke – they just don't let you see them.'

'Perhaps that's just as well,' said Edward.

She flipped careless fingers at his disapproval. 'Anyway, who was asleep?' she went on. '*I* didn't see anyone.'

'We were talking about Germany,' Jack explained. 'People over here simply don't seem to be awake to the danger.'

'Of course, in Switzerland one's ideally placed to hear all sides, French, German and Italian,' Beth said. 'We met quite a few Austrians as well. This business in the Balkans has them in uproar.'

'It's not serious, is it?' Edward said. 'After all, there's always trouble in the Balkans.'

At the end of June, the heir to the dual throne of Austria-Hungary, Archduke Franz Ferdinand, had been visiting Bosnia, which had been annexed by Austria in 1908. While riding through the streets in Sarajevo in an open motor-car, he and his wife had been shot and killed by an anarchist, who turned out to be Serbian. There were many Serbs living in Bosnia who objected to the Austrian presence, and believed Serbia should have sovereignty over Bosnia; indeed, Serbia's ambition had long been to rule over the whole of the Balkans.

'It's quite an irony that they should have shot poor old Franz Ferdinand,' Beth said. 'He was the one person who argued for some kind of federal system, to give the Slavs in the Austrian Empire a degree of self-determination. So it was foolish as well as wicked to kill him, poor old creature – and his wife, whom he loved so.'

Jack took it up. 'The Austrians we met were seething with indignation. But they also want to assert themselves, to restore their reputation as a great power. In short, they're looking for a *casus belli*.'

'I told you Latin would come in handy one day,' Edward said.

'He has you to thank for it,' Beth said. 'He told me he

32

never would have passed second-year Trials without your help.'

'So Austria means to do what? Edward asked. 'Declare war on Serbia?'

Jack nodded. 'It looks likely. And if they do, Russia is bound to come in on Serbia's side.'

'But what has Germany to do with it?' Edward asked.

'Germany's offered Austria unconditional support – I heard it spoken of as "a blank cheque",' said Jack. 'And France is Russia's ally. If Austria attacks Serbia, and Russia comes in to defend the Slavs, Germany has the excuse to attack France, which it's wanted to do ever since Unification.'

'We had a very good chat with a Swiss German,' said Beth, 'who has a friend who knows someone in the inner circle, close to the Kaiser. He hears all the gossip. The Germans despise the old nations, like us and France. They think the future lies with young, vigorous nations like themselves and America.' She wrinkled her nose at the opinion.

Edward stared into the dusk as he contemplated the idea. 'Well, of course, it may all come to nothing. International crises come and go.'

'Oh, quite,' said Jack, passing the cigarette to Beth again. 'Serbia apologises, Austria rattles the sabres a little, diplomats scurry about, all the toy soldiers go back in the box. It would be an infernal nuisance if anything did blow up, though. Most of Europe would be out of bounds, and we already had plans for next year.'

'The Ardennes and the Black Forest,' Beth explained. 'We're in a hilly sort of mood.'

'There's still Italy,' Edward said, with a hint of wistfulness. Jack and Beth romped about Europe, like children in their own nursery. It was so different when you were tied down to career, home and family. Bournemouth was about the limit to his travelling, these days. 'The Italian Alps.'

'Too close to Austria.' She sighed.

33

'Never mind, darling,' Jack said. 'We could do with a spell in England. Spend the winter in London for the shows, and do some walking in the Peaks or the Lake District next year.' They had a house in Ebury Street, convenient for Victoria Station.

'I for one would be glad to see a bit more of you,' said Edward.

Beth patted his arm. 'You're such a dear. We're going to have a few weeks in London when we get back from our lecture-tour, anyway, so we shall see you then.'

'And you'll be glad to come out here on Sundays,' Edward added, 'to get away from the grime.'

'Still promoting your rural idyll!' Jack grinned.

Charles Wroughton had learned about the missing invitation from the chauffeur, Randall.

Motor-cars being what they were, a chauffeur had to be as much an engineer as a driver. Randall had joined the household just as Charles had come home from Oxford for the last time and developed an interest in motor-cars. Randall had been more than willing to teach the young master all he knew, both above and below the bonnet, and as they were much of an age, a friendship had grown up between them.

When Lord Wroughton was made Earl Wroughton and Viscount Dene, Charles came in for the cadet title and an increased allowance, and spent what the earl considered an extravagant amount on a car of his own, an almost new Vermorel Torpedo. Charles and Randall spent many happy hours learning the anatomy of this new and exotic lady, and though the young Viscount Dene liked to drive himself, he took Randall along when it was just a pleasure-jaunt – a practical move as well as a kindly one.

Charles was not given to introspection, but if he had given it any thought, he might have concluded that Randall was the closest thing he had to a friend – though it would never have done for his father to suspect anything of the sort. Even when he had been only a baron, Lord Wroughton had liked people to know their place, whether prince or chimney-sweep. Condescension from above was as pernicious as impertinence from below.

Charles was, despite his social position, a shy and diffident man. His younger brother, Rupert, was everything he was not – handsome, outgoing, witty, popular. Charles never knew what to say to people, unless they asked him a factual question on a subject he knew about: farming, stock-breeding, the countryside, family history and so on. Then he could make a measured and thoughtful reply. But he found it hard to have opinions on abstract subjects, and was too literal to make small-talk. Though not naturally dour, he did not know how to make a joke; and while he liked and admired the fair sex, he was too self-conscious to flirt or pay compliments.

In consequence, people thought him haughty and unap-proachable. He was well aware of his reputation for aloofness, and it saddened him, though he didn't know what he could possibly do about it. The estate workers, villagers and servants – people who had known him since childhood and with whom he was much less shy – liked and admired him, but those of his own class found him uninteresting, even cold. So despite his being a very eligible *parti*, he had been more often sought by the mothers of marriageable girls than the girls themselves. At twenty-seven he was still unwed and had never been properly in love.

The nearest he had come to it was at the age of twelve, with the daughter of a local woodsman. Ruth Povey had been ten. Slim and quick-moving, utterly fearless, and unaware of the difference in their rank, she had shown him how to catch 'tiddlers' with bare hands, standing knee-deep in the stream with her skirts tucked into her knickers, how to make a 'camp' in a tree, how to snare rabbits and watch

35

for badgers. She had demonstrated the sweetness of the clover-head when sucked, the power of the buttercup held below the chin, and the wisdom of the daisy pulled apart petal by petal. When her flower had concluded 'He loves me', Charles had accepted the truth of it.

He was enchanted by her and, through one golden summer, spent every moment he could with her. He made her a rope swing on the limb of a big willow by the river; he gave her a round pebble with a hole through the middle that he had found, and she wore it round her neck on a piece of string. Once, wanting to give her flowers, he took some from an arrangement in the hall, and suffered agonies of guilt for days afterwards. When she laughed at him, it didn't wound him, and when she smiled at him, it made his heart swell with silent joy.

At the end of the summer her father had got a new position, and she and her family had moved away. He was heartbroken. His greatest sorrow was that, on the day of the removal, when he had gone to say goodbye to her – at half past five in the morning, by the thistle-patch behind the privy at the back of the cottage – and she had held up her face to him and said he could kiss her if he liked, he had not had the nerve to do so. He had, of course, never seen her again.

Now, because of his continued single state, it was generally assumed he was pledged to his second cousin, Lady Helen Hale. Indeed, his parents and hers would have welcomed the match, but those closest to him – his brother Rupert, his manservant Varden, and Randall – knew that he disliked her intensely, and only his deeply ingrained politeness hid the fact from the world.

His greatest fear was that he would somehow find himself in the position of *having* to marry her, either through some misunderstanding or from the unendurable pressure of expectation. There had to be an heir, of course, but surely

Rupert could provide one. Rupert showed no sign of wanting to settle down and, during a more than usually frank conversation a year ago, had told Charles not to depend on it. 'The duty's yours, old man,' he had said, with his customary wicked smile. 'You're not to be scraping it off on to me – though I don't blame you a bit for not wanting to be leg-shackled to Helen. That *would* be a fate worse than death.'

But Charles was nearing despair. Other girls of his class didn't like him, and he didn't much like them, either. They too much resembled Helen – he could see only too clearly that the moment the wedding was over they would turn instantly and mysteriously into their mothers. And Charles had – which would have surprised most of those who knew him – a deeply romantic seam under his prosaic exterior. He wanted to fall in love, as he had with Ruth, his wood sprite of long ago.

Then one evening, across a crowded ballroom, he had caught sight of an exquisite face, whose lambent eyes were gazing at him with an intensity he could not account for. A girl of dazzling beauty; and though she was divinely fair and Ruth had been dark, there was a delicacy about her that reminded him of the woodsman's little daughter. She seemed familiar for some reason, which added to his confused feeling that she might somehow *be* Ruth, grown up and come back to find him. She smiled, the sort of inviting smile that said, *Yes, you do know me, it's quite safe to come over.* And then he remembered that he had met her, very briefly, at the Buller-Fullertons' party a few weeks ago. Couldn't remember what her name was – it had been horribly noisy – but he had gathered that she lived somewhere near Dene Park.

He made his way through the crowds to her; acquaintance was remade. Of course, now he understood: she was the daughter of Dad's banker, Hunter, a perfectly decent chap who had taken a gun out with them on a couple of occasions. Good shot, too. And Dad valued his advice. Yes, it was safe to talk to her, but as he did so, he realised it was much more than safe: it was a pleasure. He asked her to dance. She was like thistledown in his arms. Though Charles was tall, rather heavyset and looked clumsy because of his shyness, he was actually a good dancer. Their steps suited, though she seemed tiny and fragile compared with his bulk – a creature from another world.

Best of all, though, was that she asked him only questions he could answer, and seemed fascinated by everything he said. It seemed – against all the odds – that she liked him. He was overwhelmed with gratitude.

Their dances ended and he was obliged, from courtesy, to return to the party he had come with. After that he did not meet her again – their paths were not very likely to cross in the normal course of things. It was Ruth all over again – the lost opportunity. He realised he should have made sure of another meeting before leaving her that evening. He cursed his awkwardness, and accepted the sorrowful parting as no more than he deserved . . .

Until the evening when he drove into the garage-yard at Dene Park, and Randall, coming over to him, said casually, 'Shall I put her away, my lord? Only I thought you might be wanting her again this evening.'

'I don't think I have any engagements,' Charles said, puzzled.

'Oh, I beg your pardon,' Randall said. 'I thought you might be going to the magic-lantern show in the village hall. Or, at least, to the supper party afterwards, seeing as it's Mr and Mrs Hunter who've invited you.'

'Hunter?' he said. An image streaked across his mind, like a meteor. 'You don't mean—?'

Explanations followed. The Hunters! Their beautiful daughter! The most beautiful girl he had ever met. Of course his parents wouldn't go, and would have assumed he wouldn't go either, so had not bothered to tell him about it. He was now too late for the lecture, since he would have to go up and change first, but he might still get to the supper party by a reasonable hour. He had hurried indoors, rousted out Varden (who had expected a quiet evening), got into his evening clothes and gone in a state of heightened expectation to the Hunters' house.

What luck, he thought, as he motored down the interminable Dene Park drive – a mile and a quarter, actually – to the gates. What sheer, blind chance that Randall had happened to mention it! It was only afterwards that he had wondered if it was quite as much a matter of chance as it had seemed. He was too shy to ask the chauffeur, but on reflection there had been something in his expression . . .

In fact – though Charles did not know it – Randall had learned long before from Varden that the young master had 'fallen for a pair of pretty eyes', in Varden's words, and it was a shame that their paths were not likely to cross again. Then Randall had learned from the blacksmith, Chaplin, who had had it from his aunt the charwoman, that the Hunters had invited the Wroughtons but they had not deigned to reply.

'I should have a pair of wings and a bow and arrow,' Randall said to himself, when Charles returned that evening with a look of bemused happiness. Of course, the girl wasn't of the right class, and the earl and countess wouldn't wear it for a minute, but the family was perfectly respectable and stranger things had happened. Maybe they would decide it was worth it to get an heir. It wasn't as if the girl was an actress . . . At any rate, it was good to see the viscount happy. At least Lord Dene would have had a little romance before he went to his doom with Lady Helen. Randall was not sorry about his decision to interfere.

The day after the party was not really one of Nula Wilkes's days, but she turned up anyway, saying someone was bound to have torn a hem or pulled off a button. She had a good long chat in the kitchen with Cook to hear all about it. Beattie, going upstairs after seeing Jack and Beth off on their lecture-tour, found her in the linen room, where her sewing-machine was set up, going over the previous night's finery. Beattie saw her through the open door and stopped.

'The beadwork on this bodice is coming loose,' Nula said. 'Anyone'd think you were *dancin*'. I gather it was a roarin' success. And the grand folk came after all?'

'The one that mattered,' Beattie said. 'The Viscount Dene. I was pleasantly surprised.'

'No surprise to me. If I was a man, I'd walk a country mile to see you in this gown.'

'Darling Nula, people don't even *motor* to see me any more!'

'*Do* they not? Well, and aren't you the modest one! You'd be surprised who dreams about you, little Miss Beattie Cazalet. Throbbin' hearts all round the village, so I've heard.'

'Such nonsense,' Beattie said. 'I'm an old married woman, mother of six.'

Nula smiled, taking another tiny stitch. The sewing-machine was useful, but fine work she did by hand, as she always had. 'You'll always be my beautiful young lady. I remember dressing you for your coming-out ball . . .'

'Don't, Nula,' Beattie said.

The past was a sweet drug that could waste away your life; and there was sharpness in it, too. It did not do to think about the time when one was young and every possibility in life seemed open. Doors closed, the future grew rapidly narrower until there was only one place one could set one's foot. Edward was a good man, and a good husband, and she was lucky – luckier than anyone knew – to have him. But marriage had changed her – inevitably. As a girl she had been lively, full of chatter, always singing, dancing about her domestic chores. But Edward was a serious man, thoughtful and responsible. He had fallen in love with her lightness, but it troubled him, too.

Besides, a banker was like a doctor or a lawyer: he had to keep his clients' business secret, and she had learned early in their marriage not to ask questions when he came home at the end of the day. It had placed a barrier between them. She had been so young, so grateful, so passionately eager to give him everything, and it had hurt her that there were things he held back from her. But it was just one of the adjustments of marriage. There were areas of his life where she set no foot; and a store of things she had never told him. But he loved the enigma of her. Sometimes when they were sitting silently together, he would say, 'You have your air of mystery tonight, my love.'

'Cook said the lantern show was grand,' Nula continued, obediently changing the subject. 'And the supper afterwards – fine and tasty?'

'Everything was perfect,' Beattie said. 'But what was going on with the maids?'

'That Ethel went out walkin' with a boy instead of goin' to the lantern show, and barely got back in time,' Nula said. 'That young feller from Williamson's – sure, isn't it the lure of the big white apron? Any man looks a dream in that. Same as the kilt – 'tis the romance of it.'

Beattie laughed, as she was meant to, but it did not deflect her. It was deceit, and it was taking advantage – she had granted the time off to go to the lantern lecture, nothing else. *Too sharp, that one – needs taking down a peg*: that was what Nula would have said of Ethel when she was Nanny Nula. But now she wanted only to save Beattie from being troubled.

But if Beattie didn't worry over things like that, what *was* she to do with her days? The children all grown and autonomous. Even little Peter was now away at school most of the day, and as gravely composed as an alderman about his

41

childish concerns when he was home. The children didn't need her and Edward seemed to be more preoccupied with business every year, and if the household didn't take up her time . . .

'I shall have to have a word with Ethel,' Beattie said.

Nula knew better than to argue when the lovely mouth got set like that. Miss Beattie, for all her gentle ways, had always been as stubborn as a donkey when she was set on something. 'Tell us about the grand one that came,' she suggested instead.

'Lord Dene? He seemed a pleasant, sensible sort of man. Rather grave, perhaps.'

'After our Diana, is he?'

'I wouldn't say that. He spoke mostly to the master and Mr Jack. Oh, and the rector latched on, of course. Lord Dene looked at her a great deal, though.'

'Of course he did. She wasn't made so beautiful for nothing.'

'The Wroughtons are above our touch,' Beattie warned.

'Sure, she's entitled to look as high as she likes. There's pretty girls, and then there's real beauties. Not so many of *them* around.'

They had had this conversation many times before. Beattie sighed a little. 'I'm sure a viscount meets more of them than other men.'

'But he came, didn't he? When he needn't have. And if that wasn't for Diana's sake, I don't know what.'

'Well, it's no use encouraging her until he shows his hand,' Beattie said firmly. 'Don't build up her hopes, Nula, only to have them dashed.'

Nimbly, Nula changed the subject again. 'Have you heard anything from the boys?'

'Only bread-and-butter notes to say they arrived. You know what boys are like. Writing a proper letter is torture to them. I suppose we'll hear from them when they want something,' Beattie said, with a smile.

CHAPTER FOUR

Diana went from triumph on the night of the lantern show, when Charles Wroughton had appeared, to gloom the next morning when she remembered he hadn't said he wanted to see her again. The likelihood was that nothing would come of their three meetings.

She was not in his sphere, so she was unlikely simply to bump into him. Nula insisted that he could only have come at all for her sake, but nothing he had said or done last night gave her hope. There was nothing of the lover in him. He had not spoken much at all, but he had seemed more at ease with masculine, political discussion. She was used to boys of her own age, who tried to charm her with either wit or flattery.

That was the problem, she thought, as she lay in bed staring at the ceiling and remembering. He was older than her usual beaux. The young men she knew seemed lightweight in comparison with him, their ease and chatter trivial – but pleasant and familiar. Charles Wroughton seemed so big and grown-up and serious in her memory, she felt almost afraid of him. Nothing was likely to happen, she decided, and perhaps it was just as well. She gave a convulsive little shiver, pulled the covers up over her shoulders and went back to sleep.

She got up late, having missed breakfast, and noted that neither Mother nor Nula mentioned Lord Dene. They must also have decided it was hopeless, she thought gloomily.

After luncheon, Beattie told her to go out and get some fresh air as an antidote to the late night and cigarette smoke.

Diana felt listless. 'I don't feel like a walk.'

'That's proof enough that you need it,' Beattie told her briskly. 'You're looking pale, and you have dark shadows under your eyes.'

'I'll go with you,' Sadie offered kindly.

'It's too hot to walk,' Diana complained.

'We'll go through the woods,' Sadie said. 'It'll be nice and cool in there. We'll take Nailer – he hasn't had a walk in ages.'

'That dog's out all the time,' Diana pointed out.

'Not the same as a proper walk,' said Sadie.

So they went, and she did feel better for the exercise, which annoyed her at first, but her good sense soon blew that away. She even recovered her temper enough to throw a stick for Nailer, rather than at him. He was so surprised he almost didn't chase it, which made her laugh. Thus she was in a better frame of mind when they reached home again – which was just as well because a red motor-car was parked outside the house.

Sadie said cheerfully, 'Oh, good, visitors!' and then, 'I say, isn't that Lord Dene's motor?' And Nailer ceremoniously wetted one of the front tyres before trotting busily up to the front door to see who was there.

Diana felt herself pale with nervousness. 'What can he want?' she heard herself say.

Sadie was about to say something sharp, but looked sidelong at her sister and shut her mouth. She thought him dull and old, but if Diana was fancying him she had better hold her tongue.

He was in the drawing-room with Beattie, having tea, and stood up as the girls came in. Beattie gave them a quick glance of what looked to Sadie like relief, and she wondered if the conversation had been hard going. Standing at the door with Nailer, both of them cautiously testing the air, Sadie noted that he did not smile, though he looked long at Diana – one could almost say he stared. That was not unusual, though. Even strangers in the streets of London sometimes stared at her because she was so beautiful.

Into the prevailing silence, Beattie said, 'Come and have some tea, girls. Lord Dene dropped in to say thank you for supper last night.'

'I enjoyed the occasion very much,' he said unemphatically.

Dull and old, Sadie thought. *And plain.* Without smiles or conversation there wasn't much to say about him except that he was undoubtedly *there*, taking up space and air in a very solid fashion. Perhaps, she thought, it was her awareness of his title, but he did seem to be more definite and corporeal than most people.

Diana was remembering how *big* he was – tall and heavily built. Big and grim, he seemed, with no smile to go with his staring. But her manners were automatic. 'I'm glad,' she said. 'It was nice of you to come.' Still he loomed, unmoving. 'Do sit down,' she suggested. He sat again on the sofa, but well towards one end, looking at her as if inviting her to sit beside him.

She sat obediently, but with a nervous smile, and Beattie, to give her something to do, said, 'Pour yourself and Sadie some tea, dear. Lord Dene, you remember my younger daughter, Sadie?'

'Yes, of course,' he said, and as Sadie took the armchair opposite him, next to her mother, he looked at her and smiled. It was not much of a smile, but it was a definite attempt at civility, and Sadie applauded him for it. Nailer went over to inspect his trousers – Nailer had no drawing-room manners – and Beattie said hastily, 'Push him away if he bothers you.'

But Lord Dene reached down and scratched Nailer's head in a way that told Sadie he knew about dogs and liked them.

45

Her approval rose another notch. He looked at her again and said, 'He doesn't bother me. He's a grand fellow. Is he yours?'

'He belongs to everyone,' Sadie said, 'but I suppose I'm the one who likes him best.'

'He looks like a ratter,' said Charles.

'He is – he's first rate.'

'I had a terrier like him when I was a boy. I used to rat with him in the Great Barn at Goscote.'

'Oh, I know it. I saw a barn owl there once.'

While this useful talk was going on, Diana was pouring tea and had the chance to look at Charles Wroughton without his looking at her. You wouldn't call him handsome, but he had a healthy, fleshy sort of face, pleasant enough, only rather grave and serious. His nose was big, but straight. His eyes were perhaps a little small and his lips on the thin side, but not in a mean way, and taken all together his features gave the impression of a man of breeding. His hair was fair and crinkly, subdued with macassar at the moment, except for a few errant whips at the base of his neck, which she saw when he turned towards Beattie. Now he turned towards her and as his eyes met hers she felt a little shiver run down her back and had to look away, glad of the excuse of the tea she was passing to Sadie.

'Would you like another cup?' she asked him, busy with the pot and hot water.

'Thank you, but no. I should be going,' he said. He addressed Beattie: 'I came to say thank you, but also to ask whether Miss Hunter would care to join me and a group of friends on a picnic by the river at Cookham next Saturday.'

Beattie looked at Diana, whose eyes were fixed firmly on the teapot but whose cheeks had grown pink. It seemed to Beattie an approving shade. 'How kind of you to ask,' she said.

He hastened to add detail. They would all travel down

46

together in two motor-cars, to the house of some friends of his family, the Marlowes, whose garden ran down to the river. 'Lady Marjorie Marlowe is a sort of cousin of my mother's.' They would picnic in the garden and perhaps walk beside the river before motoring back in convoy.

Beattie realised that the invitation had been carefully crafted to allay any parental unease. Everything, even the drive down, was to be done as a group, and the picnic was to take place not in some wild pocket of nature but in the garden of a senior family friend, who might be trusted to act as duenna. Diana's reputation would be protected at all times. It was unusually considerate for a young man, she thought. Diana had been admired by many, but few had been distinguished by their thoughtfulness.

Of course, Charles Wroughton was not as young as Diana's usual suitors. Beattie had looked him up in *Debrett's* (though she wouldn't dream of admitting it), and knew he was twenty-seven; his brother Rupert was twenty-four and there was a sister between them, Caroline, who had married a Lord Grosmore. Eight years was not a large gap to her, but she remembered what it was like to be nineteen and guessed that twenty-seven would seem a great age to Diana. What impressed Beattie most was that he had obviously shaped the invitation in such a way that Diana's parents would be unlikely to refuse permission, which was a sign of the seriousness of his purpose. She felt a reprehensible shiver of excitement to think that he should be so determined to see Diana again.

'It sounds like a very pleasant outing,' she said. 'I have no objection, if Diana wants to go.'

Charles Wroughton hurried on eagerly, looking now at the top of Diana's bent head. 'I will pick her up here in my motor, drive to Dene Park where the others will be waiting, and we'll motor down together,' he said. 'Shall we say ten o'clock?'

Diana raised her head, her cheeks pink, and though she still couldn't look at Charles, she said, 'Thank you. I should like that.'

Edward's secretary, Warren, came in, looking faintly worried, and murmured, 'Your sister is here to see you, sir.'

Edward consulted his watch. He had only five minutes before Sir Thomas Bromley was due, but he was generally late for appointments. 'Show her in,' he said. 'But inform me the instant Sir Thomas arrives.'

A moment later, Laura swept through the door into his office. She was tall and svelte, and the current style, which he thought of as 'tubular', suited her. She was, he thought, an extremely good-looking woman, with his own long, oval face and thick dark hair, and her energy and enthusiasm for life made her seem younger than her forty-two years. It was a terrible shame she had never married, though to his knowledge she had had offers.

He didn't approve of her working. She had inherited a competence from their mother's side, so she had no need to earn a living; and if she had, he would have supported her rather than see her demean herself. When she took a course in typewriting, Pitmanism and clerical skills, he had thought she was just amusing herself; but, with certificate in hand, she had gone and got herself a position at Carthew's in North Kensington. It was a small factory making snap fasteners, hooks and eyes, eyelets, studs and metal buttons, with an office attached where the present Mr Carthew presided over the business he had inherited from his father and grandfather. Edward had never met him, but deduced he must be an eccentric to have hired Laura instead of a man.

'Why did he do it?' Edward had asked Laura, more than once.

'He took a fancy to me, I suppose,' Laura had replied,

with a shrug. He was, according to her, 'a darling', an elderly but vigorous man given to pepper-and-salt tweeds and spats; he wore mutton-chop whiskers and always had a fresh flower in his lapel. He possessed a rather 'mashing' gallantry, but also had a shrewd business sense and a keen interest in innovation. It was the latter, she believed, that had led him to 'give her a chance'. He had taken her on on a trial basis, but had confirmed the appointment before the trial period ended and had since raised her salary, so she must have given satisfaction.

Edward was glad for Laura that she had succeeded, knowing that failure in what you had set your heart on was a miserable thing, but an entirely separate part of his brain deplored the idea of *his sister* 'going out to work'.

'But what would you have me do? Sit at home twiddling my thumbs?' was her response, when he was driven to express his doubts.

'Other ladies manage to keep themselves busy.'

'Bridge, charitable work, flower-arranging,' she suggested ironically.

'Why not?'

'Afternoon tea and gossip, and a genteel withering towards death. The pressed-flower brigade of unwanted spinsters. Thank you, Teddy. Such a tempting prospect – why didn't I think of it myself?'

It was never any use continuing an argument once she got to calling him 'Teddy'. He sometimes thought she didn't take him seriously at all, despite his position in an important private bank. She would never accept that there were things only men were good at.

'Good at wearing trousers,' was her response to that. 'And I suspect we'd look better in them, too.'

He knew she was interested in the movement for women's suffrage, and hoped it was no more than an interest. It was bad enough that she referred so lightly to 'trousers'. If she was actually a 'suffragette' as the vulgar newspapers called them, if she should get the Hunter name into the newspapers . . . Well, Hutcheon's Bank had a reputation to maintain. He could imagine all too clearly the interview with the other directors in which they suggested politely, but with all the force of a ukase, that he should consider retiring to the country.

In summary, she was his beloved sister and a constant worry to him. He came round the desk to greet her, noting that she was particularly bright-eyed that morning.

'Is that a new hat?' he enquired.

She snorted with laughter. 'This old thing? I hope you're more observant of what Beattie wears! How was your supper party?'

'Very nice. Everyone seemed to enjoy it. It was a pity you couldn't come.'

'I saw Jack and Beth at Sonia's. And I can live without the lantern show. Somehow I can never warm to mountains. They're so—'

'Mountainy?'

'Full of themselves. "Look at me, look at me!" Best not to encourage them by taking photographs. But I'm not here to talk about the Alps, my dear. I have some revolutionary news.'

'Good God!' he exclaimed involuntarily. 'What have you been up to now?'

She smiled gaily. 'I can't tell you how heartening it is, that addition of "now" to your question!'

No man likes to be teased by his sister. 'I have an important client on his way here,' he huffed, 'so please tell me in plain language what you've done.'

'Nothing illegal. I have news that I think will make you very happy. I've lost my job.'

He saw that under the flippant delivery there was hurt. So he didn't say 'A good thing, too,' but 'I'm sorry.'

'Are you?'

'I didn't approve of your working, but I was proud of you for what you achieved. I thought you were doing well – why did Carthew sack you?' An alarming thought occurred to him. 'You didn't do something outrageous, did you?'

'Your faith in me is touching! No, I didn't do anything outrageous, and Mr Carthew didn't sack me. He had to let me go. The textile industry's in a slump, and he's having to lay people off.'

'I don't see how he can manage without you,' Edward said stoutly.

'Thank you, dearest. I appreciate that,' Laura said. 'As it happens, he has a nephew who needs employment. He's going to train him on the job and pay him only pocket-money. A short-term solution and poor judgement, in my view, but I dare say family loyalties account for it.'

'He probably attracted criticism for employing a female.'

She made a movement of impatience. 'You're such a *stick*, Edward! Don't you ever want to take the world by the scruff of its neck and shake it? There's so much that needs changing!'

'You're too impatient,' he countered. 'Changing things without proper consideration leads to disaster. Look at the mess the French got themselves into. Evolution, not revolution, is the way forward.' He saw the light of battle in her eye and hurried on. 'So what will you do now? Not look for another job, I hope.'

Before she could answer, Warren tapped and put his head round the communicating door from his room. 'Sir Thomas's motor-car is downstairs, sir.'

'Very good,' said Edward. It would take Sir Thomas five minutes to extract himself from his Rolls-Royce and arrive at Edward's door – he moved with the majesty of a glacier – so he still had time to hear Laura's answer. 'You'll have

51

to be quick,' he told her, as the door shut again. 'I dare not keep Sir Thomas waiting.'

'Of course you dare not,' she said kindly. 'I'm not sure about another job. I could hardly hope to find one as congenial as Carthew's, and searching for one will bring me in for a lot of unpleasant rejection.'

Edward was relieved. 'Perhaps you should find something else to interest you. A cause of some sort.'

He meant something like orphans or old horses, but her face lit in a teasing smile. 'What a good idea! I hear the WSPU is holding a major meeting tomorrow night at Holland Park. I might go to that and volunteer my skills.'

'You know I didn't mean—!'

'You said the Cause.'

'I said *a* cause. Not the militant suffragettes.'

'They say Mrs Pankhurst is going to speak, though they may have to bring her in on a stretcher – don't you find that a shocking thing to have to say?'

'She is a convicted criminal,' Edward pointed out. 'How can you want to associate with people like that?'

'How can you be complacent about the torturing of women? The Cat and Mouse Act is a monstrous piece of legislation!'

As it happened, Edward agreed. When members of the Women's Social and Political Union were sent to prison, many of them went on hunger-strike. At first the government had felt obliged to release them when they became ill, for fear one of them should die in custody. But that rendered imprisonment futile as a sanction, making a mockery of the law.

For a time they had tried forcible feeding, but the brutality of the process had raised public outcry, so in 1913 they had passed the Temporary Discharge for Ill Health Act. When hunger-strikers grew dangerously weak they were released on licence. As soon as their health improved, they could be taken straight back to prison without the need of further trial. Thus the sanction remained effective, and the women's ill health or death was entirely their own choice. It was, the government thought, quite an elegant solution.

Edward, along with many other thoughtful people, was uneasy about it. But the suffragettes had gone from marches, meetings and shouting at political rallies to more violent action: breaking windows, arson, physically attacking policemen and MPs. Mr Asquith's car had had slates thrown down on it from a roof; Winston Churchill had been attacked with a riding-crop. Pillar-boxes had been set on fire or had tar poured into them. Eggs and flour had been thrown in courtrooms to halt proceedings. And in May of this year there had been a rash of attacks on galleries and museums, and a famous painting by Velázquez had been slashed with a meat cleaver.

Such violence was not only unfeminine, it was counter-productive, turning decent people against the movement. Edward was particularly shocked by the destruction of the painting. What would they resort to next – burning books? Civilisation itself was under threat.

He said, 'I agree it is unpleasant, and rather un-English, but what these women have done is unpleasant and un-English too.'

'But how else can women get the attention of their lords and masters? Argument has got them nowhere.'

'I don't know,' Edward admitted. 'I only know that if the matter is not capable of being decided by rational discourse, it is not worthwhile.'

'The freedom of women, not worthwhile?'

'My dear Laura, it is just that sort of intemperate language that turns people against them. Women are not slaves. They are protected by the law. And most of them are perfectly happy as they are.'

'Are they, indeed? Is Beattie happy?' Laura said.

53

'Of course she is,' Edward said at once.

And yet . . . That air of serenity, of remoteness, fascinating as it was, meant that he never really knew what she was thinking. But of course she was happy! She had a fine home, a husband, children, servants, enough to eat and drink, new hats whenever she wanted them – everything, in short, a woman could ask for. What more could she possibly want?

But there was no time for this now. Sir Thomas was on his way up. 'Laura, tell me plainly, what are you going to do?' he asked. 'You're not going to be destroying works of art? Breaking windows?'

'I don't know yet,' she said to tease him, but then, seeing his expression, sobered and said, 'No, I shan't be doing anything violent. I didn't approve of the attacks on the galleries myself. There *are* certain standards.'

'Thank God for that,' Edward said. 'You must remember my position. I can't be associated with anything scandalous. The bank wouldn't stand for it.'

She laid a hand on his arm. 'I shall keep your reputation foremost in my mind at all times. Poor Edward.'

He was annoyed. 'Why do you always call me that?'

'Because I think you have tremendous talents that you are barely aware of, and which I'm sure the bank doesn't know about. You're so shy and retiring, you think too little of yourself.'

'What would you have me do? Strut like a mountebank?'

'A little strutting might suit you,' she said. 'Do you remember the time Papa said, "Our Edward will never set the world on fire. He's such a cautious fellow"? But I don't think Papa ever understood the fire burning down below decks.'

He blushed now. 'You do talk such nonsense!' he rebuked her. But he remembered the occasion. It had been in front of company, too, and it had hurt. His father had called him a slowcoach, and Laura, who was quick like Papa, had often been impatient with him. He had wondered over the years – tortured himself about it – whether Beattie thought him dull. She had been so wildly gay that winter in Dublin when he had first met her . . .

There were footsteps outside, and it was necessary to get rid of Laura quickly. 'You had better go out through Warren's room,' he said urgently. 'I hear Sir Thomas. He mustn't find you here.'

'Nonsense. Sir Thomas is well known to have a soft spot for "the ladies",' Laura said. And she held her ground, forcing Edward to make the introduction as Sir Thomas came in and raised his eyebrows in surprise.

'My sister, Miss Laura Hunter, Sir Thomas,' he said. 'Here on a family matter – of no consequence. She's just leaving.'

'Oh, not on my account, I hope,' Sir Thomas rumbled gallantly, bowing over her hand. 'Delighted to make your acquaintance, my dear. Always pleased to feast my old eyes on a member of the fair sex. I can see the family resemblance, of course. Such good looks are wasted on your brother, though. We men must admire, but do not seek to emulate, eh, eh?'

Laura gave him an enigmatic smile. Edward couldn't bear to think what she might be about to say. She simply didn't understand his position at Hutcheon's, the importance of—

'Oh, indeed, Sir Thomas – but I have known some very beautiful men, too,' Laura said. And, seeing Edward's anguished, pleading eyes, decided she had tortured him enough, and added, 'But I must go. I have an appointment too.'

She went, leaving Edward to drag his mind back to Sir Thomas and his financial affairs, though a part of it still kept escaping to wonder why, when Laura had said the old man had 'a soft spot for the ladies', it had not sounded like praise. Indeed, it had sounded derogatory.

55

CHAPTER FIVE

The Elms was still receiving so many visits of thanks and congratulations that Beattie couldn't get out. But Sadie was more than happy to avoid the visitors by walking down to the shops for her. She was joined – suddenly, from under a hedge – by Nailer. He fell in beside her, briskly trotting, as if he just *happened* to be going the same way.

'Where are you off to?' she enquired pleasantly. 'You've got a guilty look about you.'

His tail wagged at the sound of her voice. At the other end, his nose, like a nubbin of moistened black leather, was twitching away with a life of its own. His world was an inexhaustible cornucopia of smells. Sadie wondered what it must be like to be a dog. To her there were good smells, like honeysuckle and nettles and the warm tar of the road, and bad ones, like fox droppings and the whiff of a dead bird under the hedge. To Nailer it was just smells that meant something and smells that didn't. Honeysuckle moved him not at all, but the dead bird was impelling.

'And what's the best smell in the world?' she asked him.

He looked up at her, and licked his lips. *Bitches*! he said in her mind, in a rough, growly voice. *Succulent bitches*!

'That's a very improper answer,' she said. 'You forget I'm only sixteen.'

Nearly seventeen, said the Nailer-voice. For some reason, it had always had a slight Hertfordshire accent. *And you been*

56

hangin' around farmyards since you could walk. You know the facts o' life.

'True,' Sadie said. 'And I don't think much of them.'

Come in useful one day.

'Ha! So you say. Anyway, I'd sooner not be equated with a cow, thank you.'

Nailer snorted like Munt saying, 'Wimmin!'

'There must be more to it than that,' Sadie argued. 'Why would God bother to give us brains and thoughts and feelings if all we were was breeding-stock?' She looked down at the dog severely. 'Do you ever consider that your bitches might like some say in the matter?'

Nailer paused to cough some dust out of his throat, pawed at his nose, finished up with a mighty sneeze that almost lifted him off the ground, then disappeared under another hedge as suddenly as he had come.

'You know I'm right,' she called after him.

Breeding-stock, she thought as she walked on. There was Diana hoping to 'catch' Charles Wroughton, simply so that she could be breeding-stock to a higher sort of man. Well, perhaps that was the right idea, if that *was* all there was to it. But, then, why the brain in the first place? *God moves in a mysterious way*, said the hymn in her head. But it was more than mysterious, it was illogical. It was true there was Aunt Laura, but she was in her forties and a had a private income, and even then her career was accepted only as a sort of tiresome eccentricity. If that was the only way a woman could have a brain – well, you had to ask yourself if God really knew what He was doing.

Better not try that one on the rector, she thought, with a grin. He'd done a sermon the other week about the sin of blasphemy and the hidden ways in which it could creep up on you. 'Questioning the Ways of the Almighty', as Mrs Chaplin called it, was bound to be blasphemous.

She did her mother's errand at the haberdasher's (black

thread and narrow elastic), and headed for the post office to buy stamps for her. As she approached, Mrs Oliver came out with another lady, both smartly dressed with light coats over their summer frocks, and hats of glazed straw. Mrs Oliver's was saucily trimmed with flowers, knots and an up-poking feather, but the other lady's was quite plain, with just a band of claret ribbon.

'Sadie, dear,' Mrs Oliver said. 'I was just talking about you – wasn't I, Annabel?'

The other lady turned kind, steady eyes on Sadie, which seemed to examine her with interest. 'You were indeed,' she said.

'This is my dear friend Mrs Cuthbert,' Mrs Oliver went on. 'She lives at Highclere Farm, just on the other side of Rustington.'

'Do you remember the other day, when you were riding, you were overtaken by a motor-car?' Mrs Cuthbert said, without preamble. 'That was me.'

'The Lanchester Tonneau?' Sadie said.

Mrs Cuthbert smiled. 'You know about motor-cars?'

'I have a brother,' Sadie explained. 'He's fourteen.'

'I have a husband who might as well be fourteen,' said Mrs Cuthbert, and Sadie saw it was all right to laugh.

'Sadie, dear,' Mrs Oliver said, 'Mrs Cuthbert and I were discussing what a bad thing it was for you to be riding about on that comical horse.'

Sadie felt compelled to defend her old friend. 'Arthur has a very sweet nature,' she said, and added, 'Any ride is better than no ride.'

'Oh, quite so,' Mrs Cuthbert said. 'I'd feel the same way.'

'But you're getting too old for that, dear,' Mrs Oliver took it up. 'It does present an *off* appearance in a girl of your age, and I'm sure it worries your mother.'

Sadie wanted to argue, but had nothing to say. Much as she disliked it, she knew they were right.

Mrs Cuthbert went on, 'At Highclere Farm we have no cows and pigs, just horses. Apart from our own riding horses, we keep a number at livery, and we buy youngsters, school them and sell them on. Mr Cuthbert is like a drunkard when it comes to sales – one can't keep him away! We're trying a little breeding now as well – we have two in-foal mares.'

'It sounds wonderful,' Sadie said.

'We were wondering whether you'd like to go over and help,' Mrs Oliver said.

'We always need more people than we have to exercise them,' Mrs Cuthbert said. 'It might interest you to help with the schooling, too. Fanny says you are a good rider.'

Sadie was overwhelmed. Not only to ride proper horses, but to learn about schooling! It was a dream to equal anything Diana might manage concerning weddings at St Margaret's.

'How would you get over there, dear?' Mrs Oliver asked.

'I could borrow Bobby's bicycle,' Sadie said eagerly. 'He's away for the summer.' Rustington was about six miles away. There were a couple of steep hills involved, but Sadie wouldn't let that get between her and *riding proper horses*!

'You'll have to ask your parents' permission, of course,' Mrs Cuthbert said. 'If they agree, perhaps you'd like to come over on Friday morning. Ask your mother to drop me a line, won't you?'

'Oh, yes, I will. *Thank* you,' Sadie said.

Mrs Cuthbert laughed. 'No, thank *you*. I hope to see you on Friday, then. Good day to you.'

The two ladies walked away, and Sadie had to pinch herself. Her parents *must* let her! Surely they couldn't object. She contemplated the awful possibility that her father might send her off somewhere to improve her. But surely – *surely* – she would be allowed one last summer. Just until the end of August?

Dear God, she prayed, *I'm sorry I called You illogical. If You let me have this summer riding the horses, I'll never ask for anything again, and – and I'll marry anyone You want.*

That ought to do it, she thought, though without *complete* confidence. Grown-ups – among whom she definitely included the Almighty – were unpredictable.

The meeting in Holland Park on the 16th turned out more exciting than Laura had expected. The hall was crowded, almost entirely with women, and unable to get a seat, she had to stand at the back. It was a warm evening and she wasn't sorry not to be crammed in among those close-packed chairs. While waiting for the meeting to start, she got talking to the person next to her, a cheerful, sandy-haired woman, who looked to be in her early thirties, neatly dressed in a good navy suit and rather a smart hat. She had freckles, and a wide-awake look to her face that Laura found instantly attractive.

Her name was Louisa Cotton, and she had been active in the movement for several years. 'Not the dangerous things,' she added. 'I just help with the office work. I'm not really cut out for violent action. And if I was sent to prison it would so distress my aunt. She's my only relative, and she's been very kind to me.'

'I have a brother who would be anguished if I got into trouble,' Laura mentioned. 'He doesn't even like me talking about all this.' She waved a hand to indicate the women's movement in general. 'He thinks women should be content to be looked after by men.'

'My aunt feels the same,' Louisa said. 'It's her great sorrow that I've never married. She tries hard to be understanding about the Cause, but she thinks it a poor substitute for a husband and children.'

'My family doesn't mention my single state any more. But they all deplore the notoriety of the militants. The Velázquez painting, for instance.'

60

'Yes, that *was* dreadful. And it turned a lot of decent people against us. Still,' Louisa added, 'they can repair a painting. Look at Mrs Pankhurst. Her treatment in prison has ruined her health. The strain of force-feeding has permanently weakened her heart.'

'I heard that she might be here tonight.'

'If she's recovered enough. She was released on the eleventh, and was supposed to present herself on the fourteenth, but of course she didn't. She's hiding away in one of the Mouse Holes now.' This was the term for safe-houses where hunger-strikers hid from the police after release. 'Have you ever heard her speak?'

'Once, back in February, in Chelsea. She addressed a crowd in the street from an upstairs balcony. Such an impressive voice from such a small woman! She said we were fighting for a time when every little girl born would have an equal chance with her brothers. It was very inspiring.'

Their chatting was interrupted by a rustling of movement and whispers, which grew to an excited murmur of 'She's coming!' and 'She's here!' Word came back that Mrs Pankhurst was being lifted out of a private ambulance on a stretcher, and was to be carried up to the platform. Laura turned to smile at her new friend in pleased anticipation.

And then there was a noise of several motor-cars arriving, doors slamming, shouts and police whistles.

Louisa's eyes widened. 'They must have been lying in wait for her. They knew she was coming.'

'What – the police have come to arrest her?' Laura said.

'They won't leave it at that,' Louisa said. 'They'll want to round up any other stray mice – there are bound to be some at a meeting like this. We'd better get out of here.'

'I'm not a mouse,' Laura objected.

'Neither am I,' said Louisa, 'but they'll keep us all here and take our names, and there's bound to be some scuffling. The mice will resist, and if we get caught up in it we'll find ourselves at the magistrates court tomorrow, whether we did anything or not.' She grabbed Laura's arm. 'Come on, we must get out.'

Laura looked around with alarm. The seated people were standing up, trying to see what was happening. There was a babble of voices. Those on the platform were trying to talk over it but not being heard. And by the open doors on to the street the people had solidified into a struggling mass. Some seemed to be trying to get out, others to back away. Yet others, shouting and gesticulating, wanted to get into the fray. Someone cried out in pain; Laura saw a woman hit in the face by a wild elbow; another knocked off her feet.

There was no getting out that way. Down by the platform there were exits but the aisles were blocked with people going in conflicting directions. But there was a door in the corner behind them, half hidden by a velvet curtain on a rail.

'Where does that lead?' Laura asked.

'No idea. Just pray it's not locked. Come on!'

The door opened on to a small room set up like an office, perhaps for the hall's administrator. A door on the further side gave, disappointingly, on to a lavatory.

Others had come crowding through from the hall behind them. 'We're trapped,' Laura said.

'Not us!' Louisa said stoutly. 'Window!'

It was a sash window, painted so often it was clogged and hard to move. Laura got in beside Louisa and they shoved together. The window went up crookedly and stuck, not fully open.

'I can get through that,' Louisa asserted. 'Can you?'

'I can try,' said Laura. She was bigger than her companion and had never climbed out of a window in her life, but excitement was carrying her. Louisa shoved her upper body through the gap, wriggled like a fish, and went through in a flurry of petticoats. Laura was right behind her, jaw gritted with determination. It was a tight fit, and women's clothes were not designed for the job: they bunched up around her, slowing her down. But once her hips were through her legs followed easily. Louisa caught her and helped her to her feet.

They were in a narrow alley between high walls of glazed brown bricks. To the left were the lights of the street, but before they could take a step towards them a policeman appeared in the entrance to the alley, spotted them, and shouted, 'Hey, you! Stop! Stop right there. Halt, I tell you!'

Laura's instinct would have been to obey – and, after all, they hadn't done anything wrong. But Louisa grabbed her arm again and said, 'Run!'

Down the alley she ran, faster than she had since she was a child, her heart pounding with excitement. She glanced back. There were two policemen now, one behind the other – the alley was too narrow for two abreast. They were running. She felt a swoop in the pit of her stomach: they were bound to catch her! But now someone else was struggling out through the window, awkwardly, falling to the ground, and another body right behind, blocking the way.

At the end of the alley there was a high fence of iron railings, and no other way to go. 'Now we've had it,' Laura said, panting.

'No, there's a gap,' said Louisa. 'Look!' One of the railings was missing, making a wider space.

'We can't get through there,' Laura gasped.

'Yes, we can.' Already Louisa was squeezing through, her voice coming jerkily as her body was compressed. 'My brother. Told me. If. Your head will. Go through. The rest.' A last wriggle and she was free. 'Will follow. Come *on!*'

Laura obeyed. It was a horribly tight fit. Thank heaven she was slender. Even so – what if she got stuck? The humiliation! One of the policemen had got past the blockage and was running towards them, his feet loud on the concrete. He looked so big and solid and threatening. Fear coursed through her veins and drove her struggles. She could hear his heavy breathing, see the sweat on his face.

'Stand still!' he shouted. He looked angry. He was close enough for her to smell his heat. 'Stop, you bitches!' he said.

She was shocked by the word. She had never heard anyone say it before to a lady. It inspired a last desperate wriggle and she felt herself come free with a sensation like a cork popping out of a bottle.

But his big hand shot through the gap and seized her skirt. Her heart leaped with fear.

'Got you now, bitch!' he said. His large face, ugly with anger; his hand, big as a bear's paw; his grip, too strong for her to break. She saw that his other hand was going to come through and grab her arm. She was done for.

Then there was a little dart of movement, the policeman shouted, 'Yow!' and the hand that had caught her was snatched back. She was free.

'*Run!*' Louisa cried, grabbing her hand.

'What was that?' Laura asked jerkily, as they ran.

Louisa's face turned to her, and seemed one big grin in the gloom. 'Hatpin!'

The railings had let them into a small park. They ran across it, past the rear of the buildings, until they found a gate and another alley leading back to the street. They negotiated it with caution and, emerging, looked to their left towards the crowds and the jam of vehicles around the entrance to the hall. This part of the street was quiet. Laura, all her senses buzzing, would have run, but Louisa kept hold of her and said, 'Walk quietly as if it's nothing to do with us.'

Laura's breath was returning to normal, but her nerves seemed to jump and twitch from the excitement. 'We got away!' she said. 'I never thought we would!'

'We'd better go somewhere quiet, get off the street. They

64

might send patrols to look for stragglers. There's a bus coming.'

'Better yet,' Laura said, 'there's a taxi with the flag up. Where do you live?'

'All the way out in Wimbledon, I'm afraid.'

'What about my house then? It's in Westminster.'

Laura's home was tiny, part of an eighteenth-century terrace. 'I call it my doll's house,' she said, as she searched for the key in her bag. 'But I love it so. My grandmother left me the money, and I had such a fight with my brother over living alone.'

'I can imagine. My aunt would have a fit,' said Louisa. 'You are so lucky.'

'I suppose I am,' she said. 'He's not such a bad old stick, really.'

The door led straight into the parlour. There were two rooms downstairs and two upstairs, and a tiny courtyard behind, with space for a few pots of flowers and a bench.

'This is so charming,' Louisa exclaimed. 'I see why you love it.'

'Shall I make some tea?' Laura said. 'I know I need a cup.'

There was still light in the sky, and it was a hot, still evening, so they took their tea out of doors and sat on the bench. A great graceful tree grew in someone else's garden beyond the wall, making a handsome backdrop. Laura had grown summer jasmine in a pot in a sunny corner, and the courtyard was filled with its scent.

'Well, my goodness,' Laura said, 'that was quite an adventure.'

Louisa grinned. 'But admit it, now, you enjoyed it, didn't you?'

'I'm ashamed to say I did,' Laura confessed. 'Though if I'd known what was in store for me, I'd have dressed differently.'

They exchanged histories. Louisa and her brother, Sam, had been early orphaned and brought up by their only other relative, their father's widowed sister. 'She'd never had any children and never wanted any either – and goodness! She was disconcerted when we turned up. But she rolled up her sleeves and made a go of it, as Sam would say. She did the right thing by us, and I'll always be grateful, even if she is rather strict about what a well-bred lady should and shouldn't do. Don't you think,' she added, in her quick, parenthetic way, 'that all the things we're told not to do are things the boys want to keep to themselves?'

Laura laughed. 'I've always believed that. "Don't let the girls play. They spoil things."'

'Were you a tomboy when you were little?'

'Wanted to be. Never really had the chance. Where is Sam now?'

'He's a clerk in a shipping office, and lives in diggings in Whitechapel. I'd love you to meet him. He's a darling. We've gone through so much together.'

'What were you doing when he taught you to push through railings?'

'Stealing fruit. There was a big house at the end of the street that had the most wonderful cherries and plums, and peaches under glass.' She shook her head in mock repentance. 'Dreadful of us, I know. But don't you think it terribly wrong of people to grow fruit like that in a street where children are living? Putting temptation in the way of poor weak little creatures. As bad as handing out bottles of gin in the slums.'

'The things you say!'

'Oh, I have an ungovernable tongue, I know it. Now you. Tell me about you.'

She was impressed to learn that Laura had worked at a proper job. 'A secretary! How exciting!'

'I was just a type-writer. Though it was very future-minded of my employer to take me on at all.'

66

'What will you do now?'

'I'd like to do something for the Cause – though I don't think,' she added, 'that I could smash things or attack policemen.'

'No, I couldn't, either. I was never sure, if I'm honest, that it was the right tactic. I sometimes think,' Louisa said thoughtfully, 'that Mrs P and the other extreme militants have become . . . almost addicted to the violence. That being imprisoned and starving and all the rest of it has become an end in itself.' She looked up. 'Is that a horrible thing to say? I think it makes them feel more alive to be facing danger and death. That they crave the excitement.'

Laura thought of her own excitement when the policeman was chasing her. It had been frightening, but in a strangely pleasurable way. She could see how it might become something you sought out for itself. 'I don't think it's a horrible thing to say. You may be right. But they have at least shown how hatefully men can treat women if they have the chance.'

'And they're right about one thing – that if they hadn't drawn attention to themselves, it would be all too easy to ignore us.'

'Yes,' said Laura. 'Men talk about the Cause now. They think about it.'

'Still,' said Louisa, 'I think it's time to try something different.'

'I agree. We need somehow to show men that we can do anything they can do. But, of course, they'll never allow us to. The opportunity will never arise.'

'Perhaps it may, one day. At all events, we ought to be prepared. Is there something you've always wanted to do?'

Laura thought for a moment. 'Drive a railway engine.'

Louisa laughed. 'That may be a leap too far. How about learning to drive a motor-car, to begin with?'

'I'd love to do that,' Laura exclaimed. 'But how?'

'There's a WSPU place in Surrey where they teach ladies. What do you say we both take the course?'

'I'm game if you are.'

'Then it's agreed.' Louisa held out her hand, and they shook on it.

'It's getting late,' Laura said. 'Would you like to stay the night? I have a spare bed.'

'I'd love to – but my aunt will worry if I don't come home.'

'We could send a telegram,' Laura said. 'There's an office round the corner that stays open late for the MPs. I'd love you to stay – I don't know about you, but I don't feel I've nearly talked myself out.'

'Oh, not nearly!' Louisa agreed.

CHAPTER SIX

On the day of the picnic, Diana was in a state of nerves. Had it not been for pride, she might have tried to get out of it. It seemed altogether a serious and rather frightening undertaking, not like any outing she had been on before, where she was the queen of the group, the other girls were her friends, and the boys were either current, former or potential suitors. She knew nothing about Charles Wroughton, except that he was famous for being aloof.

What had she done? What did he want of her? How could she entertain him? The more she thought about it, the more nervous she became. She could only hope that in the group she might blend into the background and pass unnoticed – something she had never hoped before in her life.

When the dashing red motor-car arrived outside The Elms, her brother William, who was watching from the morning-room window, informed her it was a 'tourer' and assured her it was 'simply topping', before rushing out to inspect it at closer quarters. By the time Diana arrived at the door, Peter had joined him, and Charles was obligingly demonstrating its salient features to an enthusiastic audience. He snatched off his cap when Diana appeared, with her mother at her shoulder, and looked at her long and carefully. If only he had smiled she might have thought him admiring her; as it was, she was afraid he was inspecting her appearance for any impropriety.

She was wearing her old-rose cotton – a colour that especially suited her – which had sleeves to the elbow, decorated by a double row of buttons all the way down, and a wide stiffened silk sash at the waist. It was quite plain, with just a little lace at the neckline and two lace inserts in the bodice: to be overdressed, Beattie had told her, would be far worse than to be underdressed. 'It is a picnic, after all.'

The skirt ended just above the ankle bone, showing her buttoned boots of grey glazed leather. Her hat was of grey felt, quite small (large hats were going out), with the brim turned up at one side, decorated with a large pink silk rose and three short feathers; and in consideration of the motor-ride, she had spent last night adding a veil, which could be tied under the chin.

She had felt quite pleased with her appearance, and Mother had told her she looked ravishing, but now uncertainty returned in the face of Charles's unwavering stare. Perhaps the females he knew wore silk all the time. And jewels. Mother squeezed her hand reassuringly, but all he said was, 'Do you have a coat? It may be quite dusty once we get going.'

Beattie had it ready. Diana put it on, and Charles helped her into the front seat, shooed William and Peter from the running-boards and got in beside her. He had left the engine running, so there was no need to crank, and with a wave, they were off. Nailer appeared from nowhere and dashed alongside, trying to bite the tyres.

'I wish they wouldn't do that,' Charles remarked, with a worried frown. 'I'm always afraid I'll run them over.'

'I assure you,' Diana said, 'no-one would shed a tear if you did. He's quite the most disagreeable dog in the district.'

'Your sister would be upset,' he said, and she felt she had exposed herself in a bad light, though she had been joking. Well, half joking.

Nothing more was said on the short drive to Dene Park.

There, on the sweep in front of the house, the rest of the party was waiting. Two young women were chattering, heads together, in the back seat of a large, heavy open motor-car, and two men were leaning against its bonnet smoking, while a uniformed chauffeur made himself invisible on the other side.

Charles performed a circle around them, came to rest alongside, and called, 'Let's get straight off! I'll just do the honours very quickly.'

The four people resolved into two couples, one apparently in their late twenties called Henry and Jane Stanton Harcourt. He was rather fat, with small eyes sunk in a doughy face, like currants in a bun; she was small and thin, with a long nose, and made Diana think of an Italian Greyhound.

'We're just here to preserve the decencies,' Henry said, in a way that made it clear it was a joke, though he did not smile. 'Old married couple. Keep you youngsters in order.'

The other two were younger, in their early twenties, and looked so alike Diana guessed they were brother and sister, both fair, thin and rather beaky. They were introduced simply as 'Katherine and James Eynsham – Kiki and Jumbo'.

Kiki was frighteningly smart, dressed in a silk foulard of black and white print and a large hat of black straw with coiled white ostrich feathers wreathing it like smoke. Both the women looked at Diana unsmilingly, and acknowledged the introduction with a bare nod. She felt suddenly horribly underdressed in her cotton, for Jane was in pale blue shantung with a wide matching hat. Their coolness suggested she had committed a terrible *faux-pas*. She was glad that Charles drove straight off, leaving them to follow.

The drive to Cookham took about an hour, but there was not much opportunity for conversation. Motor-cars were noisy, and open ones, she discovered, doubly so. She soon learned that when she pitched a remark to Charles loudly enough for him to catch it, he could not reply without looking at her, with alarming consequences for his steering. So she allowed herself to lapse into private thought, wondering what she had got herself into. Between a taciturn Charles and the two smart, disapproving couples, she did not anticipate much pleasure.

But an outing was an outing. She was not so accustomed to motoring as to be *blasé* about it, and she enjoyed the motion, the countryside unreeling around her, and the sense of adventure one always felt going to a new place.

When they reached the outskirts of Cookham there was a queue of traffic waiting to cross a narrow bridge over a river, and as they crawled along, conversation was possible at last. Charles said, 'What do you think of her?'

Diana looked at him for a moment, startled. She had been thinking of Jane's pale blue silk and opened her mouth to make a devastating mistake, then realised at the last moment that he meant the motor. She recovered herself with a gulp and said, 'Wonderful. Very comfortable. I'm sure she must be very fast.'

She had said the right thing. He seemed pleased. 'I've had her up to sixty-seven – not bad for at all for a little bus like this. If she was tuned for racing I could get her above seventy. She's French-built, of course – four cylinders, sixteen horse-power.' He continued describing the motor's finer details while they edged noisily forward over the bridge. When a pause came, and Diana realised he expected her to make some reply, she said, 'I like all the shiny brass. And, look, there's even a clock. How convenient!'

'It is indeed.' He looked at her carefully. 'Was I being a bore? I'm rather fond of the old girl, but of course one can't expect ladies to be interested in motors.'

'Not a bore at all,' Diana said, back on firm ground. One always pretended interest in the man's hobbies, drew him out to talk about them. That made one a 'splendid girl', or even 'a sport' – though one could go too far in *that* direction.

'I like motor-cars, and I wish I understood them better. I hope I can remember all those details to tell my brothers.'

'I'll gladly repeat it for you later,' he said gravely.

She changed the subject. 'Is this the River Thames?'

'Yes,' he said. 'Haven't you been to Cookham before?'

'No, never. But I know the Thames from London,' she said. 'I thought I recognised the smell.'

He looked startled, then realised she had made a joke and smiled dutifully. 'Very good,' he said.

She felt foolish. 'Where exactly are we going?' she asked.

'It's called Bell House. Olive and Ralph Marlowe will be entertaining us.'

'Are they a married couple?'

'Brother and sister,' he said, which seemed to bring that exchange to an end. She couldn't think of any more questions. But the cart in front of them moved, and they were off the bridge at last. Then Charles had to concentrate on driving through the narrow, cobbled streets lined with ancient beamed houses. They swung round a tight turn into an unpaved lane between high hedges, with a glimpse of a square church tower on the left, then round another tight turn, through a gate and on to the sweep of a large white house surrounded by trees. Charles drew up to the door, the other motor came in behind them and, as both engines were finally turned off, a delicious green silence descended, into which the sound of birdsong was threaded like gold in a tapestry.

Diana drew a sigh, and Charles turned to look at her quizzically. 'Long journey?' he hazarded.

'But so interesting,' she said quickly.

He was scanning her face as if he was trying to memorise her. He seemed about to say something, but the sound of voices and motor-car doors slamming behind them prompted him instead to movement. 'Let me help you down,' he said, and got out.

73

The girl who came running out from the house seemed about Diana's age, and was – what a relief! – quite plainly dressed in a skirt and cotton blouse. She went up on tiptoe to kiss Charles's cheek, then came straight to Diana, offering a hand and saying, 'You must be Miss Hunter! I'm Olive, but everyone calls me Obby. I've been longing to meet you. Have you had a good journey? The dust is terrible, isn't it? But at least it's better than mud! I hate winter, don't you?'

Diana was warmed by her greeting. Ralph, too, seemed pleasant and greeted her politely, but soon they were engulfed by the rest of the party, and Charles was leading Diana up to be presented to the other person who had just emerged from the house, a majestic lady in violet silk and three strands of pearls, with a front of grey curls like Queen Alexandra. He greeted her as 'Cousin Maud' but introduced her as Lady Marjorie. Did everyone, Diana wondered, go by a different name from their given one? 'Obby' had addressed her brother as 'Rolo'. All these 'nicknames' made it hard to keep track.

Lady Marjorie acknowledged Diana with a nod, and asked after Charles's mother and father. Then Charles was called away to supervise the removal of a hamper from his motor and Diana was left with the grand lady. She had always felt herself to be 'good with grown-ups': having been pretty from childhood she had always been a pet, and expected people to like her. But this one was subjecting her to an unsmiling inspection that seemed neither friendly nor welcoming.

Quite abruptly, she asked, 'How do you know Charles?'

'We met in London,' Diana began, but got no further.

'Oh, London,' Lady Marjorie said dismissively, as if that explained *everything*. 'I no longer go to London. I find one meets all too many people one does not know.'

Diana was at a loss to respond to this, but the party was on the move again and she was saved by Obby, who offered to conduct the young ladies upstairs. Jane and Kiki seemed

74

happy to linger up there a long time, fiddling with their hair, tweaking each other's gowns, and chatting to each other and to Obby about what they had all been doing, without addressing a single remark to Diana. This seemed rude to her, but she had no way of knowing if it was a deliberate snub, or simply the way they always were. She felt Obby would have liked to include her in the conversation, but she was no match for the other two.

At last they decided, languidly, to descend, to find Charles alone in the hall, watching the staircase, 'like a faithful hound', as Diana heard Kiki just behind her whisper, giggling, to Jane.

'There you are!' he said. 'The others have gone outside. What do you find to do up there for such a time?'

'You'll never know, Charles,' Jane said. 'One must keep some mysteries.'

'I find all women mysterious,' he replied.

'That much is obvious,' Jane retorted.

'You should try to learn, Charles,' Kiki said. 'Your bewilderment makes you easy prey.'

'Oh, don't tease poor Charles,' Obby said reprovingly.

Charles seemed, almost, to blush. 'Shall we join them?' he asked – and offered his arm to Diana. She took it gratefully, and walked ahead with him, feeling Kiki's and Jane's eyes like burning coals on the back of her neck.

The garden was pleasantly shaded by trees, and ran down to the river, divided from the footpath along the bank by a tall beech hedge. Lady Marjorie had withdrawn to leave the young people alone. The picnic was laid out by the footman and a maid, along with rugs and cushions on the grass. When it was all done to her satisfaction, Obby waved the servants away.

It seemed that the men would make it their task to serve the ladies, and Obby, as the hostess, was busy directing them, which left Diana with Kiki and Jane. She was prepared for them to talk to each other and ignore her, as they had so far, but now, having exchanged a significant look, they placed themselves on either side of her and catechised her.

'How do you know Charles?' was Kiki's first question. Diana wondered if she was doomed to face this opening every time.

'We met at a dance in London,' she said.

'How extraordinary,' Jane said, raising her eyebrows.

Diana would not be daunted. She might be quaking inside, but she kept a cool front. 'I should have thought that's what dances are for.'

'Not the dances *we* go to,' said Jane. 'One always knows everyone. I suppose it must have been a *public* dance. I wonder what on earth Charles was doing there.'

There was no answer to this. Diana countered with 'How do *you* know him?'

'We've known him all our lives,' Jane said. 'His mother and my mother were at school together.'

'And Daddy's hunting-box is next door to the Wroughtons' in Leicestershire,' said Kiki. 'My elder brother and sister played with Charles and Coco, and Charles helped teach me to ride.'

'Who,' Diana managed, 'is Coco?'

Jane stared. 'Charles's sister, of course.'

'Caroline Grosmore,' Kiki added. 'Haven't you met her?'

'I'm afraid not.'

'Nor Rupert, I suppose?' Another of those exchanged glances. 'So apart from this "dance"' – she said it as if its credentials were severely suspect – 'you don't know Charles at all?'

Diana desperately sought for relief. 'We're neighbours at Northcote,' she managed to say.

Kiki raised her eyebrows. 'Neighbours? Really? What's your father's place, then?'

76

'His place?' Diana queried, fatally.

Jane curled her lip. 'She means his estate.'

'My father doesn't have an estate. Just a house.'

'Goodness! What does he do?'

'He's a banker,' Diana answered.

They glanced at each other. 'How . . . interesting,' Jane said, as if she meant exactly the opposite, and Kiki giggled.

Diana's agony was interrupted just then as plates of food were brought, glasses filled, and seats taken on the rugs and cushions. Diana hoped desperately that Charles would sit by her, but he was manoeuvred away from her by Jane, and she ended with Henry at her side.

Henry didn't talk much, for which Diana could only be glad. He seemed happy to concentrate on eating; but he seemed puzzled by Diana and every now and then tried to fix her in context by asking, 'Do you know the So-and-sos?' or 'Were you at such-and-such an event?' Her answers must have been a disappointment. She didn't know anyone he knew, had never been anywhere he had been. Each failure on her part elicited a slight shake of the head, followed by more silent munching.

The conversation among the rest of the company was lively and loud but seemed to Diana to be all about people she didn't know and social gatherings she hadn't been to. They all knew each other and each other's friends: it was a closed circle of those who had played together in the nursery, been at school with each other, or were related in some degree – often all three. There was no general topic she could have joined in with, so she sat, like Henry, in silence, trying to look interested.

Charles, she noticed, did not have much to say, though he listened and nodded. He looked across at her quite often, and sometimes seemed on the brink of addressing some remark to her, but his attention was always claimed by Jane for endorsement: 'Such a funny little man – what was his name, Charles?' 'It was such fun, wasn't it, Charles?' 'That was when the rain started and we all got drenched, didn't we, Charles?'

At last the eating seemed to be coming to an end, and everyone was stirring. Obby seemed to be suggesting a game of some sort, and Diana was wondering what fresh humiliation was in store for her. She seemed to be failing miserably to make any impression on Charles or his circle. He must be regretting asking her, so obviously out of place as she was. He would never ask her again, that was for certain. At the moment, she wasn't even sure she minded.

Then, suddenly, he heaved himself up and placed himself in front of her.

'Would you care to come for a walk along the river? It seems too bad that you haven't so much as seen it yet.'

Her heart lifted: at the very least, it seemed a kindness, and would take her away from her tormentors. And it might mean he wanted to talk to her without interruptions, which was hopeful.

'I'd like that very much,' she said.

The sun was shining, the trees were waving gently, the river was sparkling and boats of all shapes and sizes were bobbing gaily on it. It was a delightful scene, and with her hand through his arm, they joined the stream of nicely dressed people strolling along the path enjoying the afternoon.

They were silent for a while, then Diana said hesitantly, 'That was a lovely picnic.'

He frowned at her, as if to gauge her sincerity. 'Are you enjoying yourself? I'm afraid we're rather a dull lot.'

'Oh, no, I wouldn't say that. Not dull,' she said. She searched for something to say about them. 'Have Henry and Jane been married long?'

'Not long. Two years – no, three. One child so far – a daughter, unfortunately.'

'They must want a son,' Diana hazarded.

He nodded. 'It's only a baronetcy, but it's an old one.'

'My aunt married a baronet,' she said, and immediately wished she hadn't. It sounded as if she was trying to compete – a feeble boast.

But he looked interested. 'Really? Which one?'

'Which aunt? Or which baronet?'

'Both.' He smiled that small, careful smile, in acknowledgement of her wit.

'My mother's sister Adelaide, and Sir John Carbury.'

'Carbury. His place is in Kildare, isn't it?'

'Yes – how did you know?'

'We have a place in Kildare too, near Maynooth, through a marriage in the eighteen-somethings. We don't get over there very often, but the shooting is good.'

They passed through a little iron gate: beyond it were water meadows on which cows grazed. A little further on, some had come down to the river under a clump of trees and were standing in the shallows. Diana was wary of cows for a number of reasons, her grey boots among them, and was glad that Charles took her no closer but led her on to a little jetty that stuck out over the river. There he stopped, leaning on the railing and looking down into the water. She leaned too. She was growing used to his silences, was less ill at ease through them. In fact, there was something quite restful about not having to sparkle and charm, as she usually did. She was always the one who had to make the entertainment. With him on his own, she felt nothing was expected of her. To be silent was acceptable.

'Look, down there,' he said quietly, pointing into the water. 'Do you see, in the shadow there?'

It took her a moment to adjust her focus from the surface to the depths and pick out a long grey fish with a pointed snout.

'What is it?' she asked.

'Pike,' he said. He turned his head and looked at her enquiringly, then looked back at the water. 'He's a big fellow. Lurking there in the shadows for an unsuspecting fish to come along – then he'll pounce.'

'Like a cat watching a mouse hole,' she suggested.

'Something like that.'

'I didn't know fish ate other fish,' she said.

'Didn't you?' He seemed to find this surprising.

'I grew up in London,' she said, then felt the need to defend herself against the constant undermining she had suffered that day. 'I know about different things,' she said. 'I can tell you what number bus to take from Kensington to Oxford Street and which line every tube station is on. I know where all the important paintings are in the National Gallery. And I could walk round the Victoria and Albert Museum with my eyes shut and tell you what every exhibit is.'

'You didn't waste your childhood, I can see that.'

As he seemed to have received that quite well, she was emboldened to ask, 'Did you grow up at Dene Park?'

'Yes. I know every field and wood and stream.'

'That must be nice,' she said. 'Tell me some more about fish. What are those ones there?'

'With the red fins? Those are rudd. And those are bream – you see, over there? Where the stream joins the river. They'll be waiting to see what gets washed down. It's a good feeding place, where two waters meet. I expect there'll be some dace, too . . .'

She could hear the change in his voice. It seemed warmer. He liked having something to tell her, and she leaned in a little closer, smiled and nodded and helped him along with questions. She felt more comfortable. She knew how to do this. It was what you did with men, encouraged them to talk about what they knew.

After a bit he stopped quite abruptly and lapsed into

silence. He glanced at her and away again, as if embarrassed. She searched around for something to say, and alighted on the cows, standing dreamily hock-deep in the brown running water under the trees' shadow. She asked what sort they were, and he hesitated, giving her a searching look. 'You aren't really interested in cattle, are you?'

It was an awkward question. She didn't want to tell a lie. She said, 'I'm interested in all country things.'

'Are you?' he said. And then, 'I've never understood how anyone could *not* be interested in country things. Our whole lives spring from the land. It made us. We're dependent on it. Yet one meets people in Town who haven't the least idea where their food comes from, let alone how history shaped their country.'

It was the most profound thing a man had ever said to her, so serious and grown-up it made her doubt all over again that he *was* a suitor. He didn't behave like any beau she had ever had. She felt terribly young and ignorant – not a feeling she was used to.

'You're quite right,' she said humbly.

And suddenly he smiled at her. When he smiled properly, it made his face look quite different – younger, and almost handsome. 'You must think me a very slow fellow to bring you here to look at cows and talk about fish.'

She blushed. 'I – I don't . . .'

'We'd better get back,' he said abruptly, straightening up, the smile gone. He offered his arm, and took her hand for a moment to put it in place. At his touch, Diana felt the warmth rush all the way to her toes. It seemed more significant than a hundred gallantries from her usual admirers.

They did not talk on the way back. In the garden, tea was just being brought out. The group absorbed them, and the conversation was as before, about people and occasions they knew and Diana did not. She fell back into silence, but it was a happier one now. If she was out of place, well, she

81

was there by Charles's desire. That gave her all the authority she needed.

When tea ended it was time to go. Obby said goodbye warmly, hoping they would meet again, and Diana was able to respond in kind. She felt that, in the right circumstances, they could have been friends. Lady Marjorie hadn't re-appeared; Ralph gave a general wave to the company and ambled off on his own pursuits.

In the noisy car going home, conversation was again impossible, but glancing at Charles, Diana thought he seemed more relaxed, even happy. He didn't quite smile, but once or twice she saw him pursing his lips as if he was whistling soundlessly, as a man does when he is content.

It felt an anticlimax when they pulled up in front of The Elms again, and Nailer came dashing out to bark at them, followed by William with technical questions in his eyes. Diana didn't want any bathos to spoil the delicate bubble of atmosphere that had built up around them. 'There's no need to get out,' she said. 'I can see myself in.'

'Are you sure?' he said. He seemed to think it wasn't right.

'Quite sure. Please don't trouble.' He still seemed uncertain so she pre-empted him, saying, 'Thank you for a lovely day. I really have enjoyed myself,' and offering her hand.

He took it, and raised it to his lips.

Sadie met her in the hall. 'I'm just back from Mrs Cuthbert's. How was it?'

Diana wrinkled her nose. 'How can you bear to grub about with horses in this heat? You smell.'

'I do not.' She sniffed her hands. 'Well, it's only horse-smell, and that's lovely. How was it? Was it fun?'

'The river was nice,' Diana said circumspectly.

'And Lord Dene?'

'He was nice too.'

Sadie examined her consideringly, trying to winkle out

information without words. She was fond of her sister, and didn't want her to be hurt. 'You know, you oughtn't to pin too much on it. I mean, he's heir to an earldom and it isn't likely he'd— Well, all I mean is, don't let your mind run too far ahead.' Still Diana said nothing, taking off her coat and brushing the dust off with the flat of her hand. Sadie handed her the clothes brush from the hall stand. 'You don't know any of the same things,' she said. 'What on earth would you have to talk about?'

Diana looked up. 'We talked about fish. And cattle.'

Sadie assumed that was a joke and a snub, and didn't pursue it. 'Why don't you come with me to Highclere tomorrow?' she said kindly.

'I have no interest in your horses,' Diana said serenely.

'It's better than frowsting indoors,' Sadie said.

'I'm going up to change,' Diana said. 'And you should wash.'

Sadie watched her go, and a worrying thought came to her. 'You aren't just going to sit around the house all the time in case he calls, are you?'

Diana sighed crossly and mounted the stairs. The atmosphere had been spoilt. Families were just impossible, with their questions and their tactlessness. Perhaps she should have let him see her in – she hadn't given him the chance to ask her out again. Oh, Lord, perhaps he thought she didn't *want* to see him again. There was no way now she could tell him she did. Had he understood her? She felt the agony of uncertainty. It was hateful being a female, always having to wait for things to happen to you, never being able to take the initiative and do the asking.

But he had kissed her hand. That was a good sign – wasn't it?

CHAPTER SEVEN

Standing, hands folded in front of her, for her daily conference over meals, Cook opined that the cold beef would not 'go round' at dinner that night. Beattie looked up, frowning, from the menu book. Cook always brought it to her, though she had usually already decided what to recommend, and Beattie, after all these years, rarely countermanded her.

'I thought there was plenty left,' Beattie said. It had been a large roast of particularly delicious beef, and though Edward was not in general fond of cold meat and salad, even in hot weather, he was always persuadable in the case of fine and rare cold beef.

'No, madam, I'm afraid not. There wasn't as much as we thought,' Cook said, meeting her eyes steadily.

Beattie read the message there: that someone had eaten it, and it would be best not to enter into the whos and the whys. They were big eaters in the servants' hall, and Beattie had never been one to go enquiring after left-overs. That had not been the way in her childhood home, and as Edward was a generous provider, she had no need to be paltry. She despised meanness.

'Very well,' she said, and would have had to be blind to miss the little movement of relief in Cook's shoulders. 'We'd better have it hashed, then, for luncheon. And for tonight . . .'

They could have something Edward liked better. Cook had her suggestion ready, but Beattie made a little gesture to stop her. A happy thought had come to her. 'We'll have curried chicken. Then we can have the salad as a side dish.'

Cook ventured an objection. 'It's rather warm weather, madam.'

'That's exactly when one eats curry,' Beattie said. 'It cools one down. Send a note to the butcher for the chicken. The salad and a dish of peas. The rest can stand as it is: the cold soup, the Cherries Jubilee – with what?'

'The Madeira cake from yesterday, madam. It'll soak nice in the juices.'

Beattie nodded. 'Very well. And the savoury. Oh, and I dare say the master will like a glass of beer with the curried chicken,' she added, as Cook was turning away. 'Wine won't go with it. Send Henry for some bottles after he's been to the butcher's.'

'Yes, madam.' Cook went out discontentedly. Every now and then the mistress ordered curry, despite anything Cook could say, and it made the kitchen reek. None of the servants could stand the smell.

Left alone, Beattie gazed unseeing out of the window for a moment. She had been born in India, and though she had only lived there until she was seven, she had vivid memories of it. Her mother had brought away many recipes when her father had moved on to a new posting – she had been a devoted wife and always travelled with him. From India they had gone to Malta, then to Dublin, where both Beattie and her sister Adelaide had had their coming-out. When their mother died, Beattie had inherited her household books. She had been pleased that, despite his reserved Englishness, Edward was quite adventurous about food, and was willing to try things for her sake.

Addie had married an Irish baronet and was settled in Kildare. Her husband demanded recognisable cuts, plainly cooked: a steak-and-kidney pie was as far as he was willing to

85

venture into the uncharted waters of 'made dishes'. 'I like to know what I'm putting into my mouth,' he was wont to say.

She was so deep in her memories that she did not hear the doorbell ring, and was startled out of a reverie when Ada announced Mrs Fitzgerald.

Not that there was much announcing to be done. The rector's wife assumed the privilege of her husband's rank to demand entry to every drawing-room, usually brushing past whatever hapless servant opened the door to her, saying, 'I shall just have a few words with your mistress,' and not waiting to hear if she was at leisure. Beattie remembered that Sadie had once said she did it deliberately to try to catch people doing something they shouldn't. Of course she had reprimanded Sadie, but secretly thought she was probably right. Sadie often was, about people: she was a noticing little thing.

Beattie met Ada's apologetic eyes over Mrs Fitzgerald's shoulder and dismissed her. At least it was early enough not to have to invite the rector's wife to stay to luncheon.

Mrs Fitzgerald waited, lips firmly closed, until Ada had gone away and shut the door, then launched her attack. 'Now, Mrs Hunter, I really must have a word with you about your housemaid.'

'Ada?' Beattie said, puzzled. Did she want to borrow her?

'Is that the one who showed me in? No, the other one, the young one. Ethel, isn't it?'

Beattie saw quite plainly that she knew Ethel's name perfectly well. This was a practised speech. She allowed herself a little coolness. 'I cannot think what you can have to say to me about one of my own servants.'

Mrs Fitzgerald was unfrosted. She gave a patronising smile. 'Yes, I know you may think it is not my business, but I like to keep an eye on all my parishioners, and you would be surprised how often it is the case that the mistress is the last

86

person to know what is going on. That is why I took it upon myself, out of a sense of duty, to call on you this morning. You must let Ethel go.'

'*Must* I?' Beattie added a raised eyebrow to the *froideur*.

'She was seen last evening with William Snow, the assistant from Williamson's, the grocer's. They were behaving in a manner – well, not to put too fine a point on it, they were *kissing*.'

'I believe they are walking out,' Beattie said.

Yesterday had been Ethel's half-day off. She didn't enquire what her servants did in their free time – though she remembered the business about the magic-lantern show. She had 'spoken to' Ethel about that, and Ethel had lowered her eyes and apologised, though Beattie hadn't sensed any real contrition. Servants, these days, were much bolder than they had been twenty years ago. Still, this was none of Mrs Fitzgerald's business.

'Kissing,' Mrs Fitzgerald went on, as though Beattie had not spoken. 'And *fondling*. William is a decent enough boy, but weak, and Ethel is leading him astray. I'm sorry to say it, but that girl is *fast*.'

'How do you know what they were doing?' Beattie asked. 'Have you been following them?'

Two red spots formed in the rector's wife's cheeks. 'Levity is not an appropriate response, Mrs Hunter. This is a serious matter. You must dismiss her before things get out of hand.'

Beattie tired of it, and she knew the only way to get rid of the woman was to agree with her. Circumspect language was called for. 'Thank you for bringing it to my attention,' she said. 'I will deal with the matter appropriately.'

'You'll dismiss her?' Mrs Fitzgerald insisted.

'I will speak to her at the first opportunity. And now I mustn't keep you. I'm sure you have a great deal more of God's work to attend to.'

Mrs Fitzgerald gave her a sharp look, testing for irony, but all she said was, 'I'll show myself out.'

When she had gone, Beattie rang for Ada, who was there in an instant, having been expecting trouble. 'What has Ethel been up to?' she asked bluntly.

Ada looked wary. 'In what respect, madam?'

That gave Beattie the clue. 'Is she responsible for the missing beef?' Ada hesitated. 'Come, I rely on you. I shan't tell anyone you peached.'

Ada flushed slightly, but that was probably her age. 'She went on a picnic on her afternoon off. With Billy Snow. Cook said she needn't have her dinner first.' She drew a breath. 'Sandwiches were made. Without supervision.'

So Edward's good roast of beef had gone down the throat of Billy Snow. A servant would have expected jam sandwiches for a picnic, or cheese at best. Taking the beef without asking was tantamount to stealing. She would have to think what to do about that. 'A picnic where?' she temporised.

'Down by the lake, madam, so I believe.' Ada looked uncomfortable.

The woods came down to the lake's edge in many parts; it was the sort of secluded place a couple might well kiss and fondle, if they had a mind. Who had seen them? It was a favoured spot for bird-watchers, of course. Mrs F fancied herself one, as it happened. Beattie had a sudden image of her sweeping the woods with the rector's binoculars in the hope of spying the lesser spotted woodpecker, and spying instead more than she had bargained for. It was a comical image and Beattie had to stop herself smiling.

Of course, with Mrs F there was never any knowing what she *did* bargain for. She liked to insert her nasal organ into every corner of Northcote. And there were rectory spies everywhere. God help anyone in Northcote who wanted to get up to anything the Fitzgeralds disapproved of.

'Very well,' she said to Ada. 'You may go. Say nothing of this.'

She ought to act, she thought. Stealing food could not be allowed. Ada and Cook both knew about it, and if Ethel 'got away with it', they would feel resentful. Then there was the kissing. If Ethel was not checked she might go too far with Billy Snow and 'get into trouble', and what would Beattie do then? Billy Snow, as far as she could judge, would not be able to afford a wife and baby, and if he repudiated Ethel . . . Pregnant maids were a mistress's worst nightmare. And Mrs Fitzgerald would have a feast of 'I told you so', enough to last for years. The thought of *that* was unbearable.

She felt a surge of revulsion. *Is this what my life has become?* she thought. If one only knew as a child how things would turn out . . .

Suddenly she was back in India: the benign dimness of the rooms, the raw-cotton blinds over the windows that muted the sunlight, the great, slow-turning ceiling fans; sitting on the verandah to catch the breeze that came up in the evening, watching the buzzards circle slowly, high up and far away, like fans in the sky. The pony-cart in which she and Addie had been driven by their governess, and the syce who had shown her how to put the tack on. The polo matches at the officers' club and the delicious cold drinks served between chukkas. The soft-voiced, soft-footed servants. The elephants, with their painted eyes, that worked in the forest. Her ayah, who had told her magical tales of princesses and rajahs, jewels and dragons, adventures and battles and, above all, love transcendent, so that she believed the whole world was full of wonder and that she would have her share of it when she grew up.

Stolen beef. Stolen kisses. Servants and suppers. Bridge evenings. Tennis parties. And love that had once illuminated

89

her like a thousand candles in a dark church – love had become a prosaic transaction, practised very briefly, with the lamps out and without words, once or twice a month. In real life, it seemed, the prince turned into a frog.

There was no magic, only domestic matters, for ever and ever.

You think too much, Addie had said to her once. Yes, God help the woman who thought! Better we should be ignorant, blindfolded, the dumb beasts treading the circle. *Thou shalt not muzzle the ox that treadeth out the corn.* Oh, muzzle us! Blindfold us! Don't tell us stories of sunlight when we must live shut away in the dark!

Suddenly she felt her own heart beating. It was like a bird battering its wings against the bars of a cage. Foolish, she reproached herself, pressing her hands to her breast. Be still. No-one is harming you. You are better off than most women in the world. Be grateful, and don't pine after things that cannot be. After people long gone and lost to you . . .

She thought of Diana and her strained hopes of Lord Dene; and Sadie, happy in the prospect of riding horses, untouched yet by longings that would undoubtedly one day eat away her peace. What should she tell her daughters? That there was magic, or no magic?

Their lives would be like hers, and there was nothing in the world to be done about it: should they not be prepared for how mundane life really was? And yet . . . would she give up the treasure in her own mind for the sake of peace? She had soared once; she had touched the sky.

Unseeing, she stared out of the window, her mind drifting here and there. 'You're far away,' Edward would sometimes say. She was too old for dreams, that was what the world would say. She rather envied Ethel her freedom to romp in the undergrowth by the lake with the Snow boy. That freedom, even for Ethel, would be very short. The flower and the bee were followed rapidly by the fruit and the withering of the leaves.

'Charles, I don't believe you're listening to me,' said the earl.

Halfway down the breakfast table, Charles jerked back from a reverie. In front of him, the bacon and eggs he had served himself were half eaten but he had no memory of any mouthful. He sought through his subconscious memory. 'You were saying something about war?' he managed.

Across the table from him, his brother Rupert sniggered quietly into his coffee cup.

The earl looked annoyed. 'The business in Ireland,' he snapped. 'This is no time for wool-gathering, Charles. We could be facing civil war, and you could be sent out there to put it down.'

Charles gathered his thoughts. The Home Rule Bill had passed in the Commons in May, offering Ireland self-rule within the United Kingdom, with a bi-cameral parliament in Dublin. It was a generous settlement, but unfortunately it settled nothing. The problem was that the north-eastern counties – most of the old Kingdom of Ulster – did not want to be ruled from Dublin. And the rest of Ireland refused to accept any compromise: it must be all Ireland or nothing. The impasse was growing steadily more bad-tempered. Both sides – Unionists and Nationalists – had now set up military wings, and already there had been some deadly skirmishes.

'Are things really that bad?' he asked.

'If you had been listening . . .' the earl said. He sighed and started again. 'There's a flood of arms being smuggled in on both sides. Militias drilling openly. The police can't deal with it. And the King's called a special conference at Buckingham Palace to try to get the two sides to agree on something – anything – that will stop the slide into civil war. That's how serious it is.'

'Have the Irish leaders agreed to attend?'

'Yes. They're meeting this morning, along with the government. The King's determined to get Home Rule, but with both sides so intractable . . .' He shrugged. 'I bumped into Asquith yesterday at the House. He said he's never felt so helpless. The question seems so small to us, he said, but it's so big to the Irish, and the consequences are unspeakable.' He frowned. 'Damned defeatist feller, Asquith. But it *is* a problem, there's no doubt about it. And if it does come to civil war, you may well be sent out there.'

'You mean the Terriers? But we're not required to serve overseas,' Charles pointed out. He was an officer in the local Territorial force.

'Ireland might be over the sea, but it's not properly overseas. It's still part of the kingdom and they may well designate it as a Home Guard matter. It's likely they won't be able to spare any more regulars.' The regular army was very small, and fully stretched guarding overseas garrisons.

'Well, perhaps the King will be able to negotiate an agreement,' Charles said. He had no wish to find himself in the middle of a civil war. How would you ever know who was on which side? How could you shoot one of your own people, even if he was shooting at you? Fighting in and around people's houses, with the women and children and old folk in the way, villages devastated, crops and animals destroyed . . . And the bitterness afterwards, whichever way it went. It didn't bear thinking about.

'Even if it doesn't come to civil war,' said his mother, looking over the top of her spectacles, 'and we all pray it won't, it will be necessary for *someone* to go over there soon and see to things at Credda.' This was the Wroughtons' estate near Maynooth. 'In the circumstances, it can't be left to the steward.'

'Wouldn't it be better for Rupert to go?' Charles objected. He had no wish to go to Ireland now, just when he was getting to know Diana Hunter.

'I shall need Rupert to go to Northumberland,' said the earl. They had a coal mine there. 'Things are still unsettled, and the last thing we want is a strike. Rupert's better with people of that sort than you are.'

Charles looked across the table at Rupert, and could not deny it. His brother had inherited all the harmonious features from his passably good-looking father, while Charles more resembled his extremely plain mother. And Rupert had an outgoing and engaging manner, and could be jolly with mine managers and pitmen alike. Charles's shyness made him seem rather stately and aloof. Estate workers and countrymen liked and admired him, but the quicker-thinking, sharper-talking industrial types couldn't spare the time to see the good intentions underneath.

'Unless there's an emergency, you had better think about going to Ireland straight after camp,' the earl concluded. The local Territorial unit held its annual summer camp in the grounds of Dene Park in August. 'Make your arrangements.' He prepared to leave the table. 'And, Charles,' he added, 'I'd like to speak to you in my room after breakfast.'

The interview was, as so often before, about marriage. The Wroughtons had always been great marriers, which was how they had not only endured but flourished when other families and titles had gone extinct.

During the religious upheavals of the sixteenth and seventeenth centuries they had married for survival and, like the Vicar of Bray, adopted a flexible posture, on or off the knees as circumstances required.

In the eighteenth and nineteenth centuries they had married for political influence: Dene Park had come with a Grenvillite Whig marriage in the 1760s, Credda with a Parnellite regrouping in the 1880s. Charles's grandfather had married property in London and a large block of shares in the Russian railway.

The present earl had married a Northumberland coal mine, a small place in Norfolk, and a factory in Leicester, which he had sold to buy the hunting-box at Melton Mowbray. The wife who came with these valuable assets was the remarkably plain and irritable younger daughter of the Earl of Hexham, but Lord Wroughton had understood the rules of the game and so had she. He had given her position and a family with a rich history; she had brought a valuable dowry. She had given him the required two sons, ran the household and performed her social duties admirably. It was a fair bargain with which they had both been satisfied.

It made it all the more incomprehensible to the earl that Charles was twenty-seven and still unmarried. He had been a biddable little boy and a quiet youth, and no difficulties had been anticipated when they had selected some very nice arable land in Suffolk for him, attached to the person of his cousin, Lady Helen Hale. Charles had known her from childhood, and she would make an eminently suitable chatelaine: it was the perfect match.

But somehow or other they had failed to get Charles up to the starting-post. He didn't make a fuss, or express defiance, which was odder: it was hard for his parents to work out exactly how he kept slipping his rope and getting away. But matters were becoming critical. Helen was not getting any younger, and the earl and his countess wanted the assurance of a couple of grandsons to give them peace of mind. They had worked hard for the Wroughton inheritance, and they deserved it. It was basic consideration that a son ought to show – damn it, it was simple good manners!

Charles, the earl thought, had a distinctly guilty look as he followed him into his business room and closed the door behind him.

'I suppose you know what I want to talk to you about,' the earl said. Charles made no answer. 'Marriage, Charles. It's your duty. I can't understand why you don't get on with it. It isn't manly to shirk your duty.'

'I'm sorry, Father,' Charles said.

The earl made a restless movement. That was no answer! It gave him nothing to get to grips with. 'Sorry? What does that mean? If you're sorry, get on with it! Helen's been waiting these five years, and her parents expect it.'

'I don't want to marry Helen,' Charles said. He hesitated, and added, 'I don't like her.'

'Don't *like* her? How can you not like her?' Charles didn't answer. 'She's not very handsome, I agree, but what's that to do with it? I married your mother. It doesn't make the slightest difference once you're married, you know, as long as she's the right sort of girl and knows her duty. Your mother runs this house like clockwork. She's admired everywhere for her skill as a hostess and her good works. *That*'s the sort of girl you have to marry. And you haven't any time to waste. There's no knowing how many girls you might get before a son comes along. Look at Henry and Jane. Look at Coco.' Charles's sister Caroline had produced two girls so far. 'You need to get on with it while Helen's still young enough to breed.' He studied his son's closed face in frustration. 'Is it her little moustache you object to?' he tried. 'But there's no need to look at her, you know. You can close your eyes when the time comes, can't you?'

'It has nothing to do with her looks,' Charles said, and added, in a low voice, 'I'm no oil painting myself.'

'No,' the earl agreed. Though in truth Charles wasn't bad and Helen really was rather a shocker. 'It's a shame Rupert didn't come along first. He has all the looks *and* all the charm. People *like* him. But facts are facts. You are the eldest.' He tried sweet reason. 'Look here, old chap, I really just want to understand. Helen's willing, your mother and I and her parents couldn't approve more. Why won't you marry her?'

'I'm sorry, Father, I just don't like her. And I don't want to be married to someone I don't like.'

The earl breathed out hard, trying to contain his fury. 'Well, who *do* you want to marry, then?' he snarled. 'Have you got someone else in mind? Because your mother and I would really like to hear about it. Do you want the Wroughton title to die out?'

'It won't come to that,' Charles said. 'Even if I didn't marry, Rupert will.'

'You can't get out of your responsibilities like that!' the earl thundered. Charles was looking down, not sullenly, but unhappily. He was such a big, strong feller, the earl thought, with frustration, much tougher than Rupert, who had always been rather slender and lightweight, but it was Charles who had always been the sensitive one, weeping when his dogs died, unable to bear being told off. The earl had beaten him for blubbing a good few times, to knock it out of him before he went off to school. Well, he didn't blub any more, but there was still that ridiculous softness in him somewhere, whatever it was. You'd never think it to look at him.

The earl tried again to be reasonable. 'Marry Helen, get an heir and a spare, and as for anything else – well, there are arrangements. These things are understood.' For many years the earl had had recourse to a pleasant young woman in a flat just across the river from the House, whom he could visit before or after sittings. He hesitated on the brink of revealing this to Charles as an example, but thought better of it. Better not to be specific.

But Charles only said, 'I don't want to do that.'

'Well, what the devil *do* you want?' The earl was back to bellowing. 'I tell you this, Charles. Things are looking bad all over Europe. War may be coming, Ireland's on the brink, and we haven't time to worry about your poetic sensitivities, or whatever they are. Marry Helen, or find someone else, but do it double quick or, by God, I'll find a way to make you!'

Charles looked up in hope. 'If I did find someone else—'

'As long as it's the right sort of gel – but, for God's sake, get on with it. And that's all I've got to say.' He pulled a heap of correspondence towards him and started reading.

Charles left the room and closed the door quietly. He took a deep breath. He hated being shouted at by his father. When he was a child, other people's anger had shaken him dreadfully, made him want to run away and hide and never come out. He had always rather be beaten than shouted at, as long as it was done cold-bloodedly, as it generally was, either at home or at school. He did not fear physical pain. It was the torments of the mind that had power over him.

He could not marry Helen. To live all his life with someone he disliked – and who would bully him, he was quite sure. She had done so when they were children; as an adult and a female she would have subtler but equally painful ways of doing so. No, it would be intolerable. He had sooner not marry, and leave it to Rupert – who, handsome and popular, would surely have no difficulty in marrying and getting the sons needed.

But he hoped – oh, he so much hoped – that that would not be necessary. Diana Hunter came back before his mind's eye, from which she had never been far away, even as he had bent his head to his father's wrath. He had not mentioned her, not to his parents or even Rupert. She was, at the moment, his treasured secret, and he would not say anything about her until and unless he felt surer of her.

She was so beautiful, like a creature from another world. Her hair like silk, not artificially gold but naturally fair, in a multitude of delicate shades, like a hayfield touched with sun and shadow. Her features so perfect she was like an alabaster sculpture of a goddess, but with the added glorious tones and textures of living flesh. Her eyes – most remarkable of all – not blue as one might have expected, but grey-gold, subtle grey flecked with gold, and with a dark blue rim to the iris that gave her a strange, other-worldly look.

He could not believe he might deserve someone like her. Yet she had seemed to like him. Modest as he was about his own meagre qualities, he was almost sure she did. She had agreed so readily to walk along the river with him, and listened to him with such attention when he talked. The girls of his own class had never listened to him like that. They were impatient with him. They called him 'slow' and 'duffer'; and outside his immediate circle they thought him cold and stand-offish.

But, oh, he groaned inwardly as he remembered the riverside walk, what had possessed him to go on and on about fish? And when he had managed to stop himself, instead of introducing any better topic he had lectured her about the importance of the land. She would think him the dullest dog in existence. He simply had no small-talk – he was hopeless!

Yet she had smiled at him – oh, her smile!

For an undisciplined moment, he saw her here at Dene, installed as chatelaine; taking, eventually, his mother's place. He loved Dene with a deep and immutable passion. It was the most beautiful place in the world to him, and she would be its crown and glory, if he could win her for it. It was one reason among many that he wouldn't marry Helen: he loved Dene too much to inflict her on it. But Diana was deserving of the throne.

He reined imagination back, and told himself sternly there were many hurdles yet to leap. He must not hope too much. But he had the whole summer. He was a slow sort of fellow, but surely he ought to be able to make some progress with the whole summer ahead.

If only he wasn't made to go to Ireland. He sent up a brief prayer: *Please, God, don't let there be civil war in Ireland.*

CHAPTER EIGHT

On the 23rd of July Austria, having undertaken an investigation into the assassination of the archduke and his wife, issued an ultimatum to Serbia. It accused Serbia of supplying the arms to the assassins and inserting them into Bosnia through its own frontier authorities. It demanded an end to all anti-Austrian activity. Hostile publications were to be banned, agitators rounded up, and anyone involved in the plot was to be brought to trial. Austria was to oversee all legal actions, and Serbia was to publish an admission and an apology in its newspapers and as a general order to the Serbian Army.

Edward heard about it from the Earl Wroughton, who called at his office the following day for, he said, 'a glass of your excellent sherry'.

'Grey said it was the most formidable document he'd ever seen addressed from one sovereign state to another,' the earl concluded. Sir Edward Grey was the Foreign Secretary.

'Designed to provoke, I wonder?' Edward hazarded.

'Serbia's got forty-eight hours to respond, and it's a great deal of bile to swallow. Wouldn't be surprising if it was enough to choke 'em.'

'Which would mean war between Austria and Serbia,' said Edward. 'And Russia's bound to support the Serbs.'

The earl almost shrugged. 'Perhaps, perhaps. Still, nothing to do with us, a lot of excitable Slavs cutting each other's throats.'

Edward thought of what Jack and Beth had said. 'But if Germany came in with the Austrians . . .'

'No-one expects that. I have it from Grey that the Kaiser himself is doing everything he can to keep the war a local matter between Austria and Serbia. The Tsar and the Kaiser are cousins. They grew up together. Germany won't attack Russia, I assure you.'

'War is a contagion,' Edward said, 'and it's a young man's sickness.'

'Well, Grey has a long head on his shoulders. He'll steady the ship. He has a lot of influence internationally.'

The earl then came to the business for which he had called on Edward – the raising of a sum of money to purchase a piece of land adjacent to his own at Dene Park. They discussed loans, and then Edward said, 'The other possibility is for you to sell some shares. If I may recommend, this might be the time to shed the Russian railway holding.'

The earl regarded him with a frown. 'Because of the threat of war, do you mean?' Edward nodded. 'But shares always go up in wartime,' the earl objected. 'I met a feller only last week who said Russian railways would go sky high.'

'They may well rise in the short term,' Edward said, 'but it would take only one campaign reversal to set them plunging, and then I'm afraid you would find it very hard to get rid of them. Better to take a reasonable profit now than to ride the rocket and be unable to get off before the explosion.'

Wroughton's frown deepened. He was not a man given to metaphor, and disliked it in other men, too. *Unmanly*, he thought any flourishes of language. But he trusted Edward's judgement – on the whole. 'You advise divesting myself of the entire holding? But that will realise far more than I need for the land purchase.'

'I would recommend investing the surplus in home-grown shares. In uncertain times it's as well to keep one's valuables close.'

100

'And what,' the earl enquired, 'would you have me invest in?'

'Iron and steel. Shipbuilding. Munitions. Stocks that rise in wartime.'

'Coal? Railways?' Wroughton asked.

'I think not. Those are industries that could be nationalised.'

'Nationalised!' The earl looked shocked, then puzzled. 'You're not talking about war between Germany and Russia now, are you?' He stared, and exploded. 'Damn it, Hunter, if you know something, you had better tell me!'

Edward spread his hands. 'You have Sir Edward Grey's ear. You must surely know more than I do.'

'Then what *is* all this old-maidishness?'

'Just instinct. A feeling one develops – a nose for the market, if you like.'

'I don't like! A nose? You can't smell war coming. Somebody must have told you something.'

Edward shook his head. 'I can only give my advice, my lord. You must decide whether or not to take it.'

The earl was silent for a while, scowling at Edward as if black looks would elicit a confession about a secret source. But Edward regarded him steadily and unemotionally, and eventually Wroughton could only sigh and say, 'Very well, have it your way. I'll sell the Russian railways. Anything else?'

'You have a small holding in German munitions.'

'And damn good shares they've been, too – you've always told me so.'

'Just as a matter of caution,' Edward said. 'They've done well, and it's a good principle to realise some profit now and then.'

'Very well, very well.' He stood up. 'And now I must get down to the House. You're a strange one, Hunter, but you've a good head on your shoulders. Wish I knew where you were getting your information. Yes, yes, I know.' He held up his hands. 'Instinct, feelings, your nose. Rot and balderdash! But if you won't tell me, you won't.'

Edward saw him to the door, and as they reached it, said, 'Oh, by the way, my lord, I must say that it was very kind of your son to take my daughter to the polo match yesterday. She enjoyed it very much.'

Just for an instant the earl's face had a 'what the deuce?' look on it, before centuries of schooling smoothed it out, and he said, 'Nonsense, nonsense. The honour was all his, I assure you.'

Warren was there to take Lord Wroughton downstairs. He descended, thinking, *Now what is that scamp up to?* He knew Rupert had played in a polo match at Radnage, but there had been no mention as far as he could remember of taking a female along. And, in any case, why that particular girl? He had no idea Rupert even knew her. *Hunter's daughter?* You didn't take your banker's daughter to polo matches. You just didn't. What was he up to? Could be damned awkward. Had been embarrassing already. He would have a sharp word with that boy the next time he saw him. A very sharp word.

There had been no question, of course, of refusing the invitation, but Diana had sighed a little at Charles's choice of outing. She was not terribly keen on horses.

Sadie had been wild with envy. 'I always wanted to see a polo match. Oh, you are lucky! There are some polo ponies at livery up at Highclere. Of course, they're not really ponies, they're full-sized horses. Thoroughbreds. They're owned by an army captain. I haven't ridden them yet, but they're the loveliest creatures. Oh, *please* ask if I can come too.'

'Of course you can't,' Diana snapped crossly. 'It's not a charabanc outing. Don't you understand *anything*?'

'I don't suppose he'd mind,' Sadie retorted. 'I expect he'd

like someone there who knows one end of a horse from the other.'

Diana didn't bother to reply to that. On the contrary, she thought, there was nothing a man liked better than explaining things. And this time he hadn't said anything about going in a party. Presumably the spectators at the match were considered chaperone enough.

But they weren't alone in the motor-car, which was a shame. When Charles had said his brother Rupert was playing in the match, she had assumed he was staying down there or would travel with the horses. It was quite a surprise when the familiar red motor drew up and two young men jumped out. It was even more of a surprise when Charles introduced Rupert to her. She had seen him once or twice in childhood at church, but for years he had been away at school and then at Oxford, and this was the first time she had come face to face with him as an adult. She had not been prepared for his good looks. She must have shown it on her face because his eyes narrowed and he gave her a very cynical smile, which shocked her into controlling her expression.

Thrown off balance, she said the first thing that came into her mind. 'Where are your horses?'

'Did you think they'd be travelling with us in Charles's motor? Rather cramped quarters, the back seat, don't you think?'

He was making fun of her, and she felt herself colour. 'I thought there were such things as horseboxes,' she defended herself.

Charles explained, 'Rupert shares ponies with another team member. Shall we go?'

He helped her into the front seat. Rupert got into the back, but not before saying *sotto voce* to Diana, 'I'm sorry if my unwelcome presence is a damper.' It was not so much what he said but the way he said it, with the same ironic

103

smile, which seemed to imply, 'I know what you're up to, and I don't approve.'

She answered with dignity, 'Not unwelcome at all. How can you think it?'

'I can think many things,' Rupert answered enigmatically. 'Some of them, alas, not fit for the ears of ladies.'

Charles had climbed in and they started off, so there was no more conversation. Diana was acutely aware of Rupert sitting behind her, and when they stopped at crossroads or slowed behind haycarts, and talking would have been possible, she found she did not want to say anything to Charles while Rupert could overhear. It *was* a damper. Fortunately, once they reached the park Rupert had to go and get changed and join the other team members, which left her and Charles alone.

They strolled round the field, and met some of the other spectators, who seemed a different sort from Charles's friends she had already met. Although they all knew each other, they did not use that as a weapon. No-one asked Diana how she knew Charles or what her father did: they simply smiled and accepted her. They talked about the game, other games, the ponies and general matters. They seemed to be mostly married couples, and many of the men were military; they had a pleasant, down-to-earth manner that Diana found easy to get on with.

The game itself she found incomprehensible, and the dashing and near-colliding horses quite alarming. Charles explained everything to her most carefully, but it wouldn't stay in her head. After a certain interval of play everyone got up and went on to the field, where Charles told her they would 'stamp the divots' – flaps of turf dug up by the ponies' hoofs. The idea was to flip them back into their hole with the tip of one's shoe, then press them in by stamping on them. 'It's fun,' he told her. She didn't see why, but since everyone was doing it, she had to. The principal idea seemed to be to give everyone a chance to move about and chat.

At the end of another period of play there was tea. Diana greeted it with relief. Charles took her to join some acquaintances, who accepted her pleasantly into the group and continued with their conversations. She found herself beside one of the military wives, a Mrs Cameron, who smiled and said, 'Do I gather you're not a horse lover?'

'I'm afraid not,' Diana confessed. 'Oh dear, does it show?'

'I recognised the symptoms,' said Mrs Cameron. 'I'm not one either, though it doesn't do to admit it. Horsy people are such fanatics, aren't they? I've never seen the attraction of them. They're so big and unpredictable. And so nervous! You go to stroke a horse, and it flinches, despite the fact it's never known anything but kindness. George's ponies, I swear, are cosseted in a way our children can only dream of, but if I ever venture near them I'm still told not to make any sudden movements.'

Diana laughed. 'I know what you mean. Though horses have never come much in my way. Except for coal horses and cab horses and the like. I grew up in London.'

'Well, count yourself lucky,' said Mrs Cameron. 'As a cavalry wife I've had all too much of them. Can't think how I got myself into it. I should have married a sailor. The high seas are about the only place that's safe from the wretched creatures.'

'My sister would boil to hear you call them that.'

'Oh, is she another one?'

'She thinks about nothing else.'

'You'll be safe enough with Charles,' Mrs Cameron observed, looking across to where Charles was talking to – or, rather, listening to – another of the group. 'He loves horses, but he isn't a bore about it.'

'Have you known him a long time?' Diana asked, half expecting to hear the crushing 'all my life' again.

But Mrs Cameron said, 'A few years, through the Territorials. He's a dear man.'

Diana would have liked to mine this promising seam of information, but at that point Rupert joined the group, and she was put on her guard again. The talk grew more lively under his influence. There was more joking and laughter. Diana saw how he teased all the women and how they loved it, clustering around him like bees around a particularly succulent marigold; and how the men laughed and shook their heads in a 'good old Rupert!' sort of way. They enjoyed him as much as their wives did.

Charles, she noticed, hardly spoke: he answered when he was asked a direct question, but he did not initiate conversation. She wasn't sure if he was more silent when Rupert was there, or if it was only the contrast between them: Rupert, glowing, glittering, brightly coloured, like a conversational mayfly flittering about, made Charles seem monochrome and taciturn. But perhaps Rupert needed to try harder: Charles was the heir, and Rupert, for all his harlequin attractiveness, was just another 'hon:' who would have to make his own way in the world.

Tea was over, the players had disappeared, and the spectators were drifting away to their places. There was to be another period of play now, she understood from Mrs Cameron, who parted from her with a smile and a hope that they would meet again, which Diana took very kindly. How different from the Stanton-Harcourts and the Eynshams!

'Perhaps during summer camp,' she added. 'We usually manage a few social engagements as a sop to the wives.'

'I thought the summer camp was only for the Territorials,' Diana said.

'It is, but there's always some training with the regular battalion as well, just so that the Terriers know what's what. Perhaps I shall see you there. We non-horse-lovers must stick together.'

Charles, who had been talking to Rupert, came back to retrieve her and said, 'Rupert isn't coming back with us. He's going to stay with Faulds – the fellow who shares his ponies with him. So we needn't stay until the end, unless you want. We could motor back slowly and enjoy the countryside.'

Diana felt a quick surge of relief. During tea, out of the corner of her eye, she had seen Rupert observing her and read no approval in his expression. A drive home without him would be much pleasanter.

It was a happy end to the day. Pottering along the lanes at fifteen miles an hour made conversation possible, and Diana drew Charles out on the countryside, the harvest, the names of different trees, and his own plans for Dene and its farms. At times he grew quite eloquent, and she was able to drift a little, listening to him with only half her attention.

It was a golden afternoon, declining towards dusk; the country was a patchwork of yellow stubble and standing corn, contrasting with dark green hedges and stands of trees in full summer leaf; the sky was deep cornflower blue decorated with dazzling white clouds. Charles had asked her out twice, and the people at the polo match had been nice to her. Life was very good.

The Buckingham Palace Conference on Ireland broke up on the 24th of July without coming to any agreement. Edward heard the next day, from one of his clients, that Asquith felt it had not been a complete waste of time: the two sides had spoken together calmly for the first time, which went some way towards allaying their fear of each other.

That was all very well, he thought, but the leaders talking to each other in a civilised way was not the same as the people on the ground getting along. Beattie had just received a letter from her sister Addie in Donadea, about the tense situation there:

The Clearys are gun-running, and everyone knows it, but catching them is another matter, and of course you

107

can't depend on the police to do anything because half of them are secret Fenians and the other half don't want to stir things up. My cook says old Mrs Cleary has been moving the guns about in the baby's pram, right underneath the baby, if you will! But who would think of stopping her, a poor old lady with no teeth wheeling her grandchild about? We sometimes feel quite isolated here. You have to watch what you say – passions run high and the Irish are so terribly touchy. We had three windows broken in the dead of night last week – three! Such a shock to the system. You wouldn't believe the noise a simple window makes when everything's quiet! And, of course, you have to rush downstairs in case they've thrown a flaming torch in. We all sleep with buckets of water outside the door these days. My nerves are in shreds, and it's all so silly because Jock is on their side, really. As the local magistrate he has to uphold the law, but he'd be happy to give them Home Rule if it was up to him.

Beattie was naturally worried about her sister and family, though this was not a new worry, but rather a nagging background fear that sharpened from time to time, then settled back again. Edward comforted her as best he could with this reflection. He could not deny that matters were very tense over there.

But it seemed that Ireland was now not the only thing to worry about. He did not share with her an intriguing piece of information he had had from a client, a retired sea captain called Willis, who was enjoying his autumn years in Weymouth and had come up to London to see to some business.

The summer exercises of the three fleets in the Channel had ended on the 23rd, and Winston Churchill, the First Lord of the Admiralty, had released the Third Fleet, which had dispersed to its home ports. The First and Second Fleets had regrouped in Portland, and Captain Willis, who liked to watch the comings and goings of the harbour, had been observing them through his binoculars.

'Red flags, Hunter,' he said. 'That's what caught my attention. First there were a lot of loaded boats coming off, and a fellow I know in the dockyard said it was personal effects being sent ashore to be put into store. And then the red flags. They have to fly those when live ammunition is being moved about. Boat after boat going off from the magazine to the warships, all loaded to the gunwales. Never seen so much activity. The whole dockyard was like an ants' nest.' The clear blue sailor's eyes looked frankly into Edward's. 'You know what it all means.'

Personal effects going into store, and ammunition being loaded? There was only one conclusion. 'The Royal Navy is getting ready for war,' Edward answered.

Willis nodded. 'Of course, the navy has to be ready, just in case, but it does mean things must be a lot more serious on the Continent than we suppose.'

Edward was puzzled. The Austria-Serbia thing wouldn't require such a level of readiness in the fleets, even if Russia got involved.

He worked later than usual that day, and the evening papers were on the street when he stepped out of the office. The Serbian deadline had expired and there was a report of the Serbs' reply to Austria. They had agreed to all but two demands: that the Austrians could oversee the trials, and that the apology should be published as a general order to the army, which it feared would cause a military uprising. Despite this surprising degree of acquiescence, it was plain the Serbs did not expect Austria to back down, because they had ordered mobilisation three hours earlier.

Edward lifted his eyes from the newspaper and sat staring at nothing as the Metropolitan line train swayed and rattled its way into Harrow station. Here there was the usual delay as the electric engine was exchanged for the steam engine, which would take the train out into the Middlesex countryside. It seemed inevitable now that Austria and Serbia would go to war, but surely it need not go any further. Russia, Germany, Britain: the Tsar, the Kaiser and King George, all cousins, childhood friends with family obligations. Messages being wired hourly between embassies to avoid any misunderstandings. Nobody wanted war.

But if his nephew was right, and Germany did, what could stop them? He thought of the long-held background assumption that sooner or later Germany would cause trouble. Had the time just crept closer? He shivered, and turned to the business page.

Bobby Hunter was staying with his schoolfriend Horsey, inevitably known as Dobbin, at the Horsey home in Grove Park, near Bromley. They had spent a happy Saturday watching the cricket, with the inestimable bonus of seeing the great W. G. Grace himself bat for Eltham. Despite his great age, he had still made 69 not out, helping Eltham to victory over the home team.

'You don't mind losing to a man like that,' Dobbin said dreamily, as they walked home in a languorous and philosophical mood induced by the long hot day.

'Fancy seeing him in person,' Bobby said. 'The nearest I've been before is having him in my cigarette-card collection! He may be ancient, but you have to say he can still bat a bit.'

'You wouldn't call it an elegant style, but there's such power in his strokes,' Dobbin mused, scuffing his feet idly through the dust of the road under the old elm trees.

'He's got a good eye, that's what it is. If you played off the back foot like that, Dobbo, you'd soon be in trouble.'

Dobbin didn't rise to the bait. 'I'm starving, aren't you?' They had taken sandwiches with them to the match, and

Mrs Horsey was an ample provider who understood young appetites, but now luncheon seemed a distant dream. 'I wonder what's for dinner.'

'You have a prosaic mind,' Bobby teased. 'Seeing old W. G. ought to lift your thoughts to nobler planes.'

'Oh? Such as what?'

'I don't know. Life in general, I suppose. Here we are at the crossroads, finished with school, off to university.' They were both going to Oxford in the autumn, Dobbin to Brasenose, and Bobby to Balliol, where his father and grand-father had gone before him. 'I'm looking forward to it, aren't you?'

'Mostly. You'll be all right – you always get on with people.'

'But you're the swot – you'll be popular with the beaks and get a first and go on to glory.'

'I don't know about that,' Dobbin said. 'It's afterwards that's really daunting. University – and then what?'

'The mysterious world of the grown-ups, I suppose – whatever that might entail,' said Bobby. 'Career and so on.'

'My pater wants me to go into his business,' Dobbin said, with a sigh. 'I suppose,' he added doubtfully, 'it's as well to have one's future mapped out, so as to avoid uncertainty and so on. But I keep thinking—'

'You do?' Bobby enquired. 'First I've heard of it, Dob, old thing.'

Dobbin punched his arm, but it was merely an automatic protest. 'D'you remember that old fellow who gave the speech at Prize Day? When he said, "If a man cannot be useful to his country, he is better off dead"?'

'Can't say I do,' Bobby said. 'I expect I was thinking of other things. It was jolly hot in the assembly hall, as I remember. Anyway, he wasn't referring to diligent fellows like you.'

'But will I be serving my country by following my pater into his business?' Dobbin asked.

'Somebody's got to make the things people buy,' Bobby said. 'That's obvious. I think you'll be jolly useful. I shouldn't take it to heart, anyway. It's the sort of thing old buffers say. He was just an old fellow with whiskers who goes about making speeches. Don't see much "usefulness" in that.'

'When you're that old you don't have to be useful,' Dobbin argued. 'You have to have *been* useful. And he was a general. Don't you remember, he talked about South Africa and the Boer War? He fought the Boers at Modder River.'

'As I said, I wasn't really listening. Look here, Dob, you don't want to be a soldier. There's more than one way to serve your country. You're too impressionable. If he'd been a bishop, you'd be nattering about going into the Church!'

Dobbin gave him a weak smile of agreement. 'I wish I was like you and didn't care about anything.'

'I care about a lot of things,' Bobby protested.

'Well, what are *you* going to do after Oxford? I suppose you'll follow your father into the bank.'

'I expect the guv'nor would like it if I went into banking, but he won't press me to,' Bobby said. 'He's a good egg. On the whole, given that guv'nors all have to sign a solemn pledge not to be proper human beings, he's quite decent. Anyway, it's not as if he *owns* the bank. It's a respectable way to earn a living, of course, but I'm not sure it's for me.'

'What do you *want* to do, then?'

'Actually, I've given it a lot of serious thought,' Bobby said gravely.

'And?'

'I want to be a lion-tamer.'

Dobbin stared for an instant before he realised he was being roasted. 'I can just see your pater's face if you told him that!'

Bobby retained his serious air. 'Assuming, of course, that I give up my ambition to be a trapeze artist.'

'Ass!' said Dobbin. 'Be serious – what would you *like* to do?'

'Something exciting,' Bobby said. 'Something *different*! Be an explorer, travel the world, see new places, discover lost tribes, climb mountains, shoot rapids, wrestle with bears. Not just go to the office on the train every morning and come home on the train every night, like the pater. Like everyone's paters. There has to be more to life than that.'

'P'raps that's what the old general meant by being useful.'

'Lord, *I* don't know what he meant. Good works and so on, I expect. Don't let it bother you. We've got three years before there's any need to think about it. In fact, there's no need to think about anything at all!'

'Don't you mean to work hard at Oxford, then?'

Bobby clapped him on the back. 'Have fun, that's what I mean to do, dear earnest old Dobbin, and I shall do my best to take you along with me, even if you are in a different college. Anyway, everyone knows that Brasenose men are sportsmen without the least academic ambition, so your job will be to chuck out the Latin verbs and get to grips with your oarsmanship. You row like a flounder in a panic, Dob, it has to be said. And your batting could do with improvement.'

'I made twenty-six not out against St John's,' Dobbin protested indignantly. 'And you were out second ball, as I remember.'

'I'll give you some coaching,' Bobby said generously. 'The secret is to enjoy yourself and not worry about the score. We've got OTC camp coming up in August. Two weeks under canvas at Aldershot! If I haven't got you enjoying yourself by the end of that, I shall give up and go into a monastery.'

CHAPTER NINE

Rupert stayed with his friend Faulds for three days, and it was not until breakfast on Sunday morning that he and the earl came face to face.

'Morning, Father,' he said cheerfully, as he walked to the sideboard.

The earl grunted in reply, then remembered the strange incident of Hunter's daughter. Neither the countess nor Charles was down yet. It was as good an opportunity as any to have it out. 'Want to talk to you,' he said.

Rupert carried his plate to his place, and the butler glided up to pour his coffee. 'Have I done something?' he asked, reading his father's scowl – though a scowl on the face of the earl was no unusual thing.

'That polo match,' said the earl. 'Damned strange thing. I was discussing business with Hunter at the bank, and he thanked me for my son taking his daughter to the polo match. Was the fellow wandering in his wits – or have you been up to something?'

Rupert raised his eyebrows. 'Not me, sir.'

'So the girl wasn't there?' the earl asked, with relief only slightly tinged with worry that his banker suffered from delusions.

'Oh, she was there all right,' Rupert said, 'but it wasn't me who invited her. You've got the wrong Wroughton. It was

Charles.' The earl could only stare. Rupert contrived a look of sad concern. 'It was embarrassing, I must admit.'

The earl was about to explode, when a horrid thought stopped him. He remembered his conversation with Charles, when he had suggested that if he married his cousin Helen, there were certain arrangements for a gentleman's comfort, which were understood by all parties. Was it possible that Charles – who was not of the very brightest – had misunderstood, and picked on entirely the wrong class of girl for the purpose? You couldn't do that sort of thing to the daughters of the middle class! It was just not on. The idea that Charles could have done something so terrible – and, worse, could think his father was actually encouraging him – was dreadful to contemplate.

He met Rupert's cool, insolent look of enquiry, and realised a lid must be put on this thing.

'Very well,' he said. 'I will deal with this. You are not to say anything to Charles, or your mother, about it. Do you understand?'

'Yes, Father,' said Rupert.

'I mean it, now – not a word.'

Rupert smiled, and bowed his head over his eggs.

Charles and his mother arrived at the same moment, and rather late, so there was no time for a private word before church. Since the family was known to be at Dene Park, the earl felt they should be seen at the morning service. There was a brake provided for the servants, following the family in the earl's Rolls-Royce.

Charles might have wondered why his father cast him several dark looks, accompanied by clearings of the throat, as though he wanted to say something, but his thoughts were elsewhere. The family pew was right at the front, so it was not possible to see who else was there without turning round, which was simply not done.

The rector, who was a keen reader of Sherlock Holmes stories, preached a sermon on the subject of 'Playing the Game for the Game's Own Sake'. This, he said, was a uniquely British virtue, an example of a higher form of consciousness, which could only arise from an old and tested civilisation. It could not be expected, he said, from the poor native of Africa (here the congregation heaved a collective sigh of relief: they knew he would get Africa in somehow so it was good to have it out of the way), who lived with the innocence of the animal, in an instinctive relationship with his great mother, Nature herself. Innocence, a state required by God if one was to pass through the eye of the needle, was harder for the civilised man to attain. It was for that that the great schools, like his own alma mater, had been founded, to guide the boyhood of this great nation to a wholesome, virtuous and Christian manhood, and through the discipline and fellowship of games to teach the greatest lesson of all, to play the game of life not for sordid reward or transitory glory, but for the game's own sake.

The earl dozed off, as he was wont to do, to wake with a start at 'In the name of the Father'. The congregation, those who had and those who had not been listening, picked up the cue, stirred and started fumbling for their pennies and sixpences, knowing that it was a downhill canter now from 'Let your light so shine before men', to 'The peace of God', the opening of the great doors to freedom, and the promise of roast beef.

As soon as the rector reached the door, the Wroughtons made their move. The rest of the congregation stood and waited in their places until the family had gone by. Outside in the sunshine the rector conversed with the earl and countess; the lesser folk hurried past, though one or two of the determined made do with Mrs Fitzgerald until they could have their turn at the pastoral ear. Charles hovered at the edge of the group looking out for the Hunters; Rupert hovered a few steps further away, watching him with private amusement.

The Hunter family came out at last, and would have passed by, but Charles caught Beattie's eye and greeted her, in his nervousness, rather more loudly than he had meant.

'Good morning, Mrs Hunter. Fine day, isn't it?'

Beattie was more than happy, for Diana's sake, to accept the opening. 'It is indeed, Lord Dene. Sunshine always makes one feel cheerful, don't you think?'

So it became necessary for the earl and countess to acknowledge Mr Hunter, since they were already acquainted with him, which further allowed Charles to make the rest of the family known. The earl and Edward found things to talk about, as men acquainted through business always will, and the countess was obliged to make some desultory remarks to Beattie, which she did stiffly and with every sign of resentment; both women were covertly watching Charles as he talked to Diana.

Good God! the earl was thinking. *What a beauty!* So this was the girl Charles had taken to the polo match, in an uncharacteristic step out of the safety and comfort of his own world. Any man might have his head turned by such a face. She seemed a pretty behaved sort of girl, from what he could see. One would expect no less from the daughter of a man like Hunter. All the same – and here his thoughts chimed with those of his wife – the middle classes were just the sort of people one had nothing to do with. The lower classes were different. One employed them in all manner of ways, and took care of them in sickness and old age. There was an historic and necessary bond between the upper and lower classes: their lives were intertwined. But the middle classes one only came in contact with on a professional basis, as doctors, clergymen, lawyers and so on. One knew nothing about their lives, and they didn't need one's help. They belonged to a different world.

The Wroughton-Hunter conjunction lasted only a few moments, before the Hunters were modestly drawing back and the Wroughtons moving away; but the earl had had enough time to see that Charles meant the Hunter girl no harm. Indeed, he saw now it was foolish to have thought Charles would make such a mistake. He was talking to her in a pleasant and friendly way, and it was plain that he simply meant to enjoy her company in the innocent way the sexes did before marriage.

As long as Charles did not let it distract him from the requirement to secure a wife, the earl had no real objection. Rupert, he had no doubt, was friendly with a large number of young females, and probably not all of them were drawn from the pool of families one had always known. No, he decided, he would not say anything about it; but if Charles did not either propose to Helen or to some other suitable girl very soon, there would have to be a further carpeting, and perhaps more stringent measures taken.

In the brief time available to her, Beattie managed to get in an invitation to both Charles and Rupert to a tennis party on the following Friday, the 31st of July. Both accepted, and though it was Rupert who expressed enthusiasm, Beattie thought it was probably just Charles's way. His manner, though polite, was naturally stiffer and more reserved. She felt a sympathy for him: she had grown up with a more popular sister, and knew what it was like to be overshadowed at social gatherings.

Then she caught herself up with an inward smile. Charles was the heir to the earldom and the estate. There was nothing about him that needed her pity.

On Monday the 27th, Sadie was up at Highclere helping Podrick, Mrs Cuthbert's head groom, lunge two of the polo ponies, Nanni and Allegro. She had told Podrick, over several days, every detail she had managed to extract from Diana about her outing to the match – not that it had been very informative.

'How can anyone be around horses and notice so little?' she complained.

Podrick, a lean and silent man with a touch of Irish in his colouring, liked Sadie and approved of her because she was good with the horses, so he accepted her chatter good-naturedly and sometimes even answered her rhetorical questions.

'Can't all be the same,' he said. 'Be a dull world if we was.'

'I expect you're right. But it is a *wonderful* world, isn't it?' she added, with passion. She was lungeing Allegro herself now, and felt the honour of it. 'I mean, here we are, on a lovely day, with all these horses . . . What more could anyone want?'

Podrick smiled to himself. 'Change rein, miss,' he ordered. 'Whip just a bit further forward. That's right.'

'He's going really well now, isn't he?' Sadie said.

'Not bad,' said Podrick. It was nearly his highest praise. Above 'not bad' came only 'pretty fair'. Below it came 'middling' and below that a wordless shake of the head. 'All right, bring him in,' he said, a while later.

Sadie called the horse into the centre. He blew the dust vigorously from his nostrils, then pushed his head into her chest and stood quietly. 'I think he likes me,' she said. She rubbed his forehead. 'He's such a lovely fellow!'

'Would you like to ride him, miss?'

Sadie's eyes opened wide. 'Really? Do you mean it?'

'Needs riding. Mrs Cuthbert said. Needs to chase a ball around, 'fore he forgets how. How'd you like to knock a few about? We'll saddle Nanni and have us a little match. The captain'll want 'em next Sat'day.'

Sadie felt elated and humbled, almost nervous. 'I don't know how to play polo,' she confessed.

Podrick hadn't thought she did. 'Soon get the hang,' he said.

They tacked the two horses. Nanni was a fifteen-two black mare; Allegro, half a hand shorter, was a bright bay. Sadie rode the gelding round the paddock for a few minutes to get the feel of him, her face a portrait of dumb bliss that amused and rather touched Podrick. Then he mounted Nanni and said, 'Come on, then, miss,' and started towards the practice field.

'Must it always be "miss"?' she asked, coming up alongside him. 'Can't you call me Sadie?'

Podrick shook his head. 'Wouldn't be right.'

Sadie was 'quite decent at tennis', as she might have said of herself, so the hand and eye co-ordination needed to hit the ball with the long-handled mallet was not too difficult to master, even though the movement of the horse had to be adjusted to. She found she didn't need to guide Allegro much: he knew the game and followed the ball without having to be told, even seemed to know before she did where it was going.

'He's enjoying himself,' she called out to Podrick, as the groom whacked the ball the length of the field and Allegro sprang after it like a cat, with a snort of excitement. Did she imagine it, or did the horse give her a disappointed look when she missed the ball, or when her strikes did not move it very far? 'He thinks me a very poor fish,' she told Podrick. She patted his neck. 'I'm sorry, old fellow. I'm doing my best.'

They had been knocking the ball up and down the field for a quarter of an hour when one of the younger grooms, Hazlett, came running up to the fence, very red in the face, and shouted out, 'Mr Podrick! Mr Podrick! You're wanted in the yard, urgent!'

Podrick turned Nanni and trotted towards him. He surveyed the lad's face as he came and, reading his expression, asked no questions. Sadie was at the far end of the field, and had to canter to catch him up. 'What is it?' she asked. Podrick made no reply, but his face was grim as they trotted together down the track, Hazlett running behind.

In the yard were the other two polo ponies, the greys Oberon and Daisy. A man in army uniform was leading Oberon up the ramp of a large cattle truck, while another groom, Baker, was gripping Daisy's halter-rope and arguing with an army officer holding a sheaf of papers. As Podrick rode up, they both turned to him in relief.

'Mr Podrick, they're taking the 'orses away,' Baker cried. 'Tell 'em they can't do it!'

The officer looked over with a sharp and noticing eye. 'Are those the other two? Er . . .' He consulted his papers. 'Allegro and Nanni?'

Podrick seemed very calm. 'You'll have to wait till Mrs Cuthbert gets back. She's out pre'nly. Nobody can't sign nothing till she gets back.'

'My name's Casimir, Captain Casimir, and I'm the requisition officer for this area for the Army Remount Service. I have the authorisation here, and I'm afraid we have to take them straight away,' the officer said. 'We've a lot to do today. Can't hang around.' He looked at Sadie. 'If you'll dismount, please, miss, and let the groom untack them.'

'Why are you taking them?' Sadie asked, and her voice came out very high, which annoyed her, because it made her sound like a child.

The soldier came back down the ramp and took hold of Daisy's rope, but Baker didn't let go. 'Mr Podrick!' Baker cried in appeal. Daisy caught the scent of something and jerked her head back, snorting.

'Now, don't upset the horses, please,' the officer said. 'That will do no good.'

121

'Have to wait till the missus gets back,' Podrick repeated stubbornly.

'What's going on?' Sadie appealed desperately.

A motor-car was heard coming up the lane, and the next moment Mrs Cuthbert drove into the yard. They all turned to her with relief. Her face looked white as she got out of the motor and took in the situation. She walked up to the officer and held out her hand. He gave her the papers to read.

'Very well,' she said, but her voice was grim. She looked at Baker. 'Let her go, and help Hazlett untack the other two.'

Podrick was already unbuckling Nanni's girth.

'Please,' Sadie appealed, now to Mrs Cuthbert, 'what's happening? Why are they taking them? They belong to Captain Davison. He's playing in a match on Saturday.'

Mrs Cuthbert came over to her. 'Get down,' she said, in a dead voice. Sadie obeyed. She held Allegro's rein and the gelding nudged her in a friendly way as Mrs Cuthbert started untacking him. 'They don't belong to Captain Davison. They belong to the army,' she said. 'It's called the "boarding-out scheme". It means an officer who can't afford to buy a horse can get the use of one for hacking or hunting – or polo. All they have to pay is its keep, and a small insurance premium. It's the way the army keeps a reserve of trained horses available.'

'Available?' Sadie faltered, rubbing Allegro's forehead. He sighed pleasurably and shifted his weight. 'But—'

'Davison signed the agreement. He should know. The army retains the right to call the animals in for a short period every year, at a month's notice.' She made a strange grimace. 'But they've never called a horse in, in living memory, so of course the officers look on them as their own property.' She pulled off the saddle and handed it to the waiting Hazlett. The soldier had boxed Daisy and was approaching with a halter and an apologetic expression. 'Come away, Sadie,' said Mrs Cuthbert.

Sadie stood to one side with Mrs Cuthbert as the business was concluded. Last to be loaded was Nanni. Podrick stroked her face and ears slowly before he handed her over. She had always been his favourite. She went up the ramp calmly, being used to boxes. The soldier raised the ramp and bolted it, the officer gave Mrs Cuthbert the requisition forms, climbed up into the cab, and the truck rattled slowly away out of the yard.

The two grooms, their arms full of tack, watched it go, Hazlett frankly in tears. Podrick's face looked as though it had been carved out of stone. 'Get inside, you two,' he said. 'Get that tack cleaned.' And he followed them into the tackroom.

Mrs Cuthbert was staring at the place where the truck had disappeared with unseeing eyes. Sadie was loath to disturb her, but she had so many questions. 'Please,' she said. Mrs Cuthbert sighed, and looked at her. 'What does it mean?'

'I was visiting Colonel Barry this morning,' she said.

'Yes, I know,' said Sadie.

'He wanted me to look out for a new hunter for him. I was with him when the telegram was brought in. He knows I have boarded-out horses at livery, so he told me what was in it.'

'In the telegram?'

'It was an alert, announcing the "Precautionary Period". It was laid down in standing orders years ago, during the army reforms. They've sent one to every army commander. It means that every serving soldier has to stand to arms. That's why they've taken the horses.'

'They're preparing for war?' Sadie asked. She felt a strange thrill of heat in her stomach. She supposed it was fear, but it felt like excitement.

'They have to be ready, just in case,' Mrs Cuthbert said. 'Colonel Barry's battalion has to move to Suffolk tomorrow to guard the coast against invasion. And the navy's oil tanks. I have to get his horses on to the train tonight. You can help me get them ready.'

'Yes, of course,' Sadie said automatically. It was good to have something to do, she thought, otherwise one might remember Podrick's face as they took Nanni away. She followed Mrs Cuthbert towards the stables, and said, in bewildered voice, 'But it's so sudden. There's not really going to be a war, is there? Nobody said anything.'

'It's just a precaution,' Mrs Cuthbert said. 'It takes time to get armies and navies into the right position, so they can't leave it to the last minute. They have to move well ahead of time.'

'But it means they think war is likely?'

'Possible,' Mrs Cuthbert corrected. 'The politicians and diplomats will be working to prevent it coming to that. And I can't believe any government will let it get as far as war – even the German government.'

'The Germans,' Sadie said. Yes, it had always been 'Germans and English'. But that was just a game. It had always been just a game.

Sadie was not able to raise much interest at home in her news. A 'precautionary period' did not cut the mustard beside news of a real, actual riot in Dublin, with bloodshed. When she arrived, she found Nula there, standing in the hallway in a huddle over a newspaper with her mother and Cook, Ada lingering in the background.

It seemed that a yacht had landed a consignment of arms – two and a half thousand German rifles and seventy thousand rounds of ammunition – at Howth, just north of Dublin. The Nationalist volunteers had mounted a chillingly military action to receive them, marching out from Dublin in an army a thousand strong, accompanied by a signalling corps, an ambulance and four food wagons.

The signallers had cut the telegraph wires to prevent communication with Dublin Castle, and a group armed with long oak staves and pistols seized the harbour and covered the coastguards while the arms were unloaded. Once the Nationalists were on their way back, the coastguards telephoned Dublin, and a company of three hundred police marched out to intercept them, while a detachment of Scottish Borderers was sent by train.

The groups had collided at Clontarf, and in the conflict that ensued, two soldiers were hit by bullets, several policemen received head wounds from rifle butts, and twenty of the volunteers were injured.

But twenty of the policemen had refused to charge, shouting, 'We're Irishmen!' and almost the whole consignment of arms was got safely away, while the volunteers had escaped by scattering through the fields.

More serious disturbances followed when the Borderers had marched back into Dublin. They were met by hostile crowds, youths throwing stones and yelling at the soldiers. A platoon was ordered to fire a volley into the air and follow it up with a bayonet charge. The crowd scattered, but the soldiers were mobbed again in Ship Street and at O'Connell Bridge, where more volleys were fired.

The disturbance had increased and spread towards the evening. The crowd wrecked a tram car, kicked and beat any soldiers who got detached from their comrades, and a mob stormed the Borderers' barracks and fired pistols at the soldiers. The hospitals received thirty cases of bullet wounds, including a ten-year-old child; in all it was estimated that at least a hundred civilians were wounded, thirty seriously, and four killed.

The horror of the events outweighed any home news. Beattie was most worried by the failure of some of the police to act. Donadea was not far from Dublin, and this sort of mutiny was contagious. Excitable elements would already be

125

calling it a massacre, and the luminaries of the Nationalist movement would not lose the opportunity to turn it into propaganda. She was desperately worried about her brother-in-law, Jock, who as the local magistrate would be in the firing line, a target for overexcited youths.

Nula was comforting Beattie as best she could. Beattie didn't know whether to telegraph Addie to ask if she was all right, or whether such an action would be provocative. That was the trouble with this sort of civil unrest: you would not know until it was too late which side the post-master was on, or the telegraph boy, or his father and uncles, or the local policeman or – Beattie trembled for Addie – even your servants. But the alternative to sending a wire was doing nothing and waiting for one from Addie. And, of course, Addie would face exactly the same questions.

It was a subdued household that evening. Sadie tried to divert attention from the Irish problem by reviving her story of the horses being requisitioned, but she could tell that no-one was listening. That Cook had been upset was proved by the potatoes' coming to the table undercooked and the mutton's appearing without its gravy. Ada served with a glum face and an air of walking on eggshells, though Ethel's head-tossing would have told anyone who happened to be looking at her that she thought the whole thing was a fuss about nothing.

It was not until the following afternoon that the telegraph boy on his bicycle brought a welcome wire from Addie, which said ALL WELL HERE STOP LETTER FOLLOWS END.

When Edward came home he read it with relief, though he knew the danger was not past. All Ireland, but in particular Dublin, was a tinderbox, which a spark could set off, and there was simply no knowing how much danger Addie and her family were in. That was the worst of it: if you knew you were in hostile country you would evacuate, but when

126

the people around you might be on your side or might not, it was hard to know what to do. And leaving Donadea might mean losing it entirely, so the tendency was to hold on and hope for the best.

Hoping for the best, he thought, was about to become a national pastime in this country too. It was announced in the newspapers that on that day Austria had declared war on Serbia, and Russia had ordered partial mobilisation in defence of her fellow Slavs.

On Wednesday Bobby came home to prepare for OTC camp. He was to leave for Aldershot on Thursday evening, and heard about the planned tennis party with faint annoyance.

'But why didn't you have it tomorrow instead, when I was still here?' he said, when Sadie told him about it. She was sitting on his bed while he unpacked his bags, throwing dirty linen into a pile on the floor.

'Don't ask me,' Sadie said. 'Mother issued the invitations. I suppose she didn't know when you'd be back.'

'Of course she did. I told her in a letter ages ago. I'm pretty sure I did, anyway.'

'Well, it's not for your sake she's holding it,' Sadie said, retrieving a book that had gone floorwards, entangled in a shirt. 'It's Diana's party.'

'I suppose it will be a parade of all the lovesick youth of the neighbourhood as usual,' Bobby said. 'I really think Di ought to be quarantined for the general good. Is she favouring anyone in particular at the moment? It was Alec Gordon when I went away. And that nephew of Mrs Oliver's – what was his name?'

'Aldis Crane,' Sadie supplied. 'I liked him. But he hasn't visited for a while. Alec still calls, among others. But she has her sights set higher now.'

'Really?' He raised his eyebrows. 'Don't tell me there's a new Adonis in town.'

Sadie grinned. 'Well, not really an Adonis. And not really new, either – just new to us. She's been out twice with Charles Wroughton.'

'What – not Viscount Dene?' Bobby stared a moment, then laughed. 'Oh dear! Poor Di! I thought she had more sense than to fall into that trap.'

'I think he likes her,' Sadie defended her sister.

'She hasn't an earthly,' Bobby said. 'Chaps like him may trifle with the likes of her, but they always settle for their own sort in the end.'

'Well, he's coming to the tennis party. *And* his brother.'

'Trifling,' Bobby scoffed, with a significant nod. 'You'll see. Now I'm really upset that I won't be there to see the fun. It's too bad of the mater.'

'It's too bad of you to be going off to camp when you've just got home. I never see you.' She thought how handsome he looked, fair like Diana but with blue eyes. People often said the good looks were wasted on Bobby when Sadie could really have done with them, but she wouldn't want him to be any different. She reached out and pushed his forelock back from his brow. 'You'll have to get this cut when you go to camp. Not very soldierly.'

He caught her hand and kissed it in a half-ironic gesture. 'It'll tuck inside my cap. Can't let them spoil my beauty when all the young ladies of Aldershot will be clustering around, hoping their mamas will invite us young heroes to tea.'

'You'd be beautiful even with an army haircut,' she asserted. 'How long is the camp?'

'Two weeks. I'm looking forward to it. Living under canvas, firing rifles, dashing about the countryside playing soldiers.'

The door opened and Ada came in. 'Have you got your things sorted out for washing, Mr Bobby? And don't forget to look out anything that needs sewing. It's no good coming to me last minute with a button off or a torn pocket, and expecting me to mend it in ten seconds.'

128

'Here's the linen, darling Ada,' Bobby said, scooping the heap from the floor into her arms. 'And I don't need any sewing. I haven't torn a thing.'

'That'll be the day,' Ada sniffed, but she smiled anyway. Everyone loved Bobby.

CHAPTER TEN

On Thursday, the 30th of July, the newspapers carried the news that, the previous day, Austrian gunboats had shelled Belgrade from the Danube. The German ambassador had asked for a guarantee of Britain's neutrality should the crisis worsen. Sir Edward Grey had sent an equivocal reply: British neutrality could not be counted on. He was still trying to arrange a conference between Austria, Germany, Russia and France, with Britain mediating. The Kaiser had sent a wire to the Tsar begging him to show restraint as he was still trying to persuade Austria to stand down.

At breakfast on Thursday, Beattie received two letters. One was from David, saying that he would like to accept the Oliphants' invitation and go to Scotland for August. Were there any family plans that required his presence, or might he go? The other was from Addie, and she read it with a mixture of anxiety and relief. The Carburys had known on Saturday that something was brewing, and Sunday had been a strange, tense day, with unusual movements and noises in the village and a sense of waiting on the brink of disaster. One of the gardeners had brought the news up to the house about the conflict at Clontarf and the rioting in Dublin: friends had sent them wires on the subject, but the Donadea postmaster had locked up his office tight and refused to pass any messages in or out, for fear of inflaming tempers on one side or the other.

When darkness fell, the family had sat together in one

room, trying to read or sew, but listening all the while to distant noises, oddly small and clear in the silence of night: a shout, a splurge of voices, the tinkling of broken glass. Some of the servants had disappeared – most alarming of all. Then the same boy, who was nephew to their cook, had come to say there was a torchlit march of Nationalists through the village; many had been drinking, and the mood was ugly.

Some of them gathered at the gates of the house, which we had shut for the first time since coming here, and were shouting for Jock to come out. He was for going, but I couldn't bear it. I'm afraid I wept and clung to his hand and begged him to think of his poor widow and orphaned children. Well, you know Jock: cool as an iceberg in a crisis. He simply reminded me he was not dead yet. He did go out at last, and I was in a swoon of fear. But by the time he got to the gate the mob had wandered off and were amusing themselves by smashing greenhouses at the market garden down the road. I suppose it was the noise they liked. None of us slept a wink that night, but in the morning all was quiet, though the village was strewn with rubbish, bricks, bottles, torn posters, broken glass and the like. Father Leak came up to see us later that morning and said he was to talk to the Fenian leaders in the village and tell them to leave us alone, and remind them that Jock was a good fellow and in sympathy with them. I hope to God it works. It's the fire I fear most – that and having Jock shot dead by some madman as he goes about his business. But we're safe for now.

Beattie told Edward what was in the letter, and read a few lines to him. 'Safe for now,' she repeated, when she had finished, looking up. 'That's what it comes to, doesn't it?'

Edward said, 'My dear, it's all any of us can say for ourselves. These are troubled times. All we can do is to live in the present and hope for the future.'

'That's not very reassuring.' Beattie gave him a shaky smile, and changed the subject. 'You don't mind if David goes to Scotland with his friend?'

'Not at all. We haven't any plans, except for our usual trip to Bournemouth, and I expect he's getting too old for that. In fact, I doubt I'll be able to join you, with things so unsettled in Europe,' Edward said.

'Oh, I don't like it when you don't come down,' said Beattie. 'People look at me so pityingly when I have to dine without a man.'

'Leave it for a few weeks, then, and see how things work out.'

'But we have to book at least a week in advance, or there won't be any room.'

'I'll bear it in mind. But let David go to Scotland, anyway.' He gave a small smile. 'Is there a girl in it somewhere? Oliphant's sister, perhaps?'

'Sophy? She's just a child,' Beattie said quickly. Actually, Sophy was seventeen, but Beattie didn't want to think about David and females, because once he started noticing them, what inevitably would follow was falling in love, marrying and going away from her. She felt fortunate that he had got to the age of twenty without seeming to care for any girl more than his sisters. She hoped that university and his studies would keep him safe at least for another year; she wouldn't have minded, really, if he had wanted to become a don and live in the all-male cloistered atmosphere of Oxford for ever. At least then he would always be her boy.

Munt was picking broad beans – not quite as bad as picking peas, but it still meant bending. His back, these days, gave him gyp. It felt as though a nail was being driven through

132

his spine. And that boy, nowhere to be found as usual! Useless! All boys were the same: full of cheek and spit, and hopping the wag if you didn't keep your eye on them. As much use as a candle on a bicycle, as his old dad used to say.

He straightened with difficulty and put both hands to the small of his back with a grimace. At the end of the bean row he saw Nailer, standing there watching him. His little round black eyes under the white eyebrows seemed to Munt to glint with sardonic amusement.

'What do *you* want?' he said. 'Think it's funny, do you? Go on, clear off!'

Nailer flattened his ears and backed a couple of steps, but he didn't actually go. There had just been a regrettable incident in the kitchen, and he had felt it wise to put distance between himself and it, and to seek out his only possible ally. The Shed Man was not always welcoming, and he threw things, too, but his aim was not as good as the Kitchen Woman's, and the things he threw on the whole hurt less. Besides, it was nearly teatime.

'Think you know it all,' Munt grumbled. 'You're all the same. Dunno what the world's coming to.'

Nailer decided to take that as a speech of welcome. He sat down on his tail, and gave a face-splitting yawn that made his ears meet behind.

'Oh, make yerself comfy, why don'tcha?' Munt enquired ironically. He looked at his beans. *Well, looking don't get 'em picked*, he told himself, and sighed, preparing to bend again.

And someone said, 'Hello, Mr Munt.'

For a confused instant he thought it was the dog speaking. But the voice came from someone who had just appeared in the gap behind Nailer, a young man in flannel trousers, tweed jacket and waistcoat, who snatched off his cap respectfully, revealing mouse-coloured hair cut so short his ears seemed to stand out. With his thin face it made him look a bit like a young deer.

'Know me now, Mr Munt?' he enquired.

Munt was struggling. There was something familiar about the face, something—

The young man grinned. 'How about if I whistle?'

It was coming now, trickling back, like blood returning to a dead limb. His memory was tingling.

The young man pursed his lips and whistled softly but as clear as a bird. The tune was 'Lillibullero'.

'God bless my soul!' cried Munt.

The young man stopped whistling to say, 'Aren't you going to tell me off? "No whistling in my garden!" That's what you always used to say.'

'Young Frank!' Munt exclaimed. 'Little Frank Hussey! Well, I'll be!'

'How are you, Mr Munt?'

Munt could only stare. 'Little Frank,' he said again, shaking his head in wonder. Then, 'You've growed.'

'Couldn't hardly help it,' said Frank. 'It's been ten years.' He looked down at Nailer, who had backed away when he appeared but was now creeping back cautiously, hearing the pleasant tone of the voices. 'And who's this little feller?' Frank asked. 'This your dog, Mr Munt? He's a grand-looking one.' Nailer wagged his tail and gave an ingratiating grin. 'Bet you're a champion ratter, eh, lad?' Frank stooped and stroked his head, and Nailer's soul moaned under the unfamiliar kindness.

Munt was too stunned to correct the misapprehension. Frank Hussey had come to him straight from school at the age of twelve, like most of the boys; but unlike most of them, he had wanted to learn. Munt had been sorry when he left two years later: his father had got him a job as a gardener's boy at a Big House. When Munt said all boys were the same, an occluded part of his brain automatically excused little Frank Hussey.

He stepped over his trug and hobbled along the row to

134

grasp Frank's hand in greeting. 'What're you doing here?' he asked.

'Got a new job,' Frank said. 'Second gardener at Mandeville Hall, in Amersham.'

Munt looked at him with respect. 'You done well. Second gardener at your age?'

'I owe it all to you,' Frank said. 'You taught me everything. If ever I get into a muddle, I always think, Now, what would Mr Munt do? And that puts me straight.'

Munt was as little used to compliments as Nailer. He had to fumble out his handkerchief and blow his nose to give himself time to recover.

Frank grinned. 'Remember when you taught me to graft apple slips? Cor, the things you called me cos I couldn't get it right! I reckon *ham-fisted vandal* was the nicest of 'em!'

'I never,' Munt said in wonder.

'Did me good. I would never've learned if you'd been soft on me. But I'll never be as good as you, Mr Munt. Gor, watching you pot seedlings, them little tiny things in your big hands . . . 'Slike magic. I still got the pruning knife you gave me.' It had been a farewell gift. Frank had been amazed and touched and, at fourteen, had been allowed to shed a few tears. Munt had had to rely on gruffness.

'I should think so too,' he gruffed now. 'Good knife that was, too good to lose. So how long you been at Mandeville Hall?'

'Just a month. Things are different there, not up to your standards, but the head gardener, Mr Orwell, he's talking about leaving in a few years, wants to open 'is own market garden, and then I hope I might get the job and start doing things your way. So, soon as I got my day off, I thought I'd pop along and say hello.'

Munt was touched. 'S'pose you think you'll come a-picking my brains every minute you fancy,' he sniffed.

135

But Frank was not a scared little boy now. He grinned, a confident man's grin. 'That's what I was planning on,' he said. 'Be daft not to, wouldn't I? I can get here easy as easy on the train on my day off. Bring you cuttings, too. You still like your chrysants? We got some fine ones at Mandeville, maybe some varieties you haven't got.'

Munt scowled. 'Don't you go taking cuttings without asking, Frank Hussey. That's stealin'.'

'Course I wouldn't,' Frank said. 'I'd ask Mr Orwell first. I know what's what.' He smiled. 'Remember when I first come and I had to dig the potato patch? It was like concrete, and I got all them blisters. Size of ha'pennies, they were. And you said, "Once you get proper calluses, then you can call yourself a gardener."' He displayed his palms. 'Got good ones now, Mr Munt. Look.'

It was fortunate that Ethel arrived at that moment, for Munt would have had difficulty finding his voice.

'Tea's ready,' she said, looking at Frank with interest. All that digging had given him good shoulders and a broad chest, and the outdoor tan of his face made his eyes look bluer.

Munt's brows snapped together into their usual position. 'I'll 'ave it in me shed,' he growled.

Ethel tossed her head, affronted. 'Well, don't expect me to carry it out for you,' she said.

Frank looked at his old mentor. 'Oh, do come to the kitchen, Mr Munt. I'd like to see the others, see if they remember me, if there's anyone still there from my time. It'd be nice to have a chinwag, and maybe they'd find a cup o' tea for me.' He turned a smile on Ethel. 'I'm Frank. I used to be gardener's boy here, but it must have been before your time. I wouldn't forget your face.'

Ethel smirked. 'Charmed, I'm sure.' She looked him up and down. 'You courting?'

'You mind your cheek,' Munt rebuked her. 'Got too much o' what the cat cleans her paws with.'

Ethel was unmoved. 'So, are you coming or not?' she asked Munt pertly.

'Ar, we're coming. Go on, run ahead.' Ethel bestowed a fascinating smile on Frank and whisked away. 'Baggage,' Munt commented, after her disappearing back. 'She'll come to no good, that one.'

They started towards the house together, and Nailer tagged along behind, enjoying the atmosphere. He'd never seen so many smiles in the vegetable garden before.

'So, is Cook still here?' Frank asked. 'And Ada, and Nellie?'

'Nellie got married. That one's Ethel. She won't stay long, neither, not if I know maids. Cook and Ada's still there, though. Got a new boy – 'Enry his name is. 'Enery the Eighth, I call him, cos he won't be here long, then we'll have 'Enery the Ninth. Don't know nothing, don't want to know nothing. Useless! Just like all boys.'

'Not me, though, Mr Munt.'

'You was different,' Munt allowed grudgingly.

That same day, a Berlin newspaper received a message that the German Army had mobilised, and rushed into print with the exciting news. It turned out not to be true, and the paper had to print a retraction some hours later. But the news agencies had seized on the original story with equal excitement and it was wired all round the world. The Tsar, who had been exchanging nervous telegrams with his cousin the Kaiser, read it, thought he had been betrayed, and ordered full mobilisation. By the time the retraction arrived, it was too late.

Edward read the news on his way home with a feeling of weight in his chest. France was required by treaty to support Russia, but if France mobilised, would Germany take that as sufficient excuse for war? And if Germany attacked France, could Britain stay out of it? He had heard from one of his clients that the German chancellor had been trying desperately

137

to persuade the Austrian ambassador to negotiate some sort of settlement with the Serbs, convinced that Britain would eventually come in against Germany. The chancellor had also met with the British ambassador in Berlin to try to find out under what inducement Britain might remain neutral in a German-French conflict. Overseas territories had been mentioned. Grey had not been encouraging. It was disgraceful even to be asking the question, he had reportedly said.

Things seemed suddenly to be moving fast, and everything was balanced on a knife-edge. As long as no-one moved, or blinked, perhaps the fragile bauble of peace might remain suspended and safe; but there were so many different factions involved, all afraid of being caught unprepared. It seemed inevitable that someone would flinch, and send everything tumbling into the abyss.

He read every page of the paper over and over, trying to filter out more information than it contained, until eventually his weary, anxious mind, longing to escape, made him fall asleep and he missed his stop. He woke as the train pulled into Rustington, stared about him in confusion, then had to rush to gather his belongings and get out, to cross to the up platform and wait for a train going the other way.

On Friday the 31st, Germany issued an ultimatum to Russia: it must demobilise fully within twelve hours, or Germany would declare war. At the same time it issued an ultimatum to France: it must declare neutrality within eighteen hours, and hand over the frontier forts at Liège and Namur to Germany as a sign of good faith. Meanwhile Britain asked both France and Germany for a guarantee of Belgian neutrality in the event of a European war. Belgium was a country Britain had been material in creating, and its first king had been Queen Victoria's beloved uncle,

Leopold. France agreed immediately; Germany did not reply.

On Friday afternoon, Diana was scowling at her little brother Peter, standing just outside the french windows with his friend Philly Tucker, who was carrying a home-made fishing rod and a jam jar.

'You promised!' Diana exclaimed.

Peter put on his most maddening expression, which was one of virtuous abstraction, as of a fully qualified seraph with terribly important things on his mind. 'I don't think I azackly *promised*,' he said kindly.

'I asked you if you would fag balls for us this afternoon and you said you would,' Diana asserted.

'Mm,' said Peter, gazing off into the distance. 'I sort of didn't say no, but then I didn't know Philly was going to go fishing.' He picked idly at a scab on his elbow, lowering his eyes.

'He can help you here,' Diana said impatiently. 'You can go fishing any time.'

'Well, the thing is, there's a *'normous* fish in Meaker's pond,' Peter said, 'and if we don't go today, it might not be there another time. And fagging balls *all* afternoon . . .'

'You can have tea,' Diana said, adjusting her position. It was true Peter hadn't actually promised, only said 'Mm' – his favourite answer to any question – which might have been mere acknowledgement that he had heard; otherwise she might have appealed to Mother on the grounds that promises had to be adhered to. 'There'll be chocolate cake.' She observed her brother closely for reaction. 'And meringues.'

'Mm,' Peter said, while Philly watched him anxiously. Tea for boys of their age was usually just bread and jam. Chocolate cake and meringues . . . ! Oughtn't they to grab the prize while it was still on offer?

But Peter was an experienced negotiator. 'You see, there's

139

a fishing rod in Parker's window, and Philly and me *really* wanted to buy it. Then we could go fishing down in the lakes, instead of Meaker's pond. It costs a shilling, and we've only got sixpence between us.' Diana underwent a struggle. Peter watched her from under his long, silky eyelashes – surely only an angel would have eyelashes like that – and added in a dreamy voice, 'Fagging for balls, when it's *so-oo* hot . . . It's nice and shady under the trees at Meaker's. P'raps we'll go there instead, and just sit and watch the fish. It's no fun fishing, really, when you've only got a home-made rod.'

Diana drew a sharp breath of annoyance. 'Threepence each,' she capitulated. 'But you fetch balls all afternoon for that, until I say you can go. And no complaining,'

'*And* tea,' Peter stipulated.

'All the tea you can eat,' Diana agreed tersely. 'Little horror,' she added, under her breath.

The young people were arriving; the garden was full of their chatter, like the sound of birds. Sadie was doing her part for the occasion, which at the moment was sitting on a bucket, writing people's names on little squares of paper and putting them into Father's old gardening hat to be drawn for partners. Diana had devised a system whereby Sadie could make sure the draw partnered Diana with Charles Wroughton.

'Look at her, queening it,' Sadie murmured to Nailer, who was sitting just behind her, in the safety of her shadow. He anticipated that the activity presaged tea in the garden, and tea in the garden offered so many more opportunities than any sort of eating in the house. The tables were lower, and people put plates down on the grass . . .

'She does look beautiful, though,' Sadie added wistfully. Diana in new tennis whites, including a subtly blue leather belt around her impossibly small waist, the skirt fetchingly

140

just above her ankles, her fair hair in a chignon into which Ethel had inserted enough pins to quill a hedgehog so it wouldn't fall down under exertion. She was greeting her old friends with all the flattering attention of someone who was not waiting for anyone more important to arrive. 'How *lovely* of you to come! What a *sweet* hat! I *do* hope it won't rain.'

The boys, Sadie thought, were mostly beaux of Diana's, former or current. Though, since Diana never discarded but only added to her hand, the distinction was no distinction. Sadie could see that most of them had not given up hope. They swung their racquets and tensed their muscles, and smiled, warmly at her and guardedly at each other, believing that a good showing on the tennis lawn might bring the wandering angel back to their side. The girls were all quite good-humoured about it. Diana had been queen for so long, and was so admittedly, undeniably the prettiest girl among them, that they did not resent her supremacy. The rivalry among them was for the men left over after she had made her choice.

'But today,' Sadie informed Nailer, 'they can have the choice of all of them because Queen Diana has her sights set higher.' Nailer sneezed. 'Yes, if he comes,' she agreed. She hoped so much that he would. It would be terrible if Diana were disappointed.

Diana approached. 'Haven't you done those names yet?'

Sadie defended herself. 'There's no hurry. You can't draw yet – everybody's not here.'

Diana's eyes went to Nailer, who was effacing himself behind the bucket. He had got into Diana's bedroom once and chewed a scarf, and she had caught him at it and managed to hit him several times with an ebony hairbrush before he got out of the door, so he held her in a certain respect. 'That dog must be tied up,' she decreed. 'I'm not having him chasing the balls and stealing sandwiches like last time.'

141

'It wasn't last time, it was years ago,' Sadie said.

'Tie him up or lock him in the shed,' Diana said. 'If he appears before everybody's gone, I shall blame you.' And she whisked away to greet another arrival.

'She's nervous,' Sadie told Nailer, not without sympathy. It must be awful to wait for someone important like that, dependent on their decision, helpless to decide your own fate. 'I hope I never grow up and start caring about men.' She sighed. 'I suppose I'll have to put you in the shed *and* tie you up.' Last time he'd been locked in he'd somehow got out of the window. She stood up, put down the hat and reached for Nailer's collar, but he seemed to dissolve under her hand, slithered several paces backwards under a laurel bush and, a moment later, was scampering at full speed across the gravel towards the gate. *How does he always know?* Sadie asked herself, and sat down to her task again.

The Wroughtons arrived at last, and in two cars, having brought some friends with them. Beattie had been lingering in the hall, worrying for Diana's sake, and hurried out to watch the elegantly clad young people spilling on to the sweep, like a flock of white pigeons. It was a moment of triumph, especially as Mrs Fitzgerald had called, managing to time her visit – 'I was just passing, my dear, and wondered if you needed any help' – for exactly the instant when Beattie would have had to admit to her that the viscount and his brother had failed them.

The extra guests were Kiki and James Eynsham and four of Rupert's friends, Lavinia and Isobel Manners, Lady Victoria Blundell and the Hon. Richard Egerton. Diana appeared, radiant and vindicated, and greeted everyone with such a seemly lack of particularity, as if she entertained such elevated folk every day, that Beattie swelled with pride and hoped Mrs Fitzgerald was taking mental notes. Indeed, the rector's wife disappeared with a muttered excuse as soon as the party had gone through to the garden. Beattie imagined her scurrying off to spread the word and was glad for a moment before whirling round and dashing to the kitchen.

'I'm sure my tea can stretch to six extra, madam,' Cook said, with just a hint of offence. She had always provided on the generous side, and privately congratulated herself on having the right kind of mistress. She couldn't have done with working in the sort of house where things were skimped and every scrap of left-over had to be accounted for. There was something unladylike, in her view, about a mistress poking about in a person's larder and enquiring after yesterday's blancmange as if she had nothing better to do.

But Beattie said, 'I'm sure it can, Cook dear, but just to be on the safe side . . . It wouldn't do to have anyone think there wasn't plenty. Some more sandwiches, at any rate – young people have such good appetites when they've been playing tennis. And cakes – what's quick to make?'

'If I might suggest, madam,' Cook said, 'scones are quick, and always go down well. Cakes I've plenty of. But there's no more bread till the baker comes tomorrow morning. Someone'll have to go for it.'

Ethel was annoyed enough to voice a protest when Beattie sought her out. It was Henry's half-day off, all right, but it wasn't *her* job to be sent on errands, and as to hurrying . . . 'I should get dusty, madam,' she objected, 'and I'll be needed to serve the ladies and gentlemen.'

'You'll be there and back before you're needed. In fact, you must be.'

'Can't Emily go?'

Beattie's expression hardened. She did not like being talked back to. 'Cook needs Emily in the kitchen. Now, stop talking and go. And be quick. I shall need you to help cut the sandwiches when you get back. *Go!*'

Ethel trailed away in a manner that made Beattie want to smack her, and wish she had sent Sadie instead. But a further

143

furious '*Go!*' at least had her whisking through the doorway, and she could only hope for the best. She must check all was well in the garden. Some of the newcomers looked smart enough to be capable of dividing the company.

CHAPTER ELEVEN

In Hetherton's Hygienic Bakery, the assistant behind the counter was young Alan Butcher, who had been teased by Mr Hetherton about his inappropriate name so often that he ought to have developed a thicker skin by now. But still he had an unfortunate tendency to blush, which had the additional drawback of making his spots stand out. He was a scrawny youth but if it hadn't been for the spots he would have been quite nice-looking: he had fair hair, blue eyes and pleasant features, and his mother had promised him that he would grow out of the spots in a little while. It was true there were fewer of them this year than last, but still he was sure that when anyone looked at him, that was all they saw. Like Mrs Oliver's Dalmatian . . .

If he had not been alone in the shop when Ethel stepped in, he would have dashed straight into the back and let someone else serve her. He had seen her at a distance before, but had never spoken to her, and the sight of her now, so trim and pretty in her afternoon uniform, with that pert, knowing look in her eyes, sent the scalding blood straight up his neck, through his face and into his ears, until he could feel them positively glowing, like two port lamps on a barge.

He swallowed a lump the size of a golf ball and managed to say, in a faint voice that squeaked at the end, 'May I help you, miss?'

Ethel noted the blush and the bob of the Adam's apple. She switched her hips just enough to make her skirt swing as she walked up to the counter. 'Miss?' she said. 'That's nice. I like a boy with manners.'

He swallowed helplessly, unable to speak. She lowered her eyelashes, then gazed up at him appealingly, the helpless female beseeching help of the all-powerful male. 'I don't suppose you could get me out of trouble, could you?'

'T-t-t—?' was all Alan could manage.

'They've sent me down here for three loaves – at this time of day! I'm sure they're all sold out and I shall have to go back empty-handed. I don't know *what* they'll say to me if I let them down.'

His chest swelled at the realisation that she wanted something from him that he could fulfil. He'd gladly have pulled the stars down from the sky for her, but that was, of course, impossible. 'We have bread,' he managed to say. There it was on the shelves behind him. It didn't occur to him that she must be able to see it for herself. He only knew she was looking at him as if he alone could save her. 'How – how – What sort?'

'Oh, white,' she said. 'White, of course. Soft white bread is what they like.' He had never heard 'soft' and 'white' pronounced like that. He stared at her lips, like a moth gazing at a flame. His blush had gone and he felt instead pale and hollow. 'Do you have three large *white* loaves for me?'

The word 'white' made her push forward her lovely lips as though she were inviting him to kiss her. He imagined, for one unwise moment, what it would be like to kiss her, and almost fainted. 'I do. I have. We have,' he stammered, and wrenched his eyes away so that he could turn and pick them out.

Ethel smiled to herself. It was rather fun teasing the poor creature. He turned back and she resumed her up-gazing pose. 'Oh, *thank* you!' she breathed, as maiden to St George over the body of the dragon. 'You've saved me.'

Have I? thought Alan. His shoulders seemed to grow broader under her gaze. 'Glad to be of service, miss,' he found himself saying, in a voice he hadn't heard before – a manly voice without a hint of mouse in it.

'My name's Ethel.'

'I know,' he said.

'You know?' She pouted, and her look was teasing now. He was in Heaven.

'You're from The Elms. Mrs Hunter's.'

'That's right. Put them on the account, will you?'

'Of course, miss. And will there be anything else?' He was flying now.

'That depends,' she said.

'Depends on what?' he asked.

'On whether you can stop calling me "miss" now. Makes me feel old and ugly.'

He blushed again. 'Oh, but you're not!' he cried ludicrously, and was angry with himself. 'Not either. I mean, you're obviously not old.' Oh, Lord, how could he be any clumsier? 'I mean, you're *beautiful*!' he got out at last.

Her eyelashes did that thing again. 'Do you mean it?' she murmured.

'You're the most beautiful girl I've ever seen in my life,' he vowed earnestly.

'Oh, you're so sweet to say so . . . ?'

'Alan,' he supplied.

'Alan. What a nice name. I've never liked my name. Ethel. Don't you think it's ugly?'

'No!' he cried. 'It's a beautiful name. The most beautiful name in the world. And it suits you,' he added daringly.

She put her basket on the counter. 'Put the loaves in there for me – Alan.'

He wrapped them in paper and placed them carefully,

147

wondering if he had the nerve to ask her if he might see her again. 'I wish I could carry them home for you,' he said boldly, 'but I can't leave the shop.'

She smiled at him, as though she were waiting for something, then lifted down the basket and walked towards the door. She was so far out of his sphere he didn't dare ask her. Why would she want to see a fool like him?

She was at the door. She turned, smiled at him again, fluttering her eyelashes.

Good Lord, she thought. *He's shy!* It was rather sweet. She hadn't walked out with a shy boy for years. 'Goodbye, then – Alan,' she said invitingly.

He swallowed and managed to say, 'Goodbye,' but couldn't voice her name.

I'll have to do it for him, she decided impatiently. 'It's my half-day off tomorrow,' she said.

He felt himself turn pale again. Was it possible he could find the courage, in this one moment of opportunity – the last, probably, he would ever have? 'W-would you – do you think you could – I mean—'

'Yes?' she purred.

'Would you like to go for a walk?' he blurted. It sounded so foolish as he heard the words that he wanted to die of shame. 'Or something? I mean, I don't expect—'

'Oh, I'd love to,' she murmured, with shy, adoring eyelashes. 'I'll meet you at the end of Highwood Road. We can walk down to the lakes and have tea at the Pavilion Café.'

He was smiling now, as though an angel had whispered in his ear, and she thought, *He's not bad-looking, if you don't count the spots.* Besides, Billy Snow was getting too sure of himself. And he was working tomorrow afternoon. He wouldn't be free until eight o'clock, and a girl had to have someone to squire her on her afternoon off. She wasn't going to spend it alone, just because *Mr* Billy Snow was foolish

148

enough to have to work when she'd told him ages ago which her day off was. And if someone reported back to him that she'd had tea with Alan Butcher from Hetherton's, well, serve him right!

Charles Wroughton was experiencing a new anxiety. It didn't matter a jot to his mother if he brought home two people or ten, whether to tea or to stay. Food was produced, beds were made up, household routines expanded or contracted according to need, and all requirements of the guests were met without so much as the flicker of his mother's eyebrow. It had never occurred to him to wonder what went on behind the scenes or below the stairs.

So he had not thought about it when Rupert proposed making up a party to go to the Hunters'. But when they had piled out of the two motors on the Hunters' sweep, and it was Mrs Hunter herself who came out to greet them, not a manservant, or even any servant at all, he suddenly wondered whether he should have asked first if it was all right to bring people.

On the other hand, *asking* might have suggested that the Hunters couldn't *afford* to be hospitable, which would be dreadful. And was probably not true anyway – weren't bankers as rich as Croesus? At that thought he managed, as he often did, to embarrass himself internally: thinking about whether or not the Hunters were rich was almost as bad as asking them. One should not think about money any more than talk about it.

So it was that as he shook Mrs Hunter's hand and received her serene smile and expressions of welcome, he was as awkward as a boy, and could only stammer something about being grateful for the invitation, while Rupert, with all his usual self-assurance, was the one who airily introduced the rest of the party. *I look a fool*, Charles thought, *and not for the first time.* He sighed, wishing he had Rupert's aplomb, and was so engrossed with his worried thoughts that when Diana appeared he was unable to manage a smile, and only shook her hand in silence, then agreed, monosyllabically, when she suggested it was lovely that the day had turned out so fair.

The other young people did nothing to help him to relax, because they were obviously of the class that he didn't usually mix with. It was not a matter of snobbery or even of design, but simply that people one did not know did not come in one's way very often. Your friends and relatives introduced their friends and relatives, and there was no need to go looking outside for new acquaintances.

In any case, it was hard for a naturally shy and reserved man to meet new people. Introductions were made and he shook hands and tried to find polite things to say, but he could see people were being turned away by his coldness – as so often happened, especially when Rupert was present. Rupert was being jolly and taking over the occasion with his ebullience, and if it was being done in a spirit of irony, only Charles knew that. The other guests clearly thought he was wonderful, flocked about him and began to enjoy themselves. All the girls wanted his attention and the boys wanted to emulate him. The Eynshams were egging him on. Victoria was looking appalled and the Manners girls puzzled at finding themselves where they were, and Dicky was flirting with girls in the sort of way that made Charles fear he was thinking of them as parlour-maids and would say something inappropriate at any moment.

Charles was wishing he had not come. He feared that he was going to hurt the family of the woman he loved, that his brother and friends would offend them in some terrible way, and he felt helpless to prevent a disaster. When the draw for partners took place, he was so glad to be paired with Diana that it didn't occur to him it had not just been luck – though there were plenty of looks that said everyone else knew it.

Playing tennis calmed his nerves: he was a good enough player, and physical activity came so much easier to him than mental. You could not offend a tennis ball or be embarrassed by a racquet. He was able to concentrate on something simple and achievable, and meanwhile be in the company of his goddess and have the legitimate excuse to look at her and speak to her. She looked divine in her tennis costume, he thought, and she played like an angel – assuming that angels *played* tennis. Actually, she had a very strong backhand, and occasionally returned shots with a ruthlessness that was a little less than angelic, which only made him love her more.

When they had won their game and retired from the lists, she suggested he might like to walk round the garden, and he accepted with gratitude. It was so much easier to be alone with her than in company. His earlier frenzied thoughts had been dissipated by the tennis. And Diana was so sweet to him! He was a clumsy, inarticulate fool, but she didn't seem to find him so – indeed, she had a knack of drawing him out so that he found himself sounding quite knowledgeable. He began to relax, and even essayed a little joke, which she laughed at generously.

Diana began by getting him to talk about flowers, trees and insects, but nature bored her so after a bit she mentioned the Territorials, and that got him going nicely. He told her that the forward party would be arriving the next day to start putting up the tents, and that the Terriers themselves would be arriving on Sunday evening for their two-week camp.

'It's rather fun,' he said. 'Scouting practice and mock battles and so on. And we have entertainments, too. We always put on a cricket match at the end, with a dance in the evening. I shall be playing in the match, of course. I don't know if you care for cricket, but it's usually quite jolly. I wonder if you would think of coming to both, and setting aside a couple of dances for me?'

151

'Of course,' Diana said, coolly enough, though her heart jumped. 'I'll enjoy watching you play. And I know you dance beautifully.'

Charles fell silent, too pleased to say anything. Diana, struggling to understand the contradictions of this taciturn man, who was so unlike any of her other admirers, slipped in another question about the Terriers' camp to set him going again.

The Hunters' garden was not large enough to make walking round it last all afternoon. Too soon, despite Diana's dawdling, they had reached the shrubbery at the end, which Charles kindly referred to as a Wilderness. Beyond it, she told him, was the footpath to the church. With an unexpected flash of courage, he suggested he might walk her home from church on Sunday.

'I'd like that very much,' she said, turning to him.

Relief made him voluble. 'I am enjoying myself today,' he said. 'It was awfully kind of your mother to invite me.'

Diana looked at him searchingly. He had been so cool and offhand at first that she had been afraid he was regretting coming; but while they played, and while walking here alone together, he had seemed to like her again. 'I'm glad you came,' she said. 'Although it's rather a noisy party, isn't it?'

'That's my brother's fault, I'm afraid,' Charles said. 'I apologise for him.'

'Oh, there's no need. But I do like having the chance to talk to you quietly, away from the others, like this.' She looked up at him, and was suddenly nervous. *Did I go too far?* she wondered.

But he said, 'Do you really?' and looked down at her for so long and so intently that she thought for one shivery moment he was going to kiss her.

But the moment passed. 'We ought to go back,' she said. It would never do for him to think her fast.

'Yes,' he said.

They walked side by side back along the path and towards the sounds of young people enjoying themselves. Diana was content, thinking there was still tea to come, when he must surely forage for her and sit by her. And then there was the walk on Sunday, the cricket match and ball. None of this was chance or idle accident. He was definitely favouring her.

Charles was content, too, but his thoughts were far more inchoate, hardly more than a golden mist over his mind. *She likes me. She likes me!*

The afternoon advanced and grew sultry. Tea was taken in the combined shadow of the house and the walnut tree. Ethel and Ada poured the tea, Emily scurried back and forth with more provisions and cans of hot water, and the young people helped themselves from the spread laid on a trestle table, then settled at various small round tables artfully disposed for sociability. Bees murmured in the marigolds, and the strong sun of late July slanted through the leaves, illuminating drifting seed heads and strands of spider silk. The conversations, even around Rupert, grew slower and quieter.

The tables were all laid for four, so Diana was not able to be alone with Charles. Alec Gordon and Alicia Harding, the doctor's daughter, joined them. Alec was annoyed by what he thought of as unfair competition for Diana's attention. Alicia had always hoped to inherit Alec when Diana tired of him, and hoped that, with Lord Dene occupying her, this might be her chance to detach him. It made for dull company: Charles, never chatty with strangers, was tongue-tied in the face of Alec's faint hostility; Alicia was being too bright and vivacious, which only made the viscount shrink more into himself.

Diana did her best to repair the situation, but it was hard going, and she was almost relieved when Rupert suddenly appeared at her elbow, leaned over her and said, 'May I get you some more tea? I see your plate and cup are both empty.'

Charles started, and began to rise. 'I'm so sorry. Let me go.'

But Rupert placed a hand on his shoulder and said, 'Not at all. It's my pleasure,' in a very firm voice. And then, to Diana, 'Won't you come with me and make your choice? I don't know you well enough to guess what you like.'

Diana would sooner have stayed, but did not know how to refuse. Rupert drew back her chair, and she walked with him across the lawn. She was glancing around to check that everyone was being taken care of, and was considerably startled when Rupert said quietly into her ear, 'You're hoping everyone's thinking you've got us both running after you. You really are outrageously vain, aren't you?' Her head snapped round. 'No, don't show yourself up. Smile, dear, that's the ticket. I mean to talk to you, come what may, and it's better that you don't spoil the party and embarrass everyone.'

Diana felt herself colour. 'What are you *talking* about?' she said.

He smiled at her with a parody of admiration. 'Oh, yes, that colour suits you. You should blush more often, Miss Hunter. Diana the Huntress. Well, perhaps not quite. I'm thinking you ought to have one of those double-barrelled names – Fortune-Hunter would suit you perfectly.'

Diana was too startled by such overt rudeness to make any retort. She stared at him, her eyes wide.

'I'm on to you,' he said, still sounding pleasantly conversational, though his eyes were hard. 'You are pitifully transparent in your scheming, but I suppose in your *milieu* it hardly matters. Your friends and neighbours would only applaud your enterprise in trying to "catch" the heir to an earldom. And I imagine your female friends would be glad to do without your competition and have their pick of your old flames.'

'How dare you?' she said angrily.

'Oh, I dare all right. Listen quietly, or I shall speak up and let everyone hear.'

Diana felt tears prickle. 'Why are you being so horrid to me?' she asked, in a small, tense voice. She simply couldn't understand his sudden, poisonous hostility.

'Because you deserve it,' Rupert said. 'No waterworks, please. I'm sure, like every spoiled beauty, you can turn them on at will, but it doesn't work with me, so save your efforts.'

'I don't understand,' she said. It sounded like a whimper and pride stiffened her. She caught her lip under her teeth to control it. 'I won't listen to your abominable rudeness any more.'

'Bravo,' Rupert said. 'I almost admire you – or I would do, if it weren't my brother you'd sunk your talons into. I am going to warn you just this once to leave him alone. I know you are only after his title and his money, and you don't care a jot about the man underneath, but I do. He's my brother, and I won't have him hurt by a tawdry suburban vamp like you. You may as well know, my parents would never consent to such a marriage anyway.'

'Then what are you worried about?' Diana retorted, through clenched teeth.

'Because before you accept that it's impossible, you might break his heart trying. So I'm telling you, as politely as my contempt for you will allow, to leave him alone. You will not pursue him, you will not see him, you will not so much as look at him if you happen to pass in the street.'

'Anything else?' she asked ironically.

Rupert gave a sardonic grin. 'Attach yourself to one of your other swains – like that poor fish at your table over there, who's glaring at Charles, considerably to Charles's bewilderment. That's your proper level in society, Miss Fortune-Hunter.'

'*Stop calling me that!*' Diana hissed. He only laughed, so

155

she tried instead to be dignified. 'I'm sure your brother is quite capable of deciding for himself who he—'

'Ah, but he's not,' Rupert interrupted. 'He gives that impression, but if you knew him at all, you would know— However, you are plainly as insensitive as a rock, so all you'll ever see is his money and title and the glittering image of yourself as Queen of Dene Park. So I'll just say this: leave my brother alone, or it will be the worse for you.'

Diana waited an instant, then said, with as much dignity as she could muster, 'Is that all?'

'That's all,' he said. 'And now I shall get you some more tea.'

'Please don't bother,' she said icily.

He smiled. 'It's no bother at all. It's a pleasure, Miss Hunter. Another sandwich? Or one of those rather wonderful meringues?'

'Go to the devil!' she told him, through gritted teeth.

He laughed. 'What a jolly suggestion! I'm sure I shall, however, completely by my own efforts, so you needn't worry.'

Diana was on the brink of losing her temper and making a scene, which she would have regretted afterwards (and later she wondered if Rupert had been provoking her deliberately to make her show herself up in front of Charles), but there was an interruption at that moment which saved her.

Alec Gordon's father stepped out of the drawing-room french windows, closely followed by Beattie, and his face was grave. Alec jumped up and said, 'Dad? Is something wrong?'

Gradually conversations fell silent as people stared across at him, wondering what had happened. It had the air of bad news.

So it was that Mr Gordon's words carried to everyone across a silent garden as he said, 'I had a telegram from a friend at my club. The news has just come through: France mobilised at five fifteen this afternoon.'

CHAPTER TWELVE

'It wasn't a full mobilisation, according to Poppa,' said Cousin Mary. 'They gave orders to their soldiers not to go within ten miles of the border with Germany.'

'That's not much,' William objected. 'You could easily fire a shell that far.'

'Well, it's not right on the border,' said Mary, impatiently. 'The idea is not to provoke the Germans, so if there *is* a war, no-one can say it's France's fault.'

'Father said Mr Asquith is still hoping we can keep out of it,' Sadie said. 'It all depends on Belgium.'

'Why Belgium?' William asked.

'Because it's neutral. If the Germans attacked Belgium we'd have to go in.'

'Oh, Lord, are we going to talk about war all day?' Diana demanded. 'There isn't going to be any war, and it's too boring to talk about it. I thought we were going to look at the shops.'

'Shops!' said Sadie, and caught the eye of Cousin Audrey, who made an identical face.

'I don't want to go to the shops. I want to go and see the *Endurance* set off,' Peter said. Sir Ernest Shackleton was sailing to Antarctica on an expedition to cross the whole continent from sea to sea. He was to leave that day from West India Dock and sail to Cowes to be inspected by the King on Monday, the first day of Cowes Week, and receive

157

a Union Jack from His Majesty to carry with him the whole way.

'Well, you can't,' Diana said, 'because *we* don't want to go, and you can't go alone.'

'It's too late, anyway,' Sadie said, more kindly, seeing Peter's lip tremble. 'We'd never get there in time. Ships always leave early in the morning. Sailors don't lie around in bed, you know.'

'Haven't got beds to lie around in,' William informed. 'They have hammocks. Wish *I* had a hammock instead of a bed. I bet it'd be cheaper for Mother,' he added helpfully, 'because there'd be no sheets and she's always complaining that I go through my sheets in no time.'

'You wouldn't if you cut your toenails,' Sadie said.

Diana made an exasperated noise. 'Sheets, hammocks, toenails – this family's conversation is enough to drive one mad!'

'Never mind,' Mary comforted her. 'There's a sale on at Barkers.'

The Hunters – Beattie, Diana, Sadie, William and Peter – had gone up to Town that Saturday morning to spend the day with the cousins at the big red-brick house in Kensington.

Aunt Sonia was Edward Hunter's youngest sister. She had made a good marriage to Aeneas Palfrey, of Palfrey's Biscuits, with a factory in Ladbroke Grove, one in Belfast and another in Edinburgh. As well as owning a biscuit empire, Uncle Aeneas was connected, through a brother who had married a Buller-Fullerton girl, with the Elphinstones, which meant the girls sometimes got invited to Society parties in Belgravia. That was how Diana had met Charles in the first place, so she was extremely fond of Uncle Aeneas, even more than of Aunt Sonia, who sent her magazines.

The cousins provided a permanent excuse to go to London, their house a perfect setting-off place for shopping, the sales, dances, plays and other enhancements of life. The

158

eldest of them was Donald, who was twenty-three and worked for the family firm; he was a solid and practical version of his father, without Aeneas's whimsical humour, loved everything about the biscuit business and was devoted to the family.

Mary and Audrey were twins of nineteen, in appearance both tall, large-boned, milky-skinned, with a hint of copper in their fair hair; in character they were very different. For at least the last nine years Mary had acted as mother to her siblings, mitigating their real mother's shortcomings, with the consequence that she seemed older than her years. Audrey was the brainy one. She had attended the North London Collegiate, and Sophie Bryant, her headmistress, was her great hero. She read extensively, wrote poetry, and was trying to teach herself Greek. She would have liked more than anything to go to university and was sometimes maddened almost to slapping point that Donald could have gone and hadn't.

Douglas, often called Duck for reasons no-one now remembered, was thirteen, and much like other boys of that age, except for an inventive bent: his 'machines' littered the house, ingenious devices that were supposed to save labour but too often fell to pieces at first use because of a lack of suitable materials. Aeneas sometimes said that if only the boy had a welding set, he could make the house servant-free.

The house, within a stone's throw of Kensington High Street, Barkers and Derry & Toms, was large and many-storeyed, had stained-glass windows in the hall and on the landings, and coloured tiles on the hall floor. It had a proliferation of bedrooms, which made it easy for visitors to be invited casually to 'stay over', and a pleasantly rackety atmosphere generated by the number of people who were always 'dropping in'. Aunt Sonia was vague in the extreme and her housekeeping erratic or non-existent, but the servants were energetic and loyal and treated her as a sort of exotic pet, to be cosseted and sheltered from harsh reality. Uncle Aeneas was large and jolly and Scottish and hospitable; and neither was ever particularly surprised to meet a stranger at the dining-table or wandering the bedroom passages looking for a bathroom.

Sadie often wished she had been born a Palfrey instead of a Hunter. Nobody in the Palfrey house ever seemed to worry about anything, and everybody – it seemed to her – was allowed to do pretty much what they wanted to. Mealtimes in the dining-room, which looked like a baronial hall, with oak panelling and deer's heads on the walls, a massive fireplace and a polished oak floor that made everyone's footsteps clash like giants', were always a happy chaos as everybody tried to tell everybody else what they had been doing, all at the same time – until Duck's new patent plate-warmer set fire to the tablecloth.

Aunt Laura had also called in that morning, and she said now, 'I'd have liked to see the *Endurance* sail. I heard that Sir Ernest almost didn't go. He was thinking he ought to cancel the expedition, because of the situation abroad, and offer his services to the Admiralty instead. But the King and Winston Churchill persuaded him to go anyway.'

'Do *you* think there's going to be a war?' Sadie asked her.

'Your father's the one to ask about that,' Laura said. 'He always seems to know everything. But whether there is a war or not, I've decided I'm going to learn to drive a motor-car. That's what I've come to tell you all. It's bound to prove to be a useful skill, don't you think?'

Her announcement caused a sensation. She explained that she and her new friend Louisa were going to a place in Surrey where you stayed for a week in a large house and learned in the grounds. 'You don't do anything else all day,' she explained, 'so, however unmechanical you are, you're bound to learn. And, of course, in the evenings there are lots of jolly ladies to chat to and have fun with.'

'All ladies?' Diana asked. 'That sounds dull. Like being back at school.'

Laura gave her a humorous look. 'I don't think we'd learn half so well if the classes were mixed.'

'I'd love to learn to drive,' said Sadie.

'They give you a certificate at the end of it,' Laura told her, 'so that for ever after you can prove to any sceptical male you meet that you know what you're talking about.'

'I've been thinking about a new kind of patent driving goggles,' Duck said excitedly. 'I'll draw it for you. It sort of has a periscope in one eye, so you can see what's behind you.'

'That sounds frightfully useful,' Laura said.

'I could make you a pair,' Duck said, 'if Mumsy's got any really strong elastic. Only without the lenses, of course.'

That Saturday, the 1st of August, talk of war had suddenly became widespread. There were discussions in the newspapers and on street corners, and so much rumour and speculation were swirling about it was hard to know what was true and what wasn't. What did seem to be a fact was that the King had cancelled Cowes Week. The Royal Navy had been officially mobilised, and the First Fleet, which Captain Willis had seen at Portland a week ago being loaded with live ammunition, had slipped away during the dark hours to steam at high speed, and without lights, through the Strait of Dover into the North Sea and onwards to Scapa Flow, its war anchorage.

Edward was at the bank all day, and received wires, telephone calls and visits from various clients who wanted advice about securing their assets, or merely to speculate with him about what they had heard.

'The railway stations are full of foreign royalties trying to get home,' he was told by Lord Forbesson of the War Office, who dropped in on his way from his club to Downing Street.

'As soon as the King cancelled Cowes, they knew the game was up. Nobody wants to get caught on the wrong side of the Channel.'

'So it's definitely war?' Edward asked, with a sinking feeling.

'Not definitely, no,' said Forbesson. 'God, I hope not! There's still a good chance we can keep out of it. If Germany will give a commitment to honour Belgium's neutrality . . . We're under no obligation to France. To say truth, it's hard to make sense of what's going on over there, with so many reports coming in from the embassies, half of them contradicting the other half, and no way to tell fact from rumour.' He stared gloomily at the floor. 'I'm half afraid we're going to get into this because of some report or other that will turn out afterwards to have been false. There comes a point, you know . . .' He raised his eyes. 'Did you play pick-up-sticks in the nursery? There's always one stick that looks all right, but when you pull it, the whole mess comes tumbling down.'

Another client, Mr Turnhouse, an industrialist, seemed not only sure war was coming, but to relish it. 'It's a struggle between civilisation on the one side, and barbarism on the other,' he said. 'Germany's a young country: she hasn't had time to develop proper ethical codes. Her extraordinarily rapid material progress of the last forty years has no solid base. Imagine if you handed out modern rifles to a primitive African tribe! That's what we're facing here. We have to put Germany in her place, to preserve everything we've worked for over the past thousand years. It won't be pleasant, but it's our solemn duty to mankind.'

Young Lord Manners said, 'I say, it'd be a bit of a lark, wouldn't it? Don't you think? Or don't you?'

Both Beattie and Sonia noticed that Diana seemed a little moody – not just in a world of her own, as would be

162

understandable in a girl who had attracted the attentions of Lord Dene, but actually out of sorts.

'You aren't worried about all this talk of war, are you, dear?' Sonia asked. 'Even if it happens – which I don't believe for a minute – it won't affect us.'

Beattie said, 'I don't remember the last war very much – the South African war. Just that there were suddenly a lot of strange places in the newspapers – Bloemfontein and Spion Kop and so on.'

'And those Boer generals, such comical names they had! Smuts and de Wet! And what was that *very* odd one – Something de la Something?'

'Koos de la Rey, do you mean?' Beattie asked.

'That's the one. Always made me think of a prize dairy bull, I can't think why. And knitting,' Sonia added. 'I seem to recall there was a lot of knitting for the soldiers. Oh, and the Queen sent every soldier a tin box of chocolate for Christmas one year. I do remember that because I thought how very *like* Her Majesty it was.'

'I don't suppose you remember Mafeking Night, do you?' Beattie asked Diana. 'You'd have been about five. Your father took you and David in a cab to see the fun.'

'I remember fireworks and bonfires and crowds and lots of shouting,' Diana said. 'I don't think I knew what it was about.'

'I never really got any of it straight in my mind, who was fighting whom and why,' said Sonia. 'Not that it mattered in the least. War is the army's business. And we have the Royal Navy to protect us – the Germans could never get past our fleet. So you can put the whole thing out of your head, my love. And, by the way,' she went on, turning to Beattie, 'you really ought to make a decision soon about Sadie.'

'I hardly like to send her abroad when things are so unsettled,' said Beattie.

'But there are good schools in this country too. In fact, there are one or two nice ones in London. There's Miss Hammond's in Sloane Street where Jean Buller-Fullerton goes – such a nice girl, and a very suitable friend for Sadie . . .'

Diana stopped listening. She sank back into her own thoughts, which revolved around the horrid and unexpected rudeness of Rupert Wroughton, which had hurt and offended her very much. She had never been spoken to like that in her life. She was used to men fighting *over* her, not to having them fight *her*. Charles might sometimes seem strangely cold and aloof, but he had never been anything but courteous.

But Rupert had said *such* things to her . . . How could he? Did he mean them? Was it some obscure kind of joke? But surely no man would be so lost to decency as to think it was amusing or acceptable to call a lady – those things. *Fortune-Hunter*. So unfair! What did any man know about the trials of being a female? They could do anything they liked, but a girl had only one career open to her. She must marry, and it was her duty to marry as well as she could. If she didn't, she'd have betrayed her parents, and the trouble and expense they had put into her upbringing.

Suburban vamp. Well, that was just mean and cruel. She would never have thought any gentleman could simply insult a girl for no reason. What had she ever done to deserve it? Conclusion: Rupert was *not* a gentleman. But it hurt all the same.

And what did he mean by 'it will be the worse for you'? What could he do to her? She had no dark secret to expose. At worst, he could try to talk his brother out of seeing her. But Charles was old enough to make up his own mind. He was not some eighteen-year-old just out of school.

My parents would never consent to such a marriage. It was flattering in a way that Rupert had mentioned marriage: it suggested he thought Charles was seriously interested in her. But surely if, at some time in the future, Charles was determined enough to have her, he would overcome his parents' objections. He was a grown man, after all. He could marry without their permission.

She would see him tomorrow after church. And she had the cricket match and ball to look forward to. She must sparkle. She must enchant him. She had never failed to enchant a man before.

Except Rupert.

Oh, God – Rupert! How could he be so rude and unkind to me? Her thoughts slid back to the gloomy bottom of the circle and started the slow climb again.

That evening the family were staying with the Palfreys for dinner. Edward arrived back from the office late, after the dressing bell. Aeneas had waited downstairs for him, having sent everyone else up.

He went into the hall when he heard Edward arrive. 'My God, you look tired,' he said, as one of the servants took his coat. 'The bell's gone, but there's plenty of time. Come into the drawing-room and have a drink before you go up.'

'Thanks,' said Edward. 'I could do with a stiffener.'

'Whisky?' said Aeneas, going towards the tray. 'Or B and S?'

'Whisky, thanks.' Edward walked to the fireplace, and stood there looking down, rubbing his hands together as though there were flames in the grate instead of a pleated fan of paper. 'Have you heard the news?' he asked, rousing himself as Aeneas put a glass of golden liquid into his hand.

'I'm only just back from the factory myself. Haven't had time to look at the paper.'

Edward took a sip of the whisky, and then a gulp. 'The Tsar point-blank refused to stand down. Germany has mobilised and declared war on Russia.'

'Good God,' said Aeneas. 'I thought for sure family feeling would keep those two apart. It was only last May that the

165

King and the Tsar went to Berlin for the Kaiser's daughter's wedding. Well, bless my soul. What next?'

'What next? I can tell you that. Belgium has mobilised, and France has ordered full mobilisation. I don't think anything can stop it now.'

Aeneas took a drink of his own. 'Perhaps it won't be so bad,' he said at last. 'We needn't get drawn in.'

Edward raised tired eyes to him. 'I expect you're right. Anyway, there's no need to talk about it tonight.'

'None at all,' Aeneas agreed. 'No need to worry the ladies.' He finished his drink. 'Another? Well, then, we'd better go up.'

On Sunday morning, the news was that the Kaiser had ordered the seizure of British ships in the German port of Kiel. In the more excitable newspaper favoured in the servants' hall, the report appeared under a fat black headline 'ENGLAND EXPECTS', with a Union Jack to either side of it. What England expected was that the Kaiser should have his knuckles rapped good and hard. Who did he think he was?

'Nasty jumped-up little nobody, with his parades and his silly uniforms,' as Cook said. 'I don't care if he is the old Queen's grandson, he ought to be put in his place.'

The boy from Stein's, the butcher's, who had brought the joint and was lounging in the doorway with his basket, said, 'We oughter get on wiv it and declare war. I dunno what they're waitin' for. The King oughter do it right away.'

'Who asked you?' Ethel interrupted. 'Cheeky monkey.'

Cook, recalled to her duty towards boys of all marks, said sternly, 'Haven't you got deliveries to make?'

He dragged himself off the door frame. 'I'm goin' up London when I done these, see the fun. But'nam Palace, Tr'falgar Square. I don't wanter miss nuffin. Cor! I hope there's a war! I couldn't half fancy a fight. Smashing!'

'Fine soldier *you*'d make, with that dirty face of yours,'

166

Cook said. 'Go on, now, get off with you, standing round like it was everso.'

He hitched up his basket and slouched away with a look of derision. He did not rub his face until he was out of sight. *Wimmin*! he thought. Fancy talking about dirty faces at a time like this!

The rector gave a more than usually stirring sermon on the subject of what he called, with definite capital letters, The National Crisis.

'This thing which is now astir in Europe is not the work of God but of the Devil. An Imp of foul aspect has been let loose, and capers and postures in Satanic glee in the courts and government chambers of our continental neighbours and, yes, even in humbler homes, beckoning weak men to do wicked things and think them right. And how should we, in this country, respond? God has given us an incomparable heritage, has bestowed on us unique blessings: a beautiful and fertile land in which, over a thousand years, we have developed a society of virtue, of truth, of justice, of every lovely and worthy aspect of civilisation. Blessings that, for His own purposes, He has given to us and withheld from others, from the simple savage in the dark interior of Africa' – the congregation braced itself – 'to the arrogant militaristic hordes of industrial Germany.' The congregation relaxed again.

The rector raised his voice to a thunder: 'We are the guardians of God's purpose for mankind! And how should we respond at such a time as this? As far as the Nation in its corporate life is concerned, responsibility must rest with those to whom, in the providence of God, it has fallen to hold the trust for Britain's well-being and Britain's honour. But each of us has a role to play, in this time as at all times: to examine our consciences, and to make and to keep our home life worthy of the great confidence God has shown in us; to be the repository of those qualities He holds dear, and to guard and keep them against the darkness.' He lowered his voice. 'It may be, it is just conceivable, that for us in England the storm clouds will roll by unbroken. We look outward among wars and the rumours of wars, uncertain what any hour may bring forth. But of this we may be certain: that our duty will be made clear to us, and that when that day comes, we must each do our duty with stern resolve and with a pure and Christian heart, trusting in God to be our guide and protector, and praying to Him always in the words our Saviour taught us: "Our Father . . ."'

'I couldn't tell if he was for the war or against it,' William grumbled to Sadie, as they walked towards the door afterwards.

'I don't think he's supposed to be *hoping* for it,' Sadie said doubtfully. Yes, they prayed every week for 'the Church militant here in earth', but wasn't that meant to be more of a spiritual crusade than actual guns and cannons?

'Well, *I* hope we get in,' William said. 'It'd be—'

'Don't you dare say "fun",' Sadie stopped him.

'I wasn't going to. I was going to say "interesting". It'd be something new to think about, something that's never happened before. I like new things.' He glanced sideways at her. 'And it might be fun too. *You* don't know.'

Sadie was about to retort when she saw Viscount Dene hovering just outside the door, his eyes fixed on Diana.

'Good job she wore her new outfit,' Sadie whispered to William, who sniggered and turned it hastily into a cough.

By dint of walking off with Charles at once, while everyone else was still milling and chatting, Diana contrived to be alone with him. Once they were in the leafy shade of the footpath, sheltered on either side by tall elms, she slowed to a dawdle, to make the short walk last as long as possible.

Charles was silent, and to start him off, Diana said, 'Quite a good sermon today, didn't you think? I wonder if the storm clouds will roll by, as Dr Fitzgerald said.'

Charles roused himself. 'I don't want to alarm you,' he said, 'but I'm afraid things are looking rather shaky. I had a telegram this morning, just before we left for church. The Territorials' camp has been cancelled.'

'What does that mean?' Diana asked. If the camp was cancelled, did that mean the cricket match and the ball were too?

Charles took her question differently. 'It's a state called pre-mobilisation. Putting us on notice, just in case. The men are to go home and wait for instructions. If we are to be embodied, we'll be ordered to report to Headquarters instead.'

'Where is Headquarters? Would you have to go?'

'Near St Albans. Yes, of course, if we are embodied I would have to go.' He looked down at her faint frown. 'Would you mind?'

'I should be very sorry to see you go,' Diana said. That did not express the half of it. It was too bad, when things had started to go so well. If he was away and unreachable she would not see him, and if she did not see him – well, 'out of sight was out of mind'. He might forget her, or meet someone else. Their meeting at all had been such chance . . . 'Will it really be war, do you think?' she asked.

'It's still not certain, but – yes, I think it will.' Privately, his CO had warned him to put his affairs in order. Whatever the politicians might think, the army was sure it was coming.

'But *you* wouldn't have to fight,' Diana said. 'The Territorials – didn't you say they only serve in this country, that they don't have to go abroad?'

'That's right. They can be asked to serve abroad if necessary, but it isn't compulsory.'

'Oh. That's good, then,' Diana said.

He stopped, and turned to face her. Her words, 'That's good', seemed a precious encouragement to him. He didn't want to go into all the probabilities now – that as trained soldiers the Terriers *would* be asked, and in terms that they could hardly refuse; and that as an officer his duty would be to go where he was most needed. What mattered was – 'You don't want me to go abroad?'

'No, of course not,' she said. Then, 'Naturally if it was your duty – a man has to do what he must – but as it is, I'm glad. I should be sorry not to be able to see you.'

He was looking at her intently, but didn't say anything. They walked on and after a bit he talked again, explaining the international situation to her as he understood it.

She nodded and said 'Yes' and 'I see', but she was only half listening. She was thinking about the Territorials moving near St Albans. If they did, surely they would still have entertainments and dances. And it was not so very far. He could come and fetch her in his motor-car. Or there were trains. If only she had a relative there whom she could stay with. She must ask if the parents had any friends in the town.

If the Terriers went . . .

CHAPTER THIRTEEN

On Sunday evening, in that quiet time after supper when the servants were off duty and the world always seemed half asleep, there was a sound of arrival: wheels on gravel, a taxicab's motor, Nailer barking, the cab door slamming and a cheerful male voice. Sadie, who was doing a jigsaw puzzle with William at the table in the drawing-room window, looked out and cried, 'It's Bobby!' She jumped up and ran out, closely followed by William and Peter. A moment later they came back leading the hero, still in his OTC uniform and looking, Sadie thought, very handsome and distinguished.

Edward looked up from the newspaper. 'I thought you were supposed to be in Aldershot.'

'Orders came this afternoon from the War Office,' he said, putting down his valise, and allowing Sadie to slip her hand under his arm and hug it. 'They said the camp was needed for other purposes, and we were to disband as quickly as possible and go home.'

'What does that mean?' Sadie asked.

'They said we had to leave the camp, the cooks and the military equipment in place. It was just us schoolboys who were sent away. So I suppose they're expecting some proper soldiers to turn up. Reservists, perhaps.'

'Pre-mobilisation,' Diana said.

Edward looked at her, surprised. Hers were not the lips upon which one expected to find those words.

171

Bobby nodded. 'That's what our sergeant said. Which means the order to mobilise could go out at any moment. It was a lark trying to get home! You never saw the trains so crowded, and uniforms everywhere. I say, Father, do you think this is it?' He didn't wait for an answer. 'I'm going to go up to Town tomorrow to see the fun. Anyone else want to come?'

Sadie, still hanging on his arm, said, 'I will.'

'Me too,' said William.

'I'll travel in with you,' Edward said. 'I have to go to the bank.'

'On a bank holiday?' Beattie said.

'There will be a lot to do, even if the bank is closed,' Edward said.

Beattie wanted to ask *what*, and *why*, but Peter was clamouring to go as well, and seeing on the faces of the others that they didn't want to be burdened with him, she had to find things with which to distract him from the disappointment of being denied.

The morning newspaper on Monday, the 3rd of August, contained a message in the personal columns that jumped out at Edward not by its size or boldness but by the heading: 'GERMAN MOBILISATION'. Underneath it said:

Germans who have served, or are liable to serve, are requested to return to Germany without delay, as best they can. For information they can apply to the German Consulate, Russell Square, London WC.

R. L. VON RANKE, Consul

He was silent as he rode into Town with three of his children, all happily chattering. In the newspaper there was a report that Germany had invaded Luxembourg, and that German troops were massing along the border with Belgium.

172

The German ambassador to Brussels had delivered a note to the Belgian government stating that the German government had 'intelligence' that the French were about to invade Belgium and march on the Meuse. The Germans were demanding free passage through Belgium for their troops to repel this invasion. In the early hours of that morning, King Albert and his council presented a reply to the German Embassy: free passage was refused, Belgium would fight to repel any invader, and Germany was reminded that it was bound by treaty to protect Belgian neutrality.

There was little doubt, Edward thought, what the German response to that would be. It was now just a matter of time. It was a lovely morning – bright, clear and glorious after the muggy, overcast heat of the last two days – but he was filled with a sense of foreboding.

He parted from his children in Trafalgar Square and walked up Haymarket and along Piccadilly, wondering at the cheerful, milling masses, who seemed to be clogging the streets in unprecedented numbers. The answer was simple, as Warren explained when he got in: thousands had arrived early at the railway termini, laden with buckets and spades and shopping bags full of sandwiches, pies and lemonade, intending to enjoy the traditional bank holiday day-trip to the seaside – only to find that all the excursion trains had been cancelled.

'They were astonishingly good-natured about it, though,' Warren said. 'When I came in through Waterloo, the station was full of Royal Navy reservists on their way down to Portsmouth.'

'That's what the excursion trains were being used for, I imagine.'

'Yes, sir. But instead of being resentful, the holiday-makers gave them a rousing send-off. The sailors looked rather bemused. They were cheered and patted on the back, and

173

everyone was singing "Rule Britannia" – or, I should say, bellowing it.'

'I see – so now they're going to have their day out in London rather than go home?' Edward said.

'Everyone seems very cheerful. I think this war news has really bucked them up. I saw a lot of Union flags being waved – they're being sold on every street corner. The ordinary people will be frightfully disappointed if we don't get in. They're longing to "biff the Bosch".'

'You sound as though you're one of them,' Edward said.

Warren took a pull on his enthusiasm. 'Oh, well, sir, you know – one's interested in international affairs, that's all.'

Edward gave him a faintly sardonic look. 'Is one, indeed? Very well. As long as you know that, whatever happens, *you* won't be going anywhere. I need you here.'

'Yes, sir,' Warren said, pleased. Those last were words one did not often hear. 'Shall I bring in the letters?'

The bank holiday was a normal working day for the post office. And for the Warrens of this world: if the boss came into the office, they came too.

The Hunters explored, entranced by the holiday atmosphere that pervaded the world's greatest industrial city. Thwarted of the seaside, the day-trippers were bent on having fun as best they could. In the parks they were already staking out picnic spots, and hardly a foot of bare grass could be seen. In Trafalgar Square, children promised a paddle at Southend or Brighton were sporting happily in the fountains.

The pubs were doing a brisk trade, and customers had spilled out on to the pavements to enjoy their pint of mild-and-bitter in the sunshine. Teashops and restaurants were packed. A solid mass of people was slowly milling between Trafalgar Square and Buckingham Palace, where they congealed a while in the hope of seeing the King and Queen come out on the balcony. Others were thronging Whitehall and hanging around Downing Street, limp Union Jacks clutched in their fists, ready to be waved violently if the announcement of war was made. Surely in Downing Street they'd hear it first.

Posters promised plenty of bank-holiday entertainments: an American exhibition at the White City, with Wild West re-enactments; sunny Spain at Earls Court, with real flamenco dancers; a flying circus at Hendon; a model-yacht regatta on the Round Pond; an afternoon concert at the Royal Albert Hall. There were the usual paddle-boats on the Serpentine and the zoo in Regent's Park; while the waxworks at Madame Tussaud's had added a topical tableau of kings and queens of Europe, including the Emperor of Austria, King Albert of Belgium and King Peter of Serbia, accompanied by 'delightful music' and 'refreshments at popular prices'.

The Hunters wandered happily, listened to the band in Green Park and fed the pelicans in St James's Park. Luckily Bobby had some jingle left in his pockets and treated them all to an ice-cream from a vendor at the park gate. They waited outside Buckingham Palace for a bit, but the windows remained resolutely closed and nothing seemed to be happening. Finally, as they were getting very hungry, they walked down to Victoria and took the Inner Circle to Kensington High Street and Aunt Sonia's.

Victoria Station was crowded too, but the atmosphere was not jubilant. Here hundreds of people were struggling along with cheap suitcases and bundles hastily wrapped in brown paper. They were Germans, fleeing the country: waiters, barbers, pork butchers, watchmakers, cobblers, musicians, tailors, governesses, teachers. They plodded their way to the boat trains in silence, bent by anxiety. At the barriers, some of the men left English wives and children in tears.

It left Sadie feeling unsettled and disturbed. If war was coming, she didn't want to think of the Enemy as those sad, shabby, worried people. She wanted him to be the Hun of the *Daily Mail*'s anathema: like the Kaiser in his spiked helmet, waxed moustache and many medals, ridiculously strutting, eminently hateable.

News came in through the day. Britain had sent a stern note to Germany, demanding an assurance that it would not violate Belgian neutrality. The Germans replied that they were fighting for their lives against French hostility and acts of aggression. It was known that the French were standing-to well within their own borders: the German lie was shocking, but not surprising.

And, during the afternoon, the British order to mobilise went out: thousands of telegrams, already addressed and waiting at the War Office, were dispatched, one for each man of the reserve, for every Territorial unit, every headquarters commander, and every police station in the land. Silent, businesslike, unperceived by the general public, they sped like poisoned arrows to their targets, bringing sober reality to the few, while the many still laughed and celebrated in the headiness of their day off.

In his quiet office, Edward went about his work, read documents, signed letters, with a faint sense of unease, a feeling of waiting for the candle to burn down and the pin to drop. *Nation will rise against nation and kingdom against kingdom . . . These are the beginnings of sorrows.* He wondered if in the future they would look back on this time, and see that it had been the End of Days. They would remember there had been portents, signs in the sky, two-headed calves and dragons that spoke like men, but with their eyes bent to the furrow they had not noticed. Only Holy Prophets ever recognised the end days, and then only with the benefit of hindsight. He firmly believed all books of prophecy were written after the event.

Outside his window the world jigged and sang in its holiday

merriment, and its voices came to him distant and clear and hollow, like the memory of children at play.

Early on Tuesday morning, the German Army crossed the border into Belgium, and simultaneously invaded France and Russian Poland.

Edward went into work to find a message from Head Office that the government had ordered an extension of the bank holiday to avoid the possibility of a bank run.

In Europe, matters pursued their now inevitable course. Belgium appealed to Britain for help, and the British ambassador in Berlin presented an ultimatum to the German government. Unless Germany undertook by midnight to withdraw from Belgium, she must consider herself at war with Great Britain and her Empire.

Lord Forbesson, with the look of a man who had not been to bed in a very long while, dropped in with the news. 'They won't withdraw, of course,' he said, 'but everything has to be done in form. So we shall be at war tonight. You can bank on that.' He gave a tired smile. 'When the banks reopen, of course.'

'That will be on Friday, I believe?' Edward said.

Forbesson nodded. 'By then there should be a new supply of ten-shilling notes and pound notes to replace the half-sovereigns and sovereigns. The Royal Mint is working full out. We have to call in the gold, of course.'

'Paper money always causes inflation,' Edward said.

Forbesson shrugged. 'Not my department. Can't have gold in circulation, that's obvious – hoarders, speculators, old ladies burying sovereigns in the garden.'

'What about silver?' Edward asked. Notes were all very well, but you couldn't hand one to a taxi driver or a newsagent.

'They'll be coining extra silver and copper, of course,' Forbesson said, 'but it will take time. Meanwhile, postal

177

orders will be recognised as legal currency – that should tide people over. Things might be tight for a few days but, frankly, that's no bad thing. Keep people quiet and at home while we get things organised. We'll have a Defence of the Realm Act by the end of the week, which should give us all the powers we need.'

He stood up to go. Edward stood too, and said, 'Thank you for letting me know.'

'You should go home,' Forbesson said. 'That's where I'm going – just for a few hours. You haven't any sons in the reserves, have you?'

'No, my lord,' said Edward. Just a nephew, he thought, remembering Jack.

'Lucky,' said Forbesson, and rubbed his eyes wearily. 'My eldest got his telegram yesterday. Gone off to Aldershot.' He tapped Edward on the shoulder in a friendly way with his stick. 'Go home, that's my advice.'

To spend the last hours of peace with the family, Edward thought. But he had a thousand things to do.

So we are at war, Sadie thought as she bicycled to Highclere on Wednesday, the 5th of August. The deadline had passed at eleven the previous night – midnight, German time – and Britain was now officially at war with Germany.

It was a baking hot day, fit only for lying about in the shade in the garden and reading, but she felt too restless for that. It was extraordinary how different she felt this morning. *At war.* What did it mean? What would happen? Probably none of it would affect her directly. War was men's business. Yet it was true, what William had said: it was something new to think about and, in a life that was very much the same day after day, one relished that.

Everything this morning seemed refreshed, clear-edged, as though she had never looked at it before. And it wasn't only her: she saw it in the face of everyone she passed. People walked with their heads up, their eyes to the horizon, their faces firm and bright, as though they had taken on a new dignity. Germany had invaded Belgium and Britain was going to drive it back and save the Belgians. That was a noble thing. She pedalled harder, wanting to burst into song. Everything was different today. Everything was *different*.

A Simpson's Dairy's cart turned out of the lane ahead of her and she slowed as Arthur plodded towards her. Mr Simpson himself was driving.

'Morning, Miss Sadie,' he said cheerfully, halting the cart. 'Heard the news, then? By golly, we'll give them Germans what-for!'

'You're driving this morning?' Sadie said.

'Ar, that boy Jesse never turned in,' Simpson said, disgusted. 'I got milk to deliver, war or no war. Business as usual, eh? That's what we says. Business as usual.'

Sadie was caressing Arthur's nose. 'I like the decorations,' she said. Arthur's browband had two red-white-and-blue rosettes fixed to it, as though he had just, by the most unlikely chance, won two prizes in the show ring. 'He looks very smart.'

'Thought I'd show the customers what we stand for,' said Simpson. 'Had 'em since the Coronation. Well, must get on. That Kaiser's not stopping *my* milk round, do what he likes. Gerrup, horse!'

Arthur drew a deep sigh and clumped on. Sadie grinned and resumed her journey. Mr Simpson plainly felt it too, this being *at war*. Defying the Kaiser made even his ordinary milk round seem special and important.

Cook had come to Beattie for the usual morning briefing looking anxious. The charwoman, Mrs Chaplin, had arrived early, big with news. Her nephew, the blacksmith, had seen a number of strangers' cars going past into the village that morning; and then the rectory's man, Fred, coming in with

179

a bent bracket to straighten, had said that their Aggie had been to the village and noticed people stocking up. She saw a queue of big motors outside Williamson's, and someone's chauffeur carrying out two whole hams from Stein's.

'It don't do to get left behind, madam,' Cook said. 'Once people get word, there'll be a run on the shops. I wish we had a motor-car, madam.'

'I'm sure there's no need to panic,' Beattie said. 'I can't see any reason the shops would run out.'

'The German blockade, madam,' Cook said. 'Everybody says they'll stop the ships getting into our ports.'

'The navy will prevent that happening. Besides, our food doesn't all come from abroad.'

Cook wasn't placated. 'No, madam. But I think it'd be best to stock up on a few things while we can. Can I send Henry and Ethel down with the handcart? Williamson's ought to favour good customers like us – people with monthly accounts.'

Beattie gave in. 'You can get in some extra butter, cheese and bacon, if you think it worth while.'

'I do, madam. Those are things that'll go quick. And flour for my baking. And rice. And sugar – there's bound to be a rush on sugar. That does come from abroad, I *do* know. And raisins.'

'Very well. But no handcart,' Beattie said. 'Only what they can carry. I don't want to set people talking.'

'The master's coffee, madam. He doesn't like tea in the morning, and coffee comes from abroad.' A thought struck her. 'Tea does, too, doesn't it? Oh, my Lord!' Without tea, how could any of them get through the day?

A thrill of alarm ran down Beattie's spine. 'Have Henry call in at the coal office at the station and ask them to deliver a ton,' she said, and added to herself, in a murmur of justification, 'I usually fill up in the summer anyway, when it's cheap.'

* * *

180

For once Ethel didn't mind being sent to the shops, even though it meant going with Henry. She told him to walk behind her, carry the baskets, and not to talk. He sulked and slouched but did as he was told: Ethel was known to slap if riled, and her hands were hard from housework.

The first thing she noticed was the crowd around the post office. There were men in army uniform, surrounded by clinging women – reservists just called up. They had to present their identity document to the post-office clerk to receive their five shillings' travelling expenses, then show it at the railway station to receive a travel warrant to their destination. The War Book had laid it all out. No reservist would be prevented from reporting to his colours by a lack of ready funds.

Others trying to get into the post office were those who found themselves short of cash because of the bank closure. Until the new notes were printed, the only paper money in circulation was the five-pound note, and anyone foolish enough to try buying anything with it in a shop had quickly found themselves red-faced. Traders were not going to part with all their change in one go.

It turned out, though, that the post office was equally unwilling to deal with 'fivers'. They would not give out sovereigns, and their smaller change was needed for paying the soldiers' expenses. One ingenious gentleman, realising that five pounds equalled twenty five-shilling postal orders, was crestfallen when it was pointed out that each postal order carried a small stamp duty, which meant they did not add up to a round sum. The clerk politely but firmly refused to part with any change, so the gentleman had to depart empty-handed.

The shops were doing a brisk trade. Williamson's had cards in the window, saying, 'BUSINESS AS USUAL' and 'GOD SAVE THE KING'. Stein's the butcher's had edged the display of chops and joints with tasteful red-white-and-blue ruffles.

Reiss, the outfitter's, had a display of items from the last war – a cap, an officer's Sam Browne, a blancoed ammunition belt, a tray of medals, a pair of crossed rifles of antique vintage and two Zulu shields.

Korder, an itinerant vendor of home-made sweets, had set up his cart on the wide corner by the Station Hotel and gathered a crowd of children. His sing-song chant rose above the chatter of the crowds as seductively as the Pied Piper's whistle:

Indian *Tof*fee!
Good for your *bel*ly!
Ask your *ma*mmy
For a *pen*ny!

Other traders hastened to make hay while the sun shone. On Goose Green, the open space opposite the station, there was a lemonade cart and a woman selling toffee apples, and Hetherton's had sent out a boy to circulate with penny buns on a tray. The Italian organ grinder, who seemed to have a sixth sense for crowds, appeared from nowhere, and soon there were people dancing to his tunes while his monkey capered and gibbered.

On the opposite corner old Mr Fields, who had taken the trouble that morning to pin his Crimea and Sudan medals to his shiny and threadbare jacket, was telling a crowd that a Tommy was worth ten Germans, and the Huns would never stand cold steel. General French would be eating Christmas dinner in Berlin off the Kaiser's gold plates, with the Kaiser forced to wait on him and light his cigar. The picture he painted was so beguiling he was obliged to repeat it for every new arrival.

Every now and then, when the children grew too rowdy, PC Whittle would make a pass and drive them, shrieking, away. His tall, helmeted figure was very noticeable that morning, pacing majestically up and down the high street, the visible symbol of nationhood, on hand to deal with any quarrels that might flare up as a result of the unusual volume of trade in the shops, or the shortage of ready change.

There was a long queue outside Williamson's, but Ethel thought it was better than housework, at any rate. Everyone was talking about the war, excited and happy, as though a fair had arrived in town. They said the Germans had 'asked for it' and must be 'taught a lesson'; and that lesson would be doled out by the British Army in double-quick time. Some said it would all be over by Christmas; others that the army would be back triumphant 'before the leaves fell'.

When she finally reached the counter, Ethel heard a woman complaining to Mrs Williamson about the lack of her usual tea and Mr Williamson telling someone else that bacon had sold out until tomorrow. But Billy Snow, elbowing the other assistant out of the way to serve Ethel himself, was eager for her to understand that restrictions did not apply to her.

'No coffee left at all, I'm afraid, madam,' he said loudly, surveying her list, 'and we're having to limit sugar to four pounds per customer.' He gave her a wink. 'On the account, of course? Let me pack all this for you, and I'll bring the baskets out to you directly,' he added, with a jerk of his head. Ethel thanked him and left. Henry was waiting outside for her. The back door was down an alley to the side of the shop, and she stationed him at the street end of it, told him to stay put, and slipped down to the door.

Billy opened it as she reached it and she went inside, into the store-room. 'I can't be long,' he said, closing the door behind her. 'You never saw such a rush as we've had this morning. Let me do your order first.' He began darting about, placing items in the baskets, while Ethel sat on a stack of boxes, watching. 'Mr Williamson told me to put some coffee aside for the gentry. I daren't give you more'n two pounds, though – Dene Park hasn't had their order yet. No trouble about the sugar. We're not rationing regular customers, but you have to say that stuff in the shop or there's arguments.'

He chattered on as he packed. Ethel thought he sounded nervous. At last he finished, and said, 'You're not carrying these home yourself?'

'No, I've got the boy outside.' She stood up, smoothing down her skirt. 'Well, I mustn't keep you,' she said demurely.

He stepped towards her. 'Ethel—' There was sweat on his upper lip. 'Someone said they saw you with Alan Butcher last Saturday, while I was at work.'

'What of it?' she said. 'Can't a girl have tea with a chap if she wants to?'

'But I thought you and me was going steady!'

'First I've heard about it,' she said, flicking imaginary dust from her glove. 'You never said.'

'But I thought you *knew*,' he cried, taking hold of her arms in anguish.

She wriggled a little in protest, but not enough to make him let go. 'I'm not a mind-reader, like that Madam Mentallo at the fête.'

'Oh, Ethel, you know how I feel about you!'

'Well, maybe I do, and maybe I don't,' she said, looking up at him from under her eyelashes. He stooped and she allowed him one kiss before pushing him away. 'Give over! Anyone might come. Haven't you got a shop to mind?'

'I've got to carry your baskets out, haven't I?' he said. 'But first – tell me you feel the same way I do.'

'Well, I don't know what that is, do I? You haven't said.'

'I love you! You're the most beautiful girl I've ever met! Ethel, will you – will you marry me?'

She laughed – not the response he'd hoped for. 'Marry you? Don't talk so daft, Billy Snow! Who d'you think you are?'

He looked hurt. 'I thought you cared for me.'

'Oh, you're not so bad,' she allowed. 'I've met plenty worse. But you've got to prove yourself before I'll say yes. The man I marry's got to be a bit special. A hero.'

'A hero?'

'You've never done a romantic thing in your life, have you? You do something romantic, then maybe I'll think about it. And that's all I've got to say.' She stepped to the door, and put on an air and a posh voice. 'Be so kind as to open the door for me, my man, if it's not troubling your manners too much.'

Bewildered and a little bruised about the heart, he scurried to obey, and followed her out with the baskets. At the end of the alley he handed them to Henry, and Ethel shoved the boy to get him moving. But then she turned back to give Billy a sweet smile and say, 'You're much handsomer than Alan Butcher,' before she tripped away.

Always leave them with a little bit of sugar, she thought. She knew how to dangle her admirers so that they kept coming back. Keep them guessing – never let them settle – but always end with a bit of sugar.

Content with herself, she walked home through the sunshine on the first day of war.

CHAPTER FOURTEEN

The shortage of change reduced Edward to having to raid Peter's money-box for pennies and threepenny bits in order to buy his daily newspapers; and the lack of proper news in them had him going to his club every day at the luncheon hour, not to eat but to talk to members who really did know what was going on.

Those who were Members of Parliament told him that the House was busy pushing through the Defence of the Realm Act, which would give the government powers to control any aspect of life deemed necessary, from taking over the railways to restricting street lighting, from imposing national prices for essential foods to requisitioning motor-vehicles.

Those who had been reservists he found in the throes of preparation, talking about the problems they were having in buying kit in the crowded stores, and competing to get tailors to make their uniforms.

'Thank God the madam and the brats are down at Eastbourne,' said Lord Henry Hastings. 'We've closed the house, and one can be more comfortable here at the club in the circumstances. I seem to spend half my day in Savile Row begging old Wilkins for preferential treatment, so I might as well bed down nearby.'

'The Americans are the problem,' said Mr Jackson Smythe. 'Town's full of 'em – got caught out on the Continent, and left their luggage behind. Now they're stranded here until

186

they can get a passage home, and they all want new suits made just when we're trying to get our uniforms fitted.'

Lord Henry agreed. 'You should hear Wilkins on the subject. "American gentlemen like a very different cut, my lord," he says. And they're such tall, strapping fellows, a suit for one of them takes up twice as much cloth.'

'Wish I'd thought of hoarding bales of cloth before all this started,' said Mr Jackson Smythe. 'More to the point than sacks of potatoes. Never cared for potatoes anyway.'

'And boots,' Lord Henry put in. 'I'll be off to France barefoot the way things are going . . .'

Lord Forbesson, dashing in at the end of the week to swallow a sandwich and a large whisky to fortify him before a Cabinet meeting, told Edward that the mobilisation was going off in exemplary fashion, thanks to the War Book.

'Wonderful piece of planning! Ever since the Agadir crisis, the Central Committee's been putting the instructions in place to deal with every possible situation. Men, stores, uniforms, transport – everything's covered. From the brigadier to the private, the bobby in the police station and the mayor in the town hall, all they have to do is turn to the right page of the Instructions, and there it is in black and white. Marvellous.' He emptied his glass and caught the waiter's eye for a refill. 'D'you know,' he added, 'there's even a reminder to the Tommy to make sure to take his library book back before leaving.'

'It's a lot of work for a war that will be over by Christmas,' Edward said.

Forbesson looked at him. 'You're a good fellow, Hunter. Just between ourselves, we're in it for the long haul. Most of the Cabinet are expecting it to last two years. Kitchener's saying it's more likely to be three or four.'

Four years? Edward was struck by the words, like a slap in the face. How could a modern war last that length of time?

187

'The old boy's shrewd,' said Lord Forbesson. 'I wouldn't be surprised if he were nearer being right than anybody. He's being appointed secretary of state for war. That's good for home consumption. The people adore him – it'll give 'em confidence to know he's at the helm. And, frankly, confidence is something we'll need. Everyone's excited at the moment, but when it grinds on we'll need determination. Morale will be all-important. That's why we're not contradicting this "all over by Christmas" rumour.'

'I won't say anything, of course. But – *four years*?'

'Germany has conscription. Every German male is liable to fight – a potential army of millions, plus vast stockpiles of armaments. We've never had conscription in this country. The people wouldn't stand for it, and quite right too. Germany's a dictatorship, we're a democracy – and the English have always hated armies, not like the Prusskis with their uniforms and parades and nonsense. So we're having to start from scratch. Kitchener wants to raise a completely new army. But our regulars will have to hold the line until we can get enough men trained, equipped and out there.'

'That will take time,' said Edward.

Forbesson grunted. 'One Tommy may be worth ten Huns, but it's still going to be one hell of a scrap. One *hell* of a scrap,' he repeated, staring at his empty glass. Then he sighed and looked up. 'We'll beat 'em all right. But it's not going to be a canter round Hyde Park, Hunter, you have my word.'

'You haven't mentioned the French,' Edward said, after a moment's silence.

'Nobody really knows how they'll turn out as allies,' Forbesson said, with a shrug in his tone. 'The only time we've tried it before was in the Crimea, and that didn't end well. Frankly, I don't have high hopes of the Frogs. Oh, they'll fight this time because their backs are to the wall. But it's still an eighteenth-century army. They treat their men like hell, don't feed 'em or take care of 'em. In a long war, things like that matter.' He smiled. 'If I was to tell you about the pages in the War Book simply dedicated to getting the soldiers' mail delivered!'

'Is that important?' Edward asked.

'Keeps their morale up – letters from home, parcels, a photo of Baby. Attention to detail, you see. This is going to be a thoroughly modern war.'

Forbesson left, and Edward felt vaguely comforted, and a little more than vaguely disturbed. *Four years?* Forbesson's confidence in ultimate victory versus his evaluation of the difficulty to come. *A thoroughly modern war.* What did that mean? Edward wasn't sure it was an entirely benign phrase, though he couldn't quite pin down why.

The war might be only days old, but Mrs Fitzgerald had never had so many demands on her attention. There was the necessity of getting provisions laid in, because you never knew what calls there would be on the rectory's hospitality. But it had to be done carefully so as not to provoke accusations of hoarding: the rectory must be above that sort of thing.

And any number of people were coming to seek Dr Fitzgerald's opinion on the morality or otherwise of public houses being open, people filling their cellars with coal, that dreadful organ grinder playing immoral tunes, not a patriotic one among 'em; demanding why the village hall wasn't being strung with red-white-and-blue bunting to show support for the British Expeditionary Force; querying whether the summer fête ought to be cancelled, whether knitting socks for soldiers on a Sunday was Sabbath-breaking, whether it would be wrong to have the Mendelssohn at Sally's wedding, because Mendelssohn was a German, wasn't he?

Dr Fitzgerald could not be expected to deal personally with every query. Mrs Fitzgerald screened the applicants and only passed those whose moral dilemma she felt beyond her

189

competence. Inevitably, she ended up taking on most of the burden herself.

She explained all this to Beattie on Thursday when she called at The Elms. 'And I know you must be just as busy, dear Mrs Hunter,' she went on, making Beattie feel instantly guilty, 'but I do want to enlist your help on a very important subject.'

Beattie tried to make a sound that was both enquiring and non-committal. She sensed an imposition on the horizon. The energy of Mrs Fitzgerald created a vortex into which one was pulled willy-nilly.

'It's the matter of the public houses, you see – and, in particular, the Red Lion.' The Red Lion was a beerhouse on the Rustington Road, patronised exclusively by the lower orders. 'Ever since the bank-holiday weekend, it's been full night after night. Drunken carousing, cheering, singing. They're using the war as an excuse, and it won't do.'

'Everyone's rather stirred up,' said Beattie.

'Becoming intoxicated is not an appropriate way to express patriotism,' Mrs Fitzgerald said sternly. 'And there are more serious problems. We have a number of reservists in the village who've been recalled to the colours. Their wives apply to the Soldiers' Families Emergency Fund – you know the committee's been sitting in the Gade Room at the Station Hotel?'

'Yes, under Mrs Prendergast, I believe,' said Beattie, still mystified. The Fund had been set up to grant the wives a sum of money to tide them over until the Army Allotment started to be paid. Few of the men had savings to bridge the gap.

'Of course, they wouldn't need the Fund,' Mrs Fitzgerald sidetracked herself, 'if they didn't live from hand to mouth. However much we urge them, they never put anything aside for emergencies.'

'Perhaps they can't,' Beattie said mildly. 'If they only earn just enough to get by.'

'There's always a way,' Mrs Fitzgerald said firmly. 'A penny here and a penny there soon adds up to a useful amount. Some of the women are simply improvident, of course, but I'm afraid I mostly blame the men. They will spend money on beer, no matter how often we lecture them about it.'

'I don't see how one can stop that,' Beattie said.

'It *must* be stopped. I want to get the Red Lion closed down for the duration of the war. The women are taking the money from the Families' Emergency Fund straight into the beer-house. It's disgraceful – women drinking themselves insensible while their neglected children sit outside on the step. They seem to have lost all restraint with their husbands going away.'

'But what do you want me to do?' Beattie asked.

'We must get up a petition to shut it down,' Mrs Fitzgerald said. 'Every decent person in Northcote will sign. I want you to help canvass them, collect the signatures. We must show a solid front on this. We—'

'I'm afraid I couldn't possibly,' Beattie said, as firmly as she could. 'I simply haven't the time.'

Mrs Fitzgerald looked both surprised and disapproving. 'My dear Mrs Hunter, we must all *make* time to do what's necessary. There *is* a war on, you know.'

'Why only the Red Lion?' Beattie asked, hoping to distract her. 'There are two other public houses, besides the Station Hotel.'

'They are rather more respectable places,' Mrs Fitzgerald returned. 'There has been a certain amount of . . . *jollifica-tion* at the Rose and Crown and the Coach and Horses this past week, but nothing like the carousing and dissipation at the Red Lion.'

'If there is misbehaviour, it's a matter for the police,' Beattie said. 'I really don't see that it's anything for us to get involved in.'

191

'You're refusing?' Mrs Fitzgerald said, in a frosty voice.

Beattie tried to placate her. She was not a woman to get on the wrong side of. 'I'm sure things will settle down in a day or two. Everyone's overexcited at the moment.'

'Very well,' Mrs Fitzgerald sniffed. 'But I must say I'm disappointed.'

'I hope she doesn't hold it against me, but I'm glad I refused,' Beattie told Edward that evening, as they dressed for dinner. 'It's not that I don't want to help the war effort. But I want to wait and see what I can most usefully do. There are bound to be lots of committees.'

'Bound to be,' Edward agreed. 'The Mrs Fitzgeralds of this world would hardly exist if it weren't for their committees. They're meat and drink to them.'

Beattie smiled, but said, 'She does an awful lot of good.'

'She's going to love this war. There'll be so many good works to be tackled. Don't let her tire you out, that's all.'

Beattie knew all the tones of his voice. 'What have you heard?'

'Nothing,' he said. 'Nothing in particular, that is. But you know, darling, where there is war, there is always hardship. And, unlike the last war, this one is going to be on our doorstep. There are bound to be refugees. They'll be a suitable subject for your efforts.'

'Refugees,' she agreed, still examining him, not entirely convinced by his answer. There was something he hadn't told her. 'And knitting,' she said at last. 'We knitted so many stockings last time, I thought we must have four-legged soldiers. Or perhaps they were putting them on the mules.'

He smiled, glad she was in spirits. 'Would you care to join me in a glass of sherry before dinner?'

She was pleased by the offer and his smile, both of which reminded her of the early days of their acquaintance, when he was courting her. The hardest thing about marriage, she thought, was no longer being courted. She wondered if Diana had really taken that into account in her longing to be wed.

As if he heard the thought, Edward said, 'Has Diana heard any more from her beau? The eminent one, I mean – the front-runner.'

'Nothing. She's rather glum about it, but it's only been a few days, and I told her he's probably busy with the Territorials and can't get away. Do you want me to tie that?'

'Yes, please.' He presented himself, chin tilted up. 'One of the great benefits of being married is always having someone to tie one's tie.'

She stepped close enough to smell, under the soap and bay rum, the scent of his skin, which had once given her shivers. It still enticed her, but there seemed so little room, once you were married, for love and its appurtenances. Not *time*, somehow, but *room* – as if everyday life expanded and filled out the whole of being, driving out everything else; until one day you stared in the looking-glass and found that you had disappeared, and a stranger was standing there in your place, a stranger with all your characteristics expunged and a bland smoothness in their place.

She tweaked the bow into suitable asymmetry, thought of kissing his chin, and didn't. 'There are always valets,' she concluded the conversation.

Luncheon had only just been cleared on Friday when there was the sound of a motor-car outside that had Diana running to the morning-room window, hoping it was Charles Wroughton's Vermorel. Her disappointment was tempered when a smartly dressed lady stepped out and she was able to cry, 'It's Beth and Jack!'

They came in, bringing as always a breath of a wider world with them. 'We've just motored down from Peterborough,'

193

Beth said gaily, exchanging kisses. 'My dears, what a journey! We're on the way to Hounslow, so we thought we'd call in.'

'Hounslow?' Beattie said. 'That's not on your lecture-tour, is it?'

'Hardly,' she laughed. 'Jack got his telegram, you see. He has to report.'

'It's been following me about the country,' Jack said, pulling off his cap. 'Of course I knew I was going to be called but I rather hoped to finish my engagements first.'

'He ought to have taken the train, I suppose,' Beth said.

'But I wasn't going to abandon the motor in some wild northern place.'

'You might as well have,' Beth said. '*I* can't drive it.'

'You may have to learn,' Jack said, with a grin, 'if this is going to be a long war.'

'Nonsense. I'll hire a chauffeur.'

'First things first,' Beattie interrupted. 'Have you eaten? We've had luncheon, but Cook could get something for you in a moment.'

Beth said, 'We didn't have time to eat.'

Jack said, 'I'm so late reporting already, a couple more hours won't make any difference.'

Beattie turned towards the bell, but Diana said, 'I'll go and tell Cook. It'll be quicker.'

Omelettes were soon on the table, followed by fruit salad, and between mouthfuls Beth and Jack told an attentive audience about their tour.

Then Beattie said, 'But what will you do, Beth, with Jack called to the colours?'

'Oh, I shall stay in London, of course, at our house. Plenty of shows and so on to keep me occupied.' She looked at Jack, her smile not quite covering her feelings.

'I'll be all right,' Jack said. 'There'll be months of training for us reservists. Who knows? The war may be over before I get sent abroad.'

'You could stay here, if you wanted,' Beattie told her. 'You'd be most welcome.'

'Thank you, dear, but I'd prefer to be at the heart of things. Better for keeping the mind off. You can visit me, though.' She looked at Diana, who seemed a little under the weather. 'I'd love it if you came and helped me settle in, Diana dear.'

Jack looked at the clock. 'I hate to dash straight after eating, but time's getting on. We really had better go.'

'No coffee?'

'Thanks, but there's too much to do.'

In the hall there were kisses goodbye, and they were gone, leaving behind them a feeling of flatness. But they always did that, Beattie thought.

When Sadie went to Highclere on Saturday, she found a state of gloom prevailing, and most of the loose-boxes empty.

'The army came,' Podrick said simply. He had his hands stuck in his pockets and Sadie could see the shape of the fists they were clenched into.

'Captain Casimir,' Mrs Cuthbert said. She was trying to be brisk, but Sadie could see that she was forcing back tears, which was terrifying. Grown-ups didn't cry: it was one of the immutable laws of the universe. 'They've left us old Captain, and Blaze, and the pony that pulls the mower and the in-foal mares. I should be grateful.'

'They took them all? The liveries too?'

'I'm afraid so,' said Mrs Cuthbert.

Sadie was bewildered. 'But they weren't – what was it? – boarded out, were they?'

'This is different. The government has been doing an annual census of all the horses in the country for years. Now they've called them in.'

'You mean they just *take* them?'

'Well, they buy them from you, but you can't refuse to

sell. The army keeps about twenty-five thousand horses in peacetime, now they suddenly need a hundred thousand. Where else can they get them from? It says on the requisition form that my darlings will be "officers' chargers", for what comfort that is, and they pay me seventy-five pounds for each, which I suppose is generous, given that they *could* just take them.' She took out her handkerchief and blew her nose briskly, then resumed in a matter-of-fact voice, 'Well, the army has to have horses, so there's no sense in complaining. I'm afraid there won't be much for you to do up here. You can have a ride on Captain or Blaze whenever you like, of course.'

'Thank you,' Sadie said, swallowing a lump in her throat. 'I wanted to help, not just enjoy myself.'

'I know. But there's nothing to do. Still, you are welcome to come up any time. I'm always glad to see you.' She scratched a bit of dried mud from her boot with the end of a stick. 'Seventy-five pounds a head!' She sighed. 'They were my whole life. I've always worked with horses, always had them around.'

'I'm sure you'll think of something,' Sadie said.

'You're very sweet,' Mrs Cuthbert said, 'but I really don't know what.'

Sadie stood with empty loose-boxes at her back, and empty fields all around. 'Highclere without horses,' she said. 'It's hard to believe.'

'I'm afraid we must all expect to make sacrifices when there's a war on,' Mrs Cuthbert said.

Sadie stayed for luncheon at Highclere – bread and cheese eaten comfortably in the tack-room with Mrs Cuthbert and the grooms – and helped with some tack-cleaning afterwards, not because the grooms couldn't manage it but for the pleasure of their company. She cycled home at teatime, and arrived so closely behind David that he was still on the front sweep, unloading his luggage from the farm cart that had given him a lift from the station, and feeling around in his pockets for a tip.

'David!' Sadie cried, with a huge surge of excitement. 'I'm so glad you're home. It didn't seem right for you to be away in Scotland with all this happening.'

'Scotland's off,' David said cheerfully. 'Oliphant's pater got called back for a government job, so the shooting was cancelled, and we all came back to Town together. Mrs O's opening up the house again so he can be comfortable.'

Beattie stood at the door, her hands clasped for much the same reason as nuns did it: the avoidance of temptation. Her heart was tripping and she was stopping herself rushing out and clasping her boy to her bosom, which would have embarrassed him. But, oh, the *love*, surging upwards like an unstoppable fountain! Her boy, her beautiful boy; her firstborn and favourite; home again, thank God!

He looked so handsome, and so heart-breakingly grown-up, dealing like a man with the carter. The children were divided in looks, as one might expect them to be. Sadie and William were like Edward, with his narrow dark face and rounded chin, his brown curly hair and brown eyes. Peter was all her, flaxen and blue-eyed, while Bobby and Diana, the good-looking ones, had managed to combine their parents' features – Diana to stunning effect. She had Edward's neat, straight features in Beattie's heart-shaped face, her hair was wheatfield gold, rather than mousy like Bobby's, and instead of ordinary blue, she had those marvellous eyes that people called hazel for want of an apt description of their uniqueness.

But David wasn't like either of them. Beattie thought he resembled her father a little. As a child, Diana had used to say he looked like a Red Indian, with his high cheekbones, jutting nose and strong chin. He even had a hint of red in his dark brown hair, which grew so vigorously from his head, as if forced outward by the pressure of the thoughts inside. (Did Red Indians have red hair? Beattie had no idea, but Diana-the-child had thought they must, to merit the name.)

He was the clever one, always so full of energy and ideas, not bubbling and charming, like Bobby, but thoughtful and determined. Beside him, Bobby seemed a lightweight, an electric brougham to a steam locomotive. And though, with his hawklike face, you wouldn't call David handsome, like Bobby, whenever he turned to look at her, he stopped Beattie's heart.

He had dealt with the carter, and Sadie had dropped her bicycle and was jumping around him like a puppy and hugging him. Others were coming to the door: Ada, dragging Henry behind her to take David's bags, giving him shy smiles that made her for a moment almost pretty. David was Ada's favourite. Nula had favoured Diana from the moment she was born, and Ada had stepped in, glad of the excuse, to ensure David did not feel ousted by his baby sister.

Diana appeared in the hall now, drawn from her listless reading on the sofa by something that promised to vary the monotony of another Charles-less day; Bobby arrived shortly behind her from the garden where he had been trying to teach Nailer tricks. Nailer co-operated in these periodical lessons because Bobby used biscuits as inducements to learn.

And here was Edward, coming to stand beside Beattie, laying a warm hand on her shoulder and squeezing it briefly in – what? – admonition? Comfort? It would have touched her, if she had had emotional energy to spare from the return of her darling.

David came towards them now, gently detaching Sadie so that he could kiss his mother and shake his father's hand.

'Good to have you back,' Edward said.

David bestowed a brief smile on Diana and Bobby, and said, 'It's good to be back. Where are the others?'

'Both out to tea,' Sadie supplied.

'Oh, tea! I'm starved. Is it nearly tea-time, darling Ada? Please say it is.'

Ada gave the impression of throwing her head back and baying with pleasure. 'I'll go and tell Cook to hurry it up. She'll be that glad you're home!'

'He's only been gone a fortnight,' Diana threw after her disparagingly, as she galloped past. 'It's not as if he's . . .' She searched around for a simile.

'Odysseus returning after ten years of wandering,' Bobby suggested.

'Quite,' said Diana, loftily, to disguise the fact that she couldn't remember anything about Odysseus. Was he the one who cleaned the Augean stables? Or was that Horatius? School seemed a long time ago. 'You haven't been gone long enough for anything to have happened. There's no news,' she told David.

Except for the war, Sadie thought.

'As it happens, *I* have news,' David said.

'Oh, what? Do tell!' Sadie urged.

'Over tea,' David said.

How typical of him, Beattie thought. Bobby would have blurted it out straight away – whatever it was. A chill thought touched her. It wasn't going to be about Sophy Oliphant, was it? Or some other young woman? *Please, God, not love already. Let me keep him a little longer.* She stepped aside to let him come past her, and touched him lightly on the arm as he passed, as if that might create a conduit to his thoughts. But she received no more than a brief smile from him as she turned to follow him.

'Where are we having it?' he asked. 'In the garden?'

'Of course,' said Sadie, appropriating from Henry the last of the luggage – a tennis racquet and a pair of cricket boots – and carrying them over the threshold. 'On a day like this? Tea under the walnut tree.'

'The English idyll,' David said.

'Complete with caterpillars and wasps,' Bobby said, following.

They chatted idly as they settled under the tree and waited for tea to appear. Family talk, satisfying and inconsequential, the small change of existence, the foundation of a balanced life. Beattie said nothing, studying her boy, wondering about the 'news', trying to discern if there was any change in him that might give her a clue. But he talked and smiled just as usual: capable, in that way he had, of holding back for his own chosen moment; showing the control that was so un-boy-like.

And at last Ethel and Ada came staggering out under laden trays. Cook had evidently felt an ordinary Saturday tea was not good enough, and had gone wild, adding cucumber sandwiches and gentleman's relish sandwiches (David's favourite), to the usual bread and butter and jam, and freshly made scones as well as cake (the rest of the ginger loaf from yesterday cut into slices, and a whole unbroached fruit cake that Beattie supposed had been meant for Sunday). The fatted calf for the prodigal returned, she thought. Diana was right, it had only been two weeks. Why did it have such an air of significance about it?

Beattie poured, watching her own hand and marvelling at how steady it was, hearing herself tell Bobby in an everyday voice to pass his brother the sandwiches. Sadie jumped up and helped hand around, then squeezed on to the short bench beside Bobby and said to David, 'So what *is* this news of yours? Come on, tell. We've all got our tea and we're dying of curiosity.'

No, don't tell, Beattie thought, in last-minute alarm. News at David's age tended to be news of change, and she didn't want change. It had been hard enough his going away to university. She didn't want him to grow up any more.

He looked around the group, seeming pleased with himself, his eyes – an intense, dark blue – alight with anticipation. 'All right, I'll tell,' he said. 'Hold on to your hats, everyone. I've enlisted!'

CHAPTER FIFTEEN

Edward almost laughed, not with amusement but with surprise, at himself more than anything. He was the only one in the family who knew either of the length of time the war was expected to last or that a huge new army of volunteers was to be sought; and yet for some reason it had not occurred to him that *his* son would be involved.

War had always been the army's business, and the army had always been a thing apart, fed largely by the same tight, impermeable community. You were either an army family or you were not. Beattie's father had been army, but the link had been broken when he'd had two daughters and no sons, and his daughters had married Outsiders. And he – Major Cazalet – was dead too long ago to have influenced his grandsons. Jack had been an anomaly and, despite him, Edward had never thought them an army family. It had never entered into his calculations.

And now here was David, beaming round at them with delight in having taken the shilling, gone for a soldier, heeded the trumpet call, joined the colours. Perhaps it was in the blood, after all. Beattie would be pleased.

'How did it happen?' he asked.

'Well, when we got back to London, Oliphant and I decided to walk from the station to stretch our legs. I wasn't meaning to come home straight away, you see. He said I might as well have a bit of a holiday in town, since Scotland was a wash-out. Had a conscience about me, you see – what a fellow he is for worrying! Talked about theatre tickets and Marie Lloyd at the Holborn Empire and a lecture series at University College. A man of wide tastes is our Oliphant. You'd never think it to look at him, but when—'

'Never mind all that,' Diana interrupted. 'Tell us about enlisting.'

'Oh. Right. Well, we were walking from the station, as I mentioned, and we bumped into a sergeant major – literally bumped, I mean. We were talking nineteen to the dozen and not looking where we were going – although,' he added thoughtfully, 'I'm beginning to wonder if it was completely an accident. He could have got out of our way all right. Anyway,' he went on hastily, as Diana glared at him, 'he was a wonderful fellow, chest like a barrel, enormous moustaches, and he sort of set us back on our feet as if we were a couple of kittens. And he said, "Now then, young gentlemen, where are you off to?" So Oliphant said, "Nowhere in particular," and added something vague about the Holborn Empire, because that's what we'd just been talking about, and the sergeant major said, "Fit young fellows like you hanging around a music hall when there's a real empire to defend? Why don't you enlist? Your king and country need you."

'Well, Oliphant and I hadn't given a thought to it, but the moment he said it, it seemed obvious. The sergeant major said he was opening up a recruitment centre at New Scotland Yard. He said there would be a general call next week for volunteers but he could take us now, if we cared to go along with him. So I looked at Oliphant and he looked at me, and we grinned like a couple of monkeys and said, "Right you are!"

'He marched off and we followed, and when we got there we found that it really was only just being set up – people moving furniture about and putting notices up. But the officer in charge was very decent, and said they had

203

everything they needed to sign us up, and made a little joke about using us to practise on.'

'Practise on!' Sadie exclaimed. 'Are you sure you've really enlisted?'

'Don't worry, it's all pukka,' David said. 'He asked us questions and filled in a form, and a medico examined us all over and said we were a couple of prize specimens. So we signed the paper and took the oath, and went to another room where a chappie measured us for our uniforms. Then we were issued with a kitbag and a list of what we can put in it, and the officer told us to go home and said we'd get a message in the next few days to tell us where to report. So I thought I'd better come straight back here, 'fess to what I'd done and make my adieux.'

He smiled around, obviously not thinking that his 'confession' would incur any penance. But in the brief silence that followed his words, before anyone else could comment, Beattie said, in a cold voice, 'No. I forbid it.'

David looked at her, puzzled. 'Mother?'

'You will *not* enlist.'

'But – I already have,' David said, hesitant, not understanding her objection. 'I've taken the oath and everything.'

'Then you can *un*-take it. I don't care what you've said, I'm not letting you join the army.'

'But I thought you'd be pleased. Grandpa was in the army. I'm following in his footsteps.'

'He was a soldier. You're a civilian – and you're just a boy. You don't know the first thing about it.'

He looked at Edward. 'Father? You approve, don't you?'

Before Edward could speak, Beattie snapped, 'I won't allow it, and that's that. Your father will get you out of it.'

'I don't want to get out of it,' David protested. 'And once you've signed—'

'You're under age.'

'Not for the army. As long as you're over eighteen—'

204

'I don't care!' She stood up, and her plate, which she had forgotten she was holding on her lap, fell to the grass. Nailer emerged from under Sadie's chair and quietly made hay. 'You're not going, and that's my last word!' She turned and walked fast into the house, leaving an awkward silence behind.

David, who had risen automatically, sat again with a dazed expression. He turned to Edward. 'I'm sorry I've upset her, but – you understand, don't you, Father?'

'I think it's what I would have done in your place,' Edward said, 'but you *are* very young.'

'They need young men, the officer said so. And I'm twenty – not exactly a boy.'

'I think it's capital!' Bobby said eagerly. 'I can't think why Mother's batey about it. You'd think she'd be throwing bouquets. Jolly well done, David old man. I'm proud of you. Off to give the Hun a bloody nose! For king and country!'

'You have another year of university to go,' Edward said, for Beattie's sake rather than from conviction.

'I can finish it afterwards,' David said earnestly. 'The war will be over by Christmas, so I'll only be losing a term. As Oliphant said, if we don't join now and get in while we can, we'll miss the whole show.' The words 'over by Christmas' touched the back of Edward's neck like a cold finger. But David went on before he could speak. 'This is more important than Latin and Greek. The honour of the country is at stake. And,' he pressed on, 'I can't get out of it, even if I wanted to. Please, Father, make Mother understand.'

'I'll talk to her,' Edward said.

'I don't want to go with her feeling bad about it. I want her blessing.'

You may have to do without that, Edward thought, but he didn't say so aloud.

He expected to find her weeping, but she was sitting on the edge of the bed, dry-eyed and stony-faced. She lifted a resentful look to him as he came in. 'I suppose you've come to talk me around.'

'No,' he said, taking the little chair beside the dressing-table. 'I don't think that comes into it. He can't take back the oath.'

'You can get him out of it.'

'I can't. And even if I could, I wouldn't. How would it look if we held our son back when others were going?'

'I don't care how it looks. He's too young.'

He stared at her. 'I don't understand why you're upset. I thought you loved him.'

'I thought you did.' The words came back as fast as a tennis volley, surprising them both. Edward opened his mouth to reply and closed it again. 'Men get killed in war,' she said. 'Had you conveniently forgotten that?'

He couldn't let that pass. 'Conveniently?' he queried, with a hint of steel under the question.

She turned her head away. 'Forgotten it, anyway. A mother doesn't forget. I gave him life. He belongs to me. I don't consent to his getting pointlessly killed.'

'He won't get killed, and it isn't pointless,' Edward said, his voice gentle again. 'We're facing a deadly danger. If the Germans take France, they'll invade England next. We have to fight for our lives, for the very existence of our nation.'

'Let someone else fight,' said Beattie. 'Not my son.'

'Every soldier is some woman's son,' Edward said.

'I don't care,' Beattie cried. 'Don't you understand? I don't *care*! Let them die. Let them all die. But not *my* son!'

Then the tears came. She turned and flung herself face down on the bed to hide them, an intemperate and strangely young movement for a grown woman with six children. He got up and went to put his arms round her, but she thrust him away with a violent hand. He stood watching her for a moment, and then some small voice in the recesses of his mind said, *Better let her have it out*. It sounded like ancient wisdom remembered from somewhere, but it might simply have been cowardice disguising itself. However, he didn't know what else to do, so he crept quietly out, closing the door behind him.

David met him anxiously at the foot of the stairs. 'Is she – all right about it now?'

Edward made a gesture that was almost a shrug. 'It's the shock,' he excused. 'None of us was expecting it.'

'I thought you'd both be so pleased,' he said, crestfallen. 'It's a good thing, isn't it? A noble thing?'

'She'll get over it. Give her time.'

'I want her to understand. You too – but her most of all.'

'Women's minds work differently.' He laid a hand briefly on David's shoulder (had to lift the hand to do it – the boy was taller than him now) and went away to his study. He needed to be alone for a while.

Beattie's tears were fierce and brief. When you got past twenty, you hadn't the luxury of long spells of weeping. It was as if the reservoir had never properly refilled from the thwarted-love years. Sorrows were felt deep, but hard and dry, more like a killing frost than healing rain. She was sitting at the dressing-table patting her face with lavender water, preparing to go down again and join her family, when the tap on the door came. She knew who it was. She could feel her heart beating light and fast, like a bird's. She said, 'Come in.'

He was carrying a cup and saucer. 'I thought you might like some tea. You didn't finish your cup,' he said. He examined her face anxiously. She hoped he didn't know her well enough to see the aftermath of tears. Children didn't really look at their parents' faces. Parents were just shapes with labels attached to them, 'Mother' and 'Father'; as flat and featureless as those cardboard figures on the beach with the hole to put your head through for the amusing photograph. She hoped she might rely on superficiality now.

'Thank you,' she said, and held out a steady hand.

He gave her the cup. 'I'm sorry I upset you,' he said humbly.

She stitched on a smile. 'It was just the shock of it,' she said. 'I'm all right now.'

Relief bloomed in his face. 'I want you to be proud of me.'

'I am,' she said. 'It didn't need this to make me proud of you.'

'But I do want you to understand, Mummy.' The childhood name, long abandoned, pierced her with the sharpest stiletto in love's armoury. Oh, children knew how to hurt you! And that they didn't mean to didn't make the pain any less real.

He sat down in the chair Edward had vacated, and folded his hands together between his knees, leaning forward a little in his eagerness to explain. She wanted to stroke the springing force of his hair, feel its unexpected silkiness and the hard curve of his skull underneath.

'You see,' he said, 'before this, Oliphant and I had been talking about things – about Life.' It was clear from his voice that the word had a capital letter. 'Being at Oxford feels so terribly sterile. We read all the time about man's aspiration, about noble deeds, making the world a better place and all the rest of it. We read about it and talk about it but we don't *do* it. I have energy and brains and strength, and to use them for nothing but writing essays seems pitiful. You do *see*, Mother? I felt – well, that there must be something *honourable* somewhere for me to do. Wasn't it Tennyson who said a man's reach must exceed his grasp, or what's Heaven for?'

It was Browning, said her mind, but she didn't say it aloud, not to inject bathos into his high moral flight. He wanted to be *good*, her boy. She had to cling to that. It was not for the swagger and the glory and the excitement that he wanted to go (well, those too, of course – he was a man, after all – but

208

not those first and foremost). The loveliest thing a man could do or be – the thing that, had they only realised, made women love them most – was *good*.

So she said, 'I do understand,' and, seeing the doubt in his eyes, she made it easier for him. 'You can't expect a mother to feel exactly the same way. We worry about your safety. We're built that way. But I do understand.'

His face cleared. She had done it for him, released him to go and take his place in the world of men. In joy, he hastened to give her something back. 'You needn't worry, I won't get hurt. I promise you. I'll come back to you safe and sound.' He flung himself down on his knees to be at the right level to put his arms round her. She put hers around him, laid her cheek a moment against his (so warm! So smooth!) and allowed herself briefly to stroke his hair. Her heart hurt so much she thought the pain would split her in two. She made herself withdraw her hands and push him gently away. Having released him, she must not make it hard for him to go. He should not remember her clinging and tearful. She was a soldier's daughter; now she must be a soldier's mother. From now on, she must only ever show pride.

'Go on down, be with the others. I'll follow in a minute.'

He went.

Everyone was out in the garden, Diana and Edward reading in an embarrassed sort of way, waiting to see how things would come out; Bobby and Sadie fooling around with the dog. Bobby looked round, his expression one of query and awkward sympathy, and said, 'I say, look, I've almost taught old Nailer to stand on his hind legs.'

'Only when you hold his front ones up so he can't help himself,' Sadie objected. 'You mind he doesn't bite you.'

'He won't bite me,' Bobby said, with that superb confidence of his. But he was still looking at David. 'Is Mother all right?'

'Yes,' David said. 'She'll be down in a minute. It was just the shock. She's quite all right about it now.'

'Oh, jolly good!' Bobby said, then lowered his voice so that only David and Sadie could hear. 'Then she'll be all right when I enlist as well. I'm glad you've paved the way.'

David shook his head. 'I'd leave it a bit if I were you. If you try it now it'll be too much for her.' He saw Bobby meant to argue and added the clincher: 'She might cry.'

Bobby looked shocked. 'Cry?' he faltered. 'Mother doesn't cry.'

'But leave it for now, anyway,' David advised seriously.

On Sunday, the first Sunday of the war as Sadie privately thought of it, the church was crowded. The pews were full. There were even some awkward-looking men not usually seen, their faces raw with shaving and scrubbing, their hair still damp from being slicked down with water, standing at the back – whether from diffidence, lack of room, or in the hope of a quick escape, Sadie couldn't tell. Some of them were accompanied by wives and children, all painfully clean and tidy in their cotton prints with scraped-back hair, the children solemn with the atmosphere they could sense.

Everyone was here, Sadie thought. Had they felt a need to communicate with God? To make a special plea, if not for peace then for swift victory, or for the protection of some family member? Some of those awkward men, she thought, might simply have felt it would be imprudent to absent themselves at such a time, or had been bullied into it by their wives, as if God might be keeping score on this morning of all mornings.

But looking around her, she decided in the end that it was simply a need to be there, with everyone else. Northcote had turned out as one: a community drawn together by this new and unknowable state of affairs. She felt it herself – a warmth running through her, a sense that she was not alone, but part of a greater thing; something that spread beyond the walls of the church, even beyond the confines of the village. Today all of England was in church, because all of England was at war. Today the English people were united in endeavour, and she was part of it.

The rector gave a sermon she found hard to follow. She assumed it was her own lack of concentration, but he seemed to veer from loving thy neighbour to condemning the aggression of the enemy, from leaving vengeance to the Lord to reviling the barbarism of the Hun; and when you threw in a diversion through the heart of the Dark Continent, memories of the South African war, notions of honour among the Zulus, and some rather incoherent references to pygmies and missionaries, it made Sadie think that perhaps it wasn't her after all. Perhaps Dr Fitzgerald was more distracted by the war than one might have expected.

As he climbed down from the pulpit, she saw him mop his forehead with a large white handkerchief. Bobby leaned towards her at that moment and whispered, 'Waving the surrender over that sermon, I suppose – and not before time.'

She pressed her fingers to her lips to stop herself giggling, and whispered back, 'What was that about pygmies? The Germans aren't small, are they?'

'I think it was a metaphor. I suspect he believes the Germans need evangelising.'

'Does he think they're heathens, then?'

'Worse than that. Nonconformists,' Bobby said, straight-faced.

Outside in the sunshine – it was a summer that seemed as though it would never end – everyone lingered, talking, no-one wanting to go home just yet. It was like a village fête, Sadie thought. There were no Wroughtons in evidence. She felt a little sorry for Diana, but managed to quell the feeling when her sister was gathered into a group of young people,

211

which included Alec Gordon and another of her young suitors, Ronnie Carruthers.

The rest of the family moved towards a knot of more substantial worshippers gathered round the rector, among whom Sadie recognised not only Mrs and Mrs Cuthbert but Mrs Cuthbert's friend, Colonel Barry of Harewood Lodge. Perhaps spurred on by the military presence, Edward wasted no time in idle chit-chat.

'I must tell you, Rector, that we are about to join that fortunate company of families with sons at war.'

Sadie, startled by the abruptness of the announcement, realised that he just couldn't wait. She had never heard his voice so brimming with pride.

Beattie laid a hand on David's arm, bringing him to the colonel's attention, and said, 'My son David has enlisted.'

Barry beamed and shook David's hand. 'Splendid, splendid! Do you know what regiment you'll be joining?'

'Not yet,' David said, and added a rather embarrassed, but circumspect, 'sir.' 'It all happened rather quickly yesterday morning. I'm just waiting to hear where to present myself.'

'We're proud of him for volunteering,' Edward said. 'He wants to serve his country, and it doesn't matter where.'

'Quite right,' Barry said. 'And they're all good, all with their own traditions. I expect you'll hear tomorrow. The War Office wants to get things moving as quickly as possible.'

'It can't happen too quickly for me, sir,' David said.

Others now offered their congratulations, and David told his story again in more detail. Some asked technical questions he couldn't answer; others were ready with advice, sometimes conflicting, on the absolute necessities a young man should pack for his departure. There was almost a party spirit, as though he had volunteered as a treat for Northcote.

'Well done indeed,' Dr Fitzgerald said. 'Showing a good example to all our young men,' he went on in a louder voice, with a glance towards the knot of sheep hanging around

Diana. 'I hope he will the be first of many. I would like to think our little community will be known in time for having done its part – and perhaps more than its part – in this great endeavour.'

So that's what it was, Sadie thought, *the war: a great endeavour.* The words connected in her mind with *Great Expectations.* She saw for a moment a big, fat book, and as it fell open, the pages riffling, instead of words there were moving pictures inside, of men in uniform marching with rifles sloped, looking proud and expectant, page after page of them, marching from the start of the book towards the finish where, instead of the two words THE END there was just one, in enormous letters, with a golden sunburst behind it: VICTORY.

Her brother was now the hero of a book, she thought. It didn't surprise her. He had always had that look about him; he had always seemed too good for dull, ordinary life.

The rest of the day passed quietly, and in many ways it seemed like any Sunday. There was roast beef and plum tart (such a glut of plums this year – there seemed to be plums in some form at every meal), and when the cheese came in Edward fetched port, and proposed a toast, which all drank – even Peter and William were allowed a sip. 'To David, our very own hero: may he serve his country with honour, and make us even more proud of him than we are already.'

'To David,' they all said.

And David said, unusually shyly for him, 'I'll do my best. I promise I'll never forget I'm a Hunter, and that you're all here at home—' He suddenly couldn't finish, and had to clear his throat and sip more port to cover it.

After dinner, Edward and David went into the study and closed the door. But they came out after a little while and Sunday went on being ordinary again. David had a couple of sets of tennis with Diana, and only just managed to beat her, then played draughts with Peter for a while. William worked on a model aeroplane he was building out of balsawood. Edward and Bobby read the papers, Beattie sewed. Sadie read a book, but didn't get very far with it. She kept stopping to look at her family, as though she had never seen them before. And at David most of all. He seemed somehow to be rimmed with light – as sometimes a cloud is when the sun is directly behind it. There seemed to be a significance about him, though he was doing things she had seen him do a thousand times before. He seemed more than her brother that long afternoon: She puzzled it out, her book lying unread in her lap. He seemed – a representative.

Beattie watched him, too, without appearing to. She felt worn out with the emotions of the day, of the two days. She looked at him as if she could store him up against the famine to come, but somehow the more she looked the less she could see him. She told herself she had grown used to his absence, at school, then at university. Why should this be any different? She didn't know. She only felt that it was.

The telegram came in the afternoon. The boy in his red cap bicycled up to the side gate, guessing they would be out there: everyone was having tea in the garden today. It was Olly Parry's's older brother, Albert, beaded with sweat from the exertion in the hot sun. He handed the telegram to Bobby, who had reached him first.

'It's for you,' Bobby said, turning to David.

There was suddenly a great stillness over the garden. Sadie thought it looked like a painting: the shadows and sunlight sharply delineated, people disposed in various attitudes, frozen in their occupations, faces turned, newspapers and books white in the shadow, the colours of their clothing strong against all the green. It would make a good picture for a jigsaw puzzle, she thought: *The Telegram*. The only movement was Nailer, sitting up to scratch violently behind his ear with a hind foot – but Nailer had always lived in a separate universe, where the rules were different and his own.

Then David rose up from the grass, where he had been stretched out in the shade of the copper beech, and stepped out into the sunshine, which dazzled suddenly on his hair, and threw his shadow blue and dense at his feet.

They gathered round him. 'It's from the War Office,' he said – as if they hadn't guessed. 'I'm to present myself tomorrow morning at St Martin-in-the-Fields, on the forecourt, at nine o'clock.'

Beattie was at his elbow, and tried to read the words over his arm, but they made no sense to her. They were just black marks.

'Tomorrow morning!' David cried. 'I'm off tomorrow morning!'

'My dear boy!' Edward said.

'Congratulations, old man,' Bobby cried, and slapped his shoulder. 'One last night of freedom, eh? You ought to make the most of it.'

But David had turned to Beattie. 'Tomorrow! I'm off tomorrow!' he crowed.

His eyes were full of stars, his lips curved in a beatific smile. His head was limned with light, his face transformed with what he was feeling. She saw it was the moment she had dreaded for years, when she would lose him to a love that would be stronger than the one between mother and son, a love that would define his adult life, as hers had defined his boyhood. He was a boy no longer. Love had carried him over into manhood. She had always assumed that it would be love for a woman; she had prepared herself for that. But he had fallen in love with war.

Still, it didn't matter: it was love all the same, and she would lose him to it.

CHAPTER SIXTEEN

David departed early in the morning, but the whole household was up to see him off. Cook needed no encouragement to have breakfast ready before the usual time. She even rousted Emily out of bed and sent her down to Stein's to get some lamb's kidneys because they were David's favourite. Stein's was not properly open, but Emily went round the back, and discovered for the first time, but not the last, that nothing was too good for 'our brave soldiers'.

'And no charge, either,' the elder Mr Stein said, pressing the pulpy package warmly into her hands. 'You tell Mrs Dunkley they're with the compliments of the house for the young gentleman.'

'Cor! I wouldn't half like to go myself,' said the younger Mr Stein.

'You got a job here,' said Stein Senior sharply. 'Just you get on with boning that lamb. I can't do everything. Only got one pair of hands.'

The sumptuous breakfast was wasted on David, who was too excited to eat much, but when everyone gathered in the hall he was careful to thank Cook specially, and her eyes grew moist as she handed him a wax-paper package of sandwiches, 'For the journey.'

'I'll send you a postcard when I'm settled in,' he promised, and completed her undoing.

He kissed his mother, but she would only allow herself

the briefest touch of her lips to his cheek, and had nothing to say in farewell but 'Take care of yourself.'

'I know,' he said. 'Get to bed early and change my socks if they're wet.' But he couldn't make her smile.

Sadie hugged him hard, and gave him a small fold of card, about two inches square. 'Keep it in your pocket,' she instructed him. 'It's a bit of my lucky white heather. I pressed it and stuck it on for you so you could take it with you.' She had bought it years ago from a gypsy who had come to the door – mainly because the gypsy had had a dog with him. Underneath she had written, *With love from Sadie*.

'I wish I'd thought of giving you something,' William wailed. 'Would you like my postcard of Monsieur Blériot?'

David grinned. 'Thanks, old chap, but you keep it. I shan't be gone that long. Just long enough to become a hero.' He was only half joking. He tucked Sadie's card into his inside breast pocket, picked up his valise, and stepped out into the pale morning sunshine. Edward kissed his wife, laid a hand a moment on her shoulder, and followed.

When Edward and David reached the assembly point, a vast crowd of eager young men had gathered, well ahead of time, each with his kitbag at his feet, a grin from one ear to the other, and a light of excitement dancing in his eyes. The noise of their chatter had sent the pigeons scattering from the roof of the famous church, and they beat endlessly round Trafalgar Square, unable to settle, the clatter of their wings adding to the background sounds of traffic.

A uniformed sergeant was taking names, and issued David with a card that revealed he had joined the North Midland Rifles. 'Pin it on your kitbag, lad,' he was instructed. The new Kitchener Army being formed would have its battalions numbered after the regulars and the Territorials of the same regiment, so David was now to be a founder member of C Company, 7th Battalion. He thought it had a good sound.

Oliphant came pushing through to claim David with relief. 'I've been here ages, looking for you. I thought I'd never find you in such a crowd! Oh, hello, sir,' he said to Edward. 'I didn't see you there. I say, isn't this splendid?' he added, in irrepressible delight. 'A chap said we're going to a camp at Clifton, near Nottingham. We have to march to St Pancras Station – that'll be a lark!'

'Rifles are light infantry, aren't they, Father?' David asked anxiously.

Edward gathered he was afraid 'light' meant 'inferior'. 'That's right,' he said. 'The light infantry is always in the forefront. They're known for their self-discipline and initiative, so they need the most intelligent recruits.'

'I say, Oliphant, it seems we're the cream!' David said.

'I never doubted it.' Oliphant grinned. 'All these chaps look like first-rate fellows, don't you think?'

David turned back to Edward. 'You needn't stay any longer, Father. I shall be all right now. Thanks awfully for coming in with me.'

Edward understood himself dismissed, shook David's hand briefly, and departed. It was rather like the first day at school, he thought: a fellow needed to make his impression, and could be embarrassed in front of his peers by lingering parents or effusive farewells.

'He's jolly decent, your pater,' Oliphant commented, when he had gone. 'Was your mater in tears this morning?'

'No, but she never cries,' David said. 'Anyway, her father was a soldier, so this is all quite normal for her.'

'Mine cries at everything,' Oliphant admitted. 'But she can't help it. I say, I'm getting awfully hungry. Did you have any brekker?'

'Not much. Couldn't face it, somehow. But I've got

sandwiches in my bag,' he remembered. 'I'll share them with you as soon as we settle down somewhere.'

The march to St Pancras – it was odd to be seeing such familiar landmarks as Piccadilly Circus and Regent Street from this new perspective – was attended by cheers and waves from those they passed, and at the terminus they were sent on their way by a band and a host of press photographers.

'I wonder which paper the picture will be in,' Oliphant said. 'I know my mater would love a copy.'

'She'll have to buy them all, just in case,' said David.

'Pity we're still in plain clothes, though.'

'Never mind. We're soldiers now. That's all that matters.'

'Soldiers!' Oliphant said, and they looked at each other, startled for a moment, then laughed. It seemed an idea both absurd and profound, strange and natural.

'I feel as if this is what my whole life is for,' David said.

'Me too,' said Oliphant.

As the train steamed northwards through the countryside, the young men settled down, lit gaspers, swapped histories. Some read papers, some played cards, some tipped their caps over their eyes and slept. David stared out of the window, gripped with an almost unbearable sense of excitement, of something wonderful beginning.

Oliphant said, 'Sounds like hunger to me. How about those sandwiches?'

A uniformed sergeant, a man in his fifties, rather fat and very knowing, came round to check everyone's names off against a list.

Oliphant gave his name. 'Initials?' the sergeant asked.

'F. A.' said Oliphant. He was Frederick Arbuthnot.

The sergeant grinned. 'I wouldn't tell anyone that if I were you, laddie. F-A stands for something else in the army.'

'What did he mean?' Oliphant asked, when he had gone. 'What does it stand for?'

One of the other lads, without removing the cap from over his eyes, enlightened him. Oliphant had not heard the word said aloud before, and blushed.

The train eventually stopped at what seemed like a country station, and there was tremendous banging of doors and shouting as they were ordered to alight. There seemed to be nothing but green countryside all around. A station-master and a porter leaned on the picket fence and a broom respectively, watching them with impassive, northern eyes. Beyond the fence was a lorry. *Oh, good*, David thought. He liked to walk as much as the next chap, but he'd done as much today as he wanted to.

The sergeant was going along the train, repeating, 'Chuck your kitbag into the back of the lorry and form up in the road.'

They obeyed, though it was rather more wandering than forming up. As they passed the lorry, David saw it was the only one there, and asked the driver, 'How far is it to the camp?'

'Six miles, chum. Give or take.'

'And how do we get there?'

'Shanks's,' he said laconically. 'What d'you think?'

'Come on, come on, my lads.' The sergeant was chivvying them. 'Let's have you in fours. It's only six miles, then there'll be a lovely brew-up.'

David hurried into position beside Oliphant, not wanting to be separated from him. Oliphant was staring sadly at his feet. David felt more cheerful for his friend's gloomy expression. 'Never mind, F-A,' he said. 'Six miles is nothing, now we're in practice.'

The camp was a field on a shallow hill, with rows of white bell-tents on one side, and some wooden huts down the other. As soon as they arrived, they were paraded, the two sergeants – old soldiers who had come out of retirement to train the volunteers – shepherding them good-naturedly into position. David glanced across the throng. Every man had been ordered to attend in plain clothes, cap, stick and overcoat, and being tall, he saw a sea of caps, almost as if that were the uniform of his new battalion. It made him smile.

As soon as they were lined up, an elderly, well-built man in khaki uniform, breeches and riding boots walked out in front of them. He had large white moustaches and looked to be in his sixties. He was followed by a lean, scholarly-looking man in tweeds.

'Well, men,' he began, and at once every lingering whisper and movement ceased, 'I am your commanding officer, Colonel W. J. Acton, and this is my adjutant, Captain Devine. You, as I am sure you now know, are the 7th Battalion, North Midland Rifles. I would like to remind you that you are associated with an old and proud regiment, the North Midland, which has a fine record, and looking at you here today . . .' he swept his gaze theatrically across them '. . . I'm sure I don't need to urge you to uphold that reputation.' He paused a moment for effect. *The old boy's a showman*, David thought, yet he felt a thrill of pride all the same that made him stand up a fraction straighter.

'Now, I don't want to keep you long,' Acton went on. 'You've had a long journey and you want to get settled in. I would just like to ask you to practise punctuality, particularly on early-morning parades. Some of you may be used to rising at a set time each day, others may not. To all of you I say, as soon as the bugle sounds Reveille, get up at once, so that you have plenty of time to get ready. Face the new day with enthusiasm, and that will carry you through whatever it brings. I want you to be out of the lines each morning *before* the actual time of parade.' His eyes swept them again, and the moustaches moved in a manner that suggested he was smiling under there. 'And I may tell you

221

that coffee will be served to you each morning before you go on parade.'

'Thank God for that,' someone behind David whispered.

The colonel marched away, and the sergeants took over. The one David had seen on the train was Sergeant Green, and he addressed them.

'Sergeant Morris is going to allocate you tents. Any groups who want to bunk together, go and see him together. Eight to a tent. But, first, anyone here know Swedish drill? Any trained teachers?' One or two hands went up. 'Come and see me. You're going to be NCOs – lance corporals, acting, unpaid, and if you make the grade, in three months' time you'll be made official, and that's an extra threepence a day on your pay. No more teachers? All right, anyone been a Boy Scout leader? Boys' Brigade? All right, we'll have you, too. See what sort of army NCOs you make. All right, the rest of you, find your tent, get settled in. And just so's you know, the next bugle call you hear means grub's up.'

Now it was Oliphant who said, 'Thank God for that. Those sandwiches seem like ancient history.'

The rest of the afternoon was spent in getting settled into their new home, filling palliasses, finding their way around, then reading and starting to learn the contents of a thick white booklet called 'Orders for Camp', which gave instructions on everything from saluting to the care of tents to hints on marching.

After supper, almost everyone spent the evening in the canteen, pints in hand, singing their way through all the latest popular songs and the old favourites. With everyone crammed together in that small space, the atmosphere was stifling, not only with heat and smoke but an excess of emotion.

David slipped out when he had finished his pint, and sat on the grass just outside, listening to his new brothers crooning 'Nellie Dean' in four-part harmony, and feeling

222

deeply content. They were all such good, decent chaps, and the whole afternoon had been marked by a complete lack of 'side', everyone helping everyone else, as if they really were brothers. No, better than that – because brothers could be difficult at times – as if they were pals.

After a bit, Oliphant came out looking for him, squatted beside him and offered his cigarettes. They lit up, and sat smoking for a while, watching the moths banging against the lit white sides of the tents. Then Oliphant said, 'Well? What do you think?'

'I think it's going to be wonderful,' David said.

That Monday, the 10th of August, the first contingents of the British Expeditionary Force embarked for France, following the advance parties that had gone two days earlier. The stations in London were crowded with khaki hordes, journeys disrupted as trains were commandeered to carry them to the ports, where every cargo ship and ferry had been pressed into service for the crossing.

Eighty thousand men, plus kit, rifles and ammunition, horses and field guns, stores, forage and sundry pieces of equipment, from a senior officer's motor-car to a farrier's mobile forge, all had to be assembled, transported and loaded. To achieve such a mobilisation in just over a week was a notable feat, and a tribute to the meticulous planning that had gone into the War Book over the last three years.

While waiting for the stunning victory that would sell unprecedented numbers of copies, the newspapers filled their space with long articles and homilies about *How To Be Useful in Wartime*. The most common advice, calculated to appeal to the Puritan streak that seemed mysteriously to underpin the hedonism of the British character, was to practise self-sacrifice and economy. There must be no waste, no extravagance, no unnecessary consumption. There were calls for theatres, picture-palaces, music halls and the like to be closed for the duration of the war so that the people might concentrate on more serious matters.

'Hoarding' was fast becoming the eighth Deadly Sin. Cook railed against it at her daily séance with her mistress when she discovered Williamson's had run out of baking powder. 'I've read in the paper, madam, about people fighting like wolves in the shops, carrying stuff off by the carload. It isn't right.'

Beattie had read the same sort of rumours; also the counter-argument, that it was a good thing for everyone to stock up while it was still possible to replace the goods. The argument only existed in the world of print, however: in the real world, either quietly or noisily, everyone laid in whatever they could get hold of.

'The government ought to do something about it,' Cook went on. 'Send the hoarders to prison, the selfish brutes, and confiscate their wicked stores.'

'But how would you be able to tell a hoarder from someone who had just prudently laid in stocks, like us?' Beattie asked.

Cook was offended. 'There's a world of difference, madam.' She changed tack. 'And look how prices are shooting up. The price of bread's nearly doubled. That's profiteering, that is.' Profiteering was set to become the ninth Deadly Sin.

Beattie could tell that Cook was just unsettled by David's going off to war, and wanted something to gripe about. She reverted to the original problem. 'We'll have to manage without baking powder as best we can,' she said. 'Can't you use bicarbonate of soda? There's a package in the bathroom cabinet.'

'I suppose so, madam,' Cook said, and turned away. 'Getting rich off the back of the war, while our boys are out there risking their lives . . .' she muttered, as she left.

I hope not, Beattie thought. *Not for a long while yet.*

'I'm stepping out for ten minutes.'

'Very good, sir,' said Warren.

Edward put on his hat and walked round the corner to St James's Street, where his wine merchant, Hoppner, had his shop on the corner of Ryder Street.

'I've been wondering,' Edward said, 'whether I ought to lay in a little extra.'

Hoppner caught his meaning. 'A number of our gentlemen have been asking the same thing. If the Germans should advance as far as the vineyards—'

'I was thinking more of the army taking up all the shipping.'

'I think,' said Hoppner, laying the tips of his fingers together, 'that capacity will be found. The governance of this country could not carry on without fine wine. The Palace, both Houses, not to mention Horseguards – pressure will be brought to bear. But if you have room in your cellars, I would advise taking delivery now, in case things get more difficult later.'

'That's what I thought,' said Edward.

Hoppner beamed. 'Very good, Mr Hunter. I still have some of the 1893 Château Margaux you liked so much. And the 1898 Ducru Beaucaillou is drinking very nicely now.'

'I'll have a dozen of each,' said Edward.

'Just let me get the order book. One dozen cases . . . Very good. And, if I may recommend – I know you are fond of Haut-Brion. The 1898 is quite excellent. It wants yet a year or two for perfection, but if it should be a long war . . .'

'You've heard that?'

Hoppner looked grave. 'I had it from Lord Overton, who is very close to Lord Kitchener, that a war of several years must be anticipated.'

'Yes, I heard the same,' Edward said.

'In which case, the very least one requires for civilisation to survive is an adequate supply of sound wines. Now, the 1899s are promising to be very good. Some are drinking now, and some want keeping. I would like you to consider the Lynch-Bages . . .'

They settled down to a satisfying conversation. There was hoarding, and then there was prudence.

Mrs Cuthbert wasn't the only one to lose horses to the army. The War Book had provided for one hundred and twenty thousand horses to be commandeered in the first instance, and these were not only officers' chargers, but heavy horses and vanners to pull the army's guns and supply wagons. Now the farmers and tradesmen were having their workhorses taken away, and there were protests and sometimes near-fisticuffs when the requisitioning officers appeared with their dockets.

On Wednesday a special train pulled up in the siding at Northcote station and the yard was full of horses being led in and tied up. Some of the bereaved had gathered there too, either to say a last goodbye or make a last protest. Elijah Parry of Parry's Farm had followed his horses down, and was now complaining to anyone who would listen, which included Sadie, even though she was only a female.

'They've took my Duke and Boxer,' he cried. 'How am I s'posed to get my harvest in?'

'If you wasn't so far behindhand,' said Phil Digby, the horseman from Sharpe's Farm, 'you'd've got it in already.'

He had insisted on leading the two they were taking from Sharpe's himself, to make sure they weren't upset, and were loaded properly. 'You can't tell if these soldiers know anything about horses,' he explained *sotto voce* to Sadie. They were beautifully groomed, as always, two grey Percheron types, and Sadie appreciated how much hard work it took to get a shine on a grey coat. They were full sisters, and identical. Dolly had a red ribbon on her forelock and Molly had a purple one, but Sadie knew Phil could tell them apart, if no-one else could. They were standing quietly, looking around with interest at this new scene, nosing at him gently from time to time as they waited to know his pleasure. Sadie had come over to stroke them, and wished she had brought something in her pockets as they whiffled hopefully in her palms.

Parry was looking sour at the implied criticism. 'Well, we all know *you*'re a parable of virtue,' he sneered. 'S'pose you tell me how *you*'re goin' to do the work without 'orses. Pull the plough yerself, I don't doubt.'

'They said they'd send us a mule,' Digby said, as though his heart wasn't breaking. 'Everyone's got to make sacrifices. There's a war on.'

'Well, it ain't *my* war!' Parry retorted. 'I never asked for it. An' sojers got to be fed, ain't they? Got to get my harvest in, got to plough an' harrow. How's a mool goin' to replace my Duke an' Boxer? You tell me that!'

'We'll just have to do our best,' Digby said quietly. He held the halter ropes in one hand, and with the other caressed a silken, firmly muscled neck. Dolly blew through her nostrils, and dipped her head to rub away an itch against her knee. Molly shifted her weight from one hind leg to the other.

One of the clerks from the coal office joined them. 'They've took two of Charringtons' shires,' he offered. 'Dunno how they'll get the coal delivered. Good job it's summer . . . An' Boyle's the greengrocer's had their vanner took. S'pose he could manage with a pony. They're not takin' ponies. Not yet,' he added doubtfully.

Captain Casimir came up to Digby at last and said, 'We're ready for these two now.' The soldier with him reached for the ropes.

For an instant Digby's hand wouldn't let go. He looked down at it as though it was not attached to him, then up at the soldier, searching his face. 'You'll be gentle with 'em?'

'Course, mate,' the soldier said automatically, reaching again.

Digby drew his hand back. 'I mean it. Don't hit 'em. They've never been hit in their lives. They'll do anything for

227

you if you're gentle and quiet. If you hit 'em it'll break their hearts.'

Casimir looked into Digby's face for the first time, and his expression altered. 'They'll be all right,' he said, briefly but kindly.

'I been wiv 'orses all me life,' the soldier said reassuringly. But they both knew – as Sadie now realised – that this was only the start. Who knew where they would go and who would handle them in the future? Horses, like men, were going to have to take their chance.

The soldier took the rope, and clicked his tongue. 'Come on, then, girlies, come along.' The mares started forward. The soldier looked back over his shoulder. 'D'you want the ribbons back?'

Digby was unable to speak, but he shook his head, and stood like a stone, his throat working, watching them walk away. They stepped delicately for such large animals – like cats, Sadie thought.

A decision had to be made about the annual holiday in Bournemouth. A telegram had come from the owner of the hotel asking them politely but firmly to confirm their usual booking, as requests for rooms were unexpectedly high. They went to the same hotel every year for the second half of August, and closed the house – Munt kept an eye on it, since he had always sooner be in 'his' garden than at home with his wife. If Edward needed to come back to Town, as he sometimes did, he stayed at his club, which had its annual closure in the first two weeks.

The servants had their holiday at the same time: Cook went to her married sister in Folkestone, and took Emily with her, since she wasn't thought fit to be left alone. Ada went to stay with a friend in Watford. No-one knew what Ethel did – she hadn't been with them last summer.

But Edward said he could not be away from the bank,

and Beattie did not like to go without him for a whole fortnight. David was away, Bobby said he was too old for sandcastles, and Diana did not want to absent herself in case Charles Wroughton called.

'I think the other three would prefer to be here,' Beattie said. 'The war is enough of a change for them.'

'Cancel, then,' Edward said. 'I'd sooner be at home than staying at the club. One's more comfortable.'

'I'm not sure that will be the case,' Beattie said. 'The servants will still have to have their holiday, you know.'

'Then how will you manage?'

'Ada says she can cook while Cook is away, as long as we don't want anything elaborate. I can help her, and she can go when Cook comes back. And the girls can do a little dusting – it won't kill them.'

But when they were asked, the servants all said they would stay too, and take their leave as days off, staggering them to cover the work. 'It's our patriotic duty, madam,' Cook said, and Ada nodded. Nobody asked Emily, but she was relieved not to have to go to Folkestone: she didn't like Cook's sister, and she was never allowed out of the house on her own, which made for very dull days.

So Beattie sent a telegram saying they would not be coming. Cook said, 'I read in the paper, madam, that there's more people at the seaside this year than ever before because of the war. I don't quite see why,' she added, in a puzzled tone, 'but anyway, you wouldn't have liked the crowds, I'm sure. Probably best you all stay at home.'

Mrs Oliver said, 'I must say I'm rather glad. Gerald and I aren't going away – it seemed wrong, somehow, with all this going on – but of course one still wants one's pleasures, and the sudden exodus in August can be rather depressing. I hate the look of empty houses. Now, we must think about what we can get up to keep ourselves amused. Parties and outings and so on.'

229

Beattie gave a small smile. 'Do you think the rector would approve? Aren't we all supposed to be practising austerity and seriousness of purpose?'

'My dear,' said Mrs Oliver, 'I don't propose to ask him.'

CHAPTER SEVENTEEN

David's first letter had been little more than an acknowledgement of his arrival. His second, which arrived on Friday
the 14th, was more detailed.

There are four companies, three sleep in tents, while
D Company sleeps in the huts. They say huts will be
built for the rest of us before the cold weather. The
other chaps are splendid fellows, all pretty intelligent.
They are mostly of the clerk sort, some drivers and
warehousemen, some teachers and quite a few
students, and in our tent we have a postman, Collins,
who ought to have the advantage of us when it comes
to marching!

So what do we do all day? Well, we are woken,
shockingly, at 5.45, to wash and shave. Eight men with
cut-throat razors in a confined space, most of them still
half asleep. It's a wonder we still have all our features!
After very welcome coffee, we parade for Swedish Drill.
Hopping round the field on one leg may look ridiculous
and far remote from the supreme object of killing
Germans, but it's important in getting us fit, and we've
all taken it up with enthusiasm. After that comes a
hearty breakfast of bread, bacon and tea, and at 9.30
we parade again for marching and squad drill, which
goes on, with a break for lunch, until 4.45. We turn in

at nine o'clock. There must be silence from 9.45 until Reveille at 5.45, which is harder on some of us than others. Why is it you always think of something you *must* say just after silence is called? However, after so much fresh air, we sleep like babes.

As you can imagine, with all this physical exercise, food is uppermost in our hearty young minds. I can report the grub here is very fair. Not, of course, up to Cook's standard, but at least there's plenty of it. Our main meal comes in the middle of the day and is usually stew – not 'like Mother makes', but we are so hungry by then we could eat a horse. Oliphant says 'we probably do'. Ha-ha. Still, when the QM comes round, there are 'no complaints'.

Two things we lack are uniforms and officers. We are constantly promised uniforms will be arriving 'soon' – army word for 'nobody knows'. Officers are to be sent to us eventually by the War Office, probably a couple of 'dugout' majors and some regular captains, but the subalterns will be volunteers like us. We have a few drawn from our own numbers, a grammar-school master, a doctor, an engineer, and half a dozen chaps who were in OTCs. Some of these wear their OTC uniforms, which at least gives us a more military look. The others wear armbands over their tweeds.

Is it all hard work for your boy? At present, yes, though the sense of brotherhood here makes the dullest task tolerable. And a Battalion Amusement Committee is to be set up, with two men drawn from each company. Oliphant says I should volunteer. I say he should. He already does a fine impression of our CO, though perhaps that should not be encouraged!

I must stop now as the post is just going. I hope you are all well and missing me.

Ever your loving son, David

232

True to her word, Mrs Oliver lost no time in arranging an entertainment. She delivered the invitation to Beattie in person that Friday.

'Such an exciting thing has happened!' she began. 'One of my young nephews, Henry Bowers, has turned up, completely out of the blue. Well, he's really the brother-in-law of my nephew in America, but he calls me Aunt Fanny so I count him as a nephew.'

'Has he come from America?' Beattie asked.

'No, from Europe. He was stranded when the war broke out, managed to get to England, and now he's dithering about what to do next. So do come and help me entertain him tomorrow evening. We'll have supper and cards and perhaps some music. Henry has a fine singing voice. You and Mr Hunter will come, won't you?'

'With great pleasure,' Beattie said, though with mental crossed fingers as Edward was not the greatest enthusiast for bridge. But perhaps there would be enough people so that he wouldn't have to play. She sought a tactful way to ask. 'Will it be a large party?'

'Oh, no, just a comfortable number, and quite informal. I've asked the Cuthberts, the Farringdons, the Frobishers and the Prendergasts, and so that it won't be too dull for Henry, the Frobishers are bringing their son and the Farringdons their daughter. I'd like it very much if Diana would come, too. She always makes a party lively, and I'd so like Henry to meet her.'

'I'm sure I can speak for her,' Beattie said, 'and accept with thanks.' She was tired of Diana's mopes – she hadn't heard from Charles Wroughton for two weeks and the rumour Beattie had gathered around the village was that his Territorials had been embodied and he had gone with them to Chiswell, the regiment's home depot near St Albans. She was sorry for her daughter, but felt she ought to shake herself out of it. A party would help.

Diana was far from enraptured by the invitation, when Beattie told her about it. 'It sounds as though it will be awfully dull,' she said. 'Just old people and bridge.'

'And music, Mrs Oliver said. The Farringdons' daughter and Eric Frobisher will be there, so it won't all be "old people" – like your father and me.'

'I didn't mean it like that,' Diana said, reddening.

'Well, I've accepted for you, anyway, so you may as well make the best of it,' Beattie returned.

On Saturday morning the post brought Beattie a letter in an unknown hand. She opened it and exclaimed, 'Good heavens! It's from Lord Dene.'

Diana jumped as though she'd touched a live wire.

Sadie looked up from her toast with interest. 'Why is he writing to you and not Diana?'

'He couldn't write to Di,' Bobby said. 'It wouldn't be proper unless they were engaged.'

'Don't call me "Di",' Diana objected.

'Is that true, Mother?' Sadie asked.

'Yes, of course. You should know that,' Beattie said, perusing the letter. 'He has nice handwriting.'

'Handwriting!' Bobby exclaimed. 'What does he say? I bet it's really a way to send a message to Diana.'

'I suppose it is,' Beattie said. 'He expresses his thanks for past kindnesses, and apologises for not being able to call because he's occupied with the Territorials and unable to leave his unit at present. And he says he hopes that when he finds himself at leisure, I will permit him to call on me again.' She handed the letter to Diana.

'Oh,' said Sadie. 'Is that all?'

'What did you expect, idiot?' said Bobby. 'A declaration of undying love?'

'Well, it has been known to happen,' said Sadie.

'Who to?'

'You mean "to whom".'

234

Diana had folded the letter without comment. Beattie looked at her bent head. 'He has nice old-fashioned manners. And it shows he has proper consideration for you, darling,' she said. 'I know it may not seem much, but it's as much as one could expect in the circumstances.'

'I know,' Diana said.

'It's awfully bad luck,' Sadie said, 'the war coming when it did and him being in the Terriers.'

'Wish *I* was away,' Bobby muttered.

And William said, 'How can you call it bad luck?'

'I mean bad luck for Diana,' Sadie explained. 'He might be away for months.'

'Well, at least he wrote,' Diana said. 'He needn't have.' And it was good to know that it was army business that was keeping him away, not simply indifference. She felt more cheerful, and all at once viewed the coming evening's entertainment with enthusiasm. Eric Frobisher was a dull dog and she didn't know the Farringdons at all, but it would be amusing to meet someone new, and any nephew of Mrs Oliver was bound to have something about him.

'What are we to wear tonight, Mother? she asked. 'Did Mrs Oliver say they were dressing?'

It was a sign, Beattie knew, of recovery.

Henry Bowers turned out to be very tall and lean, and unlike anyone Diana had ever met before. His clothes weren't cut like an Englishman's, but had a strange, loose look about them, as did he – his movements were easy and almost *over-*relaxed, as though he was always on the verge of dancing. His face was long, mobile and brown from travel, his teeth, frequently exposed in enormous smiles, were so white they seemed to glow, and his hair was thick, toffee-brown, and grew straight back from his face all round like a lion's mane. Diana thought she had never met anyone who seemed so alive.

He shook hands vigorously with Diana, seeming to devour her with his eyes. 'Wonderful to meet you!' he exclaimed, though she was sure he could not have known she existed until yesterday. 'You must call me Hank,' he added.

'Must I?' she said, puzzled.

His grin widened a fraction. 'It's what you get called when your name is Henry and your father's name is also Henry. To distinguish between you. Though in my case,' he went on, 'my grandpa was also a Henry, so my pa is Hank, and I'm Hank Junior.'

'I'm afraid it wouldn't be proper for me to call you by your first name,' Diana said. 'We've only just been introduced.'

'Oh, heck, I'm sorry. I'd forgotten you're so formal over here. Back home we all use Christian names. I beg your pardon, Miss Hunter.' And he gave her a comical bow. He was so flexible that when he bent in the middle his head went all the way to his feet.

The Farringdons' daughter, Edith, turned out to be dull, a pale, chinless girl with nothing to say for herself, so Diana felt justified in leaving her to Eric Frobisher, who was also dull but never stopped talking, thus keeping Henry, or Hank, to herself. He was certainly amusing, and had plenty to say, but not in a boring way.

At the supper table, Mrs Oliver instructed him to tell the company about his getting stranded in Europe.

He was obviously happy to oblige. 'Well, I've been over in Europe, travelling about, since early spring,' he said. 'My reward from Pops for passing all my exams. He said I should sow my wild oats and get them out of my system before settling down.'

'Where in Europe have you been?' Mr Cuthbert asked.

'Where *haven't* I been, sir! But that's another story. This one starts on board the *Hollandia*, taking a leisurely cruise down the Rhine. I was pretty done up from all the travelling, you see, and felt I needed a rest, and gliding along looking at the sights without ever leaving my seat seemed to hit the spot. But the other passengers were a pretty elderly crowd, and after a couple of days I was beginning to feel I could do with some excitement. Then on Thursday – that's the Thursday before war broke out – we hit Cologne, and we started to hear rumours that Germany was on the brink of war. Well, that gave us something to think about, I can tell you! And on Friday night we reached a place called Biebrich, and it looked as though the entire population of the town was on the streets.'

'Goodness! What was happening?' Mrs Cuthbert asked.

'We thought it must be some kind of local festival,' Hank went on, 'because of all the singing, but the captain was a wary old duck, and told us to stay put while one of the mates went ashore to find out what was going on. He came back to say that the newspapers were full of Germany's ultimatum to Russia, and the townsfolk were wild with excitement that they were going to go to war. He didn't think it would be safe for us to disembark.'

'What did you do?' asked Mr Frobisher.

'Had dinner, as usual. And as it got dark we all went out on deck to enjoy the cool air – it'd been hot as Hades for days – and we could still hear the burghers shouting and merrymaking, and singing away. Their special song, "The Watch on the Rhine".'

And to Diana's astonishment he broke into song right there at the table, in a strong baritone:

'Lieb Vaterland magst ruhig sein!
Lieb Vaterland kann ruhig sein!
Fest steht und something something,
Die Wacht am Rhein.

'Fine singers, the Germans, you know,' he concluded. 'Well, some of the older passengers were getting a bit nervous,

237

afraid the burghers might storm the ship or something, but the captain said there was no need to worry. Russia was a long way off, and *Hollandia* was a neutral vessel so we'd be quite safe on board until we got to Mannheim the next day – our last stop – where there were frequent trains to Strasbourg, across the French border. All the same, when the locals started sweeping the sky with searchlights, looking for enemy airplanes, even I wondered if I was in for more excitement than I bargained for.

'The next day we sailed early for Mannheim, and it took a lot longer than it should have because every few miles we were stopped by armed patrol boats searching for French or Russian officers.'

'My dear boy!' Mrs Oliver exclaimed. 'You didn't tell me that bit!'

'Didn't want to worry you, Aunty. It was pretty tense at the time, though. Eventually we got to Mannheim, and as soon as we docked an official came aboard and told us that Germany and Russia were at war, and that France had mobilised, so there were no more trains to Strasbourg. Well, we all got into a bit of a panic at that point. We were stranded and, boy, we felt up against it! There were mostly Dutch people on board, but quite a few English, and a couple more Americans – the Dusenbergs, awfully nice folks.'

'But England and Germany weren't at war at that point,' Edward said.

'No, sir, but we reckoned they soon would be. And there's nothing like having a German official with a gun on his hip giving you a tight-lipped once-over to make you nervous.'

'So what did you do?' Diana asked.

He turned to her. 'We just wanted to get out of there as quick as we could. The English folk could think of nothing but getting back to England, and we Yankees felt much the same! So we all jumped on the first train to Heidelberg, got there Saturday evening, and found everybody on the streets singing "The Watch on the Rhine", just like in Biebrich. Made us feel quite queer. Well, the Dutch and English were done up, and decided to stay the night, but we energetic Americans wanted to push on, so we split up, and we took a night train to Stuttgart. It was a two-hour ride, according to the timetable, but it took all night because we kept being shuffled into sidings to let the troop trains go through. What a sight! Packed to the roof, and the soldiers all singing and waving their rifles. When we got off the train at Stuttgart in the morning an officer stopped us and asked us our nationality. Mr Dusenberg said we were Americans, and the officer said, "*Sprechen sie Englisch?*" It gave us the first laugh we'd had for days. Mr Dusenberg said, "What language do you think we speak – Red Indian?" The officer looked pretty annoyed at being laughed at, but we'd proved our point because it turned out he was looking for Russian spies, and we obviously weren't.'

'How could you laugh at such a moment?' Diana said. 'I'd have been terrified.'

'Well, I was pretty scared, if I'm honest. But sometimes all you can do is laugh. Anyway, there we were in Stuttgart, feeling as if we were getting further and further away from England all the time. Also, it being Sunday morning and the Germans being at war, nobody at the station could tell us when there'd be a train to anywhere at all. So we decided to hire a motor-car. We had to get one with a chauffeur, of course, or the hire people would never have got it back. The drive seemed to take for ever,' he added thoughtfully, 'because, of course, we had no way of knowing where we were. Mrs Dusenberg was worried that the driver was abducting us. We had to stop the night in some place, I can't remember the name, and there wasn't much chance of sleep. We kept thinking the driver would sneak away in the darkness, or that he'd fetch the police and have us arrested for spies. And there was a display of shooting stars in the night,

239

and the local home guard started firing at them, thinking they were French airplanes!

'But in the morning our driver turned up right as rain, and we felt bad for having doubted him. He drove us over the border into Switzerland, to a train station, and after that it was plain sailing.'

'Plain sailing!' Mrs Cuthbert exclaimed.

'Plain,' Hank asserted, 'though darned slow once we got into France, because of the troop trains. Then we had to wait a long time to get a boat crossing. And finally, my pockets being just about empty, I thought the best thing I could do was throw myself on Aunt Fanny's mercy until Pop could cable me some dough,' he concluded, with a confiding grin at Mrs Oliver.

'Dough?' Mr Frobisher queried.

'Dough-re-mi,' Hank said.

'Money,' Edward explained. 'Likewise spondulicks.'

Diana stared at her father in astonishment, but Hank laughed. 'Exactly, sir! You speak our language.'

'I know most of the words for money,' Edward admitted.

'I thought you said Americans spoke English,' Diana teased, and Hank turned his grin on her.

'I think we did back in the seventeenth century. But we've been away from home quite a while now.'

It was a very pleasant evening. Edward was able to avoid playing bridge because Mrs Farringdon did not play so he was able to suggest Beattie partnered her husband. Diana was happy to be the centre of Hank's attention, and found him delightfully easy to talk to, full of fun and ready to engage on any subject. He told her his father owned a farm in California. 'Fruit and vegetables. Mostly citrus fruits.'

'No animals – cattle or anything?' she asked.

'No, that would be a ranch,' he said. 'We don't have many mixed farms like you do here.'

'Is yours big?'

'Fair. Most of the farms are big in Central Valley. It's four hundred and fifty miles long and fifty wide, the best farmland anywhere, flat and fertile, and the climate's perfect. You could grow anything there.'

'You sound as if you love it.'

'Ah, well,' he said lightly, 'wherever you come from is home, isn't it?'

'So you'll be in a hurry to get back there?'

He grinned. 'I'm having too much fun. I rather think I'm going to have a lot of trouble getting a passage, Miss Hunter, when there's so much going on over here! A fellow would have to be a pretty lame duck to want to miss out on it.'

Diana curled her lip. 'Why do all men love war so?'

'Would you care for us if we didn't?' he responded smartly, and she laughed.

Later he was persuaded to sing for them, and Diana was asked to accompany him on the piano. She consented, but would not be inveigled into singing with him. She had a sweet voice, but without power, and he sang like a professional. She knew better than to invite comparison.

And later again he beguiled her with stories of moving pictures and Hollywood stars, talking so knowledgeably, one would have thought he knew them personally. 'I get it all out of magazines,' he assured her. 'We're great ones for magazines back home.'

'You seemed to get on well with young Mr Bowers,' Edward observed, as the taxicab trundled them homewards.

'He's very interesting,' Diana said.

'Yes, he seemed amusing,' Edward replied. 'I hope we see him again before he leaves.'

Diana hoped he wouldn't leave for a long time. She had entirely forgotten her troubles for a whole evening.

'It says in the paper they've got all the men for the first New Army already,' said Cook to Beattie. 'A hundred thousand volunteers in ten days! They're calling it K1 after Lord Kitchener, and they're starting on K2 now.'

'That's very gratifying,' said Beattie, vaguely. She was thinking of the party last night while trying to keep still for Nula, who was behind her, pinning a dress she was going to alter.

'Volunteer fever, they're calling it, madam,' Cook went on enthusiastically. 'All over the country, it is. Everybody's joining up. And Mrs Gordon's Betty said she heard some of 'em are coming here.'

'That's right,' Nula said, with difficulty, through a mouthful of pins. 'Sure Wilkes saw them puttin' the tents up yesterday on Paget's Piece.' This was a large, rough field between Northcote and Rustington.

'Poor things, having to live in tents! Why don't they put them in the barracks? That's what I don't understand,' Cook said.

'There's no room,' said Beattie. 'As soon as the regulars move out, to go to France, the reservists and Territorials move in. So they're putting the New Armies anywhere there's a bit of open space.'

'And who are we getting, d'ye know?' Nula asked.

'Mr Hunter said it was the 9th Battalion, West Middlesex Regiment of Foot. They'll be coming in tomorrow. He thinks they may be looking to billet the officers in our village.'

'It seems a shame they didn't put the camp in Dene Park. Then the officers could have stayed in the house,' said Cook. There was a faint undertone of criticism, Beattie thought: the Wroughtons were sometimes deemed not to involve themselves sufficiently in the neighbourhood. This year even the annual Open Day at the end of August, always accompanied by a fair and various entertainments, had been cancelled 'owing to the war'. Some locals felt that was just an excuse.

Beattie answered the feeling rather than the words. 'Lord

Wroughton has made a sacrifice for the war too, you know – they've taken all his horses. That must have been a blow.' She handed back the recipe book. 'Thank you, Cook. We'll have just what you suggest.'

'Very good, madam,' Cook said, and departed.

A moment later, Nula said. 'Right, I've finished. You can take it off now. And how was your party last night? How was Mrs Oliver's young nephew?'

'He seemed very nice. Has a lovely singing voice. His father is very rich – owns a large estate in California.'

'Would he do for Diana, d'ye think?' Beattie looked at her. 'Better a bird in the hand. No good encouraging her over Lord Dene when he's disappeared.'

'I don't think Mr Henry would do,' Beattie said. 'He's bound to be going back to America soon.'

'What – with a war on?' Nula's eyebrows shot up. 'Wouldn't any red-blooded young man want to stay and fight?'

'He wouldn't be allowed to,' Beattie said. She'd had a similar conversation with Edward last night. 'If he enlisted in a foreign army he'd lose his citizenship.'

'What sort of a law is that?' Nula said indignantly. 'And since when is it a foreign army?'

'Foreign to them.'

'Sure they're the foreigners,' Nula said, indignation overcoming her usual admiration for all things American.

Beattie smiled. 'Mr Henry certainly looks foreign – bigger, healthier and with far more teeth than any man in this country.'

The new recruits – Kitchener's Mob, as they were dubbed – arrived at Northcote station on a special train, to be greeted by an eager crowd and the Boys' Brigade band playing rousing tunes, blowing with all their might to prove that it was not lack of patriotism that prevented them volunteering too but lack of years. The recruits, still in their civilian garb, formed up, grinning self-consciously, and marched off, led

243

by an elderly 'dugout', their commanding officer, on a bony white horse.

It was heaven for the small boys of the village. The volunteers might not march very efficiently, but they were still gods and heroes as they raised a dust down the high street. The boys jigged and pranced about them and tried to fall in with the uncertain beat, chanting a gleeful song: 'Join Kitchener's Army, seven bob a week, plenty o' grub to eat, blisters on yer feet!' The heroes grinned back at them in unshakeable good humour.

The camp, with a hut on one side for the battalion office, rows of tents for the men, wash tents, mess tents, cook tents, and every other appurtenance to delight the heart of a small boy, became a magnet. The newcomers were settling in, being assigned tasks and undergoing their first parades. Apart from the joy of watching former civilians learning to march and shoulder sticks (there were no rifles yet), there were all sorts of other activities going on that the boys could watch and even sometimes help with – digging sanitation ditches, fetching water, carrying messages – and the soldiers were often happy to employ a boy for a penny to run to the shops and buy sweets. Every now and then an NCO would appear and roar at the boys, sending them packing, but they never went further than the nearest cover, to ooze back again when the coast was clear.

It wasn't long before local people worked out ways to turn the camp to advantage. The sight of a man from Rustington setting up a stall opposite the camp gate selling buns galvanised them with indignation. Soon there was a row of home-grown stalls: Northcote was ready to meet all the soldiers' extra-curricular needs – including, it was whispered after PC Whittle had investigated some rustling in the bushes one evening, the carnal. But the crown for ingenuity was popularly given to a pigman, Joe Foley, who, with a pony-drawn float bearing several dustbins, got himself paid to take away the food waste every day, which he then fed to his pigs.

William and Peter were frequent visitors to the camp, and even Bobby went down one day to see the fun. But when Emily murmured that she was thinking of going to have a look when her time off came, Cook put her foot down.

'You are not!' she said. 'That camp is no place for you, and if I catch you slipping off there, I'll skin you!'

Emily's lip stuck out. 'Ah, that's not fair, so it's not,' she whined. 'I want to see. Why can't I go?'

'Because they're soldiers, and you don't know what's what,' Cook said firmly. 'You stay right away.' Emily subsided in a pout. 'And that goes for you, too, Ethel.'

Ethel, who had been smirking at Emily's disappointment, bristled. '*Me*? Why?' she exclaimed indignantly.

'Because you *do* know what's what,' Cook said grimly.

CHAPTER EIGHTEEN

Laura and Louisa spent a week at a country house near Woking called Hillside Lodge. Here a Mrs Erskine lived and conducted her driving courses for ladies, in the intervals between all the other activities she undertook for the Cause.

The house was a large modern villa set at the top of a gentle slope, with a long verandah overlooking the gardens. The driving lessons took place in some big rough fields behind the house, also belonging to her husband.

Colonel Erskine was a large, amiable man, of such equable temper that he was never put out by the disruption of his domestic scene by of gaggles of strange females. He had no strong opinion about female emancipation, preferring to borrow his wife's when he absolutely had to have one, but he supported her with a quietly fierce loyalty, which decreed that whatever Millie wanted, she should have, even if it meant changing the law of the land.

He was a familiar figure in the background, white-haired and white-moustached, though mahogany of face from long service overseas; always ambling along in the comfortable woollen cardigans he preferred to jackets when at leisure, with a pipe in his mouth and a couple of elderly spaniels at heel. He took in his stride, with a vague and pleasant smile, the strange faces and rather shrill voices that suddenly popped up in his household.

'He was exactly the same with the natives in Basutoland,'

Mrs Erskine confided. 'I think he views women as an exotic tribe, given to strange antics but not troublesome at all if you get on the right side of them.'

Laura enjoyed the driving lessons immensely. Bumping along over the grass in the bellowing, smoking motor-car, the instructor clutching the side and trying to shout at her without swearing, was great fun.

Eccles had been the colonel's soldier-servant, and had come to him in military retirement as a sort of odd-job-man-cum-valet. When the colonel bought a motor-car, Eccles had hastened to learn to drive and maintain it: he wanted to make himself so useful that the colonel would never think of letting him go. The colonel, having no understanding of the mechanical beast on any level, was glad to have Eccles take it over.

Whether Eccles would have been so eager if he had known that Mrs Erskine would one day want him to teach females could never be known. He paid lip-service to the notion that no woman could understand a machine, and that motor-driving was not ladylike, but he'd had to get used to all sorts of things that Mrs Erskine felt women should be allowed to do.

And the truth was that, though he played the curmudgeon, he had come to like the eager, strangely gallant young ladies who came under his charge. He was determined to do the right thing by them – and, thanks to his severity and perse-verance, he had never had a failure yet, though some had tried his patience to breaking point. But even little Miss Porteous, five feet nothing with wrists like tulip stems, who couldn't tell left from right, and could steer or change gear but not both at the same time, had finally made it. On her last day she had insisted on driving the motor to the station herself, and Eccles had let her, and even smiled at her shriek of pure joy when she hit thirty miles an hour down West Hill.

Laura took to driving like a duck to water – in her own

opinion, at any rate: though Eccles cursed her freely, he did that to everyone, and there were definitely whole periods when he found nothing to abuse her for. The proof came in the middle of the week when, on what should have been his afternoon off, he asked if there were any young ladies who would like to learn about the inside of the motor. He looked at Laura as he said it. She jumped up at once, and Louisa, after a hesitation, said she would too. The others only laughed, fanned themselves and said it was too hot: they intended to lounge about on the verandah and do nothing.

'Best put on some ole clo'es, then, young ladies,' Eccles said. 'You'll get mucky.'

Mrs Erskine found them old gardening jackets, hats and gloves, and they went off for a fascinating couple of hours, having the workings of the internal-combustion engine explained to them. Louisa was out of her depth, but Laura loved it all. To know how something worked was wonderful; to know how to mend it would be even better.

'I always wanted to be a doctor,' she confided.

'Doctorin's easy,' Eccles asserted. 'People can tell you where they 'urt – a nengine can't.'

When they weren't having lessons, they went for long walks over the neighbouring heathland: the colonel's spaniels got enough exercise ambling at his heels, but Mrs Erskine had two energetic Border Terriers always ready for a hike. In the evenings there were guests to dinner, and sometimes cards afterwards.

But the times Laura liked best were from tea-time to the dressing bell, which, in this gloriously warm weather, they spent on the verandah, talking, the six of them and Millie Erskine.

Miss Mackie and Miss Leake were friends and had come together. Miss Mackie was about forty, handsome and almost exotic-looking, with jet black hair and dark eyes. She had an athletic figure, and her clothes were well chosen, with a hint of fashion about them – Laura took her to be independently wealthy. She had a sharp mind, and sometimes seemed impatient of Miss Leake, who lived with her and was altogether more milk-and-water – well-meaning but, Laura thought, a bit vapid.

Miss Whittaker was a teacher, a tall, quiet woman, with a solid figure and a measured way of talking. Miss Eckersall was short and round, quick-moving, quick talking, with a snub-nosed face and a rather pugnacious manner, a factory-owner's daughter from Manchester. They had evidently met before, but whether at rallies or at Mrs Erskine's, Laura wasn't sure. Miss Eckersall was the most militant of them, and had been arrested twice, though, thanks to her father's influence, she had not been imprisoned.

Their conversations were wide-ranging, but naturally the two most frequent topics were the war and the Cause, especially where they overlapped.

The government had cleared its decks by putting aside any controversial business currently on the books, such as the Irish Home Rule Bill, and the disestablishment of the Church of Wales. In the same spirit it had granted amnesty to all political prisoners, including strike leaders and, in particular, the suffragettes. On the 10th of August the home secretary had issued a statement: 'His Majesty is confident that the prisoners will respond to the feelings of their countrymen and countrywomen in this time of emergency, and that they may be trusted not to stain the causes they have at heart by any further crime or disorder.'

'You see how well the government comes out of it,' Miss Mackie said. 'They can boast about their magnanimity, and at the same time point out that they never gave in to force. And the devil of it is that if we *don't* smile and accept the olive branch, every patriotic citizen will be shocked, and we'll lose what support we have.'

'But I suspect,' said Miss Whittaker, in her slow, deep voice, 'that the Pankhursts will be relieved to have an excuse to stop the militancy.'

Miss Eckersall agreed. 'To my mind, the whole thing's gone too far. I can't see where militancy can go next without killing someone. This way Emmeline and the others can give it up without losing face.'

'*Have* they given up?' Laura asked.

'Oh yes,' said Miss Eckersall. 'They announced straight after the home secretary's speech that it's to be suspended until the war's over.' She gave a twinkling smile. 'Between you and me, I think Emmeline and Christabel realised that anything they might manage by way of mayhem at home would hardly be noticed against the mayhem the Kaiser's going to be raising abroad.'

Miss Mackie looked disapproving. 'It's not a subject for levity. Did all those women suffer torture in prison cells to be laughed at by members of their own sex?'

'I'm not laughing at them, Miss Mackie,' said Miss Eckersall. 'What happened to them was horrible. And I'm very glad, now, I was spared it, though at the time I was peeved not to be slapped in jug so I could make a show and be famous. But it's a fact that the militants in the WSPU didn't achieve anything more than the moderates in the NUWSS. To my mind it's all to the good that it's being stopped.'

'Oh, I agree,' said Miss Leake, fervently. 'I do so hate violence of any sort.'

'Well,' said Mrs Erskine, 'Mrs Pankhurst has an easier decision to make than Mrs Fawcett. The WSPU can make a simple declaration to cease militancy on patriotic grounds, which leaves them free to work for victory, but I foresee endless arguments ahead for the NUWSS over how far to support the war effort. *They* haven't anything to give up except their agitation for the suffrage, and if they give that up, where are they?'

'In exactly the same place as the rest of us,' said Miss Mackie. 'Women without power in the men's world.'

'It seems to me,' Laura said hesitantly, since she was fairly new to all this, 'that the war may offer us a great opportunity.'

'How so? There obviously won't be any reforms to domestic law until it's over,' said Miss Mackie.

'No, but it could be our chance to prove ourselves worthy of the full citizenship we're asking for.'

'By knitting socks for soldiers?' Miss Mackie asked, with a curled lip.

Miss Leake did not catch the irony. 'Oh, I love to knit,' she said, her face brightening. 'I haven't tried stockings. I believe turning the heel is rather difficult. But I'm sure I can learn.'

'What I meant was that with so many men away,' Laura said, 'there are bound to be empty spaces at home that we women can fill.'

'You can't suppose we can be ploughmen and coal miners,' Miss Mackie said.

'We could be factory workers, perhaps,' Miss Eckersall said, then added doubtfully, 'if the unions would allow it.'

'There are plenty of unemployed at the moment to take those jobs,' said Miss Mackie.

'I don't know what form the opportunities will take,' Laura said. 'I just feel sure they will be there.' She sought for an example to save herself from Miss Mackie's tongue. 'Driving, for instance. Most of the people who can drive are men, and if they go off to war *someone* will have to take it over.'

'Well said, dear,' Mrs Erskine said. 'I think we should all decide here and now to dedicate ourselves to the war effort in any way that presents itself.'

'Obviously one would do that,' said Miss Mackie, impatiently, 'but—'

'We must prove to the country that it couldn't have won

251

the war without us. But at the same time we mustn't forget we are working to improve the welfare of *all* women,' Mrs Erskine added. 'It isn't just about the suffrage.'

'I agree,' said Laura. 'But most of all I just want to *do* something. It may or may not be our big chance, but I don't want to spend the war sitting around and talking, or handing out leaflets.'

'As it happens,' said Mrs Erskine, 'I know of something you *could* do. My cousin Margaret – Mrs Harpenden – leads a group of ladies who meet the trains bringing in Belgian refugees. What was just a trickle is fast becoming a flood, and she badly needs more volunteers.'

'What exactly do they do?'

'They meet the trains, help the poor dears to find lodgings, and put them in touch with other voluntary groups who can help them settle into a new life. It's mostly women and children, as you can imagine. There's work behind the scenes to be done as well – raising subscriptions, finding houses willing to take them in, collecting clothes and food for them.' She looked around the group. 'It's necessary work – and it's something that needs to be done *now*.'

'I'm for it,' Laura said. 'Will you put me in touch with your cousin, Mrs Erskine?'

'Oh, how dashing of you, Miss Hunter,' said Miss Leake. 'I wonder if I should volunteer for that, too.'

'You'll have quite enough to do keeping house for us,' Miss Mackie said impatiently. 'Especially when food becomes scarce and you have to queue for everything.'

'Do you really think there'll be food shortages?' Louisa asked.

'We import half our meat and four-fifths of our grain,' Miss Mackie pointed out.

'And sugar,' Miss Eckersall added. 'And tea. Factory workers practically live on bread and tea.'

'And as we are an island, it must all come by sea,' Miss

252

Mackie concluded. 'If the Germans don't try to cut our food-supply lines, I don't know what they've been building up their navy for, all these years.'

It was a sobering thought. 'Well, I'm not sure there's anything we women can do about that,' Mrs Erskine said at last.

'I didn't suggest there was,' said Miss Mackie, impatiently. 'Our strengths are campaigning and organising. It may be necessary, for instance, to impose rationing at some point.'

'Condoms,' said Miss Whittaker, startling them all. There was a brief silence.

'I beg your pardon?' said Mrs Erskine.

Everyone looked at Miss Whittaker. Laura was interested and impressed to see that she was not blushing.

'The common soldiers will be exposed to temptation in France, and if they contract a certain disease they will bring it home and spread it to our women,' Miss Whittaker said. 'A campaign to distribute free condoms, *and* to educate the women to insist on their use, will be war work of vital importance.'

Laura suppressed the urge to laugh, which would have been misunderstood, but she was imagining Edward's reaction if she told him her war work was distributing condoms. 'I think I'll leave that to you, Miss Whittaker,' she said, managing to sound suitably serious. 'It's the Belgian refugees for me. How about you, Louisa?'

'Oh, I'm game for that,' Louisa answered promptly, with perhaps just a hint of relief.

'I heard the most extraordinary thing today,' Beattie said to Edward, as Ada helped him off with his coat. He followed her into the drawing-room, where she poured him his usual after-work, before-dinner sherry.

'Well?' he invited her, taking the glass.

253

'I met Dr Harding on his rounds when I walked into the village, and he says Victor Sowden has volunteered.'

Edward sipped. 'I'm sure that can only be a good thing for the village.'

'But he's only thirteen,' Beattie said.

'He's big for his age,' Edward said. 'They only have to be over five foot three.'

'He doesn't look eighteen,' Beattie objected.

'The recruiting sergeants get half a crown a head, I believe, so they won't be too particular. And you don't have to produce a birth certificate when you enlist, you know – even supposing Mrs Sowden has one. Besides, if a lad is so eager to serve, I expect the officials feel they shouldn't discourage him.'

'It doesn't seem right,' Beattie said, vaguely troubled. 'Couldn't the Sowdens get him out?'

'I dare say they're glad of one less mouth to feed – if they notice at all,' Edward said. 'My dear, you're too sensitive. What has he got to look forward to at home, after all? Soldiering must be better for him than ending up in prison.'

Sadie was loyal to old friends, and in spite of the riding at Highclere – though there was less of that now – she was happy to oblige Simpson's Dairy and take Arthur and Blackie down to the forge for removes, especially as their stableman, Gallon, had gone off to war. Mr Simpson was having to do stable work himself. He looked rather fraught, Sadie thought.

'They've taken our two young horses,' he explained, 'and left us with these two. They're having to do extra rounds, and they're not as young as they used to be. Even then, I've had to send the drivers out with handcarts to make up the difference. I know we all have to do our bit, but if Arthur and Blackie get done up by too much work, where will we be then? It's not right, Miss Sadie.'

'Can't you get a pony or a mule?' she asked.

'You find me one,' he said. 'They're like gold dust. I wouldn't like to tell you what Charringtons paid for a pair of mules just this week.' He sighed. 'I think I'm getting too old for this game. I've half a mind to sell up.'

'Oh, don't do that,' Sadie said quickly. 'Northcote wouldn't be the same without you.'

He softened. 'It's real nice of you to do this for me, Miss Sadie. Can you get up all right? Let me give you a leg-up.'

Riding Blackie, for a change, and leading Arthur, she turned out of the yard on to the road, hoping that no-one disapproving would see her riding astride. She hadn't gone far when she saw Victor Sowden sitting on a stile, apparently holding forth to a group of older lads, who looked like the sort of 'toughs' he had always tried to emulate. They glanced at her indifferently as she approached, but she caught Victor's eye, and decided to stop and talk to him.

Probably because of the horses, he came over to her when she gestured. He walked with his usual slouch and his face wore his usual scowl, but she noticed that he took hold of Blackie's rein and caressed her nose, and Arthur's, with an almost automatic gentleness.

'I heard about you volunteering,' Sadie said. 'I just wanted to say, jolly well done.' He looked at her suspiciously. 'I think it's tremendous of you. Were you worried they'd find out you were under age?'

He shrugged, stroking the cheeks of the two horses simultaneously. 'That old sergeant give me a sharpish look, but he said, "How old are you?" an' I said, "Eighteen," and that was that. The doctor said I was a fine physical specimen, 'cause you 'ave to 'ave four teeth and I got more'n that.'

'You weren't afraid your parents would try and get you out?'

He met her eyes, and there was an unfathomable darkness in them. 'I never told me dad. He won't never miss me. Ma cried a bit, but she's in the fam'ly way again, so she don't really care. One less of us to feed.'

Sadie felt a spasm of pity. 'Well, I'm sure you'll do well in the army, and I hope when you're a big tall soldier with a chest full of medals, you'll come back and see us.'

He stroked away, staring at her wordlessly, his mind evidently working. She supposed communication with someone like her, someone outside his narrow sphere, was so unusual as to need careful assessing. The army would be a big change for him, she thought; and for the first time realised what a golden opportunity it must be for those with so few prospects.

'Gonna see the world,' he said at last. 'I ain't never been nowhere.' She nodded encouragingly. 'I might never come back,' he concluded.

'Well, good luck to you,' she said, preparing to move on. But he kept a hand on Blackie's rein. She looked at him enquiringly.

It seemed a strain to get the words out. 'D'you fink – in the army – I'd get to work wiv 'orses?'

'I don't see why not. Every unit must have drivers, for the stores and so on.'

He nodded, and released the rein. She rode on, and thought she heard him behind her say quietly, "Bye, miss.' If she hadn't imagined it, it must be about the first time in his life he'd ever called anyone 'miss'. She was terribly touched.

She was walking home afterwards from Simpson's when Nailer joined her, in his sudden way, from under a hedge. 'So what do you think about the army coming to Northcote?' she asked him.

He regarded her from under his eyebrows. *Lots more opportunities for scrounging*, he said.

'You're a reprehensible dog,' she said. 'Your mind is entirely in your stomach, isn't it?'

256

He grinned and licked his lips. *Not entirely.*

'That's even worse. What I notice mostly is that there's so much more traffic on the road since they came – carts going up and down all the time. I suppose they have to have stores delivered. And one of the officers has a motor-car. William tells me it's a "Talbot twelve horse-power". I'd like to see a tug of war between twelve horses and that motor. I bet the horses would win.'

Nailer had no opinion about that. His ears had gone back, listening for something behind them.

Sadie listened too. 'That's a motor coming. I wonder if it's the same one.'

She stopped on the verge and turned to look. It came into sight at last, and she said, 'No, it's not the same. Different colour and shape. I wish I knew the makes of cars. I must get William to teach me.'

Even as she spoke, Nailer hurtled across the road to attack the tyres. She never had a clear idea of what happened next. She shouted, the motor braked, and Nailer performed a somersault through the air to land on the verge opposite.

She rushed across the road. The motor-car had stopped a few yards further on, and out of the corner of her eye she saw the driver getting out. But her attention was on that white body on the green grass, her dog, lying so still – and just at that moment she was very clear that he was *her* dog. 'Oh, no, oh, Nailer!' she cried. 'Stupid, stupid! Oh, God, don't let him be dead.'

'Is he all right?' the man called, hurrying towards them.

Sadie saw the flank going up and down. Still breathing – not dead, then. But how badly hurt?

'I'm so sorry,' the voice said, behind her now. 'I tried to stop, but I couldn't avoid him. I think I clipped him with the mud-guard.'

'I don't see any blood,' she said. No blood from the mouth – that was good.

'Let me examine him,' the man said.

She was running her hand over the solid little body. As she touched the shoulder the dog flinched, lifted his head and then, in one lightning movement, bit her hand, striking like a snake, and was up and away, racing down the verge and through the hedge at the first weak place.

Sadie had yelped when he bit her, and now stood, shaking her hand ruefully, as she watched the dog's retreat.

'Well,' said the man, 'it doesn't look as if there's much wrong with him. Let me look at your hand.'

'Oh, it's all right,' she said, turning to him. 'It's just a scratch. He didn't mean to hurt me.'

She got her first look at him. He was lean but compactly built and, if not exactly handsome, had a very nice face, the sort you wouldn't get tired of looking at, good-humoured and sensible. She guessed he was about ten years older than her, though she wasn't very good at telling ages in grownups. He was looking at her with concern, his eyes really *seeing* her, she could tell, not just looking in her direction, as most grown-ups did with girls her age.

'He never usually bites,' she said, noticing the little creases round his eyes, as if he either liked smiling a lot, or worked out of doors. 'Or, anyway, not me,' she added, incurably honest.

'Is he your dog, then?' the man said. Despite her demurral, he had taken her hand to look at it. His was firm, dry and cool, and evidently knew what it was doing.

'He's supposed to be the family dog,' she answered. 'But really I think Nailer belongs to Nailer.'

He smiled, and all the creases came to life. 'Is that his name – Nailer?' She nodded. He gave her hand back. 'You're right, it's only a scratch. But you ought to wash it thoroughly – dogs' teeth are extremely unclean.'

Now she grinned. 'I know. I've seen some of the things he eats!'

'Dead birds?'

'Worse than that.'

There was something really nice about the moment, the two of them standing on the grass in the sunshine, smiling at each other. She had never had contact with a proper grown-up man (rather than a youth of her own age) that felt so easy.

Then he stirred. 'I really ought to be getting along. But can I drive you somewhere first?'

'Oh, no,' she said.

'Least I can do, seeing as I'm the cause of your injury.'

'Really. I only live round the corner. But thank you.'

He gave a curious little bow of the head. 'My apologies again. I hope the dog's all right. Keep an eye on him, but I suspect he's just bruised.'

'I will. Thank you,' she said, and on an impulse, 'Are you going to the army camp?'

'Yes,' he said, with an enquiring look.

'It's straight ahead, on the left. You can't miss it,' Sadie said, thinking that if he was at the camp, she might see him again.

'Thank you,' he said. 'Goodbye, then.' He turned away and went back to his motor.

'Goodbye,' Sadie said, and turned the other way, feeling oddly pleased by the incident, though she wasn't sure why.

CHAPTER NINETEEN

Oliphant and I went for a long walk on Sunday. Right out in the middle of nowhere we came across a small farm, and, believe it or not, the farmer didn't know we were at war! He hadn't heard anything about it. It seems they live mostly off the land, and only go into town two or three times a year, when they buy the bulk of what they need. He'd last been to town in June with his wife and children, and since then he'd heard no news. It's hard to believe what isolated lives these people live.

We have some captains now – two 'dugouts', one transferred from the Terriers, and C Company has an Indian Army officer named Talbot, who says he was practically kidnapped! He came home on leave to see his wife and children, and as soon as he touched dry land they told him he was transferred. Hard cheese on him, we all think. He seems a decent fellow.

Still no news about our uniforms. Our 'civvies' are starting to show the wear and tear – I'm afraid we shall look like scarecrows if it goes on much longer. Please can you send me some more underthings, and another shirt? Also my green pullover as it can be chilly at night now.

David looked up for inspiration. Next door, in the canteen, there was a warm burble of voices, but this, the smaller day room, had by custom become the quiet room, where men came to read and write letters. Here there was no sound but the turning of leaves and the scratching of pens. Oliphant was scribbling away with his tongue between his teeth and his head cocked to one side in the effort to make his hand keep up with his thoughts.

'Are you writing to Sophy?' David asked. It was a fair guess – Oliphant's letters to his parents were like school exercises.

Oliphant looked up. 'Yes – why?'

'Oh, I just thought . . . Give her my regards, will you? And say—'

'Hmm?'

'Oh . . . nothing, really.' What was there that he could possibly say through the filter of her brother? He wanted to say that he thought about her a lot, and wished he could see her, that she was really why he had volunteered in the first place – to make the world a place fit for her to live in. After so many weeks of living entirely among men, women had become almost mythical creatures: their softness, their gentleness, their delicacy, everything that was different from the hard, brash noisiness of men. When he thought of her, he saw the rounded curve of her cheek, her long white neck, the dark, feathery curls that nestled at the nape . . .

But he couldn't say any of that to F-A, good fellow though he was. He wished he had a photograph of her. If only—

'I say,' said Oliphant, 'you aren't soft on her, are you? She has a frightful temper, you know. I never knew a girl who could take offence as quickly as her.'

'You don't understand,' David said.

The war news in the newspapers came from the army communiqués passed on by the War Office, and they were unhelpfully tight-lipped. *The BEF has been in touch with the enemy near the Belgian frontier*, it said, on the 23rd of August.

261

A couple of days later, *The BEF has reached its new position.* Then, on the 27th, *British troops engaged on Wednesday against superior forces fought splendidly.* As far as it went it was reassuring: the BEF was trouncing the Germans and it was all going according to plan. But the public was hungry for more detail, more colour – more everything.

'Deliberate blackout,' Lord Forbesson said to Edward, when he met him in the club one day towards the end of August. 'Senior army chaps don't like the general public knowing too much. The War Office feels the same. And in Cabinet the consensus is that what the man in the street doesn't know can't hurt him. Tell him as little as possible and keep him happy.'

'As long as the newspaper proprietors don't break ranks,' Edward observed, and Forbesson gave him a sharp look.

'You have a way of putting your finger on the weak spot,' he said. 'We'd sooner not have to legislate censorship, but in wartime everything has to be considered, in the public good.'

In the absence of any more detailed news, the papers were filled with patriotic appeals, diatribes against the vile Hun, sad stories of Belgian citizens fleeing their homes, and helpful hints about how to aid the war effort. The French authorities were as determined as the British to keep journalists from getting anywhere near either army, and those who had crossed to France could send home only reports of gallant troops setting out for the Front, tearful farewells, and the patriotic fervour of the civilians left behind.

The illustrated weeklies were even worse off, since the British Army would not allow any photographs of British soldiers to be published, and the likes of *War Illustrated,* which had started up so eagerly when war was declared, had to make do with photographs of French troops waving from trains, and views of French towns taken from pre-war picture postcards.

262

All that ended abruptly on Sunday, the 30th of August, when, as Edward had foreseen, two of the papers broke the embargo. *The Times* issued a special Sunday edition, which coincided with a graphic report in the *Weekly Dispatch*. Their journalists, tired of kicking their heels in Paris, had travelled secretly to the war zone, and what they reported was horrifying.

The BEF had been all but overwhelmed at Mons on the Belgian border and forced to retreat. There had been terrible losses. Broken regiments were in disarray, struggling along roads crowded with civilian refugees, unable to keep formation. A second stand had been made at Le Cateau and, after a brutal and bloody battle, the further diminished army was in retreat again.

Over the next two days the other papers picked up the story and the nation reeled in shock, made all the more acute by the holiday mood that had prevailed until then. The idea that the British Army could be defeated had never crossed the national mind, and the subtle distinctions between different kinds of retreat could not be grasped. The British *never* retreated; they only went forward to victory.

Lord Forbesson assured Edward that it was merely a regrouping. 'The French fell back, so we had to fall back to keep level with them. There were so many civilians clogging the roads that the units got broken up, but they were never a rabble. They fought tremendously well against much higher numbers at Le Cateau, but the French kept falling back and they had to do the same or risk being surrounded.'

But one thing was clear: after heavy losses, the BEF was desperately in need of reinforcements. A grim determination gradually replaced the horror in the public's mind. Whatever was required to beat the Hun *would* be done. Some of the newspapers had used their editorials to put out an appeal for more volunteers, and those men who had held back so far were urged to enlist immediately. Such was the response to

263

the call that recruitment offices were overwhelmed, and the height requirement of five foot three was hastily increased to five foot five simply to slow down the flood.

Bobby was frantic. 'I can't just go off to Oxford as if nothing had happened!' he cried.

'Your business is to finish your education,' Edward said.

'But – but the *war*!' he cried, in youth's frustration at the wilful blindness of age. 'How can I sit there meekly studying with all that going on?'

'You can and you will,' Edward returned calmly. 'I haven't spent all that money on your education to have you throw it away.'

'You let David go.'

David didn't ask. But that was not something to say out loud.

'My country *needs* me, Father,' Bobby urged. 'It's my duty to go. You must see that.'

'Don't argue with your father,' Beattie intervened. 'If he says you aren't to go, that's the end of it.'

'Everybody else is going!'

'Then they won't need you, will they?' Beattie said.

The argument was renewed at intervals over the next few days, whenever the *Daily Mail* put out another heartrending piece about 'The Agony of Belgium', but Edward held firm. Having seen David off, he had no wish to put Beattie through it again.

'Where d'you think you're going?' Cook said distractedly, as Ethel tried to slip past her to the back door with her cap off.

'Just getting a breath of air,' Ethel muttered.

'You don't need air!' Cook snapped. It was a sensitive subject with her. If she kept the doors and windows shut the kitchen grew suffocatingly hot, but if they were open the flies got in, and she hated flies obsessively. 'Air indeed! If you've finished the dining-room there's all these raisins to stone.'

'Let Emily do it.'

'Emily's chopping suet. She can't do everything.'

'I'll be back in a minute,' Ethel said, and whisked herself away rather than continue the argument. Do what you want and take the telling-off afterwards, that was her philosophy.

Emily, on a trip down to the dustbin, had found Billy Snow lurking there. He had caught hold of her arm, and she had almost swooned with pleasure. He was so tall and handsome. And though he only wanted her to take a message to Ethel, it was a high point in her life when a handsome young man spoke to her.

'Tell Ethel to come out,' he had said. 'Tell her it's important, there's a good girl, Em.'

She would relive the incident later in bed. And gradually her version would change, until she became the golden-haired heroine of the story. 'Take this message to the King, Emily. There's no-one I can trust except you. The safety of the country is at stake. And when you return I will marry you.'

Ethel had whipped off her cap, pinched up her cheeks and bitten her lips to make them red. Then, having got past the dragon in the kitchen, she walked demurely down to the gate.

'I can't stay long. I'm rather busy,' she said coolly.

Billy took off his cap and stepped closer, looking down at her with a mixture of hope and doubt she found most engaging. 'I know I shouldn't call you out from your work, but it's important.'

'Why aren't you in the shop?' she asked. He had his jacket on and his apron off.

'I've been into Westleigh to do something.'

'And Mr Williamson let you?'

'Well, he sort of had to let me, really. You see, there's a recruitment office there. I've enlisted.'

She stared, unsure how she felt about the news. 'You've what?' she said, buying time.

'I volunteered. I told Mr Williamson I wanted to, and he said all right, I was doing the right thing. I did it for you, Ethel.'

'For me?'

'To make you proud of me. You said you wanted me to be a hero. So I volunteered. I'm going off to the war!'

'Well!' she said. He gazed down at her earnestly, and he looked so handsome, with his eyes bright and his cheeks flushed, that she was strangely touched. It was a grand sort of gesture, she supposed, if he'd really done it for her; on the other hand, it would mean he was going away, and she would lose one of her most constant admirers. 'I don't know what to say,' she temporised.

'But you're pleased, aren't you?' he urged. 'You are proud of me?'

'I suppose so. You'll look nice in uniform.'

It wasn't the endorsement he had hoped for. 'Ethel, don't you remember what we were talking about when you said that?' She looked blank. 'We were talking about getting married. You said you wouldn't marry me unless I did something romantic. Now I have. So *will* you marry me?'

'Don't talk so daft, Billy Snow,' Ethel said briskly, sensing a trap opening before her – though her heart tripped a little because he *was* so handsome, and almost a soldier. 'How can you marry me when you're going away?'

'We could do it tomorrow at the register office,' he said eagerly. 'I could get a special licence, and they're staying open longer for men going to war. I read it in the paper.'

Ethel's brows snapped together. 'I'm not having a wedding like that, all rushed and hole-and-corner. What would people think?'

'Lots of people are doing it – high-ups as well. You see the notices in the papers every day. Lords and everything.'

'Well, you're not a lord. And where would I live if I married you, I'd like to know, with you gone off to the army?'

'I've thought about that. You could have my room at home with Mum and Dad until the war's over. You'd be company for Mum while Dad's at work.'

At that point the shine went off the marriage proposal. 'Live with your mum and dad? What do you take me for?' He looked so disappointed she almost, for a dangerous moment, relented. Was that actually a tear sparkling on his eyelashes? Such long eyelashes for a man! 'I've got to go in, or I'll be in trouble,' she said, hardening her heart.

'Oh, Ethel, please!' he cried, catching hold of her hand. 'I love you so much. And I'm going away to the war. Anything might happen. I might – I might be killed!'

'Well, I don't want to be a widow, thanks very much!'

She was trying to tug her hand free. He was desperate for any concession. 'Will you wait for me, then? We could be engaged. I could buy you a ring when I get leave. We're bound to get leave. And the war won't last for ever. Will you be my fiancy? Then I could write to you and everything.'

'I'll think about it,' she said, pulling away.

'Oh, Ethel, I want to kiss you.'

She felt a little surge of excitement in her stomach. He was such a good kisser. 'Not here!' she snapped.

'Can you get out tonight, when you finish work? We could go for a walk and . . .' *And maybe she'd say yes.* 'It'll be our last chance to be together.'

'I'll get out,' she said. It was supposed to be Ada's evening off, but she'd make her swap – Ada never had anything to do anyway. And a soldier going off to war trumped everything. She felt the occasion would add an extra layer of thrill to what were, in any case, intensely enjoyable encounters. The woods down by the lake, imminent departure, Billy Snow and kissing . . . She might even let him go a bit further, just this once.

★   ★   ★

Standing in the churchyard after morning service, Mrs Fitzgerald was agitated.

'I know one should be pleased about the volunteering, but we've lost five of our bell-ringers. Five! They all joined up together in the hope of serving together – this "Pals" idea. Even with the reserves we can hardly manage more than a plain bob now, and it takes years to bring on a young ringer. Dr Fitzgerald is thinking it might be patriotic to silence the bells for the duration of the war, so as to save them for an alarm in case the Germans invade.'

'Making a virtue of a necessity,' Beattie observed.

'And I'm told that the entire darts team from the Coach and Horses has gone,' Mrs Fitzgerald went on. 'Not that the rector and I approve of men standing around in public bars. I always said they should have been shut down when the war started.'

'They have to close at ten o'clock now,' Beattie pointed out. New, much reduced licensing hours had been set out in the second week of the war. Previously, public houses could open from five in the morning until half past midnight.

'Still far too much time for the men to swill themselves senseless. One wouldn't mind if they would stick to non-intoxicating drinks, but it's beer, beer, beer. So damaging to the moral fibre. So unpatriotic.'

No beer and no bells, Edward thought. Was all pleasure to be labelled unpatriotic and banned? It would be a long war indeed if the intensely virtuous took it over.

'But that's not what I wanted to talk to you about,' Mrs Fitzgerald went on. 'Have you been reading these terrible stories in the papers about German atrocities?'

'I don't want to believe them,' Beattie said, 'but I suppose one must. Mr Hunter says they come from the Danish and American newspapers, and they're neutral countries.'

'Unlike us, the Germans encourage journalists to follow their armies,' Edward said. 'They want everyone to know about their military triumphs and their harshness towards those who resist them.'

'I can't see why they would want to expose themselves like that,' said Mrs Fitzgerald.

'They think fear will persuade the Belgians and French *not* to resist them, of course,' said Edward. 'It's all part of their war plan.'

The Germans called it *Schrecklichkeit*, which the papers were translating as 'frightfulness'.

At Tamines the Germans had shot four hundred civilians and burned the village down. At Dinant six hundred, including women and children, had been rounded up and shot in punishment for a bridge that had been damaged to hold up the German advance; the town had been pillaged and many buildings destroyed. Louvain had been sacked over five days of looting and mass shooting, its churches, university and library of ancient manuscripts burned and destroyed.

There were also darker whispers, rumours of rape, mutilation, crucifixion, even cannibalism – things decent people would not even voice. It was all provoking an unparalleled loathing of the Germans and a renewed determination to defeat them.

'At all events,' Mrs Fitzgerald went on, 'it's clear the Belgians have suffered dreadfully. There are hundreds of refugees pouring into the country every day, and it's time we did something for them.'

'We?' Beattie queried.

'This village. We must get up a committee at once, and raise money for them. I thought the Northcote Belgian Refugee Comforts Fund had a nice ring to it. I must have you on the committee, Mrs Hunter, and Mrs Carruthers, Mrs Ellison, Mrs Gordon—'

'Mrs Gordon won't do it,' Beattie said quickly. 'Mrs Oliver asked her the other day for a committee and she said she has far too much to do.'

'*Not* quite the spirit that wins the war,' Mrs Fitzgerald said sternly. 'However, perhaps Mrs Lattery, then. And I suppose one must ask Mrs Prendergast. Such a useful, energetic person, though she does tend to *take over* rather.' There was a long-standing rivalry between Mrs Fitzgerald and Mrs Prendergast to be Philanthroper in Chief of the village.

'But what exactly do you want this committee to *do*?' Beattie asked, alarmed that Edward was coughing into his fist, a sure sign he was trying not to laugh.

'I thought to begin with that we ought to get up a sale of work. We haven't had one for a long time, and they always raise useful amounts. I shall call the first meeting tomorrow at the rectory and we'll aim to have it at the end of the month or early in October. Now do say you will be there, Mrs Hunter.'

Beattie felt the Fitzgerald vortex sucking at her again. 'Well, I—'

'Thank you, my dear. Always such an *example* to the village.' She beamed at Edward. 'You must be so proud of your wife, Mr Hunter. And of your son, one of our *very first* volunteers! Have you heard from the dear young man lately?'

Not fair, Beattie thought, *bringing David into it*. Now she couldn't refuse without letting him down. All the same, getting up a sale of work would be a change from domestic affairs, and it was in a good cause. Perhaps she could get the girls involved. It would give Diana something different to think about. And what about young Henry Bowers? She would suggest to Mrs Fitzgerald they try to get him to help – he was bound to have some new ideas that would shake them all up.

No, on second thoughts, she would ask him on her own initiative, and only tell Mrs F when it was a *fait accompli*. Otherwise she'd be bound to end up claiming it as her own idea.

CHAPTER TWENTY

Ethel was finding the war rather distracting. She would have been happy enough playing off one local boy against another, and there was the nervous and grateful Alan Butcher in tow (she couldn't think what it was about Alan that attracted her, but there it was). But a girl would have to be made of stone not to be drawn towards a uniform. And there were so many of them around, going back and forth to the station, popping out of officers' motor-cars, buying cigarettes, newspapers and sweets in Hadleigh's. A person had only so much time off, not enough to fit in all the available men. Still, one could sometimes dawdle about an errand, or slip down to the tradesman's gate for a few minutes' dalliance.

And then there was Mr Munt's 'boy' – Frank Hussey, a boy no more; indeed, a very attractive man, which made it all the odder that he could find nothing better to do with his time off than come to visit Old Miseryguts, as Ethel called Munt in her mind, though she had never quite dared to say it out loud. Still, she wasn't complaining, because when he called on Miseryguts, he always came up to the kitchen and usually had his tea there, which gave Ethel an opportunity to flirt.

Come to think of it, perhaps the reason he visited Munt was in order to see Ethel. It made more sense to her. She wondered when he might suggest a proper walk-out. To the picture-house, perhaps. She wouldn't mind six penn'orth of dark at the Electric Palace in Westleigh with big, strong Frank Hussey. It might take a little juggling of her time: if it became a regular thing she would have to drop Alan. Oh, what it would be to be a lady! she thought. Nothing to do but polish your nails and receive gentlemen, like Miss Diana . . .

With all these concerns, as well as her job of work, Ethel had enough to be going on with, which made it not only puzzling but annoying that she should find herself thinking about her mother. It had been some time since she'd visited her: she had better things to do with her time off. But the war changed the way you thought. For some reason it made her feel uncomfortably as though she had left something unfinished. It was nonsense, of course; yet the thought nagged at the back of her mind, until one day she simply flung it out into the open and said crossly, 'Oh, all *right!*'

So one Sunday, when she could have been out sparking with Alan or flirting with soldiers, she put her hat on, begged some rock cakes from Cook and put them into a bag, walked to the end of Highwood Road, climbed the stile, and set off on the footpath across the fields to Goston.

Goston was a village two miles away, but since the railway came, the ever-expanding tendrils of Northcote were reaching towards it and would, it must be supposed, one day engulf it. It was a semi-detached part of Northcote now. Back in history, as its name suggested, it was the source of all those geese that, marching through Northcote on the way to London, had given the name to the Goose Green – probably an assembly point for different flocks. Goston was still home to several poultry farms. Ethel came from Goston, and the smell and sound of chickens still filled her with aversion.

Her mood sank as she approached the far end of the path. She had grown up in the cottage where her mother still lived: one of a terrace of four at the end of a muddy track off the village road. You saw that sort of cottage in sentimental paintings used on biscuit tins: crooked walls, small windows, thatched roof, a long garden full of cabbages and beans. In the paintings there would be hollyhocks and delphiniums in the garden too, and a cat sitting on the whitewashed doorstep, perhaps a smiling woman leaning on the gate talking to the postman. She had seen Peter doing jigsaws like that.

In reality they were old, old cottages, built cheaply straight on to the earth, and inside they were dark, cold and, above all, damp. The smell of damp got into everything, your clothes, your hair, your food; the brick floor sweated; anything left touching a wall grew mould. There were rats in the thatch, black beetles in the kitchen, and no running water. A pump at the end of the row served all four cottages. So did the privy, which was emptied by the night-soil man weekly, except when the track was too muddy to get his cart down. Even when it had recently been emptied, the privy stank.

All the cottages were in need of repair, but they were owned by an elderly spinster, Miss Deedes, who lived in genteel near-starvation. The rents – when they were paid – were not enough to cover repairs. She was a grey stick of a woman with fluttery hands, mauve lips and a drop on the end of her nose. She'd had to sell almost everything to pay her father's debts, and kept only a tiny house in the village to live in and the four cottages to give her an income.

Ethel's mother, Annie, had been born there too. Her father, a ploughman, had the cottage at a tied rent because he had worked for Miss Deedes's father. When Annie's mother had died in childbed, Annie, at the age of ten, had taken over the care of her younger siblings and her father, doing such cooking and washing and cleaning as were possible in the circumstances. When the siblings were all dead, she continued to take care of her father, until he died too.

'Lungs,' Annie had said tersely, when Ethel asked what killed them all. In that damp place, lungs were fatally weakened, and the consumption that was rife throughout the nineteenth century found easy pickings.

Ethel did not remember her own father. He must have died about the same time as she was born, she supposed, but she didn't know – Annie was not a great one for questions, asked or answered. In fact she knew almost nothing about him except that his name was Bert and he was a cowman for Mr Deedes. 'He was a bit older than me,' Annie had said once, in a rare burst of communication. When Ethel thought about it (which she didn't often, preferring to consign everything about her childhood to the darkest corner of her mind), she supposed that Bert had married Annie for practical reasons (she was occupying the cottage and would keep house for him) and she had married Bert for financial ones (he had an income and would support her).

Children had followed. Ethel did not know how many, as most of them had died. By the time she was old enough to be aware of her surroundings, there were only two left, both much older than her: Cyril by twenty years, and Edie by fifteen. Cyril had followed his father's calling as ploughman; Edie had got work in the kitchen of the Jolly Farmers, the less salubrious of Goston's two pubs.

'See how well *that* worked out!' Ethel muttered to herself, climbing the stile at the other end of the footpath.

When she was five her sister Edie had run away with a tinker, who had pulled up his caravan on the green beside the pub and was repairing the Jolly Farmers' pots and pans. How it had come about, Ethel had never been told, but she thought it was plain enough: the tinker wanted a wife and Edie wanted escape. Even a tinker's van and the uncertain life of the road must be better than what she had.

So then there was just Ma, Cyril and Ethel. She had liked Cyril. He had been more like a father to her than a brother, being so much older; and perhaps he felt like a father, too, because he had insisted that she go to school – neither he

274

nor Ma had ever been. 'But you're a pretty little thing, our Ethel, ' he said. 'You should have a chance to better yourself.' The only nice things that had ever been said to her had come from Cyril. Ma unfolded her lips only to scold.

So Ethel went to Goston village school and learned to read and write, do sums, sew and darn; also to tell the globe, and to recite the kings and queens of England and important dates. Not much of the latter had stuck. She remembered Battle o' Hastings 1066, but not the king who fought there or where Hastings was; Great Fire o' London 1666; Battle o' Waterloo 1815 – or was that Battle o' Trafalgar? Who knew or cared? Such facts stood up in her mind like ancient monoliths, erected by some unknown tribe so deep in the past that there was no guessing their significance. They were just *there*, parts of the landscape.

Geography remained a closed book to her. Apart from England, there was Abroad, which was mostly France and Germany, and there was America; but where any of them was or how far away she had no idea. It didn't seem to her to matter, anyway. Her mother and Cyril had never been further from Goston than Rustington, five miles away, for the Rustington Fair. Ethel had been to London. Edie presumably had gone further, since she had never been heard of again.

When Ethel was eleven, Cyril had died, of gangrene after cutting his foot on a half-buried ploughshare. He had died slowly at home, with Ethel and Ma tending him, and in his last lucid hours, before the fever made him delirious, he had told Ethel she must go into service.

'You'll have a roof over your head and your keep,' he said, his eyes glassy. 'You might be a parlourmaid one day. At least you'll have a chance.'

He died, and Ethel had left home to go into service, and here she was, nine years later, not a parlourmaid, but when she put on her black afternoon dress, as good as. She had never regretted going into service. She lived in a house with electric light and an indoor privy; she had a bath every week, clean sheets on the bed, and all the food she could eat. She had come so far from where she had started, she couldn't look back down without getting dizzy.

And she had turned out pretty, like Cyril had said, as the men and boys who were always after her attested. Well, having come this far, she meant to go further. Not to be a maid all her life, no: she meant to marry a man who could keep her properly, in a nice house. But not yet. She wasn't going to give up having fun yet.

Which made it all the more puzzling that she now found herself walking down the rutted lane to her childhood home. It wasn't even as if Ma appeared to enjoy her visits. Not that Ma ever enjoyed anything. A joyless woman, Ma, always ready to take offence. You knew very clearly what she disapproved of, but as to what she liked, if she had ever liked anything . . .

And the last few times she had seemed almost hostile towards Ethel, had greeted her with a glare and 'So you've turned up again. What do you want?'

It occurred to Ethel that Ma might be going a bit doo-lally. She didn't know how old she was, but she must be in her sixties, and living in that dank, dark place would be enough to drive anyone barmy. The last time Ethel had come, it had been impossible to get any conversation out of her. She'd had to do all the talking, while Ma just stared at her with that cold unblinking glare, like an owl.

And at the end, when she had got up to leave and said she'd come again some time, Ma had said, 'I don't know why you bother. I'm not your mother.' And she had given her such a look . . . It was almost as if she hated her.

Ethel came in sight of the cottage, and a sort of cold dread took hold of her. She had got out, she had escaped, and at the last moment it seemed like madness to risk Fate by coming back here, even to visit. She had an irrational fear

276

that the place would close round her and she'd never get out again. She stopped at the gate, folding her arms around herself as if she were cold. It looked even worse than she remembered. The mangy thatch, the moss growing up the chimney, the crooked walls with the render coming off in scabrous patches, the peeling paint, the garden full of weeds. Just looking at it she could smell the damp, and the thick reek of the privy; she could feel the perpetual background hunger of never having quite enough to eat . . .

Well, she'd come this far – she might as well see if Ma was all right. She needn't stay long. The door stood open, as it usually did in summer, to let in the light. She called out, 'Ma? It's me,' as she stepped in.

There was just the one room, and a lean-to scullery behind. The big bed was at one end, the table and chairs at the other. The range was in the chimney, with the shelf above it that sported the tea-caddy, the teapot and some bits of china. A door in the wall beside the range opened on to stairs that wound round the chimney to the tiny bedroom under the thatch. Ma had slept there when Ethel was a child, while she and Edie had shared the big bed and Cyril had a truckle that pulled out from underneath it. But since Ethel had left, Ma had taken over the big bed downstairs. 'I can't stand the rats up there,' she'd said. 'I hear 'em all night long, a-scuttling about, filthy beasts.'

Her life had grown smaller and smaller, lived now almost entirely between the one room and the privy. A neighbour on one side pumped her water for her and the one on the other side did her little bit of shopping in the village. What she lived on was a mystery. You couldn't get the Lloyd George until you were seventy, and Ethel didn't think she could be that old. Ethel sent her a shilling a week out of her wages; perhaps Cyril had left her something and she was eking it out. One thing was sure: old Miss Deedes couldn't be getting any rent out of her.

As her life had grown smaller, so she had shrunk away. Ethel remembered her as a big woman, with a granite face and strong forearms, always bare and usually red from doing washing, hands hard from work and quick to slap. Now she was shrivelled and shrunken, wrinkled in the face; her hair, dragged back into the same bun she had always worn, was growing thin, showing her scalp through it in places.

And today Ethel found her still in bed, sitting up with a blanket made of knitted squares round her shoulders over her nightgown. The range was lit, but burning very low, and it didn't seem to be doing anything to warm the air, which felt clammy. The penetrating smell of damp was mixed with that of dirty bodies and a whiff of urine. Coming from a clean place, Ethel noticed it as never before.

'Ma? Are you all right?'

'Oh, it's you again, is it?' Annie said. Her eyes were still bright – with malice, perhaps, but at least that was spirit of a sort – and there was colour in her cheeks, though the rest of her face was wax-yellow. Her jaw worked, clenching and unclenching, as though she wanted to bite someone. 'Turned up like a bad penny.'

'I've never seen you in bed before,' Ethel said.

'Stop in bed if I want. Please myself now, can't I? No-one else around.'

Ethel felt an unwelcome prick of guilt. 'I've not been to see you for a while. Been very busy.'

'I dare say,' Annie said.

'I brought you something,' Ethel tried, offering the paper bag of cakes. 'Fresh made.'

Annie accepted the bag without thanks, looked into it, then pulled out a cake and began to eat it with greedy haste.

Ethel watched her finish the first, then reach in for another, and said, to catch her between mouthfuls, 'So, how've you been?'

Annie waved the hand not busy with rock cake in a

dismissive way. 'You can go now. You don't need to hang around. I don't need you.'

'Ma!' Ethel protested.

'I'm not your ma!' Annie said.

'Don't be mean to me, when I've come to see you,' Ethel pleaded. Annie began to cough, spraying crumbs. The cough seemed to go on and on. 'Are you sick?'

'What do you think?'

Never answer a question straight out, that was Ma's way. Ethel came close and put her hand against Annie's brow. Annie jerked away. 'Don't!'

'You're burning up!'

'Leave me be.' She coughed again, hollowly. 'Make a cuppa tea, if you must meddle.'

Ethel retreated. Getting away from home didn't make her any more able to confront her mother. The kettle was warm and didn't take long to boil. There was tea in the caddy, and a little milk in the scullery, in the brown jug with the muslin cap weighted with blue beads – the same jug and the same cover she had known all her life. She heard her mother coughing in the other room.

'Can't find any sugar,' she said, bringing the cup back in.

Annie seemed to have lost interest. She was lying back on the pillows, her hands gripping the cake bag, her eyes fixed on the wall opposite. The colour in her cheeks, Ethel saw now, was hectic. She knew what that cough was.

'There's no sugar,' she said hopelessly, offering the cup. Annie didn't take it, so she put it down on the floor beside the bed. She hesitated, then said, 'You should see the doctor.'

Annie just looked at her, a look that said *You've been among gentry-folk too long. The likes of us can't afford doctors.* Another reason for going into service, of course – if you got sick, your employers looked after you.

Ethel swallowed. 'I'll pay,' she said. She had some money saved up. Half a crown was what they usually charged, though some did it cheaper for poor folk. Half a crown! But you had to, didn't you, for your mother? Even a mother who had slapped and belittled and ignored you all your childhood, and even now had no smile or softer look for you. She couldn't remember ever being kissed by her mother, or held in kind arms.

'Save your money,' Annie said tersely. 'Won't do no good anyway. It's the damp.' She stared at nothing a while longer, then roused herself and said, 'Where's that tea?'

Ethel handed her the cup and she sipped, grimaced, sipped again. 'I'm on the way out,' she announced, not looking at Ethel.

'Ma!' Ethel protested.

Now she looked. 'I told you, I'm not your ma. How many times?'

'You keep saying it, but I know you don't mean it.'

'Oh, but I do, Miss Fancy-ways. I had all the trouble of you, brought you up, took care of you, but you're not my daughter.'

'Don't talk so daft,' Ethel protested, but doubtfully. Ma seemed so clear about it. She asked, half defiantly, 'Go on, whose am I, then?'

Definitely malice, though there was some fever in the brightness of the narrowed gaze that absorbed Ethel's discomfiture like nourishment. 'Didn't you never guess? Gawd, you're slow, all right, for all your precious school-learning! Edie was only fourteen when she fell for you. Cyril was afraid of the scandal – thought we might lose the cottage, the Deedeses being High Church – so we put about it was me that was carrying. A whajercallit – posthumous child, that's what you were,' she sneered. 'Well, Bert'd been dead ten months when you turned up, but nobody wasn't interested enough to do the reckoning, so the story stuck all right. And *I* was stuck with *you*! Specially when Edie run off, ungrateful slut.'

280

Ethel was reeling. She stared, trying to make sense of the new information. 'But then – so you're—'

'I was near-on fifty when you was born. Had my bellyful of kids by then, an' all. Thought I was done with it. Never wanted to start all that over again. But Edie was no use, never lifted a finger for you, so I had to do it all. Well, now you know, so you can have me off your conscience. Stop coming up here and bothering me. I shan't be here much longer anyway.'

'But even if you're not my mother, you're still my—' Ethel began. Her voice sounded bewildered.

'Not "your" anything,' Annie snapped. 'Had to be done, that's all. I never liked you – too much like Edie, too mimsy-pimsy. Once Cyril sent you to that school, you thought yourself too good for your own folk. I knew you'd be off, like Edie, never give a thought to how we was to manage. Now look at you! I s'pose you think you're a lady.'

'Ma, don't talk like that.'

'I'm not your ma!'

'Well, you are to me. I don't know why you always have to be so nasty to me.'

'Cos you're my cross, that's why. You're the burden on my back. I've carried you all these years, and enough's enough. So let me die in peace. Go away, can't you?' She closed her eyes.

Ethel stood in silence, looking at her but not seeing her, trying to make sense of it. It was like having the earth pulled out from under her feet, like a rug, and finding empty space beneath. Edie, not her sister but her mother? Then Cyril was her – her uncle, not her brother. And Ma was her grand-mother. Who hated her. It wasn't fair! What had she ever done? How was it her fault?

At last another question came to her. 'Then who was my father?'

Annie's eyes opened a crack. 'You still here?'

'Please, Ma, who was it?'

'I got no patience with your questions. Go ask Edie – she's the only one that knew.'

'Do you know where she is?'

'She run off. Never heard from her from that day to this. Now go away and leave me sleep. You wear me out. You always did.'

'All right,' Ethel said. 'But I'll come and see you again.'

'Don't bother,' said Annie, eyes ostentatiously closed. '*I* don't want you.'

Outside, breathing deeply of the clean air, Ethel looked up at the sky, tears pricking her eyes. She blinked them back and sniffed ferociously. She hated to cry – it made her feel stupid and weak. She had made her own fortune since she had first gone into service, and she would continue to do so. You couldn't rely on anyone else. That was the one lesson she had learned in life. You took from those weaker than you, usually women, and manipulated those stronger than you, usually men.

Men owned the world, but if you could make them mad for you, you could own them, at least for long enough to get what you wanted. And that was what she did, and what she would do. Love didn't come into it. The likes of her couldn't afford love – not that she'd know it if she tripped over it. What she wanted was a husband who would put her in a nice house, and that was what she would get. Then she'd be safe – safe from cold and hunger, the smell of damp, the lung sickness . . .

She straightened her shoulders, and suddenly laughed. *Of course!* she thought. *Ma's gone doo-lally, just like I thought.* All this 'I'm not your mother' business – her mind was wandering. Old folk got like that. What was it the doctors called it? She'd gone sea-lion – some word like that. Old age and sickness, she was feverish – of course she'd gone dippy. It was all rubbish. Why hadn't she realised that straight away?

A movement made her turn her head, and she saw the next-door neighbour, Mrs Clark, a downtrodden woman in her forties, who looked twenty years older, having lost most of her teeth. She smiled ingratiatingly at Ethel in her neat coat, hat and good boots, not recognising her, and a moment later realised who she was.

'Been to see your mum, have you?'

'Yes, that's right.'

'She's been poorly. Took to her bed. I been doing a bit for her.'

'Yes, I'm sure. Thank you.'

'Oh, it's no trouble.' Mrs Clark inched closer. 'I'm sure she's ever so grateful. Vicar's been in an' all.'

Ethel almost laughed. Her mother had never had any time for God. 'Bet that didn't go well,' she said.

Mrs Clark looked embarrassed. 'Well . . .' she hesitated '. . . she's not quite right in the head, pore soul. Cos of being ill and everything. Vicar understood. She never meant them things she said to him, he knew that. He's a very nice man, Mr Treadgold. Said he'd come again if she got worse.' She looked up at Ethel and lowered her voice. 'Between you and me, I don't think she's long for this world, pore Christian soul. If you was to want a message sent . . . ?'

Yes, tell me when she's dead, Ethel thought.

'My youngest is a bright lad. He could take you word, if you was to tell me where.'

Ethel gave her the direction. Of course, Ma was wandering in her wits, you had to understand. But she had never been a loving mother. And a Christian soul? Ethel begged leave to doubt it. She set her face away from the cottage and walked briskly back towards Northcote, feeling her spirits recovering at every step that put distance between her and her beginnings.

CHAPTER TWENTY-ONE

'I think we should hold our sale of work in the church hall,' Mrs Fitzgerald said, firing her opening salvo.

The rectory's morning-room was so often used for parish duties, it had lost any domestic feeling. There were hard chairs for meetings, side tables covered with pamphlets and prayer books, a carpet worn almost threadbare by the passage of boots, a distinct chill in the air and, under the furniture polish, a smell of damp. It was on the east side of the rectory, but the window was obscured by a tall hedge of laurels, so the morning sun had little chance of penetrating, and the fire was rarely lit. Parish meetings, Sunday school, confirmation lessons were all held around the long oak table, its surface scarred by generations of prisoners. Those seeking pre-nuptial instruction and spiritual advice were likewise received in this punitive discomfort. Beattie sometimes thought the smell of damp must come from all the tears soaked into the woodwork.

Mrs Prendergast rolled up her mental sleeves and went in. 'I disagree. The village hall is bigger. And better placed.'

'I think we are very well placed here,' Mrs Fitzgerald returned. 'Under the aegis of the Church—'

'I meant geographically,' Mrs Prendergast interrupted. 'The village hall is central. And the extra capacity is vital. The object should be to raise as much money as possible for the poor refugees, without worrying about hurting anyone's feelings.'

Mrs Fitzgerald bristled, but Mrs Prendergast had shot her fox. 'Of course the object of the sale of work is to raise money. I think we all understand that, Mrs Prendergast.'

'Oh, couldn't we call it a *bazaar*?' Mrs Lattery interrupted. 'Sale of work sounds so dull.' She was knitting as she listened. Mrs Fitzgerald had wanted to object, but the knitting was in khaki, and therefore sacrosanct.

'"Bazaar" has an unpleasantly *exotic* ring to it,' she said sternly. 'Eastern. Un-Christian.'

Mrs Lattery flushed. 'There are Christians in the east, you know,' she defended herself. 'Copenhagen is the centre of the Orthodox Church.'

'I think you mean Constantinople, dear,' Mrs Fitzgerald said, squashing her. 'And the word "bazaar" does not conjure up proper Christian images. We are *English*, you know.'

'All the same, sale of work does sound dull,' Beattie said. 'I think we should be more ambitious, and have some entertainments, too.'

'Enter*tain*ments?' Mrs Fitzgerald made it sound like a Saturday night in Sodom.

'Oh, yes!' said Mrs Ellison, brightening. 'People will give far more if they're having fun. These sales of work can be deadly.'

'What about skittles?' said Mrs Carruthers.

'I don't think there would be room,' Beattie said.

'You could have a skittles alley outside in the yard, if the weather was fine. People do love it.'

'Madame Mentallo!' said Mrs Ellison. 'We must have her – such amusing things she says!'

'Fortune-telling is *most* un-Christian,' Mrs Fitzgerald objected.

'Surely that doesn't matter as we're having it in the village hall,' Mrs Prendergast said triumphantly.

'If we're having Madame Mentallo, we might as well call

it a bazaar,' Mrs Lattery said stubbornly. 'I'm sure more people would come if we did.'

'Skittles are as English as can be,' Mrs Carruthers put in.

'She told me I was going to travel over water,' said Mrs Ellison, 'and the next day there was a dreadful downpour and the storm drains overflowed and the gardener had to put down duckboards before I could get out of the front door.'

'Oh, that was at Mrs Oliver's garden fête, wasn't it?' said Mrs Lattery. 'I remember that storm. I was so glad the rain didn't come until the next day.'

'Bowling for a pig,' Mrs Carruthers urged. 'So traditional.'

'Why not "fête"?' said Mrs Ellison. 'We could call it a fête if Mrs Fitzgerald objects to "bazaar".'

'Or a fair,' Mrs Carruthers said. 'Fair is English enough, isn't it?'

'We could spell it with a *y*,' Mrs Lattery said generously. 'You know, "fayre".' She managed to convey the spelling in her pronunciation. 'We could call it Ye Olde Englishe Fayre.'

Beattie winced. '"Fête" seems to be a good compromise,' she said. 'Not too dull and not too exotic.'

'Why shouldn't we be exotic?' Mrs Lattery said. 'We're doing it for the Belgians, and they're not English.'

'"Fête" is a French word,' Mrs Carruthers objected.

'Well, the Belgians speak French, don't they?'

'Ladies, ladies,' Mrs Fitzgerald intervened, using her most ringing voice. 'We will get nowhere if we keep having side conversations. Now let's leave the question of what we call it for later, and talk about the stalls. I assume we'll have all the usual ones: knitting, embroidery, handicrafts, bric-à-brac.'

'I'll take that one,' Mrs Prendergast said. No-one argued – she always did.

'Clothes?' Mrs Ellison said.

Mrs Prendergast wrinkled her nose. 'They give the thing such a shabby air.'

'Home-made cakes,' said Mrs Carruthers.

'Sugar's in short supply,' said Mrs Lattery. 'Will anyone give?'

'Of course they will, in a good cause,' said Mrs Carruthers. 'It will be a chance to exercise ingenuity.'

'My cook's started to put grated carrot into the fruit cake,' Mrs Lattery said, half regretfully.

'Mine says you can use beetroot,' said Mrs Ellison. 'She hasn't tried it yet.'

'I'd have thought parsnip would be sweeter than carrot,' said Mrs Carruthers. 'If you—'

'Ladies, ladies! Please. We'll put down home-made cakes. And jams and chutneys, as well.'

'And a refreshment stall,' said Mrs Prendergast. 'Tea, lemonade and sandwiches, at least. Hetherton's will donate the loaves, and the local farmers ham and cheese.'

'Entertainments,' Beattie said firmly. 'Roll-a-penny, guess the weight, harmless little competitions like that.'

Mrs Fitzgerald gauged the temperature of the meeting, and said, 'Perhaps you'd like to take charge of that side of it, then, Mrs Hunter.'

'Certainly,' Beattie said, thinking of Henry Bowers. 'I'll form a sub-committee.' She was sure he would have some good ideas.

'Oh, I'm not sure that's—' Mrs Fitzgerald began, seeing power slipping away from her.

'Leave it to me,' Beattie said. 'I'll report back to you at the next meeting.'

'Very kind of you, Mrs Hunter,' Mrs Prendergast boomed. 'Now, shall we talk about the village hall? We ought to decorate it, of course.'

'There's plenty of that red-white-and-blue bunting left over from the Coronation,' Mrs Fitzgerald said. 'It's in the parish store-room.'

'But in what condition?' Mrs Prendergast enquired.

'We had it out last year and it was quite all right. But we can go over and have a look at it afterwards. And there's the cheesecloth we use to cover the stalls.'

'The pink and blue was all right last time,' Mrs Ellison said, 'but the white was looking awfully dingy, I remember.'

'It can be freshened up,' said Mrs Fitzgerald. 'I'll see if Baxter's laundry will wash it for us. They could make it their donation to the Fund.'

'Ah, donations,' said Mrs Prendergast. 'Now there's an area we must discuss. I thought . . .'

The meeting continued on its accustomed path.

William and Peter went back at school, and Bobby had packed his trunk and gone, complaining 'like an ulcer', as Cook said, to Oxford. Sadie was afraid that their departure might turn unwelcome attention on her, but her mother was occupied with the fête, and her father was busier than ever at work and had evidently forgotten all about sending her anywhere.

Diana was quite willing to help with the fête, especially as Henry had agreed to be involved. He had already come up with guessing how many buttons there were in a jar and guessing the weight of a cabbage, and though some of his suggestions were impractical, like a bucking-bronco competition and a shooting range, he had offered to do card tricks and even, if it would add to the jollity, to dress up as a magician for the purpose.

'And I'll go around asking folk to donate prizes,' he offered. 'I'm good at that. No-one can resist me.'

'I believe you,' Diana said, laughing.

'Gee whiz, this'll be fun,' he said. He was so successful in making it seem so, he had even persuaded Diana to go with him on his donation quest, something she would have jibbed at before as 'begging from door to door'.

At breakfast one day, Beattie said, 'Here's a letter from Beth.' And a moment later, 'She says Jack's battalion has gone to France. Of course, she doesn't know where. If only they'd let them say, at least their people at home could have an idea what they're facing.'

'Why is it a secret, Father?' Sadie asked.

'In case of spies, of course. There are spies everywhere,' William said, with relish.

'Mrs Chaplin said she heard there was a German barber in Harrow who swore if any Englishman came in to be shaved, he'd cut his throat.'

Edward looked at her. 'Use your intelligence and tell me why that can't be true.'

She thought a moment. 'Because if he killed all his customers he'd soon be out of business,' she concluded. 'But why would anyone say it if it wasn't true?'

'To foment hatred,' said Edward. 'The newspapers have discovered that "frightfulness" sells copies.'

'But shouldn't we hate them?' William asked. 'They *are* the enemy.'

'We hate the enemy, not individual Germans. We're fighting to preserve civilisation,' Edward said. 'If we become uncivilised in the process, it's all for nothing.'

Sadie said, 'It was in the paper yesterday that a mob in Liverpool smashed up a grand piano because it was a Bechstein and that's a German name.'

'Since when do you read the paper?' Diana objected, buttering toast.

'It was in Munt's shed. He uses them to line his seed trays. I was in there talking to him and I saw it. And there was a horrid bit about some poor lady's sausage dog being killed.'

Beattie folded the letter away. 'The Ellisons thought they were going to lose their governess,' she said. 'She had to register as an alien because she's a Swiss. Fortunately she's a "mam'selle", not a German Swiss. But the Frobishers have a German governess for the twins. Apparently the little boy was in tears the other day, asking if they were going to have to kill poor Fräulein. It was all very upsetting. What threat can she be? She's fifty if she's a day, and terribly short-sighted.'

'But, Mother, that's exactly the sort of person who *would* be a spy because no-one would suspect them,' William said eagerly. Boys' comics were full of such stories.

'Don't be silly,' said Beattie. 'She's been with them almost twenty years.'

'Why don't they just lock up all the Germans who live here?' Diana asked.

'Over two thousand *have* been interned,' Edward said, 'but that was mostly for their own safety. That's only about a fifth of those who've registered. The government doesn't have room to intern them all.'

'They're keeping them in the exhibition hall at Olympia, aren't they, Father?' said William. 'And Alexandra Palace.'

Edward nodded. 'But it's expensive to keep thousands locked up. Any who want to go to Germany, or a neutral country, can apply for a permit. I believe a lot are heading for Denmark. The intelligence people are keeping an eye on the suspicious characters. They know who they're after. The rest are just ordinary, hard-working people.'

'So why doesn't the government stop the newspapers trying to make us hate them?' Sadie asked.

'Because if people don't hate the Germans they won't volunteer to go and fight them,' Diana said.

'You may have something there,' Edward said. 'And there's some truth in the stories from Belgium. The German high command has specifically licensed its troops to loot – something that's strictly forbidden to our army. Besides,' he concluded, going back to *The Times*, 'we don't believe in censorship in this country.'

★   ★   ★

Mrs Prendergast called – a rare honour. Her usual way was to command people to attend her by sending a 'little note'.

'I have had an idea for the fête,' she said, glancing round the drawing-room with sharp, noticing eyes. *Looking for dust*, Beattie thought. 'No, no coffee, thank you. I cannot stay. I was thinking what a good thing it would be to have someone eminent open it.'

'Yes, that is a good idea. Did you have someone in mind?'

'Indeed I have. The Countess Wroughton!' said Mrs Prendergast triumphantly.

'Lady Wroughton? I doubt she would accept. You know they've never been very keen on local affairs.'

'Then it's time they changed. There's a war on, and everyone must do their bit. It's little enough to ask, and it will add *tone*. Now, Mrs Hunter, I think you should be the one to approach her.'

'Me?'

'Yes, indeed. Your husband is acquainted with the earl. You have an *in*.'

Beattie was so relieved that she had not said anything about Diana and Charles that she submitted rather than push Mrs Prendergast to find other reasons. 'Very well,' she said. 'I'll ask. But I don't have very high hopes. You should be thinking of an alternative. What about Mr Whiteley?'

'An MP is a poor substitute for a countess.'

'Their hats *are* much less decorative,' Beattie agreed.

Mrs Prendergast gave her a strange look, but said only, 'Do your best, that's all I ask. And as time is short, I think you should write to her straight away.'

When she had gone, Beattie sat down to write the letter, and had a sudden, extremely cunning idea. The most likely outcome of writing to the countess was that she would simply not reply, even to Beattie. But supposing she wrote at the same time to the countess and to Charles? He might press

291

his mother to accept – and at the very least it would remind him that they had heard nothing from him for almost a month.

Beattie was on her way to the village hall, where the committee were meeting to inspect the premises. In her basket she had a sheet of paper on which she had drawn a plan for the layout of stalls. Mrs F and Mrs P would argue like cats over it, she thought, but one had to start somewhere. And on the way back she would call in at Edmond's for some ink and envelopes, and at Wendell's for various things – she'd made a list on the back of the plan.

There seemed to be an unusual number of people about as she turned into the high street. Gradually she became aware of shouting somewhere ahead, the babble of a large number of angry voices. It sounded unpleasantly hostile. And further on she came up against a crowd almost blocking the road, the back markers silent but shifting about and craning their heads, trying to see what was going on. It grew denser towards the front, and she could see fists being waved.

'What is it?' she asked the man standing nearest her.

'It's Stein's, the butcher's,' he said. 'I dunno what they've done. A 'ole lot o' people come marching up the shop.'

Yes, she could see now that that was where the front of the crowd was focused. In the midst of the formless shouting she could make out some of the words: 'Hun! Hun!' and 'German bastards!'

But the Steins waren't German, she thought. Surely everyone knew that. Worried, she pushed through the outlying people to where the mass thickened. There was a man in front of her with a red kerchief round his neck. She tugged at his arm. He turned his head. It was a stranger, and a very rough-looking sort, his dark face grim. 'What's happening?' she demanded.

292

'We're gonna burn 'em down,' he said. 'Better get out of here, lady.'

Now she looked around she could see there were a lot of strange faces in the crowd, as well as some of their own 'bad sorts', like Sowden. And scattered among them, a number of people she thought of as 'toughs', all of whom were wearing handkerchiefs of different colours round their necks. She didn't know why, but it sent a shiver down her back.

'Mrs Hunter! This is no place for you!' It was Hicks, their postman, appearing beside her. 'Come away, ma'am. Do!'

She turned to him gratefully. 'These are not our people,' she said. 'I see a lot of strangers. What does it mean, Hicks?'

'I don't know where they came from. They're not from round here,' he said. 'You really must go – things are getting rough.'

'But what do they want?'

'I heard it's a gang, ma'am – them with the neckerchiefs. They call themselves the Revengers. There was trouble in Westleigh yesterday. Now they've come here, and a bad lot of people've followed 'em to see the fun.'

'Fun!'

'They get a mob together and attack anyone they think is German, to revenge the Belgians – that's what they say, but to my mind it's just an excuse for looting. Please, ma'am, come away.'

'Has someone sent for the police?' she asked. But at that moment there was a forward surge. With half her mind she registered the men with neck-cloths all moving inward at the same time. She heard the sharp sound of glass shattering, and a woman's scream. The pitch of the shouting rose.

'Oh, God!' she said. There was a boy standing near, his mouth open with amazement. She grabbed his upper arm so hard that he flinched and looked up at her with wide eyes. 'Run to the police station. Tell them. Make them come.

Run!' She added a shake and a shove and he reeled away and, thank God, started running.

Two dogs came wriggling out through the legs of the crowd. One had a lump of meat in its mouth. The other was snatching at it as they ran – a white dog with blood on its coat. It looked like Nailer.

Beattie suddenly remembered that Sadie had walked down to the village earlier to meet Anne Carruthers, with whom she had been at school. Nailer often followed Sadie. Her blood turned cold at the thought – but why would she have gone to Stein's?

There was more glass smashing, more women's shrieks. The convulsive pulsing of the crowd was in two directions now, some still pushing forward, but most, it seemed, trying to move back. A tall man with a blue handkerchief thrust himself out of the crowd. He was carrying a bulging sack, his face grim and gleeful.

'Stop!' she shouted at him. 'Stop it!' She tried to grab his arm, but he shoved her away with such force that she fell. For a moment she thought the backwards surging would trample her.

But Hicks was there, hunkered over her, almost in tears. 'You shouldn't be here! You shouldn't be here!'

'Help me up!' she gasped.

There was something else, a different voice, somewhere at the front, lighter, female, haranguing. And then – oh, blessed sound! – a police whistle pierced the air, blowing and blowing the tocsin. Here came the mighty figures in blue-black, the silver badges on their helmets glinting in the sun, tall PC Whittle and even taller PC Denton, young Andy Denton, who had arms and shoulders like a blacksmith's and opened the batting for the Northcote XI.

The back markers turned and fled, the locals to a safe distance to watch and the strangers running for the horizon. Denton had his truncheon out, and as the police advanced

294

the crowd melted like a jelly on a warm day. Hicks was still urging her to go, so anxious he had even committed the solecism of taking her arm, but she shook him off. She had to see. She saw several of the neckerchiefs running like hares. Now the crowd was thin enough for her to see Stein's, its front window nothing but a few lethal-looking shards stuck to the frame. The shouting had died down to a babble of voices at normal pitch. She heard someone call out, 'Need a doctor here! Get a doctor!' She saw a large, huddled figure on the ground, another sitting, holding his head. From their aprons she took them for Mr Stein and his assistant, Horace. She could see now that the window display had been looted, almost cleared of meat. And someone was standing in the doorway – a slight figure in a dress.

Whittle and Denton had managed to grab two bad lots and had the come-along-o'-me grip on them. There was desperate scuffling, but some Northcote people joined in now to help. One of them – Paddy Boyle from the green-grocer's next door – was built like his own horse, and subdued an arrestee by wrapping his great arms round him from behind, pinioning him.

Then Beattie's entire scalp shifted backwards in astonishment when she realised the figure in the doorway was Sadie, standing with her arms out, her hands pressed to the frame either side, her expression stunned.

My God, my God, Beattie thought, and thrust herself through the remaining bodies to get to her.

Sadie's arms came round her, and Beattie felt her body trembling. Tears choked her, though whether of love, fear or rage she couldn't tell.

'I'm all right, Mummy,' Sadie said, in a shaky voice. A moment later she detached herself. 'I'm not hurt, honestly.'

Beattie let her go. Sadie was pale with shock. 'Mrs Stein and Adella are in the back somewhere. I made them go when the men came in. Anne's there too.'

'But what are you *doing* here?'

'Anne Carruthers brought a message from her mother about a joint. I came with her. We were in here when the crowd gathered and started shouting. We were afraid to go outside then. We could hear what they were chanting. It was horrible! Then the men burst in. Two of them, toughs, not from here.' She closed her eyes a moment.

PC Whittle came over to her. 'Are you all right, Miss Sadie?'

'Yes, I'm not hurt. How's Mr Stein, and Horace?'

'Nurse Parling's with them and Dr Harding's been sent for. Can you tell me what happened, miss? Are you up to it?'

'Yes, of course,' said Sadie. She clasped her hands together to steady herself, and told about the two men bursting in. 'They said, "We don't hold with dirty Huns," and some other bad stuff. And they said they were going to string them up and burn the shop down. Mr Stein came round the counter with his boning knife and said over his dead body. Then there was a kind of struggle. Horace joined in, and a couple of men who were in here, our people, and they sort of wrestled them outside.'

'Why didn't you run away?' Whittle asked, shocked. 'It was no place for you.'

'Well, because there was a terrible crowd outside. I didn't see how we could. Anyway. Adella was behind the till crying, and Mrs Stein looked as if she was going to be sick, and I didn't like to leave them. So I made them go out through the back. Anne went with them. I was going to go too, but I saw some of our people out there, so I thought p'raps we could make a fight of it. I stood in the doorway and shouted to them but I don't think they heard. Then Mr Stein went down, and Horace, and the window was smashed, and the men were grabbing the meat and running. I could see some other people were thinking of coming into the shop to do the same, so I talked to them. I talked and talked. I said it was wrong, what they were doing, I told them the police were coming, and the ones I knew, I said their names and "Go home," and it sort of got through to them and stopped them.'

Whittle looked amazed. 'You were a very foolish young lady. You could have been badly hurt.'

Sadie didn't seem to hear him. She was talking to the air. 'It was horrible, the look on their faces. Especially when it was people I knew – sort of blank and hot and shiny, as if their souls had gone and they were filled up with hate and greed instead.'

'But, Sadie, how could you?' Beattie began to protest.

Sadie's eyes registered her. 'I *had* to help, Mother,' she said. 'The Steins aren't German at all. But even if they were, Father said if we become uncivilised, the war is all for nothing.'

'Oh, Sadie!'

'A very foolish young lady,' said Whittle. 'But very brave. I don't doubt you've saved the Steins a lot of money. It was an outside gang, so I understand,' he said to Beattie. 'They've been causing trouble in villages all around. But we've got two of 'em now. I must get 'em back to the station. You should take Miss Sadie home, Mrs Hunter – she's had a shock. A very brave, foolish young lady,' he concluded wonderingly, with a shake of the head, as if he had never seen the like.

When they got home, Sadie refused absolutely to go to bed with a hot bottle and a cup of cocoa. She also refused to tell the story all over again to the boys, the servants, or to the various people who called during the rest of the day. 'I'm not a hero,' she said stonily. 'It was all horrid, and I don't want to talk about it. I want to forget it.'

Diana and Henry came rushing in, eyes wide, having heard

confusing reports, that Sadie was dead, or had defended the butcher's shop single-handed after Mr Stein was killed.

'I think the truth is just as thrilling,' Henry said, bright-eyed. 'We have a real, genuine heroine in our midst.'

'I'm not,' Sadie said, and turned a look both worn and pleading on her mother. Beattie sent her to the bottom of the garden with a book to be out of the way, and forbade the boys to go bothering her.

Munt found her there, and gave her an apple. 'It's perfect,' he said. 'Perfect shape, perfect colour. Put that in a show, you could.'

She took it, and the love that came with it, with a tired smile. He nodded and went away. Nailer had come to him with a cut on his back. Munt didn't know how he'd got it, but he had his suspicions. It wasn't a bad cut. He'd cleaned it up for him, got the blood out of his coat. But he decided not to tell Miss Sadie about it. She deserved a bit of peace and quiet.

Mr Stein, word came, had a mild concussion, a lot of bruises, and a cut on his hand that had probably come from his own knife. Horace had a cut on his face from the broken glass, a wrenched shoulder and a black eye, but was buoyed out of his discomfort by discovering himself to be a hero. Everyone wanted to shake his hand, and girls looked at him with an unprecedented interest.

Various people in the village wanted to get up some way of honouring Sadie, perhaps with a medal and a presentation by Mr Whiteley. Beattie had to work quite hard to stop it all, and Sadie kept to the house for several days and wouldn't see anyone.

The two men arrested – one a neckerchief man, the other a low type from Westleigh – were to be charged with affray and assault. A grand policeman came down from Scotland Yard because they were investigating the activities of the so-called Revengers, a gang from London who were using anti-German feeling as an excuse to loot. Mr Stein and Horace gave statements, and the neckerchief man was taken away to Scotland Yard to see if he would peach on his fellow gang members.

'It makes one feel so unsafe,' Mrs Lattery said, at the next committee meeting. 'We've never had anything like that before in Northcote.'

'PC Whittle says that the Scotland Yard officer told him the gang never goes to the same district twice,' said Mrs Prendergast, 'so there's no need for apprehension.'

'But our own people joined in. Our own people! Men we see walking about the village every day. And one doesn't know which ones, that's the terrible thing.'

'I expect we can guess some of them,' Mrs Prendergast said grimly.

'It's the Steins we should think of,' said Beattie. 'We must all rally round them.'

The shop was closed for two days, with the broken window boarded up, giving a very melancholy feel to the high street. But Mr Stein was not one to be bullied, as his attempt to defend his shop had proved. The morning after that, a new window was in place, Mr Stein was back in his usual position cutting meat, and Horace, his arm in a sling and his 'shiner' a beacon, was working the till one-handed while Adella served at the counter. Trade was brisk, from a mixture of loyalty and curiosity. Across the top of the new window a sign-writer had painted the words 'ALL-ENGLISH FAMILY BUTCHER EST. 1878', and in the middle of the window there was a coloured lithograph of the King and Queen.

On his way home from the station that evening, Edward noticed that Reiss's had a newly painted fascia-board. In large block capitals it now said 'RICE OUTFITTERS' and underneath in smaller capitals 'LADIES' AND GENTLEMEN'S TAILORING – DOMESTIC AND MILITARY UNIFORMS'.

Edward applauded the economy of the action. Reiss had always been pronounced that way anyway, and many would not notice the change until it had been there long enough for them to forget it had ever been any different. And the 'military uniforms' reminded people that it was the *British* officer who went there to be fitted, and what could be more patriotic than that? The Union Jack bunting around the window inside completed the effect.

Edward didn't know anything about the history of the Reiss family, but he would have liked to bet they had been in England for generations. He had been into the shop many times and everyone there was as English as the King.

CHAPTER TWENTY-TWO

Beattie had a note from Lady Wroughton – typewritten, on card, with a scrawl of a signature at the bottom that could have been anyone's. It said, 'The Countess Wroughton thanks you for your invitation but regrets that she is otherwise engaged and unable to accept.' It could have applied to any occasion. Beattie imagined a small stack of them in a desk drawer at Dene Park, ready to repel boarders.

But the following day she received a letter from Charles in a very different tone. He said he thought the fête a wonderful idea and that he would be certain to come, if he could get away. He was sure his mother would be delighted to open it and lend her support to the excellent cause. And he asked after Diana (perhaps a little wistfully? Or was she reading into it what she wanted to read?) and the rest of the family and proposed his respects to Mr Hunter.

And by the afternoon post came a letter from the countess, on good paper, hand-written, saying that after all she found her engagements were altered and she could now accept the invitation to open the fête. Beattie took it in triumph to the committee.

'How gracious!' Mrs Lattery enthused. 'Don't you think she expresses herself well? And such an elegant hand!'

Beattie, on the contrary, thought the note reluctant and the handwriting careless, but only she knew the whole story.

'It will certainly add tone to the affair,' Mrs Prendergast said. 'I'm extremely glad I thought of it.'

And Mrs Fitzgerald said, 'The rector will meet her at the door on the day, and conduct her to the stage. She will be glad to have someone she knows to guide her through the proceedings.'

The whole family was invited to the Palfreys' for the day on Sunday. It had been a chilly night and the train trundled through a real autumn fog, clinging whitely to the damp sparks of gold showing among the green of the trees. When they emerged from the station in Kensington the fog was not white but grey. They walked through the suddenly alien streets, all sounds muffled, all distances deceptive, and arrived smelling distinctly of soot.

'I sometimes think I should follow your example and move out,' Aeneas said to Edward, as they shed their coats. 'The air gets dirtier, with more motors and fewer horses every day.'

'I never regret taking the plunge,' Edward said.

'But I like to be near the factory. And I'm not sure the distaff side would like it. They do love their shops.'

It was a discussion they'd had many times before, and Edward knew perfectly well they'd never move. He said, 'How is business? Have you noticed any downturn because of the war?'

'Rather the opposite. We've had a run on our tinned lines. Chaps going off to their regiments, women sending them to their men at the Front and so on.'

'What about getting hold of ingredients?'

'You've put your finger on it. That *is* going to be a problem,' Aeneas admitted. 'We've plenty at the moment. I took the precaution of stocking up before the party started. But so much of what we use comes from abroad – sugar, molasses, ginger, cinnamon, dried fruit, chocolate. They're going to be hard to get hold of, now the government's taking over all the merchant capacity for the army.'

'So what will you do? Make plainer biscuits?'

'Ah, well, as it happens, I may be taking a different path altogether,' Aeneas said. Sonia had conducted everyone else through to the drawing-room. He invited Edward into his study and offered his cigarette case. 'Care for one of these?' He favoured a special kind of thin cheroot.

'Thanks, I'll have one of my own,' said Edward, getting out his own case.

'I suppose these'll become harder to get hold of, too,' Aeneas said, examining the cheroot with a mournful look.

'I hope this war doesn't mean having to give up every comfort,' Edward said, lighting them both.

'Good God, I trust not! What's civilisation without tobacco? Doesn't bear thinking of.'

'You were saying – a new path?'

'Oh, yes. I've been approached by a chap, business acquaintance, who's now in army procurement. He suggested I tender for a government contract to make army biscuits.'

'Hard tack?' Edward exclaimed. 'A bit of a come-down for Palfrey's, isn't it?'

'It could be extremely lucrative, given that the soldier's basic diet is bully and biscuit. And I heard a rumour that Kitchener's talking about asking for a million soldiers.'

'I wouldn't be at all surprised,' said Edward.

'Well, that's a lot of biscuit! And it would solve my supply problem. An army contractor would be guaranteed ingredients.'

'It would be a big change for you,' Edward suggested.

'There'd be a small amount of re-tooling, but the basic processes are the same. It might be my wisest move in the circumstances, with a family to provide for. What do you think?'

'I think you'll make a fortune. My brother-in-law, the war profiteer!' Edward teased.

Aeneas winced. 'Don't say that, even in jest. War breeds a mob mentality.'

303

'Don't I know it!'

'Beattie told Sonia about Sadie. You must be very proud.'

'Frightened out of my wits, in retrospect. But she doesn't like it talked of.'

'Yes, so Beattie said. Don't worry, we shan't mention it. But it's sobering when that sort of thing turns up on your own doorstep – the ugly face of hatred.'

They were silent a moment, then Edward said, 'So it'll be Palfrey's Superior Army Biscuits from now on, will it?'

'I'll probably find space to make a few fancies as well, just to keep my hand in,' Aeneas smiled. 'And it may be Hobson's choice, anyway. This chappie hinted that, as the army expands, they might not bother to ask for tenders in future, just commandeer the factories.'

'In that case, I should get in at the start and negotiate a good contract.'

'Sound advice,' said Aeneas. 'Well, whatever I do, I shall never be rich, with three females at home to keep in fal-lals. They do love their little luxuries.'

In the drawing-room there was a good fire, and the lights were lit against the gloom of the day outside. Sadie thought it looked oddly as though the world had ended outside, for there was nothing to see at all beyond the window panes. *Is that what oblivion looks like?* she wondered.

Beth and Laura had both been invited for the day, and were comfortably ensconced. 'Have you heard anything from Jack?' Beattie asked.

'Just one of those field postcards,' said Beth. 'You know the sort – with printed sentences that you delete as appropriate. He crossed out everything except "I am quite well" and "Letter follows at first opportunity". I wish he'd said whether he'd received my letters. But they may be moving about too quickly for the post to catch up with them.'

From the end of August and through September, the

French and British armies had been blown like leaves on the autumn wind back from Belgium and across northern France, battle by battle and river by river – Le Cateau, St Quentin, the Marne, the Somme, the Aisne – towards Paris. It did not make very comforting reading in the newspapers for someone with a man at the Front.

'He's probably too busy to write,' Beattie said. 'I'm sure you'll hear from him as soon as they stop somewhere.'

Beth shrugged. Everyone was in the same boat, and it wasn't done to make a fuss. 'It's the nature of war, I suppose. What about David? Any news from him?'

'He still seems to be enjoying himself,' Beattie answered. 'Their huts are almost finished, which he says is a relief, because the tents are always falling down, and everything gets wet when it rains. Mostly he talks about what fun they have off duty. They've got up a couple of football teams and a choir, and there's a bridge league. Oh, and apparently when they were out on a route march one day they stopped in a village and were dismissed for half an hour. He and his friends went into a public house and had a pint of beer.' She smiled faintly. 'He waxes more lyrical about that beer than anything else.'

Edward came in with Aeneas. 'Ah, my dear brother,' Laura greeted him. 'Don't you want to know how I'm getting on in my new career?'

He sat down next to her. 'I thought it was voluntary work, not a job.'

'It *feels* like a job,' Laura said. 'Mrs Harpenden has us on the go all day – and she's a stickler for punctuality. I think I had more latitude when I was working for Carthew's!'

'What sort of a motor do you have?' William wanted to know.

'I mostly drive a Crossley Landaulette, and that feels like work, believe me! It's a heavy car to begin with, and then, of course, we load it up with more people than it was meant to carry, plus their luggage. I could hardly turn the steering-wheel at first, but I'm developing most unladylike muscles in my arms.' The girls laughed, though Edward looked slightly disapproving. 'They've more drivers than motors at the moment, so Louisa comes with me in the Crossley and helps me, which is companionable. But Mrs Harpenden says they might be getting a small Ford next week, so she'll probably take that over.'

'Is it a Model T?' William asked.

'My love, I have no idea,' said Laura.

'But what do you actually *do*?' Sonia asked.

'Well, sometimes we're just taking messages or collecting donations and ferrying them to Headquarters – clothes and cooking-pots and so on, for the refugees. But the part I like best is meeting the refugees at the terminus. They're so tired and frightened and low, poor things, it's wonderful to see their reaction when someone is kind to them.'

She paused, then went on, 'Meeting them is important for another reason. Last week we somehow lost two of the refugees, young women.'

'Lost them?' Beattie queried. 'How could you lose them?'

'We simply couldn't imagine. We met them off the train, counted them and took their names, but when we got out to the motors, two were missing. We thought they'd got separated in the crowds, and we waited, and several of us went back in and searched, but in the end we had to leave. We gave their names and descriptions to the station manager in case they turned up, but we haven't heard anything since.'

Beth looked as if she knew where the story was heading. 'Their mothers must be in a dreadful state.'

'Yes – and after all they'd been through,' Laura agreed. 'Well, anyway, yesterday when we were waiting for a train, I noticed a woman in a red hat hovering in the background. There was something familiar about her, but I couldn't place her. Then, when we were ushering our new refugees towards the exit, I saw her again, talking to two young girls at the back of the group. That's when I realised why I recognised her. I'd seen her several times before, but always in different clothes. The night we lost the two girls she'd been hanging around, only she'd had a blue hat with a half-veil. I'd noticed her because she was particularly tall.'

'White slavers,' said Beth. 'I heard they were active in London. How shocking to prey on refugees!'

'I suppose they're easy to persuade, when they're confused and have lost everything.'

'What are white slavers?' William asked.

'Bad people who take girls away with the promise of a good job, and sell them as slaves in South America,' said Laura, circumspectly.

'You should be careful,' Aeneas said. 'Some of those people can be ruthless if you cross them.'

'Oh, we're safe enough,' Laura said. 'We're always there in numbers. It's the poor girls. One shudders to think . . .' She forbore to elaborate. 'Something ought to be done.'

'Did you go to the police?' Edward asked.

'Yes, of course, but they brushed us off. Frankly, they aren't much bothered by the idea. The sergeant we spoke to said lots of girls come up to London every day looking for an easy life and get themselves into trouble. There seems to be a sense that they deserve what they get.' She shrugged. 'Policemen as a breed are not very fond of women. Or, at least, they don't take their problems seriously.'

'I suppose with so many soldiers around, girls are bound to—' Beth began.

Edward cleared his throat. 'Enough of that subject, I think.'

Obediently, Beth changed it. 'Have you heard from Addie lately?' she asked Beattie. 'No more of those disturbances, I hope?'

'No, it's quiet at the moment. She says the leaders of both sides have agreed to stop fighting until the war's over, which is a great relief to them.'

307

'So I imagine.'

'Of course, that's just the leaders,' Beattie added. 'One can only hope the rank-and-file will follow suit.'

'Why wouldn't they, Aunt Beattie?' Mary asked.

'Well, I believe there are some on the republican side who want to attack Britain while we're busy with Germany. And some who even hope the Germans will win.'

'Good heavens, why on earth would they want that?' Sonia exclaimed.

'They think they might get what they want from the Germans sooner than from Westminster,' Edward said.

'I hope these stories of "frightfulness" will put them right about *that*, at any rate,' said Laura.

Sonia sighed. 'We've always looked on the Germans as such a *cultured* nation! Beethoven and – and so on.' She couldn't for the moment think of any more of the names that were always cited. Vague impressions moved through her brain. Something that sounded like Gertie and something else that sounded like Shilling . . . She gave it up. 'But I suppose that was all a long time ago, and the Germans have changed.'

Laura said, 'Did you see that advertisement put in the paper by Lipton's the grocer's? It asserted they're completely British, and always have been. It seems they're going to sue Lyons for libel, for saying they were originally German.'

'Ah, the grocery wars,' Aeneas said, with a smile.

'I use the Home & Colonial,' Sonia said vaguely. Then she brightened. 'But I'm not to order any more of that German spa water. From now on we're only having Buxton water. That *is* English, isn't it?' she added, with sudden slight anxiety. It sounded a bit like 'Bechstein'.

'Of course it is,' Edward said, amused. 'Buxton's in the Peak District.'

Sonia looked reassured. 'And no more of that German sausage, either, which is a shame because Aeneas does like it.'

'I do,' said Aeneas solemnly. 'But we all have to make sacrifices in wartime.'

Hank, let in by Ada, came dashing past her to the morning-room where Sadie and Diana were sorting through items for the bric-à-brac stall. 'I've found a pig!' he exclaimed, his face alight with enthusiasm.

'Oh, jolly good!' Sadie said. The fête was keeping them all occupied. People were calling at all hours of the day, to hand in items for the sale of work or to ask questions or just to talk about it. Officially everything was supposed to go to the rectory, but in practice all the committee members found their houses had become depots. Sadie enjoyed sorting through the things. Sometimes what was amazing was not that they were being discarded but that anyone had ever paid money for them.

It was fun helping with the entertainments, too. The roll-a-penny and the fishing for ducks were survivals from last summer's garden fête, but the ducks needed their numbers repainting, and the fishing rods had disappeared so new ones had to be made – a short length of bamboo, a piece of string and a cup hook. Hank's idea of guessing the number of buttons in a jar had become dried peas, since no-one could be persuaded to part with buttons. Sadie had volunteered to count them in, and was the only person in Northcote who knew the total.

Guessing the weight was now to involve the more traditional cake. Hetherton's had donated it – a wedding cake had been ordered, then cancelled when they had already made the bottom tier. Mrs Hetherton had offered to ice it and write 'Belgian Refugees Fund' on the top. It would make, Beattie said, a nice centrepiece.

For other competitions there were to be needle-threading and apple-peeling, guessing a baby's name – Mr Oliver had written it on a card and sealed it in an envelope – and something Hank had devised, which involved throwing darts at playing cards stuck to a board. There was also to be a hoop-la stall – Bob Parling, the carpenter (husband to the district nurse), had offered to make the rings.

'Why don't we have a raffle?' Hank had suggested. 'They always make lots of money, and I'm sure I can wheedle up a decent prize.'

'Mrs Fitzgerald would never stand for it,' Diana told him. 'Raffles are gambling, and the rector doesn't approve.'

Hank was crestfallen. 'But what about our other competitions? Is he going to ban them, too?'

'No, they're different. They involve a test of skill, not just laying out money in the hope of winning something,' she explained.

She and Hank had been out most days, letting people know about the fête, answering questions and soliciting prizes. 'We need a lot of small things for the ducks and the hoop-la,' he said. The roll-a-penny paid for itself, of course. 'And some big things for the other games.'

He was proud of his skill in 'wheedling'. It often involved paying outrageous compliments, which he could do with a straight face, though Diana had terrible difficulty in not laughing, and several times had to resort to a pretended sneeze and a handkerchief.

'Everyone's going to think you have a dreadful cold,' Hank complained, 'and that I'm cruelly dragging you about when you should be home in bed.'

But most of all he was dedicated to the idea of bowling for a pig. He was determined to have it. He had acquired a set of skittles and, along with Bob Parling, had devised how an alley could be simply constructed; an awning of some sort to cover it if it rained would be easy to acquire. But the pig had posed problems. The farmers he had approached so far had all looked stern and told him there was a war on. Even taking Diana with him had not softened them. They wished the fête well, but a pig was a pig.

310

So Sadie was genuinely impressed. 'Where did you get it from?' she asked.

'Not from a farmer at all,' Hank said, 'Foolish me, I didn't realise that other people have pigs – including the noble and generous Mr Worritt of the Red Lion Inn.'

Sadie grinned. 'Of course, Mr Worritt! Why didn't I think of that?' Though he ran the beerhouse as his main occupation, his great passion was his four sows, which lived in a ramshackle collection of sheds at the back. Though their accommodation was makeshift, the sows – Rosemary, Gertrude, Marigold and Eglantine – were treated like royalty by their adoring owner, who would always sooner be leaning on the side of a pen scratching a pig's ear than anything else in the world. In consequence they flourished, and presented him at regular intervals with large litters of lively piglets, which grew quickly on their bountiful milk and in eight weeks were stocky little weaners ready for market.

'But how did you persuade him to give you one?' Sadie asked. 'Everybody knows he cries when he takes them to market.'

'Cries?' Diana said. 'He makes a decent living out of them!'

'Yes, but he still loves them like his own children,' Sadie said.

'No-one else could have done it. I had to employ all my guile,' Hank said, preening. 'I didn't mention at first what I was there for. I just had half a pint of his disgusting ale – I tell you, drinking that was the noblest thing I ever did.'

'You don't understand English beer,' Sadie said.

'And never will – I drank the stuff, like I said, then asked if I could see his pigs, as if I was begging for the greatest favour. Of course, nothing could please him more. Nearly an hour I spent out there in his back yard, admiring them while they looked at me as if trying to decide which bit to take a bite out of. Reminded me of the ladies of my mother's Church Circle – they've never approved of me! But it was

311

worth it. By the time I brought up the fête, I was his dearest friend. I only had to mention bowling for a pig and he was pushing a piglet down my throat.'

'Oh, no!' Sadie cried.

He added, 'Metaphorically speaking.'

'She knows that – go on,' said Diana.

'Not much more to tell. Eglantine had just had a litter of fourteen—'

'Fourteen!' Diana exclaimed.

'Even I thought it was excessive – that pig is a show-off – but he offered me a dear little spotted one as a prize. With a bow round its neck it will steal every heart away and make us lots of money.'

'It's a shame they're so heavenly when they're little and so dull when they get bigger,' Sadie said.

'Well, this one's too small to leave its mother, but Worritt said we could have it in a basket to show to everyone for a couple of hours, and the winner could collect it from him in two or three weeks when it's weaned,' Hank concluded. 'So am I the cleverest, guilingest manipulator in the whole wide world? Come now, girls, confess it!'

'He's nice,' said Sadie, when they had seen him off.

'Is he?' Diana said. 'I suppose so.'

'Oh, come on,' said Sadie. 'You enjoy his company as much as we all do. He makes everything fun.'

Diana looked at her with faint exasperation. 'What do you want me to say? Yes, I like him.' She went back to sorting.

'He likes you,' Sadie said, watching her turn a clock with only one hand round and round as if trying to find a way in. 'In fact, I'd say it was a bit more than that. I think he's sweet on you.'

'Disgusting expression,' said Diana, opening the back of the clock and peering in.

'Can't help it. Don't know any other way to say it. But, Di,

I think he thinks you're encouraging him. Are you?' Diana didn't answer, her lips pressed thin. 'What about Lord Dene?'

Diana was about to snap, 'None of your business!' but at the last minute she paused. She put the clock down absently and picked up a Chelsea dog with a chipped nose. Her feelings were in a turmoil, had been for weeks now. 'I don't know,' she said. 'How can I know when I don't even *see* him? I *think* he's interested in me, but I can't be sure. And if this war goes on a long time, what then? Do I wait for him, when he hasn't given me any reason to, really? Or do I put him out of my mind?'

'But – do *you* like *him*? Lord Dene, I mean. Are you in love with him?'

'I like him,' Diana said. 'I like him very much. I don't know if I'm in love with him. I don't think you can know that about a man until you've kissed him. Oh,' impatiently, 'you wouldn't understand. When you're older . . .'

Sadie accepted the snub. But she said, 'If you are serious about Lord Dene, I think you should be careful about Hank. It seems to me . . .' She paused, wondering how to put into words what she instinctively felt about Charles Wroughton. She remembered the way he had scratched Nailer's head. The way he looked at Diana. How much happier he had been to talk about dogs than anything else. She barely knew the man, yet she felt oddly protective towards him. She had a strong sense that, under the aristocratic enamel, there was something warm but fragile. 'I think he'd be hurt if he thought you were letting Hank run after you, and he'd go away.'

'I've always had other men hanging around me,' Diana said impatiently, to hide her unease. 'He must know that.'

'But that's different,' Sadie said. *Why?* she asked herself, and found the answer. 'They weren't serious. They were just – like puppies, playing. But Hank is a man. He . . . matters.'

'Sounds as if you've got a crush for him yourself,' Diana

said harshly. 'Do you want me to step aside and leave the way clear for you?'

'Don't be silly,' Sadie said quietly, and Diana felt ashamed.

'We'd better get on with this before the next lot arrives,' she said. 'Do you call this bric-à-brac or rubbish?'

'Oh, someone will buy it,' Sadie said, letting the matter drop.

One did not need to be a politician to know that if the Germans captured Paris it would be a terrible blow to the Allies. The armies fought mile by mile across northern France to the very suburbs of the city; the Parisians fled, like the Belgians before them, clogging the roads with their carts and children and animals. At home they waited with bated breath. Paris – the city of dreams, the first place an Englishman abroad ever went: Paris must not fall!

With a wild, heroic effort the Allies threw the Germans back, ending their terrifying month-long advance; drove them back the way they had come, north-eastwards to a region called the Champagne, where both sides dug in. The newspapers hailed the battle of the Aisne, on the 15th of September, a tremendous victory. For the people at home, it was a relief to be able to feel proud and confident again.

Cousin Jack was out there somewhere. Beth had written to say she had received a picture postcard from him of the cathedral at a place called Rheims – however you pronounced that – which said it was the capital of the Champagne country, so she concluded he was either in the city or near by. She made a little joke about how much Jack loved champagne, and said he had evidently found his spiritual home with the army.

CHAPTER TWENTY-THREE

A letter came for Sadie from Mrs Cuthbert. It was very short: 'Dear Sadie, we have horses! Come as soon as you can.'

There was speculation round the table as she hurriedly finished her breakfast, but no-one could think what it meant – except, thought Beattie, that Sadie was happy again. She had seemed a little low recently, and Beattie had put it down to the incident at Stein's. But now it seemed it was just that she had been missing the horses.

As soon as she had changed she cycled up to Highclere Farm. Bobby had taken his bicycle with him, but David's was left, and she could just about manage it with the saddle lowered as far as it would go. Breathless, she arrived at the farm, flung the machine against the fence and almost ran to meet Mrs Cuthbert, who had come to greet her, her face wreathed with smiles. 'I have tremendous news,' she said. 'Come into the tack-room and I'll tell you.'

Podrick was there, sorting through a box of odd bits and curb chains, straps and girths. He looked up at Sadie, and gave her a solemn wink.

Mrs Cuthbert perched on the saddle horse and told the story. 'It all came about because of my dear old Colonel Barry. He knows how upset I was at losing my horses, and he knows all sorts of people at Headquarters and the War Office. He got together with Captain Casimir, and – well, to cut a long story short, there's such a large number of horses going through the Army Remount Service that they can't cope. They have to set up temporary depots, and we are going to be one. We've got the buildings, plenty of grazing, and we're near the railway. They'll send us drafts of horses, and we'll get them ready.'

'What does that involve?' Sadie asked.

'The Service is still scouring the country for horses, but they've just about exhausted the supply, so they're buying them in, mostly from Ireland and India. They're sent to the depots, checked for soundness by a vet, then given some basic schooling – commands and drills, that sort of thing – before they're sent abroad.'

'Can I help?' Sadie was almost afraid to ask.

Mrs Cuthbert laughed. 'I'm depending on it! We're to have a sergeant billeted with us, a retired regular from the Remount Service, and he'll show us the proper army way to do things, and keep us straight.'

'Tell her about the bangs,' Podrick said from the background.

'They have to learn to bear loud noises, smoke and fire. So part of the schooling is letting off fire-crackers near them, and riding them between flaming posts.'

'Golly, that *will* be fun!' Sadie cried.

'Fun, is it? If you like a horse's feet waving round your ears,' Podrick commented.

'*I* think it will be fun. When are they coming?'

'The first draft is arriving today. That's why I sent for you. They could be here at any moment.'

Sadie was smiling so hard her jaws ached. 'Oh, I can't believe it – horses to school! And – I've just thought!'

'Yes?'

'Well, this will be war work, won't it? Proper war work.'

'Most definitely. The army can't function without horses.'

'Then, if you're really going to let me help, they won't be able to send me away to finishing school, will they?'

316

Mrs Cuthbert laughed. 'Are you still worried about that? I think you'll be safe enough – if they give you permission. You'll have to ask them, you know.'

'Oh.' Sadie's happiness was checked. But she recovered. 'I'm sure they'll say yes. Everyone has to do their bit. And they ought to know by now that I'm a hopeless case.'

'I heard that you did something very brave,' Mrs Cuthbert said quietly.

Sadie looked away. 'I wasn't brave. I was scared stiff.'

'That's what being brave is – doing something when you're scared stiff.'

Sadie looked at her doubtingly. 'I was shaking like a jelly. I was so scared my voice went all squeaky, just when I needed to sound determined. It was awful. And then afterwards people kept saying I was a hero. I *wasn't*! I hate it when they say that.'

'Very well, I shan't say it,' said Mrs Cuthbert. 'But you can't change what I think.' She read her young friend's face. 'We won't talk about it any more. Wait! Is that a truck I can hear?'

Into the yard came a Crossley tourer containing Captain Casimir with a uniformed driver and a sergeant sitting in the back. A large cattle truck bumped slowly in behind.

'I have your horses!' Casimir called cheerfully, as they came up to the motor. 'And your mentor. Let me present Sergeant Cairns. Cairns, this is Mrs Cuthbert, your landlady from now on. Oh, and Miss Sadie Hunter. Am I to gather that you're going to help?'

'Try to stop her,' said Mrs Cuthbert, shaking the sergeant's hand. He was short and whippy with a weathered face and calm brown eyes. Sadie liked him at once, and thought he'd be good with horses. He looked her over carefully, then shook hands with her, too.

From the truck came the sound of kicking. 'How many have you brought me?' Mrs Cuthbert asked.

'Ten this time. The vet's in the cab. He looked them over at the railway depot, so he's just here to see they've travelled all right. We had some fun loading them, I can tell you,' he added, with a grin. 'Where do you want them?'

'I thought it might be best to turn them out for the rest of the day, as they've been cooped up for so long,' Mrs Cuthbert said. 'The home paddock's nice and green. Can you back the truck up to the gate? Then we can put them straight in.'

'Right,' said Casimir, and went over to give the instructions.

As the driver prepared to turn the truck around, the door on the other side opened, and a man in civvies got down and came towards them. Mrs Cuthbert was talking to Podrick, and he reached Sadie first, took off his hat and smiled down at her. 'How's the hand?' he asked.

He had tow-coloured hair, sleeked back, and blue eyes, she saw. 'It's all right,' she said, and stupidly held it out to show him.

He took it as if for a handshake. 'And how's your little dog?'

'The same as always. So you're a vet,' she discovered.

He nodded. 'For my sins. Not yet in uniform, but the army retains me for all its horses in this area.'

'No wonder you wanted to examine Nailer,' Sadie said.

'Nailer! That was the name. I've been trying to think of it. But he certainly didn't want to be examined.' He was still holding her hand.

'He hasn't chased any cars since that day,' Sadie said.

'Perhaps he's learned a lesson, and my running him down wasn't all to the bad.'

'You didn't run him down,' Sadie defended him. 'It was his fault.'

'Courcy! Give us a hand, will you?' Captain Casimir called.

'I didn't introduce myself,' he said. 'My name's John Courcy.'

'I'm Sadie Hunter.' Then she realised Mrs Cuthbert had finished talking to Podrick, and felt obliged to introduce him to her. He let go of her hand to shake Mrs Cuthbert's, and the strangely warm and private little moment was over.

The truck's back was let down, and Podrick and Baker went to help get the horses out. They came stamping and trembling and jittering down the ramp, nostrils wide, heads high, and as soon as they touched firm ground they were away, dashing to the end of the paddock. By the time the last was out, they were galloping round and round in a wild rodeo, flinging up their heels, all tossing manes and arched tails.

John Courcy, leaning on the fence, was laughing. 'Not much wrong with that lot,' he said.

Mrs Cuthbert turned to Casimir. 'What have you brought me? Are they even broken?'

'I'm assured they are,' he replied. 'Schooled for riding, I was told.'

They were all bays and browns, though their colour had to be taken a degree on trust since their shaggy, unkempt coats were caked with mud. Their manes and tails had obviously never been pulled in their lives, and the long tail tips had been so dipped in mud they hung in separate tags that whipped together like a tangle of snakes as they charged around.

'They're from Ireland, somewhere in Kerry, I understand,' said Casimir. 'Three- and four-year-olds, all geldings. Can't tell you much more about them.'

'They look as if they've been running wild for many a merry month,' Courcy said, still grinning. 'I wouldn't set much store by that schooling, if I were you.'

'We'll need every hand to get them up to scratch,' Mrs Cuthbert said, with faint dismay. She had not been expecting diamonds so much in the rough.

Sergeant Cairns had helped get the back of the truck closed, and came to join them. 'We'll manage, all right. They're just letting off steam. They'll settle down in a bit.'

319

Even as he spoke, the wild career was slowing, and in a few minutes it had stopped and they all had their heads down, tearing eagerly at the grass. After days on nothing but hay, it was irresistible.

The truck driver, a civilian, called, 'I'll be off, then, if you're done with me?'

Casimir went over to sign his docket. The sergeant went to fetch his kit from the boot of the Crossley, and stood patiently with it at his feet, waiting to be shown his billet. Casimir came back to shake Mrs Cuthbert's hand and said, 'I'll leave you in Sergeant Cairns's capable hands. Oh, and a load of fodder will be coming later on today, with some tack, posts and rails and so on. Courcy, can I give you a lift? Where did you leave your motor-car?'

'Thank you – at the station.' He shook hands with Mrs Cuthbert, then Sadie, and said, 'I shall be popping in quite regularly to see how they're getting on, and of course if you have any concerns, send for me, and I'll come at once. We'll be seeing quite a bit of each other, I fancy.'

He said it actually while he was shaking Sadie's hand and, though it might be foolish, she felt that made it seem he was saying it particularly to her.

She was nervous when she approached her parents for permission. She was so afraid it would be no that she couldn't think what to say, and in the end she just blurted it out, then stood, dry-mouthed, wishing she had put a more eloquent case.

Her father put aside his paper and asked several worryingly well-directed questions. Sadie was sure he was going to say it was unsuitable. What her mother thought, she couldn't tell. After one look, she continued to knit, consulting the pattern, her face a serene blank as usual.

'It's a very odd request,' Edward said at last. 'Is this really what you want to do?'

'Yes, Father,' Sadie said. Her voice sounded lifeless to her ears. But would Father respond better to passion? He didn't like displays. Logic would sway him better than emotion. If only she could muster some logical arguments.

'I've been very remiss,' Edward was saying. 'There's been so much to think about since the war began that I'd forgotten all about you. I should have looked out a school for you – I meant to. But it isn't too late, you know, if you'd like to go. There are lots of good schools in England.'

This was exactly what she had feared. 'Oh, no, please, Father. I don't want to go to school. I never did.'

'Girls seem to like it. Diana did, as far as I can gather.' She was out visiting the Hardings that evening or he would have appealed to her.

'I'd much sooner do this,' Sadie said. 'And it's important work. There's a war on.'

Edward smiled. 'We can win the war without taking you away from your proper training for future life.'

Sadie said urgently, 'But this will be much better training than deportment and table-laying and that sort of thing.'

'You're very young,' he began, intending to say no. As a father he had to do what was right by his children and, unlike Laura, Sadie would not be inheriting an independence. Marriage was her only possible career and she had to be made fit for it. But she was looking at him with trapped, desperate eyes, and his heart lurched. It was the same look he had seen in Beattie that winter long ago in Dublin. Sadie was struggling against the confines of being female and, in a rare moment of sympathy, he saw how hateful it must be if your mind did not consent to it.

Almost instinctively, he turned to Beattie, and she looked up from her work at the same instant. He saw the graceful, wary lift of her head, like a deer scenting for danger. He loved her so much. 'My dear?' he enquired.

Beattie looked at her younger daughter. *We are all imprisoned in our circumstances*, she thought. Some people accepted

321

their chains more readily than others. But it was hard to see any creature's spirit crushed. Let her be a child a little longer. She said, 'Will it be dangerous?'

Sadie turned to her with wild hope. 'No!' she said. 'Just riding, schooling. Podrick and the others will do the rough work. And Mrs Cuthbert will be there to keep an eye on me.'

Beattie turned to Edward. 'She can learn the other things at home. Nula and I can teach her.'

Edward considered for an agonising moment. 'Very well,' he said.

'Oh, thank you! *Thank* you, Father!' Sadie cried.

As long as she continued to efface herself and didn't come to the table with dirty hands and wild hair, or anything of that sort, she was pretty sure the 'lessons at home' would never materialise. Her mother had never noticed her much anyway – all the care she could spare from the boys went on Diana.

Frank Hussey appeared at the kitchen door with a trug full of muddy potatoes. 'Where would you like these?' he asked.

Cook looked round. 'Emily, take them into the scullery. You can scrub 'em after tea. Where's Mr Munt, Frank? Has he got you doing his work, the wicked old man?'

'No, I offered to help. Dunno why, but somehow it's like a holiday to dig someone else's taters. A change is as good as a rest, they say. Mr Munt's coming – he's just getting the last of the beans.'

'You'll stay for your tea, Frank?' Cook invited, in a voice so different from her usual one that Ethel looked at her sharply. *Silly old fool*, she thought. *He doesn't come here for you.*

'Thanks very much,' Frank said. 'I was hoping you'd ask. I'd better wash my hands.'

'There's blood,' Cook discovered, as she glanced at the muddy paws. 'What you done to yourself?'

'Oh, it's nothing. Just caught myself on a stake.'

322

'You better wash that out properly or you'll be getting lockjaw next,' said Cook.

'I'll see to it,' Ethel said. 'Come into the scullery, and I'll make you comfortable.'

Emily was in there, having deposited the basket of potatoes, lingering in her usual absent way. She blushed richly as Frank came in, gazing at him with her mouth open until Ethel ejected her with a jerk of the head, backed up by a sharp pinch to the arm when she didn't move quickly enough.

'Come to the sink and let me clean that for you,' Ethel said, as Emily vanished. 'Make sure all the dirt's out.'

She turned the tap on and took hold of his hand, drew it under the running water and gently cleaned it with her fingertips. He was tall and she liked the loom of him over her; knew he was looking down at her and admiring her feminine tenderness and the length of her eyelashes, seen to advantage from above. A ministering angel – and actually holding his hand. How could he resist?

She missed Billy Snow, and so many of the local youths had gone now. Luckily there was the army camp on Paget's Piece. She'd never say no to a nice soldier. But sooner or later they'd go away, wouldn't they? She needed a home-based man to fill the gap. And she had liked the look of Frank Hussey from the beginning. But he hadn't made a move yet.

He noticed her, of course he did. And she felt sure she was the reason he came so often for his tea. But there was something about the *way* he looked at her that unsettled her. It wasn't the skinned-rabbit look of a hopelessly smitten Alan Butcher or the half-cocky, half-entreating look of a Billy Snow. It was almost – she hesitated even to think it, but – almost a look of amusement. She wasn't sure she liked it.

Busy with her thoughts, she had gone from washing the captive hand to stroking it absently. Now his voice brought her back. 'What do you think, then? Will I live?'

She looked up at him and saw that smile. It was – she

had it now – the smile of a man looking at a basket of kittens playing. He didn't take her seriously. She wanted him to admire her, yet be uncertain of his success. There was nothing uncertain in that smile.

She answered sharply: 'Goodness, it's nothing but a scratch!'

'You're not worried about me dying of lockjaw, then?'

'There's no lockjaw round here that I know of,' she said. 'Anyway, I've washed it clean for you. You'd better wash your other hand yourself.'

'You look very pretty when you've got your dander up,' he commented. 'Though quite what I've done to set you off I don't know.'

'You haven't set me off,' she said aloofly. 'I don't know what you're talking about.'

'Got any soap?'

She handed him the green scullery bar in haughty silence, and watched him washing. She should have stalked out and left him to it, but somehow she couldn't take her eyes off those big, strong hands. They looked so capable, the sort of hands that would know exactly how to hold a girl. She imagined dancing with him . . .

'I can manage this bit all right on my own,' he said, interrupting her daydream.

'Such a fuss over nothing,' she said. 'You'd have to put up with a lot more than that if you went to war. Yes, and that's another thing.' She thought of something to taunt him with. 'Why haven't you volunteered? All the *real* men in this village have signed up. Aren't you worried what people will think of you?'

She hadn't meant it to be as rude as that. But he went on looking down at her with that amused and – what was it? – *sympathetic* expression. As though he understood her terribly well. Something in her moved at the thought.

'No,' he said, 'I don't worry about that. Someone's got to grow the food, or what will all you people at home eat?'

'But – but don't you want to go and fight the Hun?' she stammered stupidly. *Damn you, Frank Hussey, for making me blabber like a fool!*

'I think growing food's more important. And being here in case the Hun manages to get through. You'll need some men around to defend you then.'

'I can defend myself, thank you,' she snapped.

'I expect you'd give it a good try,' he said. 'You're no coward, I'll say that for you.'

She simply couldn't think of anything else to say. Fortunately at that moment Cook called from the kitchen, 'Tea's ready. Are you two coming in?'

'Right-oh,' Frank called back. He smiled at Ethel, a friendly smile without nuances this time, and said, 'After you.'

Ethel stalked out, brushing past Emily. She was loitering just outside the scullery door, and turned into a languishing beetroot when Frank smiled at her in passing.

In the servants' hall the table was laid and the teapot was in, and Cook was placing a large fruit cake in the middle. 'Though how I've managed it, don't ask me, with sugar getting so short. I wish we hadn't made so much jam now – not but what we won't be glad of it this winter if the war goes on. Mrs Gordon's cook said she tried using honey in a cake instead but it didn't rise properly. Of course, they didn't get lots in before the war started, like we did, that's their problem. But the dried fruit – well, I hope it's all over by Christmas, like they say, because if anyone knows how to make a Christmas cake without raisins I'd like to hear it.'

'It looks lovely, Mrs Dunkley,' Frank said. 'Smells wonderful too.'

Cook was ready to swoon under his praise – no-one ever called her by her name – and Ethel gave him a sour look. *Making love to everyone! Aren't you the Mr Popular?*

'Didn't Ethel put a bit of a dressing on that hand?' Cook said, in reply.

'It's all right as it is. Just a scratch. Best to let the air get at it,' Frank said, taking the chair she indicated to him, at her right hand.

Ethel went to her own seat, noticing that Nailer had crept in and was sitting just out of Cook's line of sight, gazing at Frank with adoration. *Even the blasted dog!* she thought.

But as she sat down and looked across the table, Frank caught her eye and gave her a swift, polished and very complicit wink before addressing himself to his bread and butter, and she was undone. *He liked her! He liked her better than the others. She was the reason he came to the house.* But why did he have to be so annoying? She couldn't work him out at all.

The Germans had been halted in the Champagne, but the danger was still acute. They began a series of outflanking moves, trying to break through towards the sea. If they succeeded in turning the Allied flank and reaching the coast, they would effectively control the whole of northern France, with its large industrial capacity and fertile agricultural plains. And if they captured the Channel ports they would cut off the supply route to the BEF.

The Allies repulsed the moves, then attempted to outflank the enemy in their turn, and in a sort of leapfrog the front line extended ever further north-west. Through September and early October a series of battles took place along a diagonal from Rheims through Albert and Arras towards Nieuport on the Channel coast.

Beth had nothing but another field postcard saying, *I am quite well*; but then, suddenly, like a lifeline, came a letter, well marked with mud and what she hoped was a red-wine stain. Some of it was quite hard to make out.

Writing this on my knee by a very poor lamp, so excuse scrawl. Three of your letters suddenly caught up with me. What a blessing! Don't stop writing! And fill your

326

letters with every detail of your blissfully ordinary life. We have been moving fast, often sleeping in barns or under hedges, hence my silence. We are slogging it out with old Fritz. We make a dash, take up a position and fire a bit, then he does the same. Some of the time we're going back over ground we've marched across before. Can't tell you of the destruction! The Germans loot everything as they go, and what they can't carry they destroy. Not for nothing are they hated. My horse died under me – this life knocks them up quicker than anything. I got a replacement, a poor bony thing, with a nervous tic, sharp sideways jerk of the head. He seems to disapprove of everything, as well he might! I am getting enough to eat, though I dream of fresh vegetables. If you send me a parcel, please send beef cubes, Horlicks, chocolate, razor blades, socks, something light to read. The men are splendid, one couldn't want better. It's the most tremendous adventure. Apart from missing you, darling one, I wouldn't miss it for the world!

All my love for ever,
Jack

CHAPTER TWENTY-FOUR

Every day now the papers printed casualty lists, of those killed, wounded or missing. The latter category was very large, with the army moving so fast. Many would turn up later, or appear on prisoner-of-war lists, but many more simply disappeared into battle's maw.

Before the war, extravagant mourning – displays of grief, copious swathes of black, wreaths on the front door, elaborate funerals – were a way of coping with bereavement, but the war demanded a new way of behaving. Those who had suffered a loss were expected to react with quiet pride that their loved one had given his life for his country, and to weep, if they must, in private. It was not done, now, to make a fuss; it was almost unpatriotic.

Hospital trains were a regular sight, pulling into the London termini. Warren came in every day through Waterloo. 'It's the crowds, sir,' he told Edward unhappily. 'Hundreds of people gather to watch the trains unload. It's distasteful to my mind, hanging around like that to see the wounded. Like those old women around the guillotine.'

Edward saw it for himself when he went out to a client's house and had to pass through Victoria. It was not ghoulishness, he thought, but rather the interest of the simple nature in something new and different. No-one outside the medical profession had seen casualties on this scale before: who would not stop and look?

And he found the same need in himself, as a train steamed slowly in at the special platform where the ambulances were pulled up and the orderlies stood waiting with stretchers and chairs. It was an intense sympathy and pride, but there was curiosity too, he couldn't deny it.

The orderlies climbed into the train, then the doors opened and the Tommies appeared, on stretchers and in chairs first, then the walking wounded and those on crutches. After an initial silence (So many! There were so many!), a murmur of welcome went up from the crowd, and some applauded, but softly, as though afraid to startle them. One or two people broke from the crowd to go along the platform handing out cigarettes and chocolate. A group of women had set up a tea stall and were offering mugs to the soldiers.

And he could see how the reception had cheered and comforted the Tommies – those in a condition to notice. No, he thought, Warren did not need to fear they would be offended. He walked off to catch his own train; and was aware of a hollow space inside him, of shock. The bandages, the blood, the evidence of suffering had brought the war home to him in a way no words from the most eloquent columnist could have done.

The village had its first casualty: the Kings' son, Robert, had been a reservist, and was now in a hospital in Brighton, missing a foot and part of a leg. Beattie went with Mrs Gordon to the Kings on a visit of condolence, and met Mrs Oliver there on the same mission. They found Mr King blank-eyed with shock, and though Mrs King tried to rally for her visitors, she was evidently in the same condition. They had been to the hospital to visit their son. He was cheerful, considering, said Mrs King, and grateful for his good treatment, but he'd lost a lot of blood, and he was in a lot of pain. He thought they might have to cut more off his leg. It was a hard thing for a young man to hear. He'd been that keen on his football.

'Why Brighton?' Beattie asked, when they walked away afterwards. 'I thought the soldiers were meant to be sent somewhere near to home.'

'I suppose when a lot of casualties arrive at once, they have to be sent where there's room,' Mrs Oliver surmised.

'It will be hard for the Kings to go and visit him,' said Mrs Gordon. 'They aren't very well off. Mr King's been out of work for months.'

Mrs Oliver looked thoughtful. 'It suggests to me that there's a need for a fund, a relatives' hardship fund, to provide fares and accommodation costs for people like the Kings. We ought to get one up.'

'I agree,' said Mrs Gordon. 'We should canvass some of our people.'

'I'd like to help, but I'm fully occupied with the fête at the moment,' said Beattie.

Mrs Oliver gave a small smile. 'Yes, who'd have thought there would suddenly be so many calls on our time? Is everything going well?'

'Very well. It seems to have captured everyone's imagination.'

'There's a lot of pent-up energy,' said Mrs Oliver, 'with so many things being cancelled in August. People want a little fun, and if it's allied to a good cause . . . Henry seems to be enjoying himself, at least.'

'We're lucky to have him,' Beattie said.

'I hope you get to keep him,' said Mrs Oliver. 'He had a cable from his father this morning, asking when he's coming home.'

'Oh dear, that would be a disappointment.'

'Well, he doesn't at all want to go, and who can blame him? I think he can put a decent argument together, based on the war. It would be a heartless father who would drag his son away.'

'Could his father make him go?' Mrs Gordon asked.

'He could withhold Henry's allowance,' Mrs Oliver said. 'I hope it doesn't come to that.'

The Irish horses turned out to be a wild lot indeed, and Podrick and Sergeant Cairns agreed that if the three-year-olds had been backed at all, it was a long time ago, and they'd been running in the fields ever since. The four four-year-olds had obviously been ridden, but were over-fresh and unschooled.

'It's going to take more than a couple of weeks to have our first ten ready,' Mrs Cuthbert told Captain Casimir, when he came to see how they were settling in. She was afraid he would decide she had failed and remove depot status from her.

But he was sanguine. 'It's always a matter of luck when you're buying so many horses at once and have to trust remote agents. They're a nice-looking bunch, now you've knocked the mud off them, and worth training properly. Do what has to be done.'

With the new horses and the contract to go with them, Mrs Cuthbert had been able to rehire Biggs, one of the grooms she had previously let go, and take on two boys, Bent and Oxer. The men made a start with the six youngsters, while Mrs Cuthbert and Sadie concentrated on schooling the four-year-olds. Cairns oversaw everything and helped where it was needed most.

It was interesting work, and Sadie felt great pride at the progress of her favourite, one of the browns. She called him Conker (Sergeant Cairns was adamant they should not be named at this stage and called them One, Two, Three and Four) and he had an eager way of approaching his lessons, as though he enjoyed them, and greeted her with a glad whicker whenever she appeared.

'Don't get too fond of him,' Mrs Cuthbert said to her one day, when she came upon Sadie lingering in Conker's stall, stroking his face and murmuring to him.

Sadie had shut her mind to the fact that the end of it would be his going to the war. That was a long way off, she told herself. No need to think of it now.

'I'm just as fond of the others,' she excused herself. 'Ginger, Treacle and Nutmeg.'

Mrs Cuthbert rolled her eyes. 'Sergeant Cairns is right – you shouldn't give them names.'

The armies' Race to the Sea, as people were calling it, went on into the beginning of October, the line extending itself ever north-westwards. Antwerp was still holding out, under the tiny but determined Belgian Army, aided by the Royal Naval Division; but when it fell, on the 10th of October, they had to beat a hasty retreat to the river Yser, just north of Nieuport, and the Germans poured in behind them. With the French locked into the centre of the line in Picardy, the British had to scurry to close the gap between them and the Belgians.

On the 14th of October Jack's unit arrived at a new position and Beth received a postcard of a beautiful medieval building called the Cloth Hall in Ypres. 'These outlandish names give us headaches,' he had written on it. 'The men pronounce it Wipers, and to avoid confusion we have to follow suit. A beautiful city but already showing the bruises of war.'

Neither side was able to break through the other's line, and as both forces dug in, a Front was established that ran virtually from the Swiss border to the English Channel. France was cut in two, and only that small sector of Belgium in the far north-west remained free.

The days before the fête were grey and wet, and spirits fell a little at the thought of the village hall crowded with people in damp coats holding dripping umbrellas.

The 16th started out wet and the rain didn't stop all day, falling in a steady, workmanlike stream from a sky like a sheet of lead. Diana and Hank sat in the morning-room, staring gloomily out of the window as they went through last-minute plans. The only people who had gone by in the street had been invisible under big, depressing umbrellas; Arthur, the milk horse, had been soaked dark grey when he arrived. Sadie was in Ada's bad books for using the wrong towel to dry Nailer – who had immediately gone back out into the rain to get wet again; and Cook had warned after breakfast that there was a great deal of cold mutton to eat up before they could have anything different. It was enough to make anyone feel glum.

The 17th dawned overcast. But, leaning out of the bedroom window, Sadie decided that the sky was higher, and that it didn't smell like rain. She went down to breakfast in good spirits to spread the gospel. 'It's going to be a wonderful day and a terrific success,' she declared, over toast and marmalade. Ada, bringing in the coffee pot, said, 'I hope everyone thinks like you, Miss Sadie.'

They all went down to the village hall straight after breakfast to complete the setting-up. Those in charge of stalls were arranging and rearranging their goods to best effect. The churchwarden, Tom Begum, was up a ladder tacking up a bit of bunting that had come loose. Mrs Fitzgerald was supervising her Aggie and her man Fred in laying out the plates of food on the refreshment stall. Mrs Hetherton had brought her magnificent iced cake and was asking where to put it, and hadn't anyone thought of providing a cake-stand? Everyone looked blank for a moment, and she sighed. Little Joey Boyle, the greengrocer's son, was hanging around getting in everyone's way, so she sent him off at a run to the shop to fetch one.

Mrs Prendergast had called her bric-à-brac White Elephants, which Mrs Fitzgerald felt, like the word 'bazaar', was too 'eastern'. It was bad enough having Madame Mentallo's tent in the corner, covered with crescents, stars and vague

333

arabesques suggestive of pagan mysticism. Madame Mentallo herself – in reality Joyce Hicks, aunt to Mr Bellflower, the joiner – would be clad in gorgeous robes and a turban, but could now be seen in civilian garb, polishing her crystal ball with a yellow duster.

Beattie was arranging a vase of flowers on the table on the stage at one end of the hall, where the opening ceremonies would take place, and Diana was putting out glasses and a carafe of water. By half past ten the grey sky had withdrawn to sufficient heights for everyone to assure everyone else that it didn't look like rain, and that it was better that it wasn't too hot. By a quarter to eleven people were crowding in, eyeing the stalls and each other tensely, waiting for the off. And at eleven the committee and the rector were standing on the pavement outside the door waiting for the Wroughtons' motor-car to arrive.

A patch of watery blue had appeared in the grey, and it looked as though the sun might even break through. Beattie stood firm against an attempt by Mrs Fitzgerald to jostle her into the background, and closed her mind to the sight of a group of rough-looking dogs lurking in the alley down the side of the village hall where the dustbins were kept, one of which was undoubtedly Nailer.

Charles's urgings on the subject of the fête had coincided with Lady Wroughton's own second thoughts. She cared little for the village or its people, but she did care about appearances, and about Doing the Right Thing. Feelings were evidently strong about the fête, and it would be the right thing to lend it one's support. She was aware that there was disappointment over the cancelling of the cricket match and some resentment about the cancelling of the open day.

So, when Charles had begged her to open the fête, she had agreed without fuss. Having capitulated, she did not stint. She dressed in style, in a purple silk dress, enormous diamond brooch, long lavender gloves, fur stole and large, ostrich-feathered hat. Charles, grateful that she had taken the trouble, was equally grateful that being in uniform saved him from similar excesses: his khaki would be better received than striped trousers and morning coat, and he had always thought he looked a fool in a top hat. He had arrived home very late on Friday night, too late to call on the Hunters, so as he sat beside his mother in the Silver Ghost, his thoughts were all with Diana, what he would say to her, and what she might say to him.

The car drew up, the chauffeur jumped out and opened the door, the rector stepped forward, Mrs Eagleton's twins, Alice and Amy, carrying a bouquet between them, were given a little shove. The countess accepted the flowers graciously, then handed them to her maid, Pickering, standing behind her. The party moved in a stately manner through the hall – the countess nodding to either side without seeing anyone, Charles trying to spot Diana without seeming to – and mounted the stage. They took their seats, the crowds pushed forward and hushed, and the rector made his speech.

He thanked all those who had worked so hard to bring the fête about, spoke in moving terms about the plight of the refugees, urged everyone to spend freely to raise as much money as possible, then invited all to bend their heads. In ringing tones he spoke three prayers, first invoking God's favour on their enterprise, then His blessing on their brave soldiers far away, and lastly a general plea on behalf of the village for their sins to be forgiven and for God to look mercifully on them. Charles watched in concern as his mother grew restless but, in fairness, probably only he knew the signs – she was well accustomed to being bored in public. He had spotted Diana by now, but could not catch her eye. She had her head bent, which was seemly but inconvenient.

Finally, the rector called upon their most gracious and noble patroness to declare the fête open. The countess used the standard speech with which she opened everything, carefully crafted to fit any occasion. Her voice was harsh and toneless, but she looked the part, and no-one really cared what she said. They rewarded her with hearty applause, and Charles and the rector helped her carefully down from the stage so that she could walk among the stalls and spend a little money – *priming the pump*, Charles thought of it.

Lady Wroughton knew what was expected of her. Followed by an admiring crowd, she bought a jar of plum chutney, a pair of knitted baby's bootees and the ugliest thing on the bric-à-brac stall – in this case a vase in the shape of a bulldog in a Union Jack waistcoat – handing them in turn to Pickering to carry. She looked over the other stalls, paid a penny to guess the weight of the cake, and then, her duty done, made a slow and stately exit.

At each stage, the photographer from the *Westleigh and Northcote Chronicle* took a picture, while the reporter made notes of what she bought and everything she said. The committee followed her to the door and thanked her once more. The photographer took her shaking hands with the rector, with the committee in the background, and again getting into the Rolls-Royce.

Charles bent in before he closed the door and said, 'Thank you for doing it, Mama. I shall stay a while.' Then the motorcar moved away and he was free to follow his desire.

Sadie's stall was doing well – everyone liked roll-a-penny. You rolled your penny down a slot in a triangular block on to a board marked out in squares, the squares each bearing a number from 1 to 6. If your penny landed completely inside a square, you won that number of pennies. If any part of it was touching a line, you lost. It appeared beguilingly easy to win but, in general, the pennies were much more likely to be touching a line than not, so the lost coins paid for the prizes and made a profit as well.

Madame Mentallo had an eager queue at her tent. As Miss Hicks, she was an inquisitive spinster who knew nearly everyone, so her gypsy persona's utterances were often alarmingly perceptive. Dozens were paying a penny to guess the beans, the cake or the baby's name, and there was a hilarious group gathered around the needle-threading and apple-peeling, mostly of men egging each other on to display their clumsy ineptitude. Mrs Frobisher and Mrs Gordon, who were running those two competitions, were quietly discouraging the dextrous women who wanted to compete to win. *That* was not in the spirit of the thing.

The children in the crowd were mostly gathered around Hank in his corner, excitedly watching his card and conjuring tricks and debating fiercely how they were done. Hank was wearing a long black robe, a pointed sorcerer's hat, made out of black cartridge paper and decorated with silver stars, and a false moustache and goatee beard that gave his long face a thrillingly sinister look. He accompanied his tricks with a patter of which Sadie could overhear bits, and which she thought amusing. Behind him, Diana at the upright piano was playing a suitable background accompaniment, like a pianist at the cinema.

Charles had felt it incumbent on him to do his duty by the fête, and had visited every stall, except Madame Mentallo's, and spent a pocketful of change. He came to Sadie last, and greeted her with a shy smile. 'What do I do?' he asked.

'Have you a penny?' she enquired, aware that she did not have his whole attention. He kept glancing over her shoulder towards Hank's corner.

He felt in his pocket. 'Only a sixpenny bit.'

'I can give you change,' she said kindly. She supervised his six attempts to beat the system.

As the last penny trembled and dropped on its side over a conjunction of lines, he said, 'I'm not very good at it.'

'It's not you, it's just luck,' she assured him. 'It's very hard to get the penny inside the lines. That's the point. It makes money for the cause.'

'Oh, I see.' He looked at her properly. 'Thank you for reassuring me.'

'But don't tell anyone.'

'I won't. How are you? Are you well? And your family?'

'We're all well, thank you. How are the Terriers?'

'Coming together as a unit, now. I'm very proud of them.' He glanced again and bit his lip. 'Your sister is in very fine looks.'

Sadie looked at her, playing a drum-roll with both hands and laughing at Hank's gestures. 'She is,' she agreed. She observed his expression a moment, and said, 'Why don't you go and say hello to her? I'm sure she'd be pleased.'

'I don't want to interrupt when she's busy.'

'Oh, Hank will want a rest anyway. I can hear he's getting hoarse. Do go.'

Gratefully, he went.

Diana had seen him arrive, and had tried to be dignified, not to look as if she were courting his attention. But then he had wandered about the stalls for such ages, as if supporting the cause was the whole reason he had come, and her heart had sunk. He had not dashed over and claimed her in front of everyone. Perhaps, after all, he did not care for her.

But then he was talking to Sadie, and looking at her as he did so. And finally, finally, he was approaching her. He looked, she thought, very fine in his uniform. Lots of soldiers had come up from Paget's Piece for the fête, and a few officers as well, but their uniforms did not fit them as his did. It outlined his figure beautifully, and was obviously made of superior materials. And the khaki suited his weightiness of character. People naturally stepped back to let him pass, affected by his air of grave authority. Hank suddenly seemed like a will-o'-the-wisp in contrast.

She stopped playing. Hank glanced back, and went on with the trick he was performing.

'Hello,' Diana said cautiously.

'Miss Hunter,' Charles said. He cleared his throat. 'I trust you are well.'

'Very well, thank you.' She sought for something to say. 'It is very nice that you were able to come to the fête after all.'

'You think so?' he said, with curious eagerness. 'I did write to your mother that I would, if I possibly could.'

'Yes,' said Diana. She felt ridiculously shy with him.

'I was able to get a short leave of absence. Forty-eight hours,' he said. 'I arrived late last night. I have to be back by tomorrow night.'

'Did you drive down? In your motor-car?'

'Oh – yes. It doesn't take long. It isn't very far, really.' *What a ridiculous conversation*, he berated himself. *She'll think you an idiot.*

Think of something witty to say, Diana told herself savagely. *You sound like a simpleton.*

Hank finished the trick, pocketed his cards, shooed the children away, and joined them, with a pointed look at Diana.

'Oh – er – I don't think you know . . .' she began awkwardly. 'May I present Mr Henry Bowers, from America? Lord Dene.'

The men shook hands while inspecting each other keenly.

'Whereabouts in America?' Charles enquired politely.

'California. Do you know it?' said Hank.

'No. I've never been to America.' Which killed that line. 'Are you over on business?' he tried next.

'Vacation. But I got caught in Germany just as the door

was shutting and had to make a run for England. I'm staying with my aunt, Mrs Oliver.'

'Oh, yes, I know Mrs Oliver,' Charles said. Why was this man standing so close to Diana? Was there – oh, Lord – something going on? But Diana was looking at *him*. He cleared his throat again and addressed her. 'Would you care to accompany me round the stalls?'

'I'd like that,' she said at once. 'I've been playing all this time, so I haven't seen anything.' The headlamps of her eyes swung round on Hank. 'You probably ought to look in on your pig, don't you think?' An expression of baffled annoyance crossed his face, but he gave them a slight bow to share between them and went away.

Charles offered her his arm and, feeling with relief her slender hand slip into it, said, 'Pig? Is that some kind of slang?'

'No, it's a real pig. You bowl for it.' She turned him in the other direction. 'Tell me about what you've been doing all this while. You've been gone such a long time.'

Her words quickened something in him. He looked down at her, and dared to say, 'Did it seem a long time to you?'

She coloured, and lowered her eyes, which was answer enough for him. Suddenly he felt happy and relaxed. 'Would you like to try rolling a penny?' he invited cheerfully. 'I'm told there's no skill in it – it's just luck.'

She smiled. 'Don't let the rector hear you say that,' she said. 'That would make it gambling.' They presented themselves at Sadie's stall. Charles made her change a shilling for him, and they each had six goes; and then, as Diana declared she was determined to win *just once*, another shilling's worth. They were laughing together by the end of that, and Sadie, pleased, surreptitiously nudged Charles's last penny over a fraction and declared he had won twopence. He seemed terribly pleased, and gave them both to Diana, who immediately lost them.

They walked on, arm in arm, from stall to stall, spending his money. He bought a jar of lemon curd and a little china powder-box and gave them to her; at the refreshments stall he bought two glasses of lemonade, but somehow they put them down without drinking them. They were not aware of the eyes of the room watching them; they were hardly aware of the room.

Finding themselves at the door, they stepped outside without thinking. The clouds had broken up and there were patches of pale blue and a drift of hazy sunshine; the warmth brought out the smell of dying leaves, and a piquant hint of woodsmoke. 'Such a *blue* smell, I always think,' she said.

He turned to look at her. 'Miss Hunter,' he said. She felt suddenly tremulous inside. 'I want you to know that it wasn't my intention to stay away so long without word. But I couldn't get away from my duties. And it wouldn't have been proper for me to write to you.'

'I understand,' she said, and dared to look up. In its earnestness his face was almost handsome. *This was Lord Dene!* she reminded herself. 'Would you have?' she asked. 'If you could have?'

He didn't seem to know how to answer that. 'I—' He cleared his throat. 'I think very highly of you. I had hoped you realised that.'

At this delicate moment, Hank emerged, minus his sorcerer's robes and looking smilingly determined. *Damn the man!* Charles thought, though lifelong training kept it from showing in his face.

'Miss Hunter, Lord Dene! You must come and bowl for the pig. I absolutely insist. You've patronised every other stall. You can't leave him out.'

He urged and ushered them back through the hall to the door into the yard. A large crowd, mostly male and working class, was gathered round the latest contestant, jacket off and sleeves rolled up, shouting encouragement. The soldiers among

341

them fell silent when Charles appeared and drew themselves up to half-attention, and following their eyes, the others gradually quietened down and fell back. The man who was bowling threw his last ball almost at random and stepped aside, touching his cap. Diana was rather thrilled at this evidence of Charles's power. Hank, on the other hand, looked annoyed.

'Come now,' he addressed Charles, holding out a handful of balls. 'You must show us how it's done.'

Charles knew when he was being made a fool of. His lips tightened. 'I'd really rather not.'

Diana looked at him in concern. It wouldn't do for him to appear a rabbit in front of everyone. She thought she spotted Ethel somewhere in the background, which would mean it would spread like wildfire. 'I don't think Lord Dene wants to bowl, Henry,' she said.

Henry? Why the dickens was she calling him by his first name? Charles thought. He met Hank's narrowed gaze and sardonic smile.

'Of course, if he doesn't care to, there's no need,' said Hank, with heavy kindness. 'I thought he might like to support us, that's all.'

'How much?' Charles said tersely, and handed over his last sixpence in silence. There was an expectant hush. Men are men the world over, and when a pretty woman comes on the scene, they are quick to spot which stags are clashing antlers over her. There were some sharp looks, some smiles, but a few concerned brows – the men in khaki in particular didn't want this unknown captain to be made a fool of.

Charles transferred two of the balls to his left hand, settled the other in his right. He put his foot to the line, bent, sighted the pins, and bowled.

The instant the ball left his hand Diana's shoulders went down with relief. The movement looked *right*. And, the next second, eight of the pins had gone clattering over; the ninth rocked a moment on its base, and then toppled too.

The crowd erupted in cheers and applause. Charles straightened. He would never have bowled at all if he had not been challenged. He had an extremely good sports eye, was a fine cricketer, and had bowled for prizes at country fêtes since he was a boy.

Frankie Parling, who was running the lane, bent to set the pins up again, but Charles gave the balls back to Hank. 'It's enough,' he said. 'I don't really want a pig.' And addressing the crowd with the effortless ease of long practice, he said, 'Please carry on – enjoy yourselves! Remember, it's all in a good cause.'

And he offered his arm to Diana, and walked away. Every man there understood that he was walking off with the prize, pig or no pig.

They sat on the wall of the house next to the village hall for a long time, talking. He told her more about life in the Terriers. She listened attentively, feeling her heart sing with triumph. *He must like her! He had bowled for her.* She didn't know if he had known he could do it, or if it was Fate taking a hand, but she felt it was significant.

At last he asked, 'That fellow, Bowers.'

'Yes?' she said.

He hesitated, not knowing how to ask. 'You seem to know him awfully well.'

'We've been working together on the fête for weeks,' she said. 'One becomes friends in such circumstances.'

'Friends,' he repeated thoughtfully. Then, 'Is he going back to America?'

'I don't know,' Diana said, trying to sound indifferent.

It seemed to cheer Charles. 'I was thinking of asking my mother to hold a ball,' he said.

'What a good idea! Do you think she would?'

'I think we owe it to Northcote, after cancelling the last one. I think I can persuade her. And if I do – Miss Hunter, will you open it with me?'

343

She hardly knew what to say. This was distinction indeed – he was singling her out. He was giving his preference for her official status. She examined his face – unsmiling now, heavy with earnestness. There was a trembling inside her at the thought that he cared for her, that *he*, the Viscount Dene, cared for her over all the other girls.

'I'd be very glad to,' she said. She didn't smile either, but gave him a look of such sincerity that he took her hand and raised it to his lips.

'When I go back,' he said, in a gentle voice, 'I wish you won't think that I am ignoring you if I don't write to your mother. It is very hard to find the leisure – even off-duty there is always someone asking me to do something.'

'I understand,' she said.

'I had better take you back in,' he said. 'People must have missed you.'

'I have to play the piano for the closing hymn,' she admitted.

'And I really should go home – my mother has hardly seen me today. Will you be at church tomorrow?'

'Yes. Will you?'

'I shall make a point of it.'

'Will you come to luncheon afterwards?'

'I wish I might, but my family will expect me. And then I'll have to leave. But I'll walk you home after church, if I may?'

'I'll look forward to it,' said Diana.

CHAPTER TWENTY-FIVE

Lady Wroughton received the suggestion about a charity ball with equanimity, until Charles added the clause about wanting to open it with Diana Hunter. But though black fury and instant refusal flooded her mind, she clamped her mouth shut and did not vent them – proof, if it were needed, of the iron quality of her self-control.

It had long been apparent to her and the earl that there was some difficulty about Charles and women. Despite his birth and potential position, he just didn't *take*, as they used to say in the countess's youth, with the young ladies. And he had never seemed to care much about them, either. If he continued to refuse to marry Helen, it was a relief that he was finally interested in *somebody*. One could only deplore his choice.

'But she's pretty,' the earl remarked to his countess, in her bedroom that night.

'What on earth has that to do with it?' the countess retorted. Her maid had departed and she was sitting at her dressing-table rubbing Pond's into her face. Pickering had lately urged her to try it against the dryness of her skin, which cracked painfully in the cold winds of autumn and winter. The countess had no time for beauty and would have been horrified at the idea of trying to enhance it artificially, but Pickering had promoted it as a therapeutic measure.

The earl forbore to answer the question. Men liked pretty

women, that was just a fact, but there was no point in trying to convince his lady of it.

Instead, he tried tentatively: 'Could be for the best. New blood and so on. Too much marrying of cousins is bad for the stock.'

'We are not horses, Wroughton.'

'Principle's the same.'

'Helen's only a second cousin.'

'Bound to have very plain children, though,' the earl mused.

Lady Wroughton put down the pot with an exasperated bang. 'Charles can't simply go marrying anybody who takes his fancy. The girl may be pretty, but who are her people?'

'My dear, you know Hunter. He's a very decent sort. And the wife I believe comes from an army family.'

'They *may* be tolerable – just – but you know very well these people always come with dozens of utterly unsuitable hangers-on. Ghastly cousins and mad aunts. Who else would we be forced to notice?'

'Every family has its oddities,' he reminded her. 'Look at Helen's uncle Lucius.'

'That's exactly the point, Wroughton,' the countess cried. 'We *know* them. If Charles married one of our own sort we'd know all about them and be prepared for the worst. And they're *our* people. I simply can't be expected to tolerate an endless succession of vulgar and freakish connections, just because Charles won't do his duty and marry a decent girl. It's so *self-indulgent* of him!'

The earl agreed with her but, unlike her, he didn't see what could be done about it. You could bring a horse up to the start, but if it wouldn't run, it wouldn't run. His wife believed whip and spurs would do the trick, if applied long enough and hard enough. But Charles had inherited his mother's stubbornness, though it exhibited itself in a different way.

'Quite so, m'dear,' he said. 'But what will you do? Refuse to throw this ball for him?'

'No,' she said calmly. 'I *shall* hold the ball. I shall invite every eligible girl I can find, and he shall dance with them all. I shall baffle him with choice. When he sees how many there are, and compares them with this – this *Hunter* girl, he'll see the error of his ways. He'll drop her like a stone.'

The earl considered. There was something about the picture she had painted that was oddly familiar, almost like a story he had heard before. But as a plan it had possibilities. The girl, though pretty, would be at a disadvantage in such high company, and might be shown up to be awkward and gauche. Men liked pretty ladies, but they equally disliked being made to look foolish. And if Violet could wean Charles off the Hunter girl, he would be just as pleased as she was. Though he wouldn't like to upset Hunter himself too much. The fellow was a fund of good advice – and, besides, he rather liked him.

Ethel did her work on Sunday morning automatically, her mind elsewhere. Despite several of her usual suitors and the sprinkling of soldiers, she had found the fête rather dull. There was nothing on the stalls that she wanted to buy, the competitions did not interest her, and going to Madame Mentallo was not worth the queue unless you went in with a man. Mentallo was good at giving useful hints when a girl took a chap into her tent and gave her the wink, but Ethel didn't want encouragement for any of those who were hanging around her. They all said the same silly things to her, and had the same nervous laugh and the same damp hands, and looked at her with the same calf eyes. Where was excitement? Where was the thrill of danger? She wanted to be swept away by a man she couldn't resist.

Alan Butcher, who was becoming dangerously proprietorial, had gone to get her some lemonade, and she had taken the chance to escape outside for a breath of air. As she shoved her way out she collided with the considerable chest of a tall man in khaki.

'Whoa! Steady the Buffs,' said a big, deep voice – a voice she could tell instinctively was built to be heard across wide open spaces. Big hands caught her upper arms to save her from falling. 'No need to go knocking a bloke about – we're not married yet, y'know!'

Ethel looked up into a broad, fair face, hard and handsome, with hair, cut soldier-short, that glistened silver and gold in the sunlight. The blue eyes against the brown skin made the face look spuriously boyish, but there was nothing boylike in their expression.

'Beg pardon, I'm sure,' she said haughtily, to cover the fact that her heart had tripped. The presence of this man was so great he hardly needed the uniform – oh, but the uniform suited him!

He released her arms and invited her by a gesture to step to the side of the door, out of the flow. 'No need to apologise. It's a pleasure to be bumped into by a lovely young lady like you. Cigarette?'

'I don't smoke,' she said coolly. 'What d'you think?'

He winked. 'That you don't in public. Fair enough. Have a sweet instead.' He pulled out a paper bag. She took one, while he lit a cigarette. 'Oh, where are my manners? The name's Wood, Andy Wood – Miss?'

'Lusby. Ethel Lusby.'

'Ethel! Now there's a name I've always been partial to.'

'Have you really? How interesting,' she said, with devastating irony.

He was unwithered. 'Yes, I've always thought an Ethel would be both beautiful and bold. I can see you're beautiful, Miss Lusby, and I'm guessing you're bold.'

'What do you mean by "bold"?' she enquired suspiciously.

'Full of spirit. Ready to try new challenges.' He drew on

his cigarette and blew the smoke to the sky. 'I been watching you,' he said.

'Oh? And what did you see?' She liked this line of conversation.

'A young lady bored to death with all the weedy youths. A young lady that wants a proper man.'

People were pushing past them, and he used the excuse to step closer. He smelt clean, and his hard, tanned face, bending towards her, was smooth and healthy. But most of all he gave off such a sense of power and masculinity that she felt herself weakening in the stomach and knees in a most alarming way.

She clung to scorn as her only weapon. 'See that, did you? I think you need specs. And what do *you* want, pray?'

He laid a hand over hers. It was hard, and amazingly hot. 'I think you know the answer to that. And I'm thinking you want the same thing.'

Her mouth dried, and her insides whimpered. But she rallied. She didn't give in *that* easily. She snatched her hand away. 'Well, aren't you the presumptuous one?' she returned with spirit.

'Presumptuous!' He grinned. He had nice teeth, but it was rather a lupine smile. 'I like a lady with education. How about bowling for the pig? That's about the most exciting thing this do has to offer.' He crooked his arm to her, and she took it without hesitation. For her, *he* was the most exciting thing the do had to offer.

'Now, I'm guessing you're a school-teacher – am I right?' he said, as they walked towards the alley.

She was flattered, but tried not to show it. 'Not even warm,' she said. 'And what are you?'

'I'm a reservist, called back from my honest pursuits in Civvy Street to teach these lucky lads how to be soldiers, Gawd help 'em.'

'I mean, *what* are you – like, a private or a general or what?'

'Halfway between. I'm a sergeant. Don't you see my stripes?' He cocked his upper arm a little towards her.

'Don't mean anything to me. I don't know anything about the army,' she said loftily.

'Then I shall have the pleasure of teaching you. Can't not know about the army when there's a war on! See, a sergeant, he's the most important man in the whole set-out. The officers depend on him, the men can't live without him, and the generals all wish they *was* him, so's they could be in the thick of it, 'stead of stuck at their desks.'

Ethel was entranced by his way of speaking. 'Don't the officers make the decisions?' she asked.

'Once they've run it past the sergeant,' he answered. '"Sar'nt Wood," they say to me, "ought we to mount an attack on that post over there?" And I say, "Yessir, if you want your bloody head shot off. Give me four men and I'll take it from the rear." And he says, "Jolly good, Sar'nt Wood. Carry on."'

She laughed. He had imitated an officer's voice so well. 'You ought to be on the stage.'

'Waste of my considerable talents, when there's a war on,' he said.

'Why aren't you an officer, if you're so clever?'

'I'm a damn sight *too* clever to be an officer. Us sergeants have all the fun and get all the prettiest girls – don't you know that?' They were about to reach the back yard, where the sounds promised a merry crowd; there was no-one else in the alley. He pushed her gently back against the wall and she felt the hardness of his thighs against her, keeping her there. 'Oh, Miss Ethel Lusby,' he crooned, 'this is our lucky day.'

She mounted one last, desperate defence. She pushed against his rock-hard upper arms and said, 'You think a lot of yourself, don't you?'

'No sense in holding back when you see what you want,' he said. He looked down into her eyes and she was helpless. But he *had* held back. He hadn't kissed her. He'd smiled, released her, and taken her hand through his arm again. 'Let's go and get a pig.'

Now she went back over her memories as she did the fires and made beds. Why hadn't he kissed her? She couldn't have resisted him. Maybe he was afraid someone would come, and make trouble for her. But she had an idea that he didn't mind trouble on his own behalf and would care less about it on hers. She had a sense that this was a dangerous man. But it was what she had been wanting, wasn't it, the instant before she'd bumped into him? The thrill of danger.

That was why she was seeing him next Sunday, on her afternoon off. She was meeting him outside the church and going for a walk. He had said he didn't know the area, and she thought she might show him the woods and the lake; but even as she thought it, she shivered with delicious apprehension.

She had never properly had a mother, and there was nothing inside her that told her not to do this. But her own instinct of self-preservation, developed over a lifetime of having no-one to care for her but herself, seemed to have fallen asleep. *Why hadn't he kissed her?* She worried at it all day as she went about her work. He could have – why had he stopped?

Ethel thought herself sophisticated and up to the rig, but she had never been interested in fishing, or she might have understood the nature of a lure.

'The fête seems to have been a grand success,' said Hank to Diana, when they met at Mrs Oliver's at a tea-party a fortnight later.

'Mother says it made a lot of money for the refugees. It's all being paid into the rector's bank account, and then he's going to draw a cheque to present to the War Refugees Committee in London. They co-ordinate all the efforts. Father offered to take it to Lady Lugard on behalf of the committee, because he knows her through her husband, but Mrs Fitzgerald and Mrs Prendergast insist on doing it themselves.'

'Yes, I don't suppose they'd want to give up that treat,' Hank said. He thought she might laugh, even just smile at his daring satire, but she only said 'Hmm,' in an absent sort of way. There was something different about her, ever since that business at the skittle alley. Before that, he'd really felt he was getting somewhere with her. Now when she looked at him she didn't really see him any more.

He supposed she was pitching for the lordship, and he was disappointed, but not surprised. You wouldn't call Lord Dene a prize in the matter of looks, and he was as dumb as an ox when it came to charming conversation, but he *was* a lord, and he was also in uniform. Coming from a society without titles, he was inclined to put more emphasis on the latter than the former.

'It all seems a bit flat, now it's over,' he said. 'Don't you think?'

'I suppose so,' said Diana. 'But Mrs Fitzgerald says we mustn't rest on our laurels. We need to be thinking of what to do next. And there are lots of other good works.'

'Aunt Fanny thinks we should be doing more for the wounded,' Hank said. 'But I was thinking more along the lines of fun. Working for the fête was *fun*, didn't you think?'

'Hmm,' said Diana again, far off in her dream. Then she brightened. 'Of course, there's the Wroughtons' ball to look forward to. They haven't set a date yet, but Lord Wroughton said they would definitely do it before Christmas.'

'Oh, yes,' Hank said. 'The ball.' He'd heard as much about that as he wanted to. Besides, if it was a private Wroughton thing, chances were he wouldn't be invited. He sighed loudly to try to attract her attention. 'I'm thinking of volunteering.'

That did it. She looked at him now. 'Wouldn't you lose your citizenship?'

'You can't think about that when it's a matter of duty,' he said seriously. 'Every man is needed to fight this evil.'

For a moment she regarded him with something like the old warmth. 'I think that's splendid.' But then her eyes slid away again to contemplation of her inner landscape. 'When will you go?'

'Oh, I don't know,' he said, disappointed. 'Soon. I must talk to Auntie about it first.'

At last David's unit were getting their uniforms. 'And not before time,' Oliphant grumbled. 'My jacket's on its last legs.'

'And the way they're going about it is crazy,' David agreed.

The shortage of khaki cloth still persisted, and the uniforms were arriving not all at once but in batches. Every day, at drill, certain men would be ordered to fall out and report to the quartermaster's stores. It would be because, for instance, a bale of size 38 tunics had arrived, and they were the men who measured 38 inches around the chest. Or perhaps a cargo of size 6⅞ caps had come in, and they took a 6⅞ hat. These random individuals would march off as civilian scarecrows, and march back as semi-soldiers.

'Look at me!' David said, throwing out his arms. 'An army tunic and civilian trousers! I look ridiculous. And when are we going to get boots?'

'Be grateful B Company got them first,' said Oliphant. The first batch to come in had been of very poor quality, and the heels kept falling off, sometimes when the unlucky owner was miles from camp, so that he had to hobble home alone, and hope not to get lost on the way. One poor fellow hadn't got back until the early hours of the morning, though in his case it was because he had fallen accidentally into several village alehouses. Out in the country, they didn't worry too much about licensing hours.

Their colonel had indignantly sent back the whole

353

consignment of boots with a fierce complaint, and a new supplier had now been found, one who had lost the tender first time round to a lower bid.

'You can't make boots for ten shillings a pair,' Oliphant concluded. 'That should be obvious. Captain Talbot said the new ones'll cost fourteen and six d.'

'These were thirty shillings, F-A,' David said mournfully, looking down at their ruin. 'Thirty shillings!'

Oliphant inspected them carefully. 'I think you were gypped, old man,' he said solemnly, and received a punch on the arm for reward.

The next day, however, they and several other C Company men were issued with lace-up breeches and puttees, and had to learn how to put the latter on.

'You want to get 'em tight enough so's they don't fall down, but not so tight they cut off your calculations,' Sergeant Green informed them jocularly. 'Step forward, Adamson, you lucky lad, put your foot up on this here box, and I'll demonstrate on you. Pay attention, the rest of you. Now, you start down here, round the top of the boot. Make sure you get a good overlap, or you'll get mud inside your boots. Fold like this. Twice around. Then away we go. Round and round the lovely limb. You got a leg like Vesta Tilley, my son! And tie off up here, under the knee, like so. All right. Carry on.'

It was a tricky business to get right. The first time David overlapped his turns too closely and ran out of material before he reached the top. Oliphant, by contrast, had his turns too far apart, and the whole thing sagged sadly in concertina fashion to his ankle as soon as he moved. Adamson, for his second attempt, made the elementary mistake of rolling the puttee up with the tapes on the outside, so when he reached the top, after a laborious effort with tongue sticking out, he had nothing to tie up with.

'What the devil are the damned things for, anyway?' Colbert snarled, as he tore another failure from his lower limb.

354

'Cheaper than gaiters and easier to march in. Warm, waterproof and washable,' David replied. 'I think I've got it now . . . Except that my toes are going dead. Too tight.' He sighed and started to unroll again.

Oliphant, his foot up on a box, had made a discovery. 'I say, it's much easier if you start at the top and work down. Look – I've made a pretty decent job this time, I think.'

Sergeant Green, strolling by again, goggled at Oliphant's leg and said, 'Where d'you think you are, the bloody cavalry? Take it off and do it right!'

'Sergeant?'

'Only cavalrymen in riding breeches tie their puttees that way. You're infantry,' the sergeant explained patiently. 'Unless you've got a horse concealed in your tent I don't know about.'

'No horse, Sergeant,' Oliphant said sadly. 'I just thought it was easier this way.'

Green laid an enormous hand on his shoulder. 'If it was easy being in the army,' he said, with fake sympathy, 'anyone could do it.'

After the dribs and drabs, there was a sudden cascade in early November, and in a matter of days everyone was fully kitted out. The difference was amazing. Now they looked like soldiers. They felt like soldiers too. They marched more smartly, held their heads up, swung their arms. When the sergeants shouted, 'Left, right, left right – come on now, bags of swank!' bags of swank was what they got. The noble crusade they were involved in deserved a noble look, and their pride in the army and what it was doing increased tenfold.

There was a sudden craze for photographs, now they looked the part. Each company was assembled and photographed officially by a photographer sent down by the War Office, and some local pressmen were allowed to come in and take formal pictures, to encourage recruitment.

355

But every group of friends, every tent, every platoon, every team within the greater team, wanted the moment commemorated. Captain Lorrimer of B Company had a camera of his own, a 35mm Leitz he had bought in Germany the year before for a walking tour in Hesse. He was willing to let anyone use it, provided they paid for the film, and the photographer from the *Clifton Gazette* offered to develop the films and make prints for a reasonable fee. Soon everyone was sending pictures home. David sent one of himself with F-A, Adamson, Collyer, Colbert and Giles 'Dicky' Byrd, his particular friends, all in a row, leaning on their walking-stick rifles, each with a comfortable cigarette between his fingers and a grin on his face.

'As photographs go,' he said, as he put it in the envelope, 'it's pretty near perfect.'

The Salient of Ypres was important for reasons of morale, as the last bit of Belgium in Allied hands, and because it was keeping the Germans from taking the Channel ports. The fighting went on through October and into November. At home they heard of fierce attacks and desperate defences, wild heroic charges and strategic retreats fought every foot of the way. Sometimes lines were held by a last-minute dash from reinforcements; sometimes lines were broken with staunch regrouping at a new position.

The confusion of movement, of advance and retreat, of the focus of attack shifting about from one spot to another, made it hard even for someone with an atlas to make sense of. And then was the spelling to cope with, the outlandish names whose pronunciation could only be guessed at: Nieuport, Langemarck, Poperinghe and Passchendaele; Poelcapelle, Gheluvelt, Dixmude; Zandvoorde, Zonebeke and Kortekeer.

All the average person could say for sure was that the Germans were throwing everything they had at the Allies, and the Allies were repulsing them. The Germans outnumbered the Allies by a huge margin, and they had vast quantities of artillery and shells, yet in spite of this superiority they had not broken through in any significant way. Stories abounded of small forces of British soldiers holding off mass German attacks. We were winning, they said at home, that was what mattered – or, rather, the Germans were *not* winning, despite their boasted military prowess.

Oh, but the casualties! The cost of such desperate conflict was in blood, and as the hospital trains rolled in, and as War Office letters arrived at addresses all over the country, those directly involved, at least, knew with what pain the enemy was being thwarted. The newspapers reported casualties in a matter-of-fact way, and always made the point that German losses were greater, but still British losses were in the tens of thousands. The tight, skilled, experienced regular army that had gone across in August had numbered ninety thousand; more than fifty thousand of them had been killed, wounded, or were missing.

Such a running total was not to be found in the papers, of course – it might have led to a loss of public morale. But in mid-November, when the Flanders front seemed to be falling quiet again, Edward called at Lord Forbesson's London house, at his request, to discuss his securities; and over a glass of sherry in his study, his lordship told him some of the realities behind the triumphant headlines.

Though there had been sharp clashes since then, the last mass German attack had ceased on the 11th of November. The British had held them off long enough to be able to fall back to a position of their own choosing where they could dig in and hold on.

'The Germans don't look like renewing the large-scale fighting,' Forbesson said. 'The weather's turned – hard frosts and some heavy snowfalls already. And they've taken a hell of a beating. We estimate their casualties are twice what ours have been, and ours have been pretty damned heavy. This is not warfare as any of us have known it before. But one thing we've learned: in the trenches, it's a damn sight easier to defend than to attack.'

'I imagine so,' said Edward

Forbesson rubbed his temple absently. 'We're not in too bad a case, all things considered, and the men have been splendid – splendid! But we're damnably short of shells and ammunition. We've got to get on top of that problem before the spring.'

'And short of men?' Edward suggested. 'I heard a rumour that the Territorials were going to be sent out.'

'Eight battalions,' Forbesson admitted. 'Well, at least they're not completely raw. And with luck it may only be a matter of holding the line for the winter. But we'll have to do something about recruitment. Can't go on with this piecemeal volunteering. We need a steady stream of trained men. Some of the battalions out there are down to the strength of companies, and companies are little more than platoons. Sir John French is collecting together odds and sods of survivors and cobbling them into new units. But it's the shortage of officers that hits hardest. So many of our best chaps gone. The Royal West Kents have only four officers left – all subalterns. The First Coldstream is down to two and a quartermaster.'

'I knew things were grave,' Edward said, 'but I didn't know *how* grave.'

'We've performed miracles in the Salient, Hunter, I don't mind telling you. The Germans pounded us with the most powerful artillery the world's ever seen, but our line held. They outnumber us two to one, but they couldn't take Ypres. By those measures they're losing, and losing badly.' He drew thoughtfully on his cigarette. 'All the same, I think even the man in the street is starting to understand the war won't be over by Christmas.'

'Perhaps that's a good thing,' Edward said. 'The nation needs to concentrate. We may have been taking it too lightly until now. What did Johnson say? "When a man knows he is to be hanged in a fortnight, it concentrates his mind wonderfully."'

'You're right,' Forbesson said. 'A dose of reality is hard medicine, but this war is going to be won by grit, and our people have that.' He lapsed into thought. The fire under the chimney leaped and crackled, its shifting light picking out gleams from brass and silver around the room, and the gold on the spines of the books that lined the walls. The clock on the mantelshelf dropped its measured strokes like small pebbles into the pool of quiet.

The large dog basking on the hearthrug rolled on to its back, yawning noisily, and Forbesson shook himself back to the here and now. 'To personal matters, Hunter,' he said. 'I wanted to talk to you about my place in Hampshire. I can't see myself being able to get much use out of it for the duration of the war. I'd like to rent it out – frankly, I could do with the money. Do you think you could find me a suitable tenant?'

'As it happens,' Edward said, 'I do have a client, a wealthy Belgian businessman, who's looking for a country property. He wants to get his family out of London. What were you hoping to realise?'

They settled down to a comfortable discussion.

CHAPTER TWENTY-SIX

One of the three-year-olds – Cairns called it 'Number Seven' but Sadie called it Star, for a white mark on its forehead – had injured itself trying to jump out of the paddock. It had hit the top rail and fallen badly on one knee.

John Courcy was sent for. Sadie volunteered to hold the gelding for him, so that the others could get on with their work. 'Are you sure?' said Biggs. 'He might get a bit rough, miss, being frightened like.' He hadn't known Sadie as long as Podrick and Baker.

'He'll be all right with me,' Sadie said. 'He knows me.'

The gelding was feeling very sorry for himself, holding up the injured leg and trembling, nostrils flared and eyes wide. Sadie clipped a rope to his head-collar and took a good grip, stroking his neck and cheek and talking to him softly. John Courcy came into the box with his bag and assessed the situation. He didn't quite ask if Sadie could manage, but he said, 'Do you want to put a twitch on him?'

'I don't think we'll need it,' she said.

Courcy looked back at Cairns, who gave him an infinitesimal nod, swung a bucket of hot water inside, closed the half-door and leaned on it to observe.

'All right,' Courcy said. 'Let's have a look.' The gelding swung his head up as he took hold of the leg below the knee, but settled as Sadie soothed him. The big brown eye looked down into hers and found reassurance there, and his head came down a little. 'He's made quite a mess of himself, hasn't he? Exposed the joint capsule and the tendons.'

'Will he be all right?' Sadie asked. 'He will heal?' A horse with a broken leg had to be shot – she was afraid this might lead to the same result.

Courcy felt around the wound with careful fingers. 'The joint capsule and tendon sheaths are intact – he hasn't lost any fluid. I think he'll be all right. Let's get it cleaned up, to start with. There's grit in here.'

'He came down on the gravel,' Sadie said. 'Poor old boy.' She stroked the star on his forehead, and he lowered his head and snuffled at her other hand gratefully. She watched with keen interest as Courcy swabbed out the wound with hot water and cotton wool, noting gladly that he was making a thorough job of it, getting into every cranny. The gelding flinched once or twice, but otherwise submitted quietly.

When the wound was clean, Courcy disinfected it with iodoform powder, using a puffer to get it into every recess, and said, 'Right, I'm ready to stitch. It'll be a long job. Are you still comfortable holding him?'

'Yes, we'll be all right. He's happy enough with me.'

The horse was, in fact, now leaning his face against her while she drew gently on one ear. Courcy smiled. 'You have a good way with horses, Miss Hunter. It's a gift.'

She blushed with pleasure. 'Oh,' she said, not used to compliments. 'Well, I like them.'

'They always know,' Courcy said. It was a sign of his confidence in her that he sat down in the straw to settle for what was going to be a long job. Cairns had long since come to the same conclusion and gone away to his work. Courcy chose a fine suture needle and thread, and began pulling together the ragged shreds of skin.

'It's like a jigsaw puzzle,' Sadie said, after a while.

'Luckily there don't seem to be any pieces missing,' Courcy

said. And after a moment, 'Don't feel you have to keep quiet. I can talk and sew at the same time. In fact, I prefer it.'

Of course, the instant she was licensed to talk, she couldn't think of anything to say. But after a moment she asked him if he had always wanted to be a vet.

'Always,' he said. 'It didn't go down well at home. My father's a doctor and it shocked him terribly. He thought his the more noble calling. But I said God put animals under our dominion so we owe a duty of stewardship to them.'

'Did he try to stop you?' Sadie asked.

'Oh, yes. But when he saw I was determined, he agreed to it, as long as I studied at the Dick.'

'The what?'

'The Royal Veterinary College in Edinburgh. It was founded by a man called William Dick, so it's always known as the Dick Vet. You see, students there have to attend lectures in human medicine at the Royal College of Surgeons as well, so my father thought if I was exposed to the right influences, I would see the error of my ways.'

'But you didn't.'

'No. He thought it shaming to have a son who was a mere horse doctor. So I came as far from home as possible to practise, so as not to tread on his toes.'

'Where is home?'

'Northumberland.'

'I've never been to Northumberland. Well, I've never been anywhere, really. Do you miss it?'

'Yes, sometimes. It's wild and bleak, not like here. But this country is very beautiful – more beautiful in the aesthetic sense.'

'But not really home?'

He glanced up at her. 'It's beginning to feel more like home,' he said. 'Of course, there's a little bit of one's heart that always wants to go back. I miss the wide openness, and the bare, grim hills with the wind romping over them.'

'You say it so beautifully,' Sadie said.

He took another tiny stitch; the horrible gape was beginning to disappear behind black silken skin. 'You're remarkably easy to talk to, you know,' he said.

Sadie's heart sang. But of course, she told herself sternly, he didn't mean anything by it. 'People often say things to me because they don't really notice I'm there,' she said.

'I'm sure that's not the reason,' he said. Sadie turned her head away slightly, occupied herself with crooning to the horse.

He saw that she was a child still in most ways, but trembling on the brink, on the edge of the precipice that was adulthood, and he felt a sudden, piercing sympathy for her. In some ways she was an exile, like him – a person out of their place, always looking in through a glass pane at the warm, cheerful precinct where everyone else lived their lives. It made, he felt, a bond between them.

'I think people tell you things because you're intelligent,' he said, trying to make it matter-of-fact, as though they were discussing horses. She looked at him warily. 'Intelligence is a rare gift,' he went on, 'and too often undervalued.' Particularly in females, he thought, but he did not add that bit aloud, for fear of making her shy away.

She had nothing to say to his last remark, but the thoughts that occupied her seemed happy ones. After a moment he said, 'How is the schooling coming along?'

And after that they talked about horses.

The war quietened down as the weather grew too bad in France for any large-scale fighting. As the men settled in one place, there was a sudden splurge of letters home, and a reciprocal scramble to send out parcels of little luxuries to make their lives better and tell them those at home were thinking of them.

At the beginning of December the great oblivion that was

363

war spat out a letter from Jack. From its condition, it had obviously gone astray – a rare occurrence, the army postal service being usually a model of efficiency. Only a few days later, it spat out Jack as well. Beth had a telegram, telling her he was coming home. She rushed about, ordering his favourite foods, arranging flowers, telephoning friends, instructing Mrs Beales, the cook-housekeeper she had engaged. And then he was there, actually on the doorstep, looking strange in his uniform, carrying a leather hold-all and a small box wrapped in pink paper.

'I was going to bring you flowers, but it's the wrong time of year,' he said, by way of greeting. 'Nothing but chrysanthemums.'

'I bought chrysanthemums,' she said, trying hard not to cry. She didn't want to waste time with weeping. 'I thought you should have flowers in the house to come home to.' There was a big arrangement of bronze and deep red ones on the small table opposite the door. Mrs Beales was hovering, waiting to take his bag. 'Come in, don't let the fog in.' It wasn't quite a pea-souper, but it was a raw, grey afternoon, everything dripping, the paving stones glistening with sooty moisture. She had had the lights on all day.

He stepped in, put down his bag, and Mrs Beales scurried past to shut the door, pick up the bag and disappear with it. Jack grinned. 'Was that monumental tact? Leaving us alone in case you want to kiss me?'

'I *do* want to, so much, but you look so strange in your uniform. So – *other*.'

'You look pretty "other" without one,' Jack said. 'You can't think what it does to one's perceptions to be in a totally male environment for weeks at a time.'

She knew they were talking to cover their sudden shyness. The war had placed a barrier between them, through which they could see but not touch each other. 'Come in to the fire, and have a drink,' she said.

364

'Excellent idea,' he said, following her upstairs. The drawing-room looked cosy, with a good fire leaping energetically under the chimney, the lamps lit, the well-worn leather sofa drawn up to it, the table with the decanter tray handily placed. 'My God!' he breathed, pausing at the door. She stopped and looked back at him enquiringly. He couldn't tell her what a contrast it was, what he was seeing compared with what he had been seeing day after day for the last three months. He felt, paradoxically, a hollowness, like great sorrow, at the sight of this comfort and luxury – as though, like the Little Match Girl, it was not for him.

He shook himself, and held out the box to her. 'For you. All the way from the Continent. *Marrons glacés*. Well, the chestnut is a tree, if it's not a flower.'

'Chestnut trees have flowers,' Beth said, trying to understand this strange distance that was between them, when they had always been as close as twins. 'Thank you. I love *marrons glacés*.'

'I know.'

'Whisky or brandy?'

'Whisky, please. We had brandy in France, but whisky is harder to get hold of, not being their drink.'

'France?' she queried. 'Weren't you in Belgium last?'

'Generic term,' he said, 'for where the war is.'

She gave him his drink, and took hers to the sofa, sitting at one end, legs tucked up under her, so she could face him. He sat leaning forward, elbows on knees, turning his glass in his hands, watching the spitting firelight catch the crystal. Beth wanted to talk, felt it welling up in her, but knew it would be meaningless chatter. She didn't want to chatter, not to Jack, her love, her husband. So she sat in silence. After a bit he roused himself and said, 'Have we got any music?'

'Yes, the gramophone still works. What would you like?'

'You choose,' he said, almost tersely.

She had a fancy he was keeping her occupied, but it suited her to be busy about some small task. She had no idea what would suit his mood – or, indeed, what his mood was; it seemed dark just now. She didn't think he could bear Brahms, his favourite. She chose in the end Arthur Rubinstein playing Liszt.

They sat listening until Mrs Beales announced dinner. At the table he was light, amusing, made her talk about the London scene, reminisced about plays they had seen and places they had been, and she knew he just wasn't there. She wanted to cry out, 'You don't need to pretend with me!' But she loved him enough to see that pretending was his only defence against some emotion so overwhelming he dared not admit it. He ate at first with frightening speed, but caught himself up and slowed down, though she could see it was an effort.

After dinner he said, 'I must have a bath. Is the water hot?'

'Yes. I'll go and draw it. You go up to the bedroom. Your dressing-gown is behind the door.'

'Dressing-gown!' he said, as though she had suggested something impossibly exotic.

She thought the bath was another way of avoiding her, but when it was ready, he said, 'Come in and talk to me. Give me five minutes to wash, then come in.'

She took him in another whisky, and found him lying back in the soapy water, his hair and eyelashes wet. She thought him thinner than when he had gone away. 'Are you going to shave?' she asked.

He ran a hand automatically over his jaw. 'Do you mind? I'm not too bristly. I shaved this morning – no, last night, but it was late last night.'

'I don't mind. Jack, I have to ask – how long have you got?'

He grinned, and it was almost his old look. 'Eager to be

rid of me, eh? I suppose the other bloke's waiting impatiently at some hotel round the corner.'

'Not at all. I've put him in the spare room. How long?'

'Four days. We're all getting four days' leave at some point in December. I'm afraid it's a case of last in, first out. The regulars are getting the days nearer Christmas. Those who are left.'

She held her breath, but those words seemed to have unblocked something, and he began to tell her about his war, slowly at first, and then with increasing fluency, and all she had to do was sit on the edge of the bath and let him do it. There was anger there, and sometimes his words were like blows; but as the stream thickened and flowed the anger washed away, and there was sadness and pride, love for his fellows and grief, and, at last, gladness to be home.

'Do you remember I sent you a picture postcard of the Cloth Hall in Ypres?' he said.

'Yes, of course. I have it in my writing case.'

'It's gone now. They shelled it and shelled it – Ypres. My God! When we first saw it, it was a pretty place, all Gothic spires and curlicues – we laughed a bit, it was so outlandish, but it was pretty. When I left it was just ruins, a chimney sticking up here and there, or a wall with gaping windows not attached to anything. The buildings that are left are chipped and broken, the roads pitted with shell holes. People live in their cellars like rats; only the rats run about in the streets. We were in the line on the 11th of November, up the Menin road, we'd been there seventeen days, and they sent up some Territorials to relieve us. Poor beggars, they didn't know what they were getting into. They were full of talk about how they'd been brought up from Poperinghe by a fleet of London omnibuses – thought it great fun. So we made our way back down the road, diving into the ditch when a shell went over, and there in front of us the Cloth Hall was burning. It was the biggest building left standing, so you couldn't miss it. It was a sheet of fire, flames leaping out of the windows, great gouts of sparks exploding from the roof. And, God help me, my first reaction was how pretty it looked, just like fireworks.' He stopped.

'Darling,' she said, but had no other words.

He drank whisky. 'But we kept the Germans out. They smashed Ypres but they couldn't take it. The line held. We still hold the Salient.'

And you survived, she said in her head.

'It's a different kind of war, and I think some people are only just coming to terms with it. No more cut and thrust, no cavalry charges, flashing swords and flying pennants, bugles and drums and glory. All those battles fought across France and back again – Le Cateau, the Marne, the Aisne and the rest – they're like something out of history now. And most of the men who fought them are dead and gone, too. It's up to us, now – all of us.' He looked up and held her eyes. 'The people here at home have to know that. They have to understand.'

She wanted desperately to hold him. 'You mustn't feel guilty for having survived,' she said.

He grimaced. 'Dammit, Beth, you have a way of sticking your finger right on the sore point. I can't help it – I do feel guilty. But I'll try not to let it get me down.' He drained the glass. 'I think I'm a little bit drunk, but it's nice. Smoothes the raw edges. I'm glad to be back, darling – don't know if I've mentioned that.'

'Not so far,' she said. 'I'm glad to have you back. And talking of backs, let me scrub yours for you.'

He sat forward and she soaped and scrubbed his back, feeling his ribs through the skin, and noting the thickening of his shoulder and arm muscles. In a purely physical way, he *was* a stranger to her. She rinsed him off, and as she straightened, he reached up a wet hand to her face, cupped her cheek, and drew her down to be kissed. She felt his lips come alive under hers, and thought, with relief, that it was going to be all right. They would go to bed, and it would be all right.

On the 16th of December, Scarborough, Hartlepool and Whitby were shelled from the sea by German battleships. The attack came without warning to an unprepared population: it was centuries since the mainland of England had been struck. Streets of houses were destroyed, churches, schools and public buildings; 137 people were killed and almost six hundred wounded, mostly civilians. The newspapers were full of shocking reports and photographs.

'This is not warfare, this is murder,' the editorials cried.

Anathema against the Germans for this foul attack on innocent civilians was almost matched by outrage against the Royal Navy for not having prevented it. The army was all very well, but the army was always 'over there', and that was where warfare belonged, too. The navy had been Britain's bulwark. But now the Huns had shelled England itself, and got away with it. Why hadn't the navy blown them out of the water? There was some terrible mismanagement here!

The news scared Cook and Ada almost into hysterics. The shores of Britain, the line that separated her from the rest of the world, had been breached; her sea defences, which had kept her safe from time immemorial, had terrifyingly failed. If the Germans could bombard English towns with impunity, what was to stop them landing? And if they could land on the North Sea coast, no place in England was safe. Suddenly the war had arrived on the doorstep.

'They'll be turning up here next,' Cook cried, at teatime, as she and Ada huddled over the newspaper reports. 'And us all undefended, our men gone away to France! All we've got is the police, three of them to guard the whole of Northcote!'

'We'll be murdered in our beds,' Ada moaned.

Munt did all he could to stir them up, shaking his head and sucking his teeth over the desperate state of home defence. 'Government's not give a thought to it,' he said. 'So set on saving Belgium, they don't care what happens to our own country. Course, they've always believed the navy'd keep us safe. We all believed that. Got to think again now, haven't we?'

'Oh, Mr Munt, what are you saying?'

'Stands to reason,' Munt said. 'The navy was supposed to keep the Germans out of England, so they've not put a penny into civil defence. Sent the Territorials to France, now, so there's 'ardly a fit man nor a gun that'll fire in the 'ole country. All that's left, to defend you women,' he managed to put a quaver into his voice, 'is old men and boys, like me and Henry here.' Henry looked startled but gratified to be so elevated to Mr Munt's level. 'We'll do our best, o' course, but . . .' He shrugged helplessly.

'Oh, Mr Munt!' Ada cried, half alarmed, half touched.

'We won't be able to hold out long,' he went on tremulously. 'Not against fit young Germans, we won't. They'll kill us right off. But at least it's a quick death. It's you women I worry about. They'll keep you alive for their own evil purposes.'

Ada gave a little scream, which made Emily jump. She squared her sparrow's shoulders. 'They won't get me,' she cried. 'I'll defend meself. There's plenty o' knives in the kitchen.'

'Oh, Emily, don't say such things!' Ada cried, though curiously comforted by Emily's courage. 'We could all have knives,' she suggested hesitantly. 'Take 'em up to bed with us, in case. Keep 'em under our pillows.'

'You'd cut your ear off,' Ethel said, coming back from a reverie about her last evening out with Sergeant Wood. 'Don't pay no attention to him. Germans, indeed! He's having you on. It's miles to the sea from here.'

'They march fast, them Germans,' Munt said. 'Be here in no time.' He leered sidelong at Cook. 'Looking for nice plump English virgins.'

Cook squeaked, though this time more at the word 'virgins', which was not suitable for the tea-table, than the threat of invasion. 'None of that talk in my kitchen,' she said, rallying a bit. She was starting to think Ethel was right.

Ethel was scornful. 'Germans come here, with a whole camp of soldiers on Paget's Piece? I don't think so.'

'Oh, I'd forgotten the camp,' Cook said, with relief. 'You're a wicked old man, Mr Munt, and you'll go to Hell.'

'I'll see *you* there, then,' he retorted, pushing his chair back. 'Well, I better be gettin'. Got to fortify me shed, case the Germans come. Build the barricades.'

Henry pushed his chair back and said he'd better be gettin', too.

'Why? What you got to do?' Cook asked sharply.

'Help Mr Munt,' Henry said. 'Build the barricades.'

'Oh, get in that scullery and don't talk so far back,' Cook snapped, herself again. 'You've got all them knives to clean.'

And she heaved herself up from the tea-table to start the creation of a steak and kidney pie for the family's dinner.

It was Mrs Oliver who persuaded Lady Wroughton to alter the nature of her proposed ball. They met at Lady Smith-Dorrien's house, at a meeting for the Blue Cross Fund. There was an excellent tea laid on, as usual, and finding Lady Wroughton enjoying a slice of particularly fine Madeira cake, she took the opportunity to recommend a charity event over a purely social one.

The countess's horror at the idea of ordinary people trampling all over her house – she had always kept open days to the minimum, and confined them to a very few rooms – was counterbalanced by the obvious need to raise money for the comforts of the wounded. Their local hospital, Mount View, which had been set up in a breezy spot for consumption sufferers, was gradually emptying itself of lung cases and taking in lightly wounded and convalescent soldiers.

The whole nation had been shocked out of its complacency by those hospital trains, those casualty lists, and the sight, growing more frequent on London streets, of men on crutches and men in wheelchairs and men with bandaged heads. And the aristocracy had paid a disproportionate share of the blood price: officers led by example and were always first into the fray. The Cecils, Cholmondeleys, Crichtons, Dawnays, Desboroughs, Fitzclarences, Gordon-Lennoxes, Worsleys and Wellesleys had suffered such losses that the next edition of *Debrett's* would need wholesale rewriting. At such a time, a purely private ball would not only look wrong, it would *be* wrong.

The ball was fixed for the 19th of December. The countess comforted herself that the riff-raff would be kept out by the price of the tickets; and if she had to accept a tiresome number of the affluent middle classes, she could at least ensure that the right people came as well. A little subtle blackmail by letter, together with the lure of her unwed sons, would have the mamas buying tickets for their daughters.

The preparations for the ball brought joy to the tradesmen of Northcote, and interest to the lives of the whole village. Even those who could not go could enjoy a long gossip about who would, and on the night could gather outside the gates to see which famous people went by.

Edward, Beattie and Diana were going. Nula and Beattie had been busy making Diana's new gown.

'Aren't you sorry not to be going?' Diana asked Sadie one day, when she paused by the door, watching Nula pin a sleeve.

'Not me,' Sadie said. Her seventeenth birthday was not until January, and she was not 'out' – with the war on, she wondered if she ever would be. 'I can't see the point of balls,' she said. 'You have to dance with so many people you don't like just because it's polite, and you can't go and ask the one person you want to dance with because it isn't done.'

Diana rolled her eyes, but she was too happy to be unkind. 'When you come out, I'll let you borrow my garnet necklace,' she said. 'It will suit you, with your brown eyes and hair.'

Sadie was touched. 'I hope you have a lovely time,' she reciprocated.

'I will,' Diana said superbly. But inside she was nervous. Suppose there were lots of very upper-class girls there, like Kiki Eynsham and Lady Victoria Blundell? Suppose she made a fool of herself and they were cruel and sneering? Suppose Charles danced with them and ignored her?

But he *had* asked her to open the ball with him. It must mean something, mustn't it? In the little time she had spent with him, she had never gained the impression that he was unkind. Whatever Bobby said, he wouldn't simply toy with her and hurt her.

And she loved her new gown. The long, slender line with narrow skirt and draped bodice suited her figure perfectly. It was in cream brocade, with oversleeves of gold silk net, and gold-coloured gathered lace on the bodice. Most fair girls would have looked washed-out in such a colour scheme, but it made her glow richly, and brought attention to her unusual eyes. Her hair was to be dressed with silk roses, and she was to wear her mother's pearls and small pearl earrings – nothing else.

'You look . . . enchanting,' Edward said, when she came down the stairs on the evening of the ball. 'Like a fairy princess.'

For once Diana had nothing to say, and gave him a small, almost shy smile. Her beauty hurt his heart: there was something so vulnerable and frightening about a beautiful young girl. The sight of his eldest daughter come to this threshold moved him, more than her coming-out had, for that had seemed a beginning and this felt like an end. You made your sons tough and ready for life, if you could, but you tried to protect your daughters from it. And when they stepped out into it, so absurdly confident in their own power to conquer, you lost them.

CHAPTER TWENTY-SEVEN

Dene Park sent a motor-car for the Hunters. It was not the Silver Ghost but a smaller Wolseley, though Lord Dene's chauffeur was driving. Edward concluded from this that it had been Charles's idea to send it.

Dene Park was a Palladian house by Giacomo Leoni, with an enormous Corinthian portico on the front, the better to intimidate visitors, Beattie thought, as they drove up to it. It looked splendid, with the windows lit up and a stream of motor-cars disgorging finely dressed people. The doors opened into a huge, square hall rising the height of the building, with a gallery around three sides and a staircase on either side. The original, to the right, gave access to the gallery and the upstairs rooms of the house; that to the left led straight up to the ballroom.

At the door two footmen were checking tickets, while in the hall a small army of servants and hired maids were taking coats. As it was not a private ball, there was no receiving line, but at the top of the stairs there was a large landing and an anteroom before the ballroom itself, and both were crowded with friends and acquaintances of the family, lingering and chatting noisily with each other while lesser mortals passed straight through. Edward spotted the earl over the heads, and he nodded civilly though he appeared unable to break away; he could not see the countess.

'We'd better go through,' he said to his womenfolk. 'We're blocking the way.'

Diana was piercingly disappointed to discover herself one of the unimportant people, doomed to pass through un-noticed, but she swallowed her feelings and put her head up. Beattie, with a fair idea of what she was thinking, squeezed her hand comfortingly. Whatever else did or did not happen, a ball at Dene Park was something to be savoured.

But at that moment Charles came struggling out through a crowd of very smart ladies, looking a little flushed. He came straight to the Hunters, shook hands with Edward and bowed to Beattie, while saying, 'I'm so sorry, I meant to meet you down in the hall but I was detained.' He cast a frustrated half-glance behind him, as if his detaining had been much against his will. And to Diana he said, 'Miss Hunter, I hope you have remembered your promise? You did say that you would give me the opening dances.'

'I hadn't forgotten,' Diana said, putting her hand on his offered arm. From the depths she had soared again to the heights. They walked through the anteroom into the ball-room, from which music could already be heard. People parted in front of them, then closed in behind to follow. Conversation dropped, then rose again in their wake. She felt eyes on her, but had no leisure to look, concentrating on managing her train and her feelings.

Of the ballroom she had only an impression of lights, colours and a certain amount of glitter as they walked to the far end; she could feel Charles's arm under her hand, hear his breathing, smell the French chalk on the floor, his bay rum and a hint of cloves from his hair oil. Her nervous-ness made her feel disembodied; she couldn't really believe this was happening, that she was here at all.

At the top he stopped, turned to her; the music struck up with a waltz; he slipped a gloved hand round her and rested it in the middle of her back. His other hand took hers, and she dared at last to look up at him. There was no transformation: it was the plain, unsmiling Charles Wroughton she had known these months past; but he met her eyes and set her pulse jumping again. 'You look very beautiful this evening,' he said. 'I am the luckiest man in the room.'

Then his hands tightened and they were moving – dancing, it seemed to her, in a luminous mist.

Charles danced well, as she now remembered, and she was able to relax into his guiding hands. Other couples had crowded on to the floor. Charles did not seem to want to speak, and as her senses cleared she could look around, take in the scene and savour her moment.

During one turn she passed the earl and countess, standing together in a corner with a group of very glittery people – the women in diamonds and the men in orders. They did not look at her, but she felt terribly visible to them, as though she had forgotten some essential piece of her clothing.

She swallowed nervously: this was not her milieu, these were not her people; she was dangerously out of her place, flying too close to the sun. For one instant she wished she was back at The Elms with Sadie, doing a jigsaw puzzle. Then she shook the thought away. Ridiculous! What girl wouldn't want to change places with her: dancing in a beautiful new gown at a grand ball with Lord Dene?

Charles looked down at her, and his left hand slightly squeezed her right. 'Is everything all right?' he asked. 'I thought you seemed – troubled, for a moment.'

She was touched that he was so sensitive to her. He must have felt her momentary qualm. For that, he deserved honesty. 'Not troubled,' she said. 'Just for a moment I couldn't believe I was really here.'

'I'm glad you are,' he said. He had been feeling much the same – that he couldn't believe she was here, in his arms, dancing with him. 'I would like to go on like this for ever,' he added.

Heat flooded her. It was not possible to misinterpret that comment. She sought for something to say. 'It was kind of you to send the motor-car for us.'

'For you,' he said. He swallowed. She saw his rather prominent Adam's apple jerk up, then down. He said, rather low, 'I was so afraid you wouldn't come.'

They danced in silence after that. She was used to her suitors chattering to her, trying to be charming, to impress her, to make her laugh. But Charles's silence seemed more of a tribute. When the set ended, he did not take her to the side, but remained standing where the music had beached them, holding her loosely, telling her about a concert his men had got up, and when the music started again, his grasp firmed and he danced her away again. She wondered for a startled moment if he meant to dance with her all night. *That* would certainly raise eyebrows.

When he ran out of subject matter, she told him about Sadie's war work, and that got him talking about horses. The Remount Service had taken his hunters, but he had been able to keep his hack and take it with him to Chiswell. 'It's good to have a friendly face there,' he concluded. 'Sometimes it can be strangely lonely, being surrounded by hundreds of men in uniform. They're all splendid fellows,' he added hastily, 'and so eager to get sent to France. There's a new rumour every week, that the battalion is on its way, and they're so disappointed when it turns out to be false.'

The music stopped again, and this time, before Diana had had time to draw breath, Rupert appeared at their side, and said, in a voice that seemed to her to drip poison, 'Charles, you can't keep the loveliest girl in the room to yourself all evening. I simply insist on the next dance. Move aside, there's a good fellow. Miss Hunter, may I have the pleasure?'

Diana's comfort was that Charles looked annoyed at being

interrupted. For herself, she could do nothing but consent. Rupert danced her away, and she waited, her scalp tingling, very conscious of his hands touching her, for the attack.

'Good work!' was what he said. 'And quick, too. Everyone's noticed that you danced two sets. Now they're all asking, "Who is that female who's got her claws into poor Charles?" No, no,' he went on quickly, tightening his grip as she tried instinctively to pull away, 'don't give them any more food for gossip. Dance nicely, Miss Fortune-Hunter, or you'll scotch your own campaign. Wait! What am I saying? Do behave as badly as you wish! Stamp your foot, slap my face and storm off the floor – please! You'll be doing my work for me.'

'Your work?' she said angrily. 'And what is that? To make trouble and unpleasantness?'

'No, no, that's your job. Mine is to save my brother from a besotted mistake. I told you, didn't I, to leave him alone?'

'You should have told him to leave me alone,' Diana said, trying for haughtiness. '*I'm* not pursuing *him*, I assure you.'

'Oh, quite. Like Old Man Kangaroo, you want to be very truly run after. And poor old Yellow Dog Dingo will chase you until you catch him.'

'I have no idea what you're talking about,' Diana said icily, 'but if you are referring to me as a dog—'

'No, you are the kangaroo. Charles is the dingo. Do pay attention.'

'I don't think he would like it if he knew how rude and unpleasant you are being.'

'Don't worry about that. He's dancing with Georgy Pargeter now, and she's a nice, sweet, adoring sort of girl who would make him the perfect wife. There are plenty of nice girls to take his mind off you, as long as I can keep you two apart.'

'I think you are a cad,' she said in a low voice.

'Better a cad than a harpy. No, don't pull away. Remember

379

people are watching. I'll stop being a cad if you promise to leave Charles alone. He won't be allowed to marry you anyway, as I've already told you. He relies on my father for his income, and that can be cancelled in a trice.'

'Then what are you worried about?' Diana said loftily. Her stomach was churning unpleasantly with emotions.

'I'm not worried about his marrying you, because he can't. I'm worried about his having his heart broken. If you had the slightest womanliness about you, you would promise to let him go.'

'I'm not promising anything to you. It's none of your business,' Diana ground out, between clenched teeth.

He smiled horribly. 'Then I shall just have to keep dancing with you all evening, and show you up to Charles as the heartless flirt I know you are.'

She would have pulled away from him then and walked away, whatever the scandal, but he anticipated her and gripped her so tightly she couldn't release herself. He was hurting her hand; his right hand was crushing her ribs; but short of screaming, there was nothing she could do about it. But when the dance ended, she was determined to get away, whatever it took – even if she had to stamp on his foot, or bite him. Her temper was up. She would sooner make a scandal and have to leave than let him get his way.

The music did stop and she wriggled, felt him trying to hold her yet tighter, heard him growl, 'Oh, no, you don't!'

And then, thank God, Charles was there! How had he got away from his partner so quickly? He laid a hand on Rupert's shoulder and said, 'Sorry, little brother. This dance is promised to me.' For an instant Rupert didn't release her, but Charles didn't move, simply stood like a rock, and in the end he had to let her go. Diana wanted to rub her crushed hand, wanted to cry, to sob and shout hateful names at Rupert as he walked away. But she couldn't, of course. It was all she could do not to wince when Charles took her wounded hand. In her relief at being rescued, she felt suddenly quite weak. She wanted to collapse bonelessly on Charles's chest. But she couldn't do that, either.

At the end of another set, Charles said, 'It's very hot in here. Would you like a breath of air? A glass of champagne?'

'Thank you,' Diana said. At the other end from the ante-room there was a door beside the dais where the orchestra sat, which led into a further room, where supper was being set up. A few people, evidently on a similar mission, were standing about talking, fanning themselves, some with glasses in their hands.

Charles, however, seemed to have something else on his mind. He said, 'There's something in particular I want to talk to you about. Would you think it very wrong of me to take you away somewhere more private?'

Her heart seemed to be beating uncomfortably in her throat. 'Where?' was all she managed to ask.

'The picture gallery. It's bound to be quiet there. Would you care to come and see some of my ancestors?' It was plain from his tone that he meant it as a joke – the first she had heard him make.

At the far end of this room there was another doorway, which led on to a staircase hall, and they trod in silence up to the next floor and through a door into a long gallery, dimly lit, lined with pictures interspersed with bookcases. Along the centre were reading tables, and at the end a group of sofas and chairs around a lit fire. It was cold up there, especially, after the heat of the ballroom, for someone in a ballgown. Diana shivered, but Charles didn't seem to notice, though he led her towards the fire. He didn't refer to the ancestors, and she didn't particularly want to look at them.

He said, 'This wing was added in the middle of the last century, with the orangery below the ballroom, and this gallery above. I like to come here and read, so I always

381

have them light a fire. I feel comfortable here with the ancestors watching over me. Rupert says their eyes follow him reproachfully.'

'Perhaps Rupert's conscience is not clear,' she said, rather daringly.

But, again, Charles didn't seem to notice. He evidently had something on his mind. He led her to the sofa, and sat beside her, turning to face her, his look grave and earnest. *He's going to say something bad,* she thought. *That he doesn't want to see me any more. That he's engaged to someone else.* She waited nervously.

At last he said, 'The rumours about going to France aren't all untrue. But at the moment, the men don't know what I've been told – that we will be going in January.'

'Oh,' said Diana. And then, 'You must be excited.'

'I suppose I must,' he said. 'But I'm sorry, too.'

'Sorry?'

'That it will take me further away from you.' He swallowed visibly again. 'It did occur to me that – that if we were engaged, I could write to you. We could write to each other.' She didn't know how to reply to that, and waited, her eyes wide, for him to put it in unambiguous terms.

How delicate she was, like a wary fawn, he thought. *How little she knows her own power! Even now* . . . He cleared his throat. 'Miss Hunter,' he said, 'we haven't known each other long, but I've come to feel – to admire you very deeply. In fact – the truth is, I love you very much. Will you consent to be my wife? Will you marry me?'

The moment had come, and she didn't shout *Yes, yes!* or feel a surge of triumph, or peals of victory in her head. She felt suddenly very small and rather humble and very scared. She wanted to cry. She didn't know how to answer him, what to say.

There just was one thing she could do. She stood up, which made him stand, too. She looked up into his face searchingly, seeing his nervousness, his uncertainty of success. It was so very far from the arrogant, cold Lord Dene she had once believed him. She said, 'Will you kiss me, please?'

He hesitated a moment, faintly puzzled; but took the other step to her, put his arms carefully round her, lowered his head to hers, laid his mouth against her mouth.

Her first real kiss. It was like a bolt of lightning going through her, the touch of a man's lips – *this* man's lips. She felt as if she might fall, closed her hands on his shoulders, felt him tighten his grasp. He would always hold her up, she thought. He was no Rupert. He would die rather than hurt her.

After a moment he lifted his head, released her carefully, looked down at her with painful enquiry.

'Thank you,' she said, and her voice sounded, to her, like someone else's, coming from very far away. 'Yes, I will marry you.'

He closed his eyes. 'Oh, thank God!' he said. He opened his eyes and took both her hands. 'I will give my life to making you happy.'

'I know you will,' she said. The hand Rupert had crushed was being hurt by Charles's ardour, but she hardly noticed at that moment.

When Charles came towards her, escorting that Miss Hunter, and followed by the Hunter parents looking lightly stunned, the countess's heart filled with fury. But she knew a *fait accompli* when she saw one. It was simply not possible to make a fuss, in a ballroom, in front of everyone. Had it not been that her elder son had always been remarkably incapable of guile, she would have thought he had designed it that way.

Swallowing her feelings made black spots dance before her eyes, and for a moment she thought she might swoon. A thousand thoughts flashed across her mind as she swung her eyes briefly to her husband's face, to see a similar look of bafflement there, swiftly concealed. It would be possible to coerce Charles by withdrawing his allowance and altering the will to deprive him of those parts of the estate not entailed, but not now he had made his desire known to all the world. Everyone must know what this procession meant. They would be laughed at, and that would be even worse than taking the Hunters into their bosom. Their only course now was to put a good face on it and pretend to the world that the girl had hidden depths that only *they* were insightful enough to discover.

So she brushed cheeks with the chit, relieved at least to see she had no unseemly look of triumph on her face – indeed, she looked stunned too, as well she might – then shook hands with the parents, and trooped off with them to the dais, where Wroughton stopped the orchestra and got up to make the announcement. Charles, with the girl's hand through his arm and firmly gripped by his other hand as though he feared she might run off, or dislimn, was smiling – widely, fully, ecstatically – and that sight alone gave the countess pause. She had never seen him smile like that, not since . . . well, perhaps when he was five or six, and had been given his first pony.

The ballroom erupted into applause and an excited babble of comment, and those acquainted with either family pressed forward to give their congratulations and scrutinise the happy couple, some with kindness and pleasure, others with curiosity. Diana felt herself raked by the sharp eyes of disappointment looking for faults, but she didn't care. A June wedding, he had said to his parents: in the summer, at any rate, as soon as he got leave. No hasty register-office affair squeezed in before he went to France: she was to have full honours. It didn't occur to her that this was a concession from him to his mother to sweeten the deal.

The orchestra was striking up again, a waltz, and she

understood that they must circle the room in each other's arms and be admired and applauded. As Charles was about to lead her out, Rupert reached them, shook his brother's hand and, with a malicious glare, took Diana's and said, 'My dear Miss Hunter. I think you know everything I'm wishing you right at this moment.'

She retrieved her hand and was led away. It might have disconcerted Rupert if he had known that in her bewildered rapture she had barely registered his presence, let alone taken in what he said.

'Well, you'll be moving up in the world, then,' said Sergeant Andy Wood, as he and Ethel walked through the woods, crunching the rime-edged leaves under their boots. It was a crisp, blue winter day with weak sunshine sparkling through the bare branches and dazzling on the waters of the lake. 'I suppose you'll be a lady's maid next, to a real lady.'

'Ada says she'll need a proper trained one,' said Ethel. 'Anyway, I don't mean to stay in service for ever. I'm just waiting for the right offer to come along.'

He didn't bite. He said, 'I'm surprised you got time to come out with me, with all the hobnobbing there must be going on, high-ups popping in and out.'

'Oh, it's not like that. *He* had to go straight back to camp the next day. He's getting some days off at Christmas, and we won't see any of 'em till then. The earl and countess have invited the whole family over on Boxing Day. Well, all except Mr David – there was a letter this morning. He's not getting Christmas off. They all get four days, but his aren't till after, and then he's going to stay with his pal's folk, the Oliphants. The missus is in a rare state about it. She never shows, but she didn't eat a thing at breakfast.'

'Her favourite, is he?'

'Oh, the sun shines out of his eyes. But between you, me

and the bedpost, his pal's got a sister – that's the real attraction, if you ask me.' She sensed his attention wandering. He wasn't terribly interested in the doings of the family, though they naturally formed a large part of her life. The rapture 'below stairs' over Miss Diana's engagement had transformed all their lives. Any engagement would have been exciting, but *this* one . . . !

Still, her companion couldn't be expected to share it. She chose another question – one that concerned her more nearly. 'So what you doing at Christmas? You getting leave?'

'I am, my girl, and what's more I'm one of the lucky ones. I get off Christmas Eve so I get the 'ole thing.' He smiled at the horizon, a tight, pleased look that gave her a thrill she felt all down her legs.

'And what you going to be doing?' she asked, with a modest smile.

He looked down at her, and a dark imp danced in his eyes. 'Why, I'm going home, what d'you think? Going home to see the wife and kids.'

The whole world seemed to stand still: leaves paused in their rustling, birds held their breath, the sun stopped sparkling on things and stared at Ethel to see how she would react. She answered, through a dry mouth, 'You didn't tell me you was married.'

'Didn't I? Didn't come up, somehow, I s'pose. Too many other things coming up, eh?' And he squeezed her arm against his side. 'What – you didn't think a handsome bloke like me would still be available, did you?'

'I never give the matter any thought,' she managed to say, from a great distance, as she frantically rearranged her interior landscape.

He grinned, and the imps capered with glee. 'Thought I was goin' to marry *you*, did you?'

She could not allow him the triumph. '*Marry you*? You think a lot about yourself, Andy Wood, and no mistake! I wouldn't marry you if you was covered in gold. Don't flatter yourself. I'm just after a bit o' fun, that's all.'

He turned to face her, and put his arms round her. 'Ah, well, now, fun – that I can offer you. Come 'ere, you gorgeous hussy!'

She arrived home much later, her outside somewhat rumpled and her mind sore. She had so been enjoying going out with an older man, one who knew what was what, and had assumed her wiles would work on him as on the youth of Northcote. She had even made enquiries about a sergeant's pay, had learned that in civilian life he was in the printing trade, which was a good line to be in. She had thought he might do very nicely. And now . . .

She had been made a fool of. But at least she had covered herself. He would not have the satisfaction of knowing it.

Nailer was hanging around the kitchen door when she reached it, hoping for someone to open it so he could slip in. 'Get away from here, you mangy hound!' she snapped. She aimed a kick at him, and managed to connect the toe of her boot with his ribs, though not very hard – he was an expert in avoiding blows. It was dark now, and the frost was falling. She could see her breath clouding the air, and the lights inside looked welcoming to the weary pilgrim from the Land of Disappointment.

Cook looked up as she came in, and said, 'There was a boy here today, brought a note for you. It's behind the tea-caddy. I give him a penny for bringing it – you can pay me later.'

Ethel reached up to the high mantelshelf, retrieved it and opened it with one hand while she took off her hat with the other. It had no envelope – just a folded piece of cheap paper, very grubby. The writing inside was in pencil, hard to make out, obviously wielded by an inexpert hand.

In the background she heard Ada say, 'Who's it from, Ethel?'

387

And heard Cook reply, 'One of her fancy men, I don't doubt.'

Ethel tilted it to the light, and slowly deciphered the painful scrawl. *Yor mother dide Mundy nite. Vicar has took over, also things. I am sory. E. Clark*

'What is it, Ethel?' Ada said again.

She folded the paper and pushed it into her pocket. She felt a strange emptiness, like hunger, only it wasn't. 'Nothing,' she said. 'What's for supper?'

The front line was not where Jack would have liked to be at Christmas, but at least Fritz had stopped shelling for the time being. There had been nothing over since the middle of the day on Christmas Eve, and the snipers had packed up at dark, too. The weather was clear and cold, the best one could hope for in this basically sodden place. The mud was crisp in places, and the puddles had a skim of ice.

The air was so sharp, sounds carried a long way. Last night, when he had done the round of his line at midnight, one of the men, Harper, had said, 'Listen, sir! Listen to that!'

Far away, but clear as a bell, had come the sound of German voices singing a carol in pleasant harmony.

'It's 'ole Fritz in his dugout, sir,' said Harper, wonderingly. 'D'you hear what they're singing? Flippin' cheek, singing one of ours!'

'It's one of theirs too, Harper,' Jack had said, and he sang a few words in German.

> *'Stille Nacht, heilige Nacht*
> *Alles schläft; einsam wacht . . .'*

'Blimey, is that German, sir?' Harper seemed dumbfounded.

'That's German,' Jack confirmed.

'Well, who'da thought it? Dunarf sound queer! And they have Christmas and everything, same as us?'

'Wonders will never cease,' said Jack, solemnly. Then he started singing too, softly, but in English, and one by one the men had joined in, crooning along with the distant enemy. It had been a bizarre, yet touching moment.

And this morning, Christmas Day, was the stillest, quietest day he had ever known. Some genius at the commissary had sent sausages along with the breakfast bacon and bread. They were not very good sausages, but the smell of them frying was heavenly. Jack sat in the door of his dugout, to get the light while he shaved, and savoured the aroma, and the smell of real coffee that his servant was brewing up behind him. He'd brought some back with him from leave. Coffee, sausages, this lovely pale, frail sunshine – and no shells. One thing about being in the front line: your pleasures narrowed and grew proportionately sharper.

No shells. There had been no exchange at stand-to. Jerry didn't send over any hate all morning, and the British Army was so short of ammunition it wasn't going to fire first. By eleven there was even a little warmth in the sun: in a sheltered spot, you could feel it on your skin if you turned your face upwards.

It was Sergeant Agar who interrupted him as he was writing to Beth – part of a marathon letter that he would post when he came out of the line in two days' time. 'Better come outside and see this, sir,' he said.

'What is it, Sergeant?'

But Agar only shook his head and retreated. Outside there were more men in the trench than were on duty, and they were all crowding on to the firing step, elbowing each other out of the way to crane over the parapet. Jack heard voices in the distance, not singing this time, but calling.

'What's going on? You men, get down!'

'It's Fritzy, sir,' said one eager lad, turning a shining face to him. 'They're calling out to us.'

'Let me see.'

389

He got up on the step and eased his head cautiously out. It might have been a trick, but it didn't sound like one. The voices from over there sounded like ordinary cheerful men, not soldiers. He saw them poking their heads up, waving, and with his head out, he could hear them clearly. 'Tommee! Tommee! Merry Christmas, Tommee! Good time! You hear?'

So he shouted back, '*Frohe Weihnachten!*' There was a huge cheer, and one of the heads grew a body as a grey-clad soldier heaved himself cautiously up, put a knee on the top and slowly stood upright, hands raised to chest height, palms out, to show he was not armed. It was a perilous moment. If any fool had taken fright and fired, all hell would have been let loose. But this was Christmas Day, the Saviour's birthday, and all hell stayed confined.

The German, finding himself still alive, gave a little capering dance, and even from that distance you could see his foolish grin. 'Tommee! Tommee! Come out! Make friendship! We have beer! We have sausage, *ja*?'

Further down the trench he saw one of his own start to climb out. It was madness. It was unmilitary. The Brass Hats would definitely frown on it. Couldn't you get shot for fraternisation? But a strange happiness gripped him. This war was not war as anyone had ever known it, so why not this, now, on Christmas Day? He heaved himself slowly up, saw a stir of excitement across the way, and a German officer raised himself, too, matching Jack's movements.

The floodgates were opened. Everyone was spilling out. Men were advancing towards the middle of no man's land, grinning at each other in enormous good will. Cigarettes were offered. Bully beef was swapped for German sausage. Hands were shaken. Few of the men spoke German, but there were enough English speakers on the other side, and the evincing of friendship seemed to need no translation, anyway. Over to his right, a group of men from both sides started kicking a margarine can about in an impromptu game of football. He heard someone shout, *'Tott'nam 'Otspur!'* His opposite number shouted, *'Bayern Munich!'* and they all laughed.

He came up to the officer, a man younger than him, with golden down on his cheeks and eyes as blue as the unblemished winter sky. Shyly he offered Jack a cigar, examining his face with a frank curiosity that Jack knew he was echoing.

'Danke schön,' Jack said, and the boy – for he was little more – looked pleased. Jack pulled out his own lighter and lit both cigars. 'Very good,' he said.

The officer pulled out a silver flask, and offered it. 'Schnapps,' he said. 'From *mein Vater*. Very good.' Jack thanked him and took a pull. 'Leutnant Gruber,' the young man said, offering his hand.

'Captain Hunter,' said Jack, shaking it.

The German smiled delightedly. *'Weihnachten,'* he said. 'Peace. No more war.'

'No more war,' Jack agreed.

It was as easy as delightful to exchange these sentiments, here and now, on this day, in this place. War was an absurdity. Why should you ever kill another man who had never done you any harm? If this was all it took, this smiling, handshaking, exchange of cigarettes, then let peace break out here and now, let it spread all the way along the line, until everyone had laid down their arms. Let it fill the whole world.

Others came up, and he left his friendly officer to wander among the other groups, marvelling at how men who did not speak each other's tongue could yet communicate. He came to one group where a German was translating for his fellows. At the sound of his accent, which was pure London, Jack stopped and touched his arm. The German turned in enquiry.

'You speak very good English,' Jack said. 'Where did you learn it?

The German soldier grinned. 'Blimey, sir, I should hope I speak it all right! I was born in Peckham. When the war broke out, I was a waiter at the Dorchester. My uncle was a barber in Jermyn Street.'

'I think he may have cut my hair,' said Jack.

He wandered from group to group, feeling a detached, almost paternal fondness for all these fellows, from both sides. Then he left them to go down and finish his letter. He sat on an upturned ammunition box in a sunny spot, leaning his back against the dugout wall, with his writing case on his knee, but the pencil lay slack in his fingers, and his mind wandered. He lit a cigarette. He could hear the men's voices, clear on the clear air as they chatted and laughed. The sun was declining now, the short day fading. Soon the dark would come, night with its hazards and doubts, and who knew what tomorrow would bring? In his heart he knew this was only a hiatus, that there had not been enough suffering yet for it to be all over. But he was grateful even for this. He wondered what Beth was doing. And he wondered where he would be this time next year. He hoped it might be *home*.